The Scum Villain's Self-Saving System

REN ZHA FANPAI ZIJIU XITONG

1

墨香铜臭

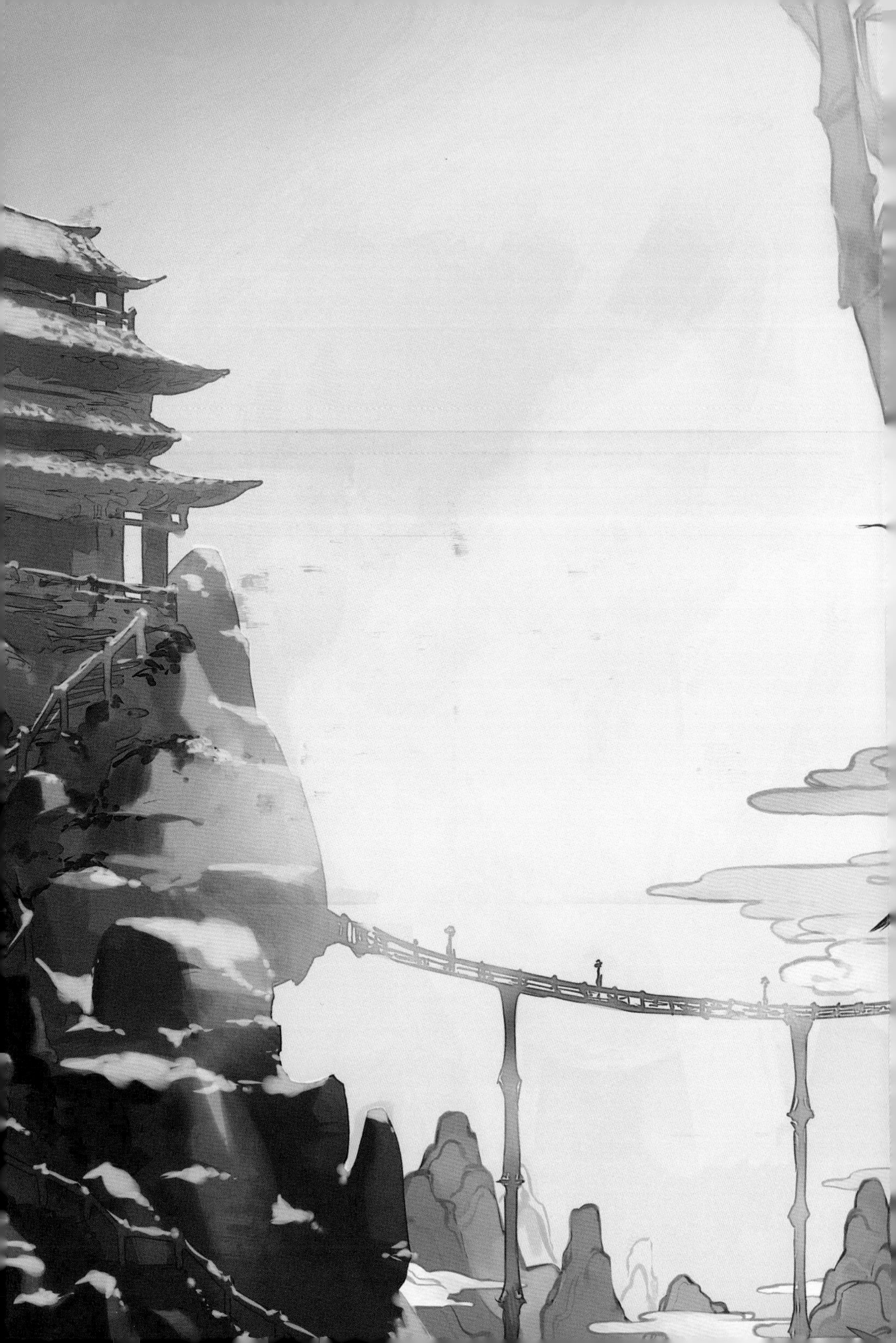

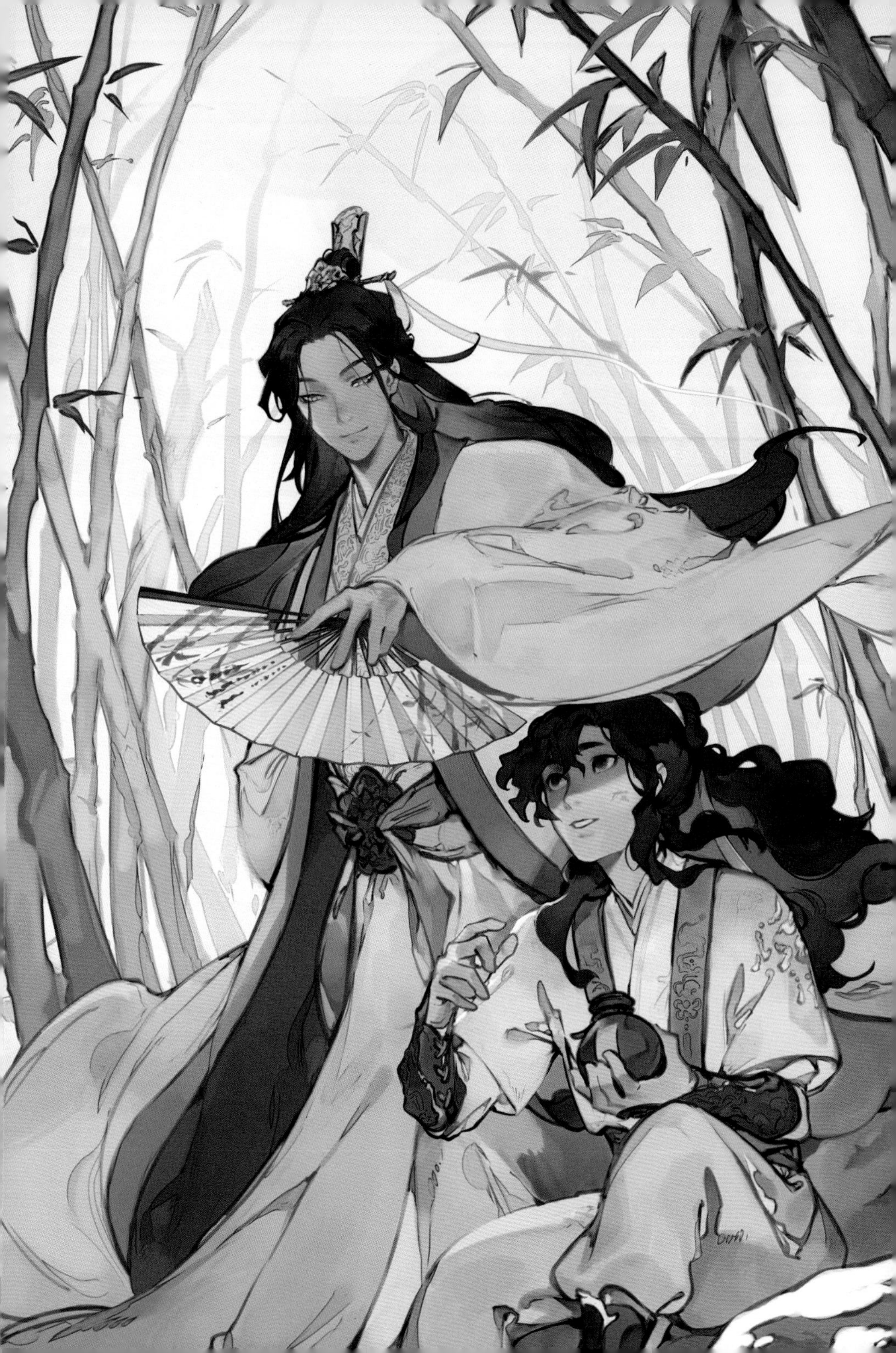

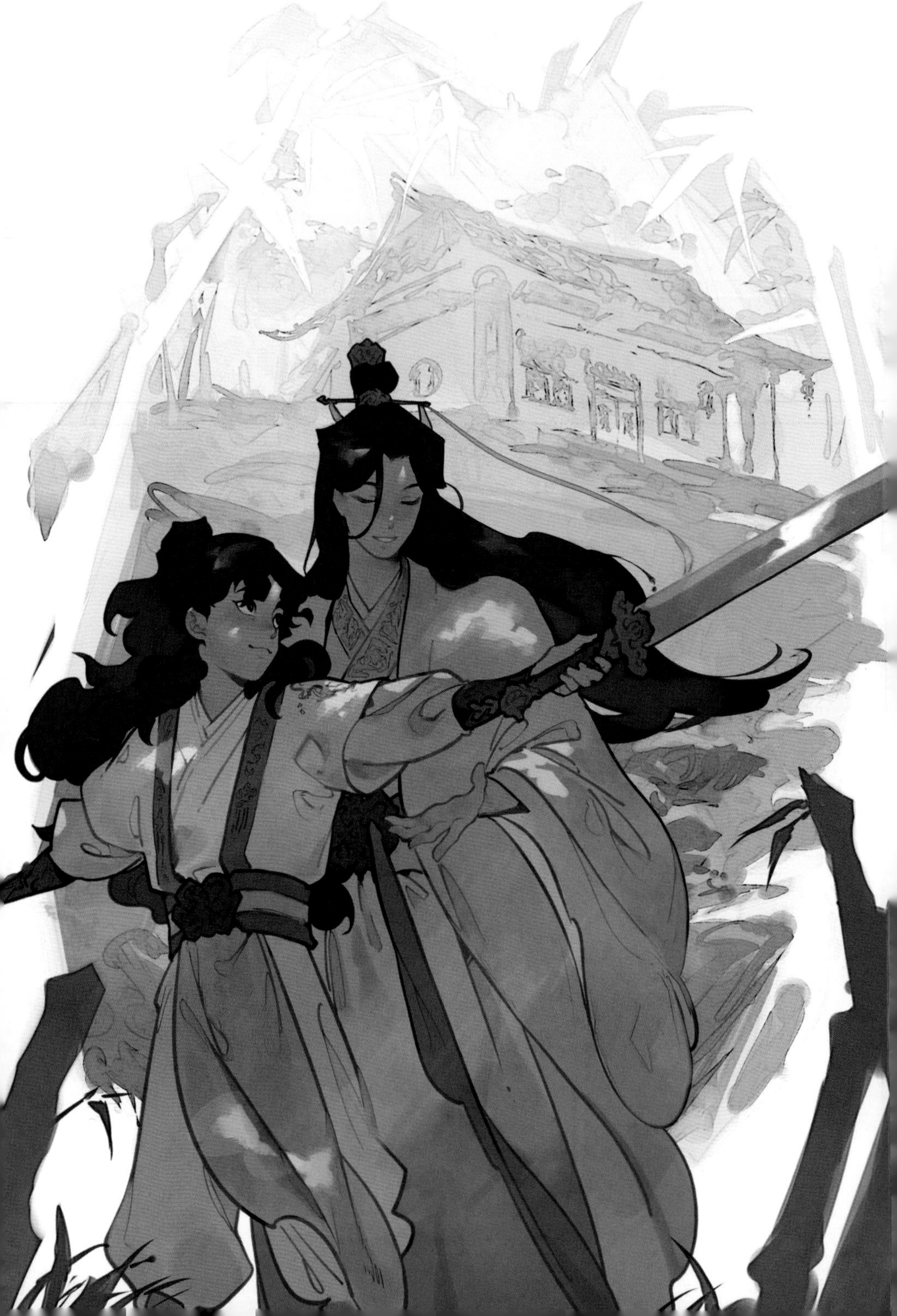

The Scum Villain's Self-Saving System

REN ZHA FANPAI
ZIJIU XITONG

1

WRITTEN BY
Mo Xiang Tong Xiu

TRANSLATED BY
Faelicy & Lily

ILLUSTRATED BY
**Xiao Tong Kong
(Velinxi)**

Seven Seas

Seven Seas Entertainment

THE SCUM VILLAIN'S SELF-SAVING SYSTEM:
REN ZHA FANPAI ZIJIU XITONG VOL. 1

Published originally under the title of 《人渣反派自救系统》
(Ren Zha Fan Pai Zi Jiu Xi Tong/The Scum Villain's Self-saving System)
Author ©墨香铜臭(Mo Xiang Tong Xiu)
English edition rights under license granted by 北京晋江原创网络科技有限公司
(Beijing Jinjiang Original Network Technology Co., Ltd.)
English edition copyright © 2021 Seven Seas Entertainment, LLC
Arranged through JS Agency Co., Ltd
All rights reserved

Illustrations by Xiao Tong Kong (Velinxi)

Seven Seas press and purchase enquiries can be sent to Marketing Manager Lianne Sentar
at press@gomanga.com. Information regarding the distribution and purchase of digital
editions is available from Digital Manager CK Russell at digital@gomanga.com.

Seven Seas and the Seven Seas logo are trademarks of
Seven Seas Entertainment. All rights reserved.

Follow Seven Seas Entertainment online at
sevenseasentertainment.com.

TRANSLATION: Faelicy, Lily
INTERIOR LAYOUT & DESIGN: Clay Gardner
PROOFREADER: Jade Gardner
COPY EDITOR: Dawn Crane
IN-HOUSE EDITOR: M. Suyenaga
BRAND MANAGER: Lissa Pattillo
PRINT MANAGER: Rhiannon Rasmussen-Silverstein
MANAGING EDITOR: Julie Davis
ASSOCIATE PUBLISHER: Adam Arnold
PUBLISHER: Jason DeAngelis

ISBN: 978-1-64827-921-8
Printed in Canada
First Printing: December 2021
10 9 8 7 6 5 4 3 2 1

THE SCUM VILLAIN'S SELF-SAVING SYSTEM

CONTENTS

Contents based on the Pinsin Publishing print edition originally released 2017

1

Scum

*P*ROUD IMMORTAL DEMON WAY was a male power fantasy of a stallion novel.

To be more specific, *Proud Immortal Demon Way* was a monster-fighting, escapist cultivation novel with an incomparably ridiculous length, a golden finger that broke every rule, and a harem size nearing three-digits, seeing as every single female character fell for the protagonist. The year's hottest stallion novel—there was no other!

The male lead of this novel, Luo Binghe, was neither the kind who started heroic and invincible, like a proud dragon of the heavens, nor the kind who was a loser, a good-for-nothing without merit—yet he managed to trend with tens of thousands of readers on Zhongdian Literature, inspiring countless other male fantasy novels to follow in his footsteps.

He was the kind of lead who was pitch-black, dark, and vicious, though before his heart blackened, he was the kind who suffered misery after misery.

Next, let a veteran reader of this novel, Shen Yuan, omit the countless fanservice-y details and concisely summarize the million-word epic for everyone...

Immediately after birth, Luo Binghe was abandoned by his parents, swaddled in white cloth, and put in a wooden basin that was lowered into the Luo River. This occurred on the coldest days of the year, and it was only thanks to fishermen pulling him out of the water that he didn't freeze to death as a baby. Because he'd been drifting along the Luo in the season when it was choked with thin ice, he was given the name Luo Binghe.

Luo Binghe spent his early years wandering the streets, hungry and cold—a dreary childhood. A washerwoman who worked for a wealthy family took pity on him, and since she had no children of her own, she adopted and raised him as her own. Mother and son were poor, and they suffered much humiliation at the hands of their rich patrons.

Growing up in such an unhealthy environment became the foundation of Luo Binghe's future twisted personality post-darkening—his inclinations to fight over every scrap, seek revenge for the smallest grievance, and hide murderous intent behind a smile.

Once, he withstood the beatings of the family's young masters for a bowl of lukewarm meat congee. In the end, he was still too late, and he failed to give his adopted mother even a single taste before she died.

By complete coincidence, he was selected for training by one of the cultivation world's four great sects, Cang Qiong Mountain. There, he apprenticed under the "Xiu Ya Sword," Shen Qingqiu.

Luo Binghe thought he could finally start down the righteous path. He couldn't have expected that Shen Qingqiu was fair without but foul within, trash of the lowest caliber. Shen Qingqiu was jealous of Luo Binghe's unparalleled and exceptional talent, and he secretly feared his disciple, whose cultivation improved by leaps and bounds every day. He always found new ways to taunt and demean Luo Binghe, even enlisting the boy's peers to belittle him.

Throughout these years of studying, Luo Binghe endured every humiliation. It was another heart-wrenching arc in his story, filled with blood and tears.

After much difficulty, Luo Binghe managed to turn seventeen, at which point he finally participated in the event the cultivation world held once every four years: the Immortal Alliance Conference. However, at the conference, Luo Binghe fell victim to Shen Qingqiu's scheming, and he tumbled into a crack in the boundary between the Human and Demon Realms—the Endless Abyss.

That's right, only then did the story truly begin!

Not only did Luo Binghe survive, but within the Endless Abyss, he found his personal sword, the peerless mystical blade "Xin Mo." He also learned the truth of his origins.

As it turned out, Luo Binghe had been born to the Demon Realm's Saintly Ruler and a woman of the Human Realm; within his veins flowed the blood of the ancient, heaven-fallen demons as well as that of the human race. His birth father, Tianlang-Jun, had been sealed beneath a great mountain, trapped for all eternity. His birth mother had been a disciple from a righteous cultivation sect, but shortly following Tianlang-Jun's sealing, she had been expelled on suspicion of having secret ties to demons. She had died from a postpartum hemorrhage after giving birth to Luo Binghe, but prior to her death, she had set her son adrift from the lonely ship she'd birthed him on. It was the only way she had been able to give Luo Binghe a chance to survive.

Luo Binghe used Xin Mo to release his body's seal on his demonic blood. Then, within the dark abyss, he single-mindedly cultivated and enlightened himself to otherworldly techniques before heading back to Cang Qiong Mountain Sect. From there on out, Luo Binghe steadily headed down his dark path, never looking back.

Every single one of his old enemies suffered great torment and died a horrible death by his hand. With his steadily improving ability to lie and scheme, Luo Binghe won the trust of many people, feigning compliance while secretly plotting against them. He seized power and rose in position, beginning a reign of terror.

As the story unfolded, Luo Binghe's heart blackened further and further. He returned to the Demon Realm and inherited the position of Saintly Ruler. Yet unsatisfied, he began to eradicate each one of the Human Realm's great righteous sects, bathing them in blood, annihilating all who opposed him.

In the end, Luo Binghe became a legend spoken of for generations of immortals and demons, hailed for his unification of the three realms, the uncountable size of his harem, and his boundless number of descendants!

"Dumbfuck author, dumbfuck novel!" With his dying breath, Shen Yuan spat this final curse.

Who could have imagined that an upstanding young man like him—who had properly purchased the website's VIP currency and read the novel's official version—would find himself persevering before his untimely death to finish a novel so stallion, so money-grubbing and overly padded, that it left him speechless with rage? How could he not curse?

Proud Immortal Demon Way, by Airplane Shooting Towards the Sky. Just looking at that euphemistic handle smacked you in the face with a dirty feeling. Grade-school level writing with landmines everywhere, breaking all suspension of disbelief. And Shen Yuan couldn't bear to call that incoherent mess of a world the author had built a cultivation setting.

What kind of cultivation world had people using horses and carriages all day? What kind of cultivation world had people who, after achieving inedia, still needed to eat and sleep? What kind of cultivation world had an author who occasionally mixed up even the stages of Foundation Establishment and Nascent Soul?

When faced with the protagonist, every single character acted like his total edgelord aura had devoured their intelligence—especially Luo Binghe's master, Shen Qingqiu, that idiot among idiots, scum among scum! His only purpose was to dig his own grave, and he hadn't even managed to finish before he was killed by the protagonist instead.

So why had Shen Yuan started this book, even going so far as to read it to the very end? Don't misunderstand, Shen Yuan didn't enjoy degrading himself. The reason he had persisted was also what had caused him the most frustration.

This novel had an incredible amount of foreshadowing, plotlines everywhere, mystery after mystery, layer upon layer of red herrings. And at the very end—not a single one paid off! It was enough to make him want to puke a fountain of blood.

Why were priceless herbs, spirit elixirs, and peerless beauties everywhere, like they didn't cost a cent? Why were the villains' speeches and poses as they dug their graves and got offed all exactly the same? The dozens of maidens barely glimpsed, all of whom agreed to enter the harem, what happened to them...?

All right, skipping that last one for the moment—who had been the culprit behind the scores of atrocities? Exactly what was the purpose of the unending list of characters so hyped up for being awesome and without equal? Why did none of them make an appearance, even at the very end?!

Towards the Sky-bro, Airplane-bro, "Great Master": Can we have a discussion? Fill! In! Plot holes! Okay?!

Shen Yuan felt like he could have come back to life with the power of sheer rage.

In the endless darkness, a mechanical voice sounded by his ear:

〔Activation code: "Dumbfuck author, dumbfuck novel." System automatically triggered.〕

The tone reminded him of Google Translate.

"Who is this?" Shen Yuan looked around. It seemed like he was floating in a virtual space, one so dark that he couldn't see his hand before him.

The voice came from all directions.

〔Welcome to the System. This System operates in line with the design concept "YOU CAN YOU UP, NO CAN NO BB"[1]; we hope to provide you with the best possible experience. It is our sincere wish that during your time, you can fulfill your desires and, in accordance with your wish, transform a stupid work into a magnificent, high-quality, first-rate classic. We hope you enjoy.〕

In the midst of his ensuing vertigo, a man's voice asked lightly beside him, "...Shidi? Shidi, can you hear me?"

Shen Yuan shuddered and settled his mind, forcibly peeling open his eyes. The scene that appeared before him was a massive, whirling flurry. It took a while for everything to finally coalesce and slowly become clear.

He lay on a bed.

---

1   A common Chinese meme. This is a deliberately (and entertainingly) bad translation of the phrase 你行你上, 不行别比比. Basically, "If you're capable, then you do it; if you're not, then stfu."

Looking up: a white, gauzy canopy hung overhead, with finely crafted perfume pouches dangling from the four corners.

Looking down: he wore a white robe of an ancient style. Next to the pillow lay a paper fan.

Looking to his left: a handsome, elegant young man dressed in xuanduan formal robes sat by his bedside, looking at him with concern.

Shen Yuan closed his eyes, then sharply reached for that folding fan and opened it with a snap. He lightly waved it, fanning away the cold sweat pouring down his face.

The man's eyes lit up with joy. "Shidi finally woke up," he said warmly. "Do you have any discomfort?"

"Nothing too bad," Shen Yuan said with some reservation.

The information overload was a bit much. He dazedly tried to sit up. As he did, the man quickly reached out to support his back, letting him lean against the headboard.

Having read many of Zhongdian's transmigration novels, Shen Yuan had long ago resolved that, if he one day woke up to find himself lying in a strange place, the first words out of his mouth before he understood what was happening definitely wouldn't be a carefree giggle and, "Are you filming a movie? The props look so real—your crew's really giving it their all!" I.e., the words of a person slow-wittedly trying to find their footing.

Rather, Shen Yuan concentrated on acting like he'd just woken up, expression absentminded. "I... Where is this?"

The man startled. "Did you sleep yourself into a trance? This is your Qing Jing Peak."

Internally, Shen Yuan was shocked, but he continued to act muddled. "Why...why was I asleep for so long?"

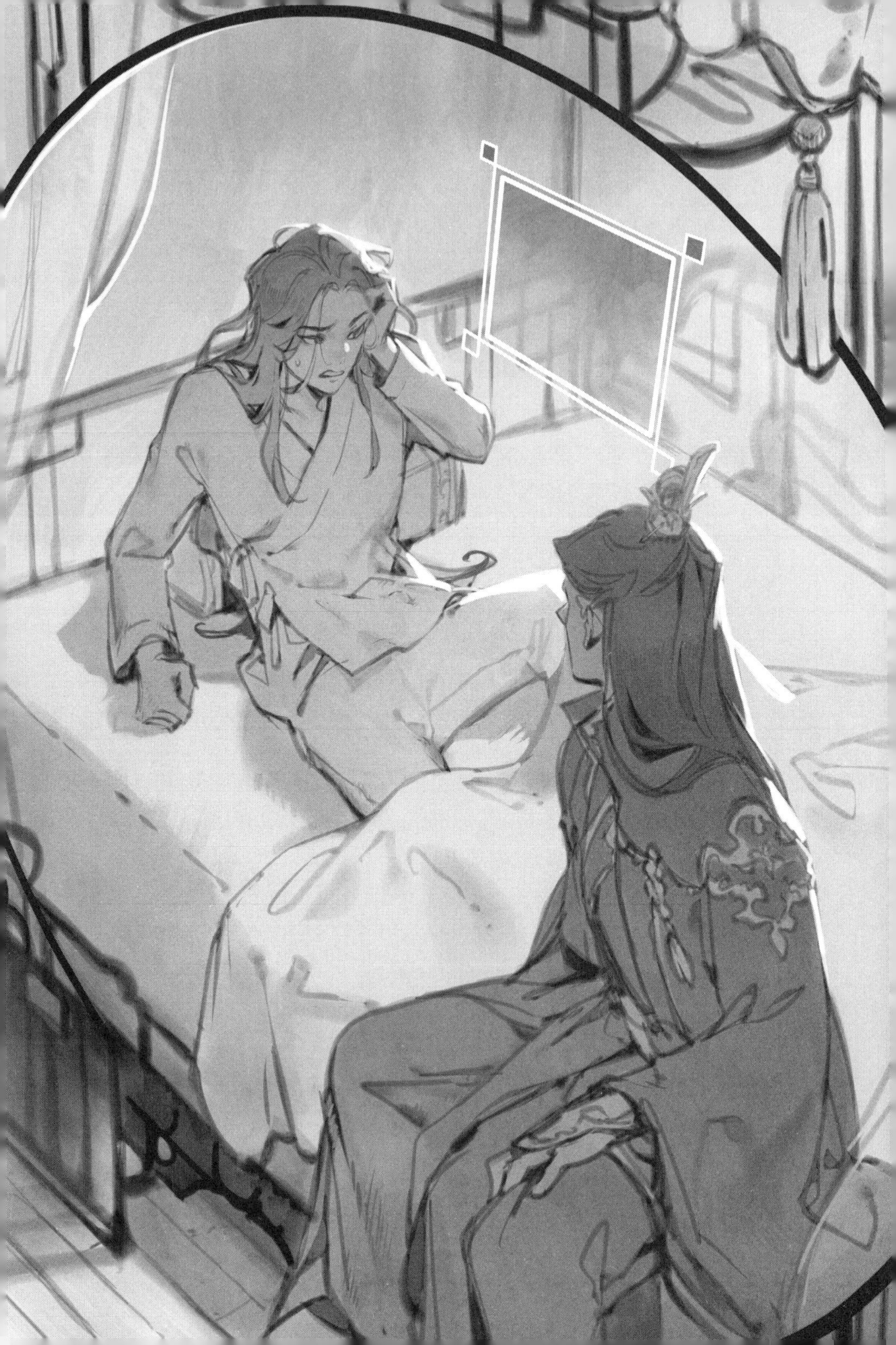

"That's what I wanted to ask you. You were in perfect health, so how did you suddenly come down with a high fever? I know that with the Immortal Alliance Conference approaching, you've been training your disciples and are anxious to see results. But with Cang Qiong Mountain being such a well-established and renowned sect, even if one of our own didn't attend this time, no one would dare question us. Why concern yourself with empty words?"

The more Shen Yuan listened, the more something felt off. Why did these lines sound so familiar? No, why did this *setup* seem so familiar?

The man's next sentence, single and earnest, confirmed all his suspicions. "Qingqiu-shidi, are you listening to Shixiong?"

At this moment, something dinged, and the mechanical, Google-Translate-like voice from his dreamscape spoke again.

[The System was successfully activated! Bound Role: Luo Binghe's master, Cang Qiong Mountain Sect's Peak Lord of Qing Jing Peak, "Shen Qingqiu." Weapon: the sword Xiu Ya. Starting B-Points: 100.]

"Fuck, fuck, fuck, what bullshit is this? How come you're speaking directly into my brain? Does Airplane Shooting Towards the Sky know you're plagiarizing *Proud Immortal Demon Way*'s setting like this?!"

Of course, Shen Yuan didn't say this out loud, but the voice swiftly responded.

[You have triggered the System's execution command and have been bound to the Shen Qingqiu account. As the plot progresses, various point types will gradually become available. Please ensure that no score falls below zero, or the System will automatically mete out punishment.]

Stop. Enough. Shen Yuan was sure now. He'd hit the jackpot—he'd transmigrated!

Transmigrated into a story he'd just finished, moreover, even if it was a pitch-black stallion novel he'd hated, and even if it came with some kind of shitty "system." As a 21st century veteran VIP reader of Zhongdian Literature, Shen Yuan had read various types of do-over and transmigration male power fantasy novels year in and year out, so theoretically, he could have happily and easily accepted this fact. But of all people, the shell he was borrowing just happened to belong to the male lead's scum villain master, Shen Qingqiu. This... uh, made the situation rather complicated.

The amicable-looking elder-brother type beside him was Cang Qiong Mountain Sect's current sect leader, Shen Qingqiu's shixiong, the "Xuan Su Sword," Yue Qingyuan. Fuck.

There was a very important reason Shen Yuan emphatically thought "fuck" at the sight of Yue Qingyuan. In the original work, Yue Qingyuan's death had been caused by his good shidi, Shen Qingqiu, okay?!

And what a horrific death it was. Tens of thousands of arrows had pierced him until not even his bones remained!

At this moment, the victim was facing his own "murderer" and showering him with concern. The pressure was immense.

On second glance, though, the story hadn't yet unfolded to that point. Yue Qingyuan was still in perfect health, meaning that at this point in time, Shen Qingqiu had yet to reveal himself as a hypocrite, and his reputation was still pristine. Yue Qingyuan was a bleeding heart, nothing to be afraid of. Though his character ended up suffering quite a bit, during his read, Shen Yuan had been rather fond of him. He was just about to relax when a string of words floated eerily to the forefront of his mind.

...Within the dark, gloomy room, a metal chain hung from a beam. At the end of the chain dangled a ring. The ring was fastened around a person's waist—if it could still be considered a "person." This "person's" appearance was filthy and disheveled, like that of a madman. The most frightening thing about him was that all four of his limbs had been severed. His shoulders and thighs were only four bare knobs of flesh. When touched, he would let out a hoarse "ahhh" sound. His tongue had been torn out too, rendering him unable to form complete words.

—Proud Immortal Demon Way, a selected passage on Shen Qingqiu's fate.

Shen Yuan—ah, no, Shen Qingqiu—rested his forehead on his hand. He was in no position to lament the horrors of other people's deaths—the most horrific death was his own, okay?!

Henceforth, he had to avoid any critical errors!

First: eliminate any mistake at the root.

Second: from now on, cling madly to the male lead's thighs.

Third: be a good mentor and helpful friend who is earnest and gentle in his teachings; meticulously show the male lead every kind of concern.

The moment Shen Qingqiu had these thoughts, a long string of alarms erupted in his mind, as if one hundred police cars carrying one hundred shrieking divine beasts were zooming past. It was so cacophonous that he shuddered, clutching his head in pain.

"Shidi, does your head still hurt?" Yue Qingyuan asked worriedly.

Teeth clenched, Shen Qingqiu didn't answer.

[Warning,] the System shrilly notified him. [This proposed plan is incredibly dangerous and qualifies as a violation. Please do not attempt, or the System will automatically mete out punishment.]

"How was that a violation?"

[Currently, you are at the beginner level, and the OOC feature is frozen. You must complete a beginner-level quest to unfreeze it. Before unfreezing, any act in violation of the original Shen Qingqiu character settings will result in a deduction of a fixed number of B-Points.]

As a semi-otaku, Shen Qingqiu had seen a number of fanwork-related terms here and there—you know what I mean—so of course he knew the definition of OOC: adj., acronym for "out of character," defined as breaking character or acting in a way inconsistent with the character's canonical personality.

"In other words...before that whatever-feature gets unfrozen, my behavior and actions can't differ from what 'Shen Qingqiu' would do?"

[Correct.]

This System had already let him transmigrate into Shen Qingqiu's shell, replacing him, but it still cared about a detail like being OOC?

"You just said something about how...the points can't fall below zero. If they do, what happens?"

[You will automatically be deported back to your original world.]

Original world? But in Shen Yuan's original world, his body had already expired. In other words, if he lost all his B-or-Whatever-Points, what awaited him was, in short, death.

Well, if he just ignored the male lead and avoided doing anything, things would be fine, right?

He raised his head and scanned the room, but among the disciples waiting on him by his bedside, he didn't see anyone that matched

Luo Binghe's description. Feigning unconcern, he said, "Where is Luo Binghe?"

Yue Qingyuan paused, giving him a strange look.

Shen Qingqiu remained straight-faced but was secretly filled with glee. Was it possible that the time wasn't ripe? That the male lead had yet to apprentice to Cang Qiong Mountain Sect?

"Shidi, don't be angry," said Yue Qingyuan.

An ominous premonition stirred in Shen Qingqiu's heart.

Yue Qingyuan sighed. "I know you don't like him. But that child's already worked hard enough, and he hasn't made any significant mistakes. Don't punish him any further, all right?"

Hearing this, Shen Qingqiu's lips felt dry. He wet them and said, "...You can just say it. Where is he?"

Yue Qingyuan was silent for a moment. "Whenever you finish stringing him up and beating him, haven't you always shut him in the woodshed?"

Shen Qingqiu's vision went dark.

In his previous life, Shen Yuan had been well-off growing up, and he'd basically qualified as a modest example of a second-generation rich kid. His two older brothers had been set to inherit the family business, and he'd doted on his little sister. The entire family had been very close.

From early on, he'd known that even if he idled the rest of his life away, he'd never want for food. Perhaps due to this carefree upbringing, devoid of either competition or pressure, he came to believe that ranking in the top ten of a competition was good enough, so long as it had more than ten people.

Therefore, he'd never understood what scum villains like Shen Qingqiu were thinking as they dug their own graves.

The original Shen Qingqiu had both training in cultivation and the qualifications to prove his experience, not to mention the self-restraint to put up a facade. He wanted for neither standing nor reputation, and with the support of the world's largest sect, he would never want for money either.

So why did he have not even a speck of the poise expected of an immortal? Why did he act like one of those bitter courtyard-complex concubines[2] with too much time on their hands? Why was he so unable to tolerate the main character no matter how innocuous his behavior, and why did he spend day in and day out scheming up new torments for him, even getting others to do so in his place?

Even if Luo Binghe was blessed with heavenly talent, and even if his aptitude was exceptional to the point that he was more or less cheating...there was still no need to envy him to that extent, you know?

Still, the blame didn't really lie with Shen Qingqiu—it lay with the author. These types of villains were everywhere in the novel, as numerous as carp in a river. It was just that Shen Qingqiu's character had been especially detailed *and* especially rotten.

What could you do, though? The ultimate boss in this book was the protagonist himself. How could a firefly outshine the sun and moon?

The cultivation world had dubbed Shen Qingqiu the "Xiu Ya Sword," so naturally he had the appearance and bearing to match. Even now, glancing left and right into a blurry bronze mirror, Shen Qingqiu was quite satisfied with what he saw.

---

2   深宅大院 *refers to the complicated courtyard compounds of rich families in old China. Generally, once a concubine enters a family, they can't leave this area, which can contribute to bitterness and a feeling of being trapped.*

It was a fine-featured face with pitch-black eyes and brows, thin nose and lips, and a most scholarly air. Combined with a slender body and long legs, he could more or less be considered beautiful. Though his real age was unclear, this was a cultivation novel: Shen Qingqiu had achieved Mid Core Formation, which meant he'd perfectly preserved his youthful appearance. He was certainly many times better-looking than Shen Yuan's headcanon for him.

He still couldn't compare to Luo Binghe.

The moment Shen Qingqiu thought of Luo Binghe, he was instantly struck with a pounding headache. He wanted to go see Luo Binghe, who was currently shut in the woodshed, but as soon as he took a single step, that ear-piercing notification rang once more in his mind.

[Warning! OOC Warning! Shen Qingqiu would not take the initiative to visit Luo Binghe.]

"Fine. I'll get someone else to bring him. No problem there, right?" Shen Qingqiu snapped. He thought for a moment, then called, "Ming Fan!"

A youth around sixteen years old, tall and thin, promptly ran in through the door. "This disciple is here. What instructions does Shifu have?"

Shen Qingqiu couldn't help but send a couple more glances his way. Ming Fan's appearance was respectable enough, it was just that his face was a bit unfortunate, with a sharp mouth and sunken cheeks. Internally, Shen Qingqiu tsked and lamented. *As expected for classic cannon fodder.*

This was the most senior of the original Shen Qingqiu's disciples, Luo Binghe's shixiong, Ming Fan. *This* was also the legendary lowest level of cannon fodder!

Needless to say, when it came to things like locking Luo Binghe out of the dorms late at night or feeding him false techniques on purpose, Ming Fan was the ever-present perpetrator. Whenever Shen Qingqiu felt inclined to torment Luo Binghe, Ming Fan was always his most useful assistant and most enthusiastic supporter.

Knowing that this child's fate in the original work wasn't much better than his own, Shen Qingqiu couldn't help but look at him with the pitying gaze of a fellow victim. "Go bring Binghe here."

Ming Fan was plainly unnerved. Whenever Shen Qingqiu had called for Luo Binghe in the past, he'd always referred to him as "that little beast," "ungrateful brat," "this wretch," or "whelp." He'd hardly even used Luo Binghe's full name more than a few times. Where had this sudden change come from?

But Ming Fan didn't dare question a command from his shifu. He jogged to the woodshed right away and kicked the door twice. "Get out! Shizun's calling you!"

Shen Qingqiu paced within his room, exhaustively examining the System within his mind.

[B-Points, also known as points awarded for being a badass. The more B-Points one accrues, the more magnificent, high-quality, and first-rate the work has become.]

"Then how can I raise my B-Points?"

[One, change the nonsensical plot and raise the average IQ of the villains and supporting characters. Two, avoid landmines that break suspension of disbelief. Three, ensure the main character's satisfaction points. Four, discover and finish hidden plot events.]

Shen Qingqiu analyzed each option one by one.

In short, not only did he have to clean up the original Shen

Qingqiu's messes—the Shen Qingqiu who'd had a veritable mob of enemies coming for his ass—he also had to stop other characters from creating *more* messes.

He didn't even know if he could preserve his own sorry life, and here he still needed to ensure that the main character preserved his OPness, time in the spotlight, and harem size.

All those unsolved mysteries, those plot holes the author had neglected to fill, and now Shen Qingqiu had to grab a shovel and sweat away, filling them in himself.

Ahhh...

"Great Master" Airplane Shooting Towards the Sky had claimed that *Proud Immortal Demon Way*'s purpose was perfectly clear, and that each word had been written with a single goal in mind: to satisfy the reader.

This was especially evident in how, in the future, the OP male lead would play innocent, a wolf in sheep's clothing hunting other wolves, exacting revenge against lowlifes, generating enough satisfaction to overturn the heavens. Thus the work's popularity had swelled rapidly as it grew longer and longer, until no foot-binding cloth could compare to its length.

Keeping track of the plot had been stressful even as a reader. Insane landmines were everywhere—how could he manage to avoid all of them?!

"What kind of plot would qualify as *not* nonsensical?" Shen Qingqiu asked.

〔The standard is subjectively determined; it depends on the readers' reactions.〕

"Then how many points do I need to collect to launch a beginner-level quest?"

[The timing is situationally determined. When the requirements have been met, the System will automatically notify you.]

Subjectively determined, situationally determined—what an all-purpose remedy. Shen Qingqiu scoffed, then upon hearing the door open, looked back to see a youth slowly walk in.

"Shizun." The youth spoke respectfully even though his movements were unsteady, and he still managed to stand perfectly straight.

The small smile that had been forming at the corner of Shen Qingqiu's mouth froze.

He was definitely dead! Before him was the face that would, in the future, infatuate everyone who saw it, from eighty-year-old women to infants still in their swaddling clothes, the Gary Stu protagonist's face—and he'd beaten it to this extent?! He was *dead*!

But even though this face bore clear evidence of abuse and was covered in injuries, the protagonist was, as expected, still the protagonist. Luo Binghe's two eyes were as bright as morning stars—a tender shoot of a handsome young man.

That firm yet humble countenance, demonstrating his noble and unyielding spirit. That pencil-straight back and stance, evincing a proud core that would rather break than bend!

In that instant, a flood of parallelisms and other stylistic devices flooded through Shen Qingqiu's heart, passage after passage jumbling together into countless stanzas of praise that almost spilled forth out of his mouth.

Luckily, Shen Qingqiu managed to rein it in, albeit while internally yelling about how close he'd come. The underlying hardware of this protagonist's halo of excellence was really too much—he almost couldn't hold back!

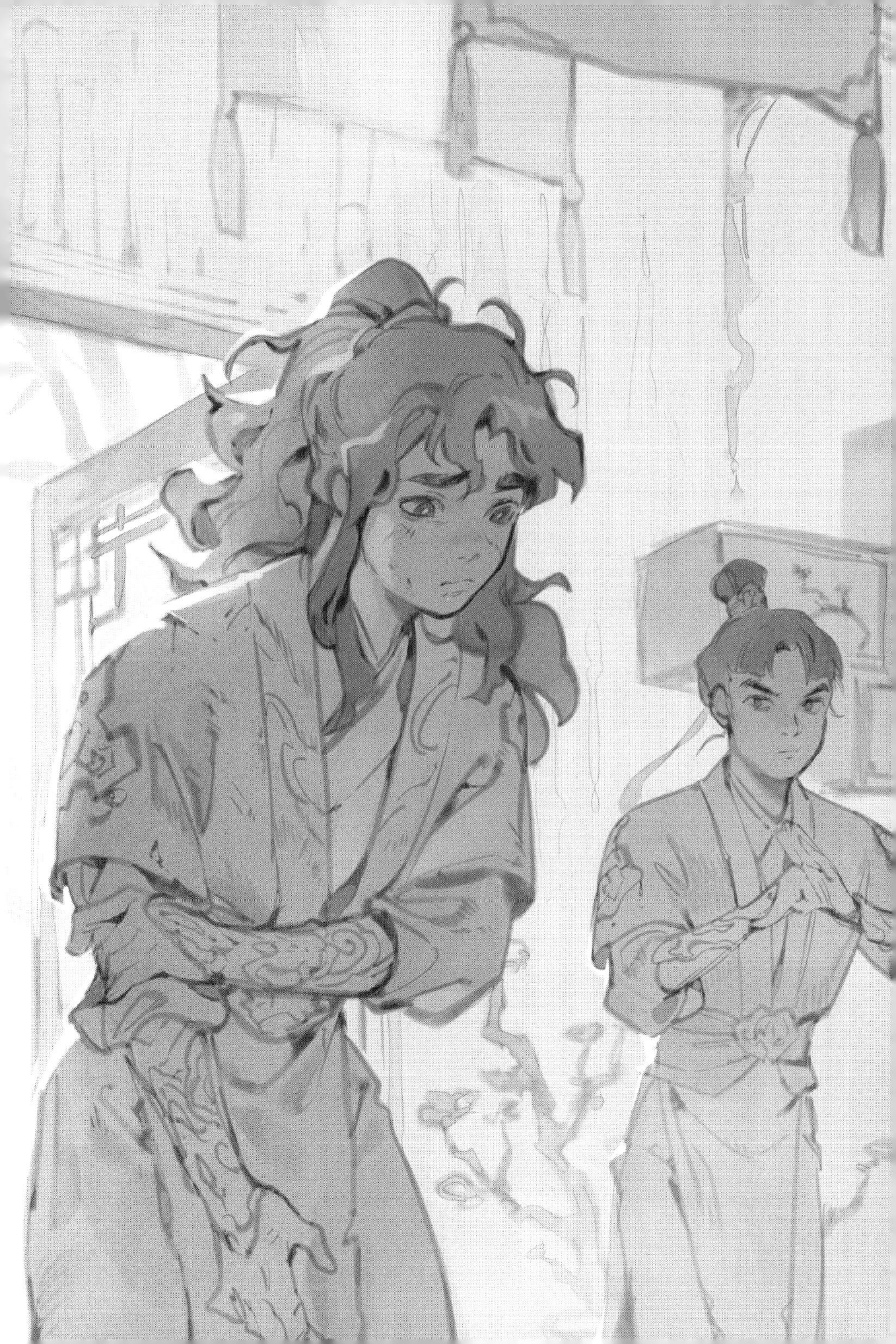

Shen Qingqiu's mouth twitched as he watched Luo Binghe limp through the door, then struggle to kneel. *I can't afford your submission—if you pay respects to me today, you are definitely going to kneecap me in the future.*

"No need." Shen Qingqiu stopped Luo Binghe, and with a flick of his wrist, he tossed over a small bottle. "This is medicine." He paused before adding in a mocking tone, "Don't let anyone see; they might think my Qing Jing Peak abuses its disciples."

Shen Qingqiu had assumed his role quickly. Even though he'd done something daringly subversive by handing over medicine, he'd also done it with a nasty attitude. Therefore, it was passably in line with Shen Qingqiu's hypocritical nature—his tendency to do evil while he simultaneously feared others finding out.

Indeed, the System didn't send an OOC notification. Shen Qingqiu let out a sigh of relief.

Luo Binghe had expected that his master had called him for further "instruction." He never would have thought he would be offered medicine. At first, he froze, then he respectfully received the small bottle with both hands and said, with honest gratitude, "Thank you for the medicine, Shizun."

At this point in time, Luo Binghe's face was still full of innocence, his smile sincere and gentle like the warm dawning sun. Shen Qingqiu stared at it for a while, then turned his head away.

Prior to his darkening, this male lead's personality was that of a model and upright youth; shine a bit of sunlight on him and he'd glow, give him a scrap of goodwill and he'd return it tenfold—that type. It would not have been an exaggeration to call him a little lamb.

"This disciple will henceforth redouble his efforts and not let Shizun be disappointed," Luo Binghe happily continued.

Eh, no, if you redouble your efforts, I'm guessing your original master would really *be disappointed...*

If Shen Qingqiu hadn't read *Proud Immortal Demon Way*, he would have found the sight of this scene heart-wrenching, and he probably would have shed a couple of sympathetic tears for Luo Binghe's plight.

As it was, he'd seen everything from beginning to end from an omniscient perspective, so he'd been privy to Luo Binghe's plentiful and colorful thoughts post-blackening.

To wit, Luo Binghe's current pitifulness directly correlated to the future ferocity of his wanton laughter as he ground his foot into your head. Though he would wear the mask of a kind and humble gentleman, inside, all his thoughts would be about how he'd rip out your tendons, pull out your bones, peel off your skin, and hang it all out to dry.

> **Luo Binghe smiled. "Today, the humiliation this disciple once suffered will be returned one hundredfold. For injuring my hands and feet, I'll tear off your limbs and grind them to dust."**
>
> **—Proud Immortal Demon Way,**
> **selected passage number two.**

After that, he had in actual fact carved Shen Qingqiu into a human stick.

"Binghe, how's your cultivation progress?" Shen Qingqiu asked in a deliberately aloof tone as he moved to sit in a sandalwood chair. With that single "Binghe," he terrified himself to the point that frightened goosebumps rose all down his back.

Luo Binghe's back also shook with a clear shudder, but he still managed a smile tinged with shyness. "This disciple is stupid and still...failed to understand."

That was about right. With a fake cultivation manual, the fact that he hadn't yet suffered a qi deviation was all thanks to his incredible protagonist-level durability. If he'd actually understood anything in that manual, it would have been a miracle.

Boy, come hang out with me! Shen Qingqiu yelled within his heart. *This master will deliver unto you the correct techniques!*

That demonic System's warning notification started blaring incessantly.

"I was only thinking about it," Shen Qingqiu said to the System. "Of course I know it would be a violation!"

Out loud, he spoke casually. "Today, this master punished you out of his own impatience. After all, time waits for no one. Now that I think about it, you've been under me for a while—how old are you this year?"

"This disciple is fourteen," Luo Binghe obediently replied.

Eh? Fourteen, huh?

That meant that at this point, this master and this disciple, Shen Qingqiu and Luo Binghe, had already passed the incident at the mountain entrance. There, the latter had been forced to kneel as punishment.

It meant they had also passed the incident where Luo Binghe's fellow Qing Jing Peak disciples had pummeled him en masse, as well as the incident where he'd "backtalked" Shizun and been strung up and beaten, in addition to the incident where he'd ruined the peak's talismans and been punished with hard labor... Such a glorious track record.

(Shen Qingqiu waved goodbye to his last hope of survival.)

Shen Qingqiu rested his forehead on one hand and waved Luo Binghe away with the other. "I wish to be alone."

Shen Qingqiu was an easygoing person.

Since his residential address had already changed to *Proud Immortal Demon Way*, and since he'd already kicked the bucket in his original world, he figured he might as well try making it work here.

He'd arrived in a cultivation setting, received a body with decent martial ability and swordsmanship for free, and was also part of a famous righteous sect. If he wanted to stand out, he could stand out, and if he wanted to lie low, he could hole up on Cang Qiong Mountain Sect's Qing Jing Peak and be a recluse. What was there to complain about?

The only slightly difficult thing would be finding a girlfriend. In this sort of male power fantasy stallion novel, any woman inevitably belonged to the male lead, as long as she wasn't ugly. Everyone knew this.

Still, Shen Qingqiu was a man of few needs; he would have been satisfied just idling away to a ripe old age. In that way, it wouldn't be that different from how his previous life had been going.

However, while Luo Binghe was a factor, making a name for himself was right out. If Shen Qingqiu remained anywhere near the original work's setting, even if he found some non-existent paradise to seclude himself in, once Luo Binghe took power, he'd still be able to carve Shen Qingqiu into a human stick.

"It's not that I don't *want* to cling to the male lead's thighs, but who made him so damn black-hearted? He's the type who seeks thousandfold retribution!"

After his daily cursing at "Great Master" Airplane, Shen Qingqiu quickly set some goals: in short, familiarize himself with his environment, work with the System as much as possible, diligently pursue more accomplishments, earn B-Points, and unfreeze the OOC function as soon as possible. If the situation started looking grim, he'd have to seek out an alternative strategy.

Cang Qiong's twelve peaks were like twelve giant swords forged by nature, steep and magnificent, piercing the skies.

Shen Qingqiu's Qing Jing Peak wasn't the tallest, but it was the most tranquil, heavily forested with tall bamboo. On top of that, as basically all of Shen Qingqiu's disciples needed to learn the four scholarly arts of guqin playing, Go, calligraphy, and painting, from time to time the clear sounds of reading and the murmur of the guqin would drift on the breeze. It was an excellent destination for scholarly youths, steeped in ancient arts and literature, and perfectly aligned with the needs of the original Shen Qingqiu—that poser.

As Shen Qingqiu passed a group of disciples, they respectfully asked after his health; he schooled his countenance to match the original's cold, aloof look, nodding slightly while walking with his hands clasped behind his back. He managed to get by with this, troubled only over how he was supposed to match the book's names to these wavering faces.

This wasn't Shen Qingqiu's most pressing concern, however. That was self-defense, and for that, he needed to figure out how to employ the original flavor's martial ability and swordsmanship.

If he remembered correctly, before Luo Binghe darkened, Cang Qiong Mountain Sect suffered a succession of significant incidents, things like demonic incursions and the Immortal Alliance Conference. Shen Qingqiu would have to deal with all of them.

If all he had to work with was a shell with no cultivation ability, forget following the plot, the male lead wouldn't have to lift a finger before an insignificant no-name monster got him killed!

Shen Qingqiu walked deep into the forest, alone. Only after confirming no one was in sight did he remove the sword at his waist. He held the scabbard in his left hand and the hilt in his right, and he slowly pulled it out.

Xiu Ya had been with Shen Qingqiu since he was young and newly known, and it could have been considered prestigious unto itself. The flash of its blade was snow white, luminous but not blinding, definitely a top-class armament. When one channeled spiritual energy into the weapon, the blade glowed faintly. As Shen Qingqiu pondered exactly *how* to "channel spiritual energy," the sword in his hand began to shimmer white.

It seemed like he'd inherited the original's cultivation and martial abilities as well. His mind had filled in the gaps without him needing to consciously remember.

Wanting to see Xiu Ya's power, Shen Qingqiu casually slashed once.

Who knew a single slash would be so terrifying? The sword's arc dazzled like a flash of lightning released from his palm, so bright that even UV 400 sunglasses wouldn't have saved him if he hadn't closed his eyes. When he opened them again, he beheld a deep ditch that had been carved into the ground, as if it had been split by lightning.

"Holy shit!"

Shen Qingqiu remained expressionless, but his heart surged with exhilaration.

So damn awesome! Power worthy of a character who was a peak's sole master. With this level of cultivation, if he diligently trained for the next twenty years, then maybe in the future—as a last resort, if he absolutely *had* to face that overpowered Luo Binghe—he might just be able to flee in disgrace!

Yes. All he wanted was to be able to flee in disgrace.

He wanted to practice more, but he heard the sound of subtle footsteps snapping dry twigs.

In truth, that sound was still a long way off, but his five senses were highly sensitive, and it would have been difficult not to notice. Shen Qingqiu studied that deep ditch in the ground, then sheathed his sword with a clink before hiding himself within the greenery.

The footsteps came closer and closer; there was more than one person. As expected, a moment later, the first face to appear was Luo Binghe's, seeming to shine with its own light. The first sound, however, was the crisp, delicate voice of a young maiden.

"A-Luo, A-Luo, look, there's a huge ditch in the ground here!"

Upon hearing this nickname, Shen Qingqiu almost staggered from his hiding place.

[Shen Qingqiu's youngest female disciple, Ning Yingying,] the System said concisely.

"What use was that introduction?" Shen Qingqiu hissed. "Everyone knows that only one person addresses Luo Binghe that way!"

The pretty girl following Luo Binghe came into view as well. She looked slightly younger than Luo Binghe, lovely and adorable, her braided hair bound with orange ribbons as she ran and skipped, brimming with naivety. Every proper cultivation novel had to have a charming young shimei-type.

This young shimei inspired some complicated feelings in Shen Qingqiu. This was because he had designs on Ning Yingying—ah, no, more like the *original* Shen Qingqiu had designs on Ning Yingying.

Shen Qingqiu's character settings were stuck on "shady hypocrite." Since on the surface he looked pure-hearted, free of desire, and immune to wicked temptations, then beneath that surface he had to be immoral, shameless, scummy, and despicable. He was a teacher, but he harbored filthy intentions toward his obedient and cheerful disciple. He tried to carry them out several times in the story, and he very nearly succeeded.

One can, however, imagine the result of daring to try to get a taste of the male lead's woman!

While reading, Shen Qingqiu had thought it a little strange that Luo Binghe hadn't tried to castrate the creep. His failure to do so absolutely didn't jive with Bing-ge's dark charm! So, he'd gone to the comment section and joined the mob in flooding it with posts to the tune of, "Please castrate Shen Qingqiu! No castration, we unsubscribe!"

Upon reflection and closer consideration, Shen Qingqiu was profoundly terrified. If the appeal had succeeded then, he'd absolutely have had to chop off the hand with which he had made those posts!

Luo Binghe glanced over once and offered only a half-hearted smile.

But Ning Yingying wanted his attention, and she fumbled around for something to say. "Tell me, A-Luo, which shixiong was practicing their sword glares out here?"

"On Qing Jing Peak, I'm afraid only Shizun has this level of cultivation," Luo Binghe answered as he picked up an axe and started chopping at a tree.

He only spoke one line, then paid her no more heed. His focus was entirely on his own actions as he raised and lowered the axe, chopping in earnest.

These trees were neither thin nor weak, and the axe was half-rusted. At this time, Luo Binghe was only fourteen years old, so chopping was tremendously taxing. Soon, sweat poured down his face.

Ning Yingying sat on an old log, watching him with her face propped in her hands. After a while, she was bored again and wheedled. "A-Luo, A-Luo, play with me!"

"I can't." Luo Binghe didn't even have the time to wipe away his sweat; he continued to swing the axe as he spoke. "Our shixiong told me that after I finish chopping today's wood, I also have to carry the water. If I finish chopping quickly, I can clear out some time to meditate."

"Our shixiong are really awful! Always making you do this and that. It looks to me like they're bullying you on purpose." Ning Yingying pouted. "Humph, I'll go back and tell Shizun. Once I do, they won't dare bully you anymore."

Until this point, Shen Qingqiu had been treating this experience like he was at a shoot for a scene of a *Proud Immortal Demon Way* drama—just passing through!—and enjoying a tale of two childhood sweethearts. Upon hearing this, he paled in shock.

No, no, no, you absolutely can't come tell me! What am I supposed to do?! I can't be OOC—who exactly should I punish?!

But at this time, even while the young Luo Binghe was experiencing the full depth and breadth of humanity's hardships, he still had the pure heart of a white lotus. He shook his head at Ning Yingying. "Absolutely don't. I don't want to trouble Shizun with these small matters. Our shixiong don't mean any harm, they just see that I'm young and want to give me more chances to train."

In that instant, Shen Qingqiu could almost see ten thousand rays of light behind Luo Binghe. He couldn't help but back up three steps, unable to look directly at a male lead who had achieved such a transcendent state of being—who'd attained such profound enlightenment!

While Ning Yingying chattered, Luo Binghe finished chopping his quota of wood. Putting the axe away, he found a random patch of relatively clean ground and sat down cross-legged with his eyes closed.

Inside his heart, Shen Qingqiu released a long sigh.

In truth, even during the early, misery-ridden part of the storyline, the protagonist's overpowered nature had already started to emerge. The cultivation manual Ming Fan had given Luo Binghe was a fake. The more he trained by following it, the more his techniques should have degraded until they were absolute rubbish. But with his peerless talent and his body's half-demon blood, Luo Binghe had managed to eke out a path of his own by complete accident... It was entirely unscientific!

While Shen Qingqiu sighed, there came the sound of another set of jumbled footsteps.

As soon as he heard them, Shen Qingqiu knew that what was coming wouldn't be good.

Ming Fan stepped out into the clearing, leading several low-ranked disciples. Upon seeing Ning Yingying, he delightedly strode up and grabbed her hand. "Xiao-shimei! Xiao-shimei, I finally found you. How could you come to a place like this without saying anything? The back side of the mountain is so large—what if some dangerous beast or poisonous snake leapt out? Come, Shixiong has something fun to show you."

Naturally, Ming Fan saw Luo Binghe silently sitting nearby, but he ignored the other boy as if he were nothing but air.

However, Luo Binghe, being very well mannered, opened his eyes and spoke. "Shixiong."

"I'm not afraid of poisonous snakes or dangerous beasts," Ning Yingying giggled. "Besides, isn't A-Luo with me?"

Ming Fan swept his gaze toward Luo Binghe, squinted, and scoffed.

To Shen Qingqiu, Ming Fan's thoughts couldn't have been clearer. He heard the affectionate way Ning Yingying addressed Luo Binghe and, in that moment, his annoying shidi had become even more irritating.

In the end, Ning Yingying had a young girl's disposition, completely unable to take a hint or read the room. "What fun thing does Shixiong have?" she asked, head tilted. "Hurry up and show me."

Ming Fan became all smiles. He unfastened a deep green jade ornament from his waist and held it in front of her. "Shimei, my family just came to visit, and they brought me lots of high-quality and interesting little trinkets. I thought this one was particularly pretty; I'll give it to you!"

Ning Yingying took it from him and examined it closely in the sunlight shining through the leaves.

"Well? Do you like it?" Ming Fan asked eagerly.

From his hiding place, Shen Qingqiu finally remembered—this was *that* scene!

Not good! He shouldn't have come! Danger!

He couldn't be blamed for not remembering clearly. How could someone who'd cursed "dumbfuck author, dumbfuck novel" remember ancient content from the beginning of a serialized novel that had been running for four years and covered an in-narrative span of two *hundred* years? He'd spent twenty days binging the novel from start to finish, so he had clean forgotten that whump-filled arc of pointless abuse that covered Luo Binghe's beginnings at the sect, okay?!

Ning Yingying had absolutely no idea what was high quality and what wasn't. After looking nonchalantly at it for a while, she tossed the jade ornament back.

Ming Fan's smile froze on his face.

"What? This color is so ugly. The one A-Luo has is prettier," Ning Yingying said carelessly as she wrinkled her nose.

Not only did Ming Fan look unhappy, but Luo Binghe, who'd been wisely pretending to not exist, trembled lightly as his eyes snapped open.

"Does Shidi also wear this kind of thing?" Ming Fan spat through gritted teeth.

Luo Binghe hesitated slightly.

He hadn't managed to answer when Ning Yingying barged in. "Of course he does. Every day, he wears it close around his neck. It's his treasure. He refuses to even let me look at it."

Although Luo Binghe was usually so composed, at this point his expression also changed. He unconsciously clutched the goddess of mercy Guanyin pendant around his neck, hidden beneath his clothes.

Your IQ and EQ, young lady! The male lead is taking all the collateral damage!

Ning Yingying absolutely hadn't considered the consequences of these words as she said them. She'd only been thinking of how she always saw Luo Binghe wearing that jade Guanyin close to his skin, never parting with it. Girls in particular invariably wanted to get their hands on the things their crushes treasured, which they hoped would confer upon them the satisfaction of being in a "special position." But

Luo Binghe simply refused to give her that recognition. Displeased, she'd brought it up in this half-sweet, half-brazen manner.

Of course he'd refused, okay?! Luo Binghe's washerwoman mother had spent almost her entire life savings to finally, with great difficulty, give her son the consecrated protective charm she wanted for him. It was the only bit of warmth in Luo Binghe's dark world, always by his side, and even in the future when he was at his darkest, it could summon up his last dregs of humanity—so how could he randomly hand it to anyone else?!

Ming Fan, both angry and jealous, advanced a few steps. "Luo-shidi, you sure are stuck-up, refusing to show Ning Yingying-shimei your pendant," he snarled. "If this keeps up, when we face strong enemies in the future, will you refuse to even lend a hand?!"

Young man! There's definitely a logical gap between your first and second lines!

"It's fine if he doesn't want to. Shixiong, don't bully him!" Ning Yingying hadn't thought things would turn out like this, and she anxiously stamped her feet.

How could Luo Binghe best Ming Fan at this point? Not to mention a group of junior disciples who were Ming Fan's lackeys were also ganging up on him.

In a moment, that jade Guanyin fell from Luo Binghe's neck into Ming Fan's hands. Ming Fan raised it up for a look, then suddenly laughed loudly.

"Why...why are you laughing?" Ning Yingying said, confused.

"I thought it had to be some rare treasure, for him to protect it so fiercely. Shimei, guess what it is?" Ming Fan tossed the jade pendant into Ning Yingying's hands, positively gleeful as he chuckled. "It's a counterfeit..."

"Counterfeit?" Ning Yingying asked. "What's that?"

"Give it back." Luo Binghe enunciated each word. His fists slowly clenched, a treacherous undercurrent surging in the depths of his eyes.

Shen Qingqiu's fingers involuntarily twitched once, then again, and again. Naturally, he remembered that the jade Guanyin was a counterfeit—he also knew that it was Luo Binghe's biggest berserk button.

For an entire year, the washerwoman had scrimped and saved on food and utilities, but because she lacked experience, a con-man had tricked her into paying a high price for a fake charm. Heartbroken after this, her body had steadily deteriorated. Luo Binghe would undoubtedly be unable to forget this pain for the rest of his life. Thus, this was the one insult that Luo Binghe could never tolerate.

As a bystander, Shen Qingqiu desperately wanted to reach out, beat up Ming Fan, snatch back the jade pendant, and toss it to Luo Binghe.

Also, if he did that, maybe Ming Fan wouldn't thoroughly offend Luo Binghe? Then, later on, he could keep his paltry little life.

[OOC.]

"Thank you. Shut up."

"You want it back, I'll give it back. Who knows which street stall this cheap thing was purchased from?" Ming Fan plucked the pendant from Ning Yingying's hands, disgust in his tone. "I'm afraid giving it to Shimei would dirty her hands."

So he said, but he had not the slightest intention of returning it.

Luo Binghe's face was tight. Suddenly, he struck out with both fists, hitting the couple of low-ranked disciples restraining him.

Enraged as he was, his blows were not directed by technique;

they were random strikes fueled by the anger within. At first he managed to cow these low-ranked disciples, but they quickly realized that he was in truth incredibly weak and that only his demeanor was impressive.

Also, Ming Fan was snarling at them. "What are you standing there for? He dared to attack his shixiong—teach him what it means to respect seniority!"

At this, they all regained their courage and surrounded Luo Binghe, clobbering him.

Ning Yingying was scared stiff, her pitiful brain capacity still not understanding how things had progressed to this state. "Shixiong!" she cried. "How could you do this?! Hurry up and tell them to stop, or—or I'll never talk to you ever again!"

"Shimei, don't be angry," Ming Fan said in a panic. "I'll tell them to stop hitting this guy, okay?"

He was distracted. Before he finished speaking, Luo Binghe broke free from the many arms and legs entangling him—and sent a fist into Ming Fan's nose.

A wild wail. Two twin streams of fresh blood jetted from Ming Fan's nostrils.

Although she had been about to burst into tears, at the sight of this, Ning Yingying couldn't help but let out a stifled laugh.

Sister, really, do you like Luo Binghe, or do you want to screw him over?! Shen Qingqiu howled in his mind.

Before this point, Ming Fan might feasibly have let Luo Binghe go, but now that he'd been humiliated in front of his crush, he couldn't back down, no matter what.

The two boys twisted into a fighting heap, but no matter how exceptional Luo Binghe's talent, he was still young, and he hadn't been cultivating with proper instruction. It was, for the most part, a one-sided beatdown. Yet Luo Binghe remained silent, teeth clenched.

Shen Qingqiu wanted desperately to intervene—but the System exploded with a terrifying cascade of alarms.

[Severe OOC! Severe OOC! Severe OOC! Important things must be repeated three times! In this situation, Shen Qingqiu would choose to smile! He would watch from the sidelines, hands in his sleeves! Or personally beat Luo Binghe himself!]

Was it really going to make him look on while a child was being abused? This was really too much… Even so, Shen Qingqiu couldn't afford to take risks.

While he was anxiously fretting, a compromise suddenly came to him.

Cang Qiong Mountain Sect had a minor technique, "Plucking Leaves, Flying Flowers." At a glance, it wasn't very useful, just aesthetic and interesting. The novel had described how Luo Binghe used the technique to win the nth woman's affections. As Shen Qingqiu had, since his arrival, been furiously reviewing various manuals, he had also recently seen a description of it.

He plucked a nearby leaf and channeled a touch of spiritual power into it. The first time, he channeled too much. The leaf couldn't withstand his power and instantly split into several pieces. He succeeded the second time, held the leaf between his fingertips, and gently blew, letting go.

The leaf shot toward Ming Fan like an airborne knife.

As Ming Fan's long and horrible scream split the air, Shen Qingqiu shook out his hand and wiped a bead of sweat from his forehead.

No wonder they said that to an expert, even a flower or tree could be used to hurt people! But he hadn't killed Ming Fan just now, right...?

Luo Binghe had suffered quite a few punches and kicks, but suddenly it was Ming Fan who staggered backward. Luo Binghe looked up. Fresh blood dripped from his forehead past his eyes, but he hadn't expected to see Ming Fan stretching out his own hand, his palm also covered in blood.

Ming Fan stared in disbelief. "You *dare* to use a knife?"

Due to its fierceness, Ning Yingying hadn't risked coming close to their fight, but now she hurried to throw herself between the two. "No, no, A-Luo didn't use a knife. It wasn't him!"

Luo Binghe also had no idea what had happened. He closed his mouth tightly and tried to clean the blood from his face.

"Did you see clearly? Was he holding a knife?" Ming Fan interrogated the other disciples as blood seeped out of his back—like he'd been cut with the edge of a sword.

The disciples looked around at each other in complete disarray, some shaking their heads, some nodding.

Ming Fan was a spoiled and pampered young master, and he had never suffered this level of physical pain. The sight of his own hand covered with blood sent panic surging through his heart. The puzzling thing was that there was no evidence of a weapon either on the ground or on Luo Binghe's slender person. It couldn't have vanished into thin air, right?

Shen Qingqiu held his breath. His vision suddenly flashed red, and a huge line of floating text popped up before him in a blood red as eye-catching as it was bone-chilling.

[Violation: OOC. B-Points -10. Current B-Points: 90.]

Shen Qingqiu released his breath, relieved. He'd been prepared for a deduction in the realm of fifty, or even to lose everything. Only ten was much better than he'd thought. He'd take the loss for now. There would be future chances to earn those points back.

Then, shortly after he let out that breath, Ming Fan pointed to Luo Binghe and yelled, "Get him!"

Shen Qingqiu nearly vomited a mouthful of blood straight from his chest.

The gang of disciples heard the order and tackled Luo Binghe. Shen Qingqiu unconsciously tore off a nearby handful of leaves and sent them all singing through the air.

He regretted it as soon as they left his hand.

The fuck am I doing? No matter what happens, Luo Binghe is the magnificent male lead. It's not like he's never been ganged up on before. Like they could beat him to death! Like hell you need to worry, self!

He might have gotten away with the first interference, but now? Fantastic, even an idiot would notice something was off!

Numerous disciples were splattered with blood. They anxiously gathered around Ming Fan, no longer daring to gang up on Luo Binghe.

"Shixiong! What's going on?!"

"Shixiong, I've also been cut!"

Ming Fan's face was green and white. Only after a long moment did he yell out. "Go!"

Leading his group of lackeys, all covering their backs and holding their arms, he frantically withdrew. They truly came like the wind and left like it too.

Only Ning Yingying remained, standing there dumbly for a while. Then she shouted, "A-Luo, were you the one who sent them running just now?"

Luo Binghe shook his head, expression gloomy. He stood up, straightening with difficulty. Then he bent down again with a tense look, searching the ground for something, turning over fallen leaves, dry twigs, and mud this way and that, over and over again.

Shen Qingqiu knew what he was looking for. Naturally, it was that jade pendant, which had been lost in the confusion.

He saw it, clear as day. Before fighting, Ming Fan had swung out his arm, and as he did, the pendant's red string had snagged on a branch high above their heads. But Shen Qingqiu couldn't point that out.

Also, just after he'd sent the leaves flying, he'd heard that heart-shattering System scream.

[Violation: OOC. B-Points -10 x 6. Current B-Points: 30.]

In an instant, he'd fallen below a passing grade!

So one leaf equals ten points? Don't use such simple, crude arithmetic!

Ning Yingying didn't dare speak. After all, she had caused this entire affair. If not for her big mouth, Luo Binghe would never have suffered a beating—and on top of that, he'd lost his pendant for no good reason. She swiftly began to help Luo Binghe search.

They of course remained empty-handed, even as it became dark.

Luo Binghe stood dumbly in place, staring at the mess of the ground. They had overturned every speck of dirt in sight, but still they hadn't found it.

"A-Luo, if we can't find it, let's just let it be," said Ning Yingying, a little frightened to see him so dazed and out of his mind. She took his hand. "I'm sorry, I'll buy you another one later, all right?"

Luo Binghe paid her no heed. He slowly withdrew his hand and walked toward the forest's edge, head lowered. Ning Yingying hurried after him.

Shen Qingqiu was truly impressed with himself. These two children had searched for an entire afternoon, and he'd actually gone and watched the whole time... How could he explain that to himself, other than to say that he had too much fucking time on his hands?

He waited until they'd gone a good distance, then finally emerged from his hiding place. He raised his head and looked about, then tapped his foot on the ground. In that moment, he experienced what it meant to have "a body as light as a swallow," and with great ease, he rose and plucked that jade pendant from where it was caught on a branch.

In truth, Shen Qingqiu wanted to secretly return it to Luo Binghe, but he was now familiar with this System's rules. That would definitely count as a violation. He didn't have any B-Points to squander.

After some thought, Shen Qingqiu decided to keep it for the time being.

Maybe later, this jade pendant would be of great use. For example, perhaps during a critical moment, when his fate hung by a thread, he could bargain it in exchange for his life? Shen Qingqiu gave this possibility serious consideration.

Right then, a line of green text with a pronounced 3D effect jumped into view.

[Congratulations! Obtained key item: Fake Jade Guanyin x 1. For changing the storyline, Shen Qingqiu IQ +100. Current B-Points: 130. Please continue to work hard!]

All the points that had just been deducted were not only restored, he even got more!

On top of that, given the influence this jade Guanyin had on Luo Binghe, it was definitely a high-level item, and it *could* be used preserve his life! What a happy surprise!

A rush of satisfaction flowed through Shen Qingqiu, cleansing him of the gloom that had set in while he crouched in the dark for a whole afternoon. At this moment, even the System's eminently punchable, Google Translate-like voice was melodious beyond compare.

Meanwhile, outside the forest, Luo Binghe had already left the back of the mountain, and he slowly unclenched his fist.

Lying in his palm was a whole green leaf. Its edges were sharp and stained with blood.

In the days of Shen Qingqiu's recuperation following his awakening from that inexplicable fever, Yue Qingyuan came to visit him many times. As the sect leader of the world's foremost major cultivation sect—which might be likened to being the principal of a comprehensive cultivation university—his workload had to be heavy. Yet he was still so considerate to his shidi. As a stranger in a strange land, Shen Qingqiu practically wanted to shed tears of gratitude.

That the original flavor had actually turned on such a kind superior and fellow disciple, that he had breached their brotherly covenant just like that—it just made clear how much of a scumbag he was!

"Now that Shidi has rested for several days, has your health improved?" Yue Qingyuan asked, his eyes full of earnest concern as he held one of the Bamboo House's porcelain tea bowls.

"I have long since recovered," said Shen Qingqiu, lightly waving his folding fan and feeling at home in the atmosphere of brotherly love. "I've caused Shixiong such trouble, making him worry."

"Then I suppose it's about time for Shidi to leave the mountains," said Yue Qingyuan. "Is there anything you need?"

The hand Shen Qingqiu was using to fan himself froze. "Leave the mountains?"

"Did the illness make you forget?" Yue Qingyuan asked, surprised. "Didn't you tell me before to leave the matter of Shuang Hu City to you, as a training opportunity for your disciples?"

So it was some troublesome project undertaken by the original flavor. But while Shen Qingqiu had been familiarizing himself with this body's spiritual power and techniques, they still weren't second nature. How could he take disciples down from the mountains for training? Just as he was about to summon his resolve and embarrass himself, to renege and say that his body wasn't well after all, the System's unfeeling voice reverberated in his skull.

[Beginner-level quest issued. Location: Shuang Hu City. Quest: Complete the training. Please click to accept.]

At the same time, the quest synopsis popped up before him with two options on the bottom, the left saying "Accept," the right saying "Reject."

So this was a beginner-level quest. Shen Qingqiu's gaze lingered on "Accept" for a while.

The option blinked green, a ding sounded, and the System said, [Quest successfully accepted. Please thoroughly read the provided files and make your preparations. We wish you a swift success.]

Shen Qingqiu came back to himself. "Naturally I remember," he said while smiling. "It's just these days I've rested too much and grown slow. I had almost forgotten about this matter. I'll head out in a few days."

Yue Qingyuan nodded. "If you're not completely recovered, there's no need to force yourself. There's no rush to train your disciples either. You especially don't need to personally take care of this matter."

Shen Qingqiu agreed, still smiling, but he couldn't help giving Yue Qingyuan two extra glances.

Zhangmen-shixiong, your current role, it's getting a bit too much like a quest-giving NPC...

All affairs on Qing Jing Peak, whether large or small, were handed to and looked after by Shen Qingqiu's trusted subordinate, Ming Fan. Shen Qingqiu had discovered that in matters that didn't involve a certain protagonist, Ming Fan was surprisingly efficient and intelligent. They were able to set out the following day.

Before leaving Qing Jing Peak, Shen Qingqiu briefly inspected his appearance. Teal robes, loose sash, sword at left hip, fan in right hand, elegant, cultured, reliable, graceful! A properly otherworldly being!

In short, absolutely not OOC—perfect!

At the bottom of the long, hundred-step stone stairway, waiting by the mountain gates, was the carriage prepared for Shen Qingqiu, as well as a collection of horses for his accompanying disciples.

"Are you kidding?" Shen Qingqiu muttered in his head. "In the end, this is still a cultivation setting. Why aren't we flying on swords?"

[Even in a magical setting like *Harry Potter,* not every wizard goes out riding brooms,] the System coolly replied. [It would be too conspicuous.]

"You sure are knowledgeable," Shen Qingqiu muttered. "Did you do business over at Harry Potter's before?"

The System typed out a giant line of hovering symbols: [...]

In all these years of the System's operation, Shen Qingqiu might have been the first person bored enough to act so familiarly with it, let alone to fuck around with it.

On the other hand, if he thought about it, this setup made sense. This trip down the mountains was for the sake of training, and the majority of these disciples were young and lacked experience. They hadn't even claimed their personal swords yet. According to the traditions of Cang Qiong Mountain Sect, only once a disciple's cultivation reached a certain stage could they go to Wan Jian Peak—one of the Twelve Peaks—to pick a suitable blade.

Though it was said that the person picked the sword, in truth, the sword also picked the person. If a person with subpar talent insisted on taking a top-class sword capable of condensing spiritual energy collected from the heavens and earth, it would be the equivalent of a beautiful woman marrying an ugly man or arranging fresh flowers in cow dung. As you can imagine, the sword would be entirely unwilling.

Luo Binghe's real golden finger only activated when he came upon his own personal sword, the mystical Xin Mo.

Shen Qingqiu entered the carriage. Its appearance wasn't especially ornate, but the interior was both spacious and comfortable, and a small incense burner faintly smoldered within.

Once he sat, Shen Qingqiu had a sudden premonition that something wasn't quite right. He abruptly poked out his fan and raised it to lift the curtains. The second he looked outside, he felt he should have been struck blind by the sight.

No wonder he'd thought that the silhouette hurrying back and forth around the carriage seemed familiar—the person everyone was ordering around to do miscellaneous tasks was none other than the great male lead, Luo Binghe.

Just then, Luo Binghe hauled the last item onto the carriage— a white jade chess board that was mandatory luggage on all of Shen

Qingqiu's trips (though it usually went unused). He raised his head to see Shen Qingqiu observing him with a complicated expression and jolted slightly. Respectfully, he said, "Shizun."

The injuries Luo Binghe had received from Shen Qingqiu's pre-fever discipline were just about healed. The bruises on his face had vanished, and one could finally clearly see what he looked like. Even though he was young, his features still soft and immature, no degree of youth could conceal the handsome grace within him. On top of that, he walked and moved with a shining air. Who would ever guess that this was Qing Jing Peak's most miserable flower bud, which had been ravaged by wind and rain for many years?

Although Luo Binghe was doing the rough work of moving luggage and equipment, his attitude was meticulous. It was hard not to be moved by that earnest and focused bearing—it was especially hard for Shen Qingqiu, who already had some fondness for this male lead.

He was, indeed, *very* fond of this ruthlessly decisive protagonist, who was so clear-cut with who deserved his kindness and who his hatred.

After staring for a moment, Shen Qingqiu made an "oh" sound, then pulled back his fan, dropping the curtains.

It had to be said, the male lead was inescapably the male lead. Even with how downtrodden this kid was, with no history, no prospects, nor parents to love him, it was no wonder that there were still so many first, second, third, and fourth female leads ready to hang off his every word, trail in his wake, and otherwise throw themselves at him. Good looks were the true way of the world!

This also explained why there was always some cannon fodder or another who found him an eyesore, and who wanted to vent by beating him until his head looked like a pig's.

Then something else occurred to Shen Qingqiu: *That's not right.*

If the total number of traveling disciples, including Luo Binghe, was ten, and there were only nine horses, then weren't they missing one?

All right, even if he'd thought with his toes, he'd have known who to blame.

As expected, Ming Fan's gleeful voice cut through the snickering outside: "Actually, we're short on horses, so we have no choice but to inconvenience Shidi this time. Although, since Shidi's foundation is poor, it's perfect—you can also take this chance to train."

Short on horses my ass.

In recent years, of all the major sects, Cang Qiong Mountain Sect had become number one when it came to cultivation; it had no real business rivals. That it was overflowing with wealth could be left unsaid. In short: Like they'd want for even a single horse!

"What?" Ming Fan paused, truly well versed in digging his own cannon fodder grave. "What sort of expression is that? You dissatisfied?"

"I wouldn't dare," said Luo Binghe evenly, neither haughty nor humble.

At this point, a young girl's bell-like laugh cut the air. Ning Yingying had arrived. "Shixiong, what are you two talking about?"

Shen Qingqiu held his forehead. *Really, young lady, your timing!*

Ning Yingying was a powerful catalyst in the continued worsening of Ming Fan's and Luo Binghe's relationship. Whenever she appeared, Luo Binghe was in for no shortage of suffering, and Ming Fan was in for an equal amount of personal grave-digging.

Once again, Shen Qingqiu tentatively lifted the carriage curtains a little, dithering over whether he should speak.

As expected, he beheld Ning Yingying excitedly waving her hand. "A-Luo, not enough horses? Come ride with me!"

She really does bring a lot of hatred down on Luo Binghe.

So it is known: although this type of plot, wherein the downtrodden protagonist receives special attention from a beauty, is a satisfying trope often seen on Zhongdian Literature, it is also the likeliest to incite the envy of others and subsequent persecution.

In this moment, if Luo Binghe accepted Ning Yingying's suggestion, he could forget about getting any peace on this trip.

Shen Qingqiu could no longer sit by and bear it. "Yingying, don't make a fuss. Men and women mustn't be too intimate. No matter how close you are with your shidi, there ought to be limits. Ming Fan, we're dawdling. Why haven't we set out yet?"

Ming Fan was overjoyed, no doubt thinking, *Shizun and I are on the same page!* He hastily urged the group to depart.

Ning Yingying pouted but said nothing.

That little skit over for now, Shen Qingqiu let his mind wander from it and returned to silently reading the files spread out on his System desk.

This trip wasn't to commemorate the first plotline to take him down the mountain. It was, most importantly, concerned with a beginner-level quest that would determine whether he could unfreeze the OOC function. Shen Qingqiu couldn't afford to treat it with anything but the utmost seriousness.

The file described the location, a small city several tens of kilometers away from Cang Qiong Mountain Sect. Recently, a number of murders had occurred within it. Already, nine people were dead.

Every victim shared a common fate: the skin on their body had been completely, meticulously peeled off from head to toe and with prefect precision, as if the skin had never been attached to the deceased body at all. It was enough to horrify anyone. Therefore, the murderer had come to be known as the "Skinner Demon."

The Skinner Demon's chosen victims were all young, beautiful women. Therefore, in Shuang Hu City, every family with daughters, wives, or concubines shut and locked their doors the moment night fell. Despite this, they had been unable to stop the Skinner Demon from coming and going as it pleased.

A succession of nine horrible deaths, yet the officials had no idea what to do. The city's people were in a state of panic. There were even rumors that it was the work of a ghost—otherwise, how could the culprit come and go without a trace?!

Several influential families had met together and at last decided to send someone to Cang Qiong Mountain Sect to plead for assistance from the immortal cultivators.

Shen Qingqiu had already read this information multiple times. But no matter how many times he read it, it wasn't the least bit helpful.

The hell is a Skinner Demon?! Never heard of it! Is this a newly added plotline or a hidden one?! Is it dangerous?! Is it strong?! Am I even going to be able to deal with it?! This isn't what we agreed to!

In response to these questions, the System said: [What isn't? You were once a novel reader. Novels are a type of artistic creation, and in any artistic creation, there are always decisions that must be made and things that must be left out. Now that you've become part of this world, you naturally have to experience everything yourself, regardless of importance—you must follow every plotline to the very end, even ones omitted from the original work.]

Shen Qingqiu had no say in any of it. As such, he had diligently trained for numerous days, single-mindedly seeking to make his abilities second nature, lest he croak at the hands of some no-name monster before he ever had the chance to die beneath the male lead's feet, like a general passing away before his first victory.

Luo Binghe was still outside, so at no moment did Shen Qingqiu dare to relax his vigil, keeping an eye out for any untoward activity. At the same time, he rummaged through the carriage interior. Every comfort one could imagine was on hand. Shen Qingqiu managed to dredge up five or six different tea sets, and he was speechless at the sight of them. No matter that in his past life he could have counted as a wealthy second-gen, he still hadn't been this pointlessly indulgent in his pursuit of first-world affluenza, okay?

At this time, a wave of cackles rolled in from outside the carriage. He swept a glance outside.

Luo Binghe trailed alone at the back of the group, at times walking, at times running. From time to time, horses encircled him, purposely kicking up a cloud of dust until he was filthy and caked with it.

Shen Qingqiu couldn't help clutching the handle of his fan, knuckles itching faintly.

This was only a book, and all the people were constructs, imaginary characters. Logically, Shen Qingqiu was very clear on this fact... but when a character was actually being taunted and bullied right before his eyes, it was just flat-out unrealistic to expect him to be completely unmoved.

Having attempted to dissuade them several times to no avail, Ning Yingying finally realized her interference only made things worse. She anxiously urged her horse toward the carriage and called out. "Shizun! The shixiong, look at them!"

"What about them?" Shen Qingqiu asked placidly. Though his heart was moved, he didn't show it.

"They're bullying someone so viciously, yet you're not telling them off," she said defiantly, her voice carrying with the strength of her indignation. "If they keep on like this—Shizun, what are you teaching your disciples to become?!"

Even though she was directly tattling on them, Ming Fan and his lackeys didn't feel any pressure at all. They were all used to the prior Shen Qingqiu silently permitting these actions. The harsher their bullying of Luo Binghe, the happier they made their teacher. Why would they exercise restraint?

Ming Fan was happiest of all. He was so sure that on that day at the back of the mountain, Luo Binghe had used some manner of sorcery he'd learned from who-knew-where. Today, Shizun was here, and he'd be crushed!

Shen Qingqiu made an "oh" sound. Then he spoke a single line: "Luo Binghe, come here."

Luo Binghe's expression went blank. Accustomed to this call, he gave his quiet assent and walked over.

At first, everyone was still riding high on schadenfreude, thinking that Shen Qingqiu was calling Luo Binghe over to grab him by the ear and discipline him.

What happened next shattered their entire worldview.

Shen Qingqiu used his fan to lift the curtains, then jerked his chin at Luo Binghe before shooting a glance at the carriage interior. Even though he didn't speak, the meaning couldn't have been clearer.

"A-Luo, hurry and get on!" Ning Yingying said happily. "Shizun is letting you ride with him!"

Like! Thunder! On! A! Clear! Day!

If they hadn't known their master so well and for so long, Ming Fan and his fellows would have suspected that Shen Qingqiu had been possessed by a demon.

Luo Binghe had also frozen in astonishment, but his reaction was nevertheless swift. He paused for only a second before saying, "Many thanks to Shizun."

Then he stepped into the carriage, ever conscientious, and sat straight-backed in a corner. His hands and feet remained tucked in, like he was afraid that his patched clothes would dirty the interior.

[Warning...]

"Warning rejected," said Shen Qingqiu. "I wasn't OOC."

[Shen Qingqiu would never do anything to alleviate Luo Binghe's troubles. Verdict: OOC level 100 percent.]

"Have you carefully examined this character's complicated inner world?" Shen Qingqiu countered. "Of course he would never do anything purely to alleviate Luo Binghe's troubles. But right now, my goal is to prevent Ning Yingying from losing faith in me as her teacher. Yingying is my dearest little disciple, and she begged me! How could I let her plea go unheard?"

[...]

"So my actions are completely in line with 'Shen Qingqiu's' internal logic," Shen Qingqiu declared. "Your warning is invalid!"

During their exchanges over the last couple of days, Shen Qingqiu had gradually figured out a handful of the System's quirks. It had rules, but these rules were not rigid. As that was the case, there was a bit of leeway for bargaining.

As he'd hoped, for the time being, the System couldn't think of an argument to enforce its deduction.

Riding high on the delight of victory in this first battle, Shen Qingqiu couldn't help but laugh.

However, Shen Qingqiu had in that moment been quietly sitting in the carriage, seemingly meditating with his eyes closed in a trance. When Luo Binghe suddenly heard him laugh, he couldn't resist stealing a glance at him.

To tell the truth, it would have been a lie to say that Luo Binghe wasn't surprised. Even though he'd always revered Shen Qingqiu, he had no illusions about how his master treated and looked at him.

At first, he'd thought that if Shen Qingqiu asked him to get in the carriage, there must be something even more terrible waiting for him within, and he had mentally prepared himself for it. He hadn't expected Shen Qingqiu to not bother with him at all, instead focusing only on himself as he began to meditate.

Luo Binghe thought for a moment. It seemed to him that he had never been this close to his teacher before and that he had never had an opportunity to carefully examine Shen Qingqiu like this.

Appearance-wise, you couldn't complain about him. Perhaps Shen Qingqiu couldn't qualify as supremely beautiful, but he was certainly good-looking, and you wouldn't tire of looking at him. The profile of his face, in three-quarter view, seemed to have been carved by creeks and mountain springs, and when not fixed in a cold scowl, it became gentle and bright.

As soon as Shen Qingqiu opened his eyes, he found Luo Binghe staring at him. He saw a glimpse of the future Luo Binghe's unique grace, that of "eyes like cold stars, a soft and radiant smile, with muted words and quiet laughter."

Luo Binghe had been caught red-handed, and right as he was struck, lost as to what to do, Shen Qingqiu smiled at him.

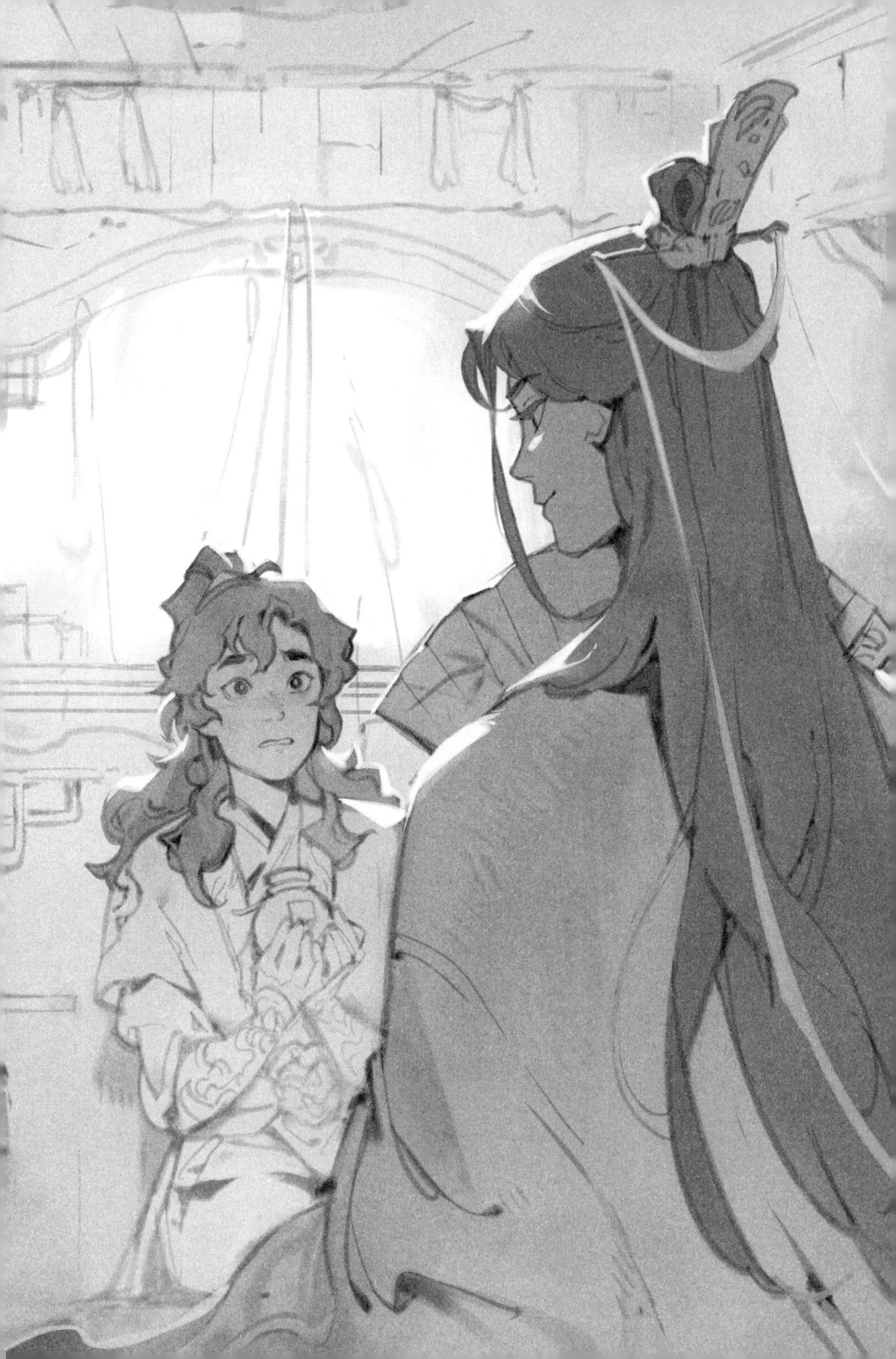

This smile was purely unconscious—but Luo Binghe felt like he'd been pricked by a small, fine thorn. He quickly averted his gaze and became increasingly awkward, unsure of what he was feeling.

Very soon, Shen Qingqiu couldn't bring himself to smile anymore.

The System had delivered a notification. [Violation: OOC. B-Points -5. Current B-Points: 165.]

Sayeth Shen Qingqiu: "Even a brief smile warrants a deduction?"

Sayeth the System, most righteously: [OOC is OOC.]

Having learned his lesson, Shen Qingqiu spent the rest of the trip stone-faced until they finally arrived at Shuang Hu City without incident.

Although the city wasn't large, it was reasonably bustling. After gaining entry, they took up residence at the mansion of Old Master Chen, the city's richest man. He was also the one who'd facilitated sending someone to Cang Qiong Mountain Sect to plead for assistance.

Two of Old Master Chen's beloved concubines had died horribly at the Skinner Demon's hands, so he'd been desperately looking forward to Shen Qingqiu's arrival. He rubbed his beautiful third concubine's small, white, jade-like hands as he moaned and groaned to their whole party, eyes overflowing with tears.

"Immortal masters, you must help us! Nowadays I dare not let Die-er leave my side for a second, for fear that the moment she's careless, she'll be killed by that wretched monster!"

At these NPC-like lines, a powerful sense of déjà vu made Shen Qingqiu's face twitch.

He very much did not enjoy the sight of a sixty-year-old coot and a young girl in her teens cooing at each other right in front of him.

Luckily, Shen Qingqiu retained the divine air of a lofty master. After this perfunctory meeting, he aloofly took his leave to his room, leaving Ming Fan to make small talk with Old Master Chen. Certain privileges came with simply being a master; no matter how aloof you were, no one dared say anything. In fact, the more aloof, the more respectful the gazes that trailed after you.

Soon, Ning Yingying knocked and entered. "Shizun, Yingying wants to go and walk around the market," she said sweetly. "Would Shizun like to keep me company?"

Speaking truthfully, no man could dislike being so prettily cajoled by a young girl. When she entered, Shen Qingqiu had his back facing her, but upon hearing her plea, his heart half-melted. He steeled the remaining half and glanced back with the air of one looking up from a book—the essence of a cold and detached intellectual—and said blandly, "If Yingying wants to go and walk around, she may ask several shixiong or shidi to accompany her. This master still has things to do before confronting the Skinner Demon."

Who else would she ask to keep her company? How could Shen Qingqiu not know?!

At the same time, how could he not want to go out and play? Up until now, he'd been hunkered down inside Qing Jing Peak's Bamboo House, forced to fake being an awesome master of arts and literature, meaning everything he did had to be done "blandly": blandly speaking, blandly laughing, blandly practicing the sword, blandly being a poser—bland to the point that he often had the urge to scatter a handful of salt over his head! What a damn pain!

And now when he finally got a break to take a trip down the mountain, he was still trapped in his room because of the System's stance that "the original Shen Qingqiu liked quiet and would be unwilling to mingle."

Shen Qingqiu didn't even want to pretend to meditate, so he lay on the bed, just pretending to be dead.

Shortly before sunset, Ming Fan entered the room to deliver a report.

Finally, someone had come to talk to him—to keep him company. Shen Qingqiu couldn't help but want to weep for joy. Every perk belonged to the male lead, every loneliness to the cannon fodder. Accompanying young girls to view colored lanterns and such—none of that was for their lot.

"This disciple has closely examined the corpse," said Ming Fan. With a solemn expression, he presented the items in his hand.

Shen Qingqiu took a closer look. They were two stacks of yellow talismans, written upon with cinnabar ink. The paper had blackened to a shade akin to necrosis.

"You used these talismans to assess the corpses for demonic energy?" he asked.

"Shizun's eyes see all. This disciple used these talismans in two locations. The first at the soil near the grave of a victim who'd been buried, the second beside a yet unburied corpse still at the coroner's."

If even the grave soil was this saturated with demonic energy, then that confirmed that the Skinner Demon was undoubtedly of the demon race. Finally, Shen Qingqiu knew what they faced.

He cleared his throat, which made his following humph sound even colder. "They dare to harm the lives of people within a hundred kilometers of Cang Qiong Mountain? Since these demonic lowlifes came to our door, they can't blame our disciples for enacting justice on behalf of the heavens."

Listen, he really didn't want to say this corny line so full of hot air. But he'd have been OOC if he didn't!

Ming Fan gazed at him reverentially. "Shizun is wise! If Shizun took action, that demon would be taken care of in one strike, ridding the people of evil!"

Shen Qingqiu could say nothing. It seemed this master-disciple duo was right in the mold of "you reign, I'll worship." A most joyous union.

To tell the truth, Shen Qingqiu was extremely satisfied with Ming Fan as a disciple. Even though he was a rich young master and spoiled rotten, he was never even a little arrogant in front of his teacher. Instead, he was absolutely obedient and incredibly respectful. A man could never dislike being worshipped like a god.

Ming Fan had also single-handedly handled the travel preparations, from arrangements of food to lodging. If his IQ hadn't inevitably plummeted whenever he laid eyes on the protagonist, transforming him into a schoolyard bully capable of any misdeed, he would also be a promising young sprout!

And moreover, as a fellow victim, Shen Qingqiu always felt a kind of pity for this cannon fodder disciple who, in the end, Luo Binghe would throw into an ant pit so that he would be bitten to death by tens of thousands of ants...

"This trip down from the mountain is for the sake of your training. Unless as a last resort, this master will not assist you. Ming Fan, as the most senior disciple, you must design careful strategies, lest you let that demon harm your fellow disciples."

"Yes! This disciple has already devised a tactical formation. As long as that demon—"

Before Ming Fan could finish, a person rushed into the room, interrupting him.

"Shizun!" Luo Binghe's face was stark white as he yelled.

Shen Qingqiu's heart thumped once, but he feigned indifference. "What has happened to make you shout so loudly and in such a panic?"

"Ning Yingying-shijie went with me to the city's market earlier today," Luo Binghe said. "Once evening fell, I urged Shijie to return, but she refused—then somehow she suddenly vanished. This disciple...searched the entire street once but couldn't find her, and he could only come back to plead with Shizun for help."

If Ning Yingying had disappeared at this critical moment—this was no joke. Night had almost fallen.

Ming Fan leapt up right away. "Luo Binghe! You—"

Shen Qingqiu promptly flicked his sleeves, and the tea bowl on the desk exploded. As a deterrent, it wasn't OOC, and more importantly, it prevented Ming Fan from further digging his own grave.

Shen Qingqiu assumed an expression of barely suppressed anger. "If it's already come to this, there's nothing more to say. Luo Binghe, come with me. Ming Fan, take a couple of shidi and ask Landlord Chen for assistance, then go look for your shimei."

Ming Fan sent a hateful look at Luo Binghe but nodded and hurriedly left.

Luo Binghe remained, his head lowered, not saying a single word.

Shen Qingqiu knew this absolutely wasn't Luo Binghe's fault. Ning Yingying's role as a female character wasn't just to be lovable and cute but also to dig her own grave and be a burden.

In the original work, the number of plot twists caused by her sudden disappearances, blunders, or other messes, had allowed Airplane Shooting Towards the Sky to drag out the plot for hundreds of chapters.

At times, Shen Qingqiu had been rather impressed with Luo Binghe's fortitude when it came to accepting harem members. He never refused anyone, daring to accept even the most troublesome of women, and he did this without being screwed over or killed. Shen Qingqiu could only say that, as expected, the brilliant protagonist truly was overwhelmingly cool, awesome, insane, and badass, with a dick longer than the heavens. A normal person definitely couldn't have put up with such things.

Luo Binghe, who thought Shen Qingqiu had ordered him to stay so as to beat and yell at him, said quietly, "This entire affair is this disciple's fault. If Shizun wishes to punish this disciple, he will neither resent nor regret it. He only wishes for Ning-shijie's safe return."

He looked incredibly pitiful. Shen Qingqiu wanted to pat his head, but as the System's existence obstructed this, he forcibly held himself back. "Come," he said coldly. "Take me to the place where your shijie vanished."

Luo Binghe and Ning Yingying had lost each other at the most bustling corner of the market.

Shen Qingqiu closed his eyes, and he sensed a barely perceptible thread of demonic energy. He followed that thread, which seemed like it would at any moment fray or snap, until he opened his eyes again and found that he stood at the doors of a cosmetics shop.

Shen Qingqiu stared at it silently.

Could it be that the murderer worked here? Would it be that easy?

However, upon entering the cosmetics shop, the thread of demonic energy snapped, dissipating completely. Perhaps the murderer wasn't hiding in the shop and had just come at some point recently? If they had patronized a cosmetics shop... Was the Skinner Demon a woman?

Shen Qingqiu made these stabs in the dark, and he sent Luo Binghe inside to ask a few questions, but this yielded no results.

This quest had been offered to him expressly so he could level up. Thus, none of its scenes had been in the original work, so he had no point of reference. Shen Qingqiu furthermore acknowledged that he wasn't a master of deduction capable of deep analytical thought, who could infer a multitude of facts from a single clue. When playing room escape or detective games, he'd always run into dead ends.

As he was agonizing, the System thoughtfully notified him: [We notice that you have encountered difficulties. Would you like to spend one hundred B-Points to activate easy mode?]

"Shit, if there was something like an easy mode, you should have said so earlier!" Shen Qingqiu snapped. "Activate, activate, activate!"

He fixed his gaze on the "Yes" option for three seconds. The option blinked green and disappeared.

Then something in the air sent goosebumps all down his back.

Such—such palpable demonic energy!

As if they were afraid that otherwise no one would find the target!

Calling this easy mode was no lie!

Shen Qingqiu wasn't the least bit ashamed about using easy mode, and with spirits soaring, he strode in the direction from which the demonic energy emanated. A mere five hundred steps later, they had left the central district and arrived in front of an abandoned, neglected house.

This has to be the place! Just look at those ghastly white paper lanterns! Look at those dilapidated gates! A proper haunted house, don't you see?!

Shen Qingqiu schooled his expression and turned to Luo Binghe, who'd been silently following behind him. "Return to Chen Manor and notify Ming Fan to bring all the disciples and their talismans here."

Luo Binghe had yet to speak when his pupils suddenly contracted.

He was staring straight at something behind Shen Qingqiu. That didn't bode well.

However, it was too late in the end, and a gust of foul wind blew past, slamming the gates open.

"Shizun, Shizun, wake up, quickly!"

Shen Qingqiu woke up.

Upon opening his eyes, he saw Luo Binghe opposite him, looking awfully distressed, arms and torso bound. As Shen Qingqiu roused himself, Luo Binghe heaved a sigh of relief, eyes brightening. "Shizun..."

"Shizun..." Ning Yingying echoed. She was tied up with Luo Binghe, her expression miserable.

Shen Qingqiu was a little dizzy, and he had no idea if whatever crap the demon had sprayed on them had any side effects.

He was in a foul mood.

This easy mode was straightforward to the point of mercilessness! It had delivered him straight into the boss's mouth!

The worst part was that the dignified Peak Lord of Qing Jing Peak had been unexpectedly struck down by a mini-boss, and thus, shortly after he woke up, the System shrilly declared: [OOC, B-Points -50.]

He'd just spent one hundred B-Points to activate easy mode, and now in a flash he'd lost another fifty. How could he not be distressed?!

The original Shen Qingqiu's skill at facing down demons should have made this quest as easy as killing a chicken with a knife. Shamefully, the knife had failed to even hit the chicken.

In seconds, Shen Qingqiu discovered something that made his mood even worse.

His body felt a little strange. He was chilly, and he had a slight ache all over. Upon lowering his head, he almost couldn't stop a "fuck" from leaving his mouth.

He'd! Been! Stripped! Naked!

Only his upper half had been stripped naked, but that was already horrifying enough.

Regardless of everything else, Shen Qingqiu was still a peak lord! This appearance, with his upper half stark naked, his lower half wearing only a pair of pants and white shoes, and his four limbs bound tightly with a thin rope as he lay sprawled on the floor—

What! Was! This?! He looked exactly like a tender pretty boy caught in bed during an illicit act. No wonder the System had deducted fifty points straight off the bat—it was deserved! Even taking him to zero would have served him right!

Shen Qingqiu's face went from red to white and back. He wanted to dig a hole in the ground with his sword and bury himself for a while, but his sword had disappeared without a trace.

Of course Luo Binghe looked both worried and a little embarrassed. He definitely assumed that having seen Shen Qingqiu in such a sorry state, he would inevitably suffer more vicious retaliation once they got back.

"Shizun, you finally woke up," Ning Yingying sobbed. "Yingying is so scared..."

Scared? If you're scared, then don't go running off whenever you feel like it, young lady!

Shen Qingqiu gave up.

At this time, an unsettling chuckle came from behind him. A tall, dark silhouette emerged from the pitch blackness.

"The great Cang Qiong Mountain? The great Peak Lord of Qing Jing Peak? *This* is all you amount to. If the so-called greatest sect in the world is full of your sort, the day the demon race conquers the Human Realm is just around the corner." This was followed by another bout of crazed laughter. The speaker's head and face were covered with a black veil, and their voice was hoarse and unpleasant, as if their throat had been ruined by opium smoke.

Shen Qingqiu squinted. "The Skinner Demon?"

"That's right! That's me, I'm the Skinner Demon! How wonderful that the illustrious Xiu Ya Sword has fallen into my hands today! Shen Qingqiu, ah, Shen Qingqiu, even if you think until your wits give out, you won't be able to guess my identity!"

"Why wouldn't I be able to guess?" asked Shen Qingqiu.

The Skinner Demon said nothing.

"You're Die-er, aren't you?"

The Skinner Demon said nothing again as they lifted their veil—then she snapped in irritation. "Impossible! How did you guess?!"

Shen Qingqiu was speechless.

Did she think he was blind? That he couldn't tell from her figure? Men loved to look at bodies first before the face, okay? With that curvy bust and bottom—plus that tiny waist in between—she could only be a woman. Also, the room's furnishings *smelled* rich, and you couldn't find that just anywhere. Of course he knew that they'd been transported back to Chen Manor! And while Chen Manor had many women in residence, he'd only seen a couple and only been introduced to Die-er, so if he had to guess, of course he could *only* guess Die-er. He didn't know anyone else's names! How could he guess them?!

But who knew you'd lose your cool so quickly, without denying it even a little, and jump right to lifting your veil?!

Could he say this? Could he?! Listen, how could he say this out loud?! He could only swallow it all down.

Die-er—or to be clear, the Skinner Demon—quickly adjusted her posture and donned the face of Old Master Chen's beloved concubine, thusly recovering that infinitely tender, stunning, and delighted smile.

"Not bad, it was indeed me! But Shen Qingqiu, even if you guessed until your wits gave out, you couldn't possibly imagine why a weak and delicate woman like me would be the culprit, right?"

Shen Qingqiu straightened, struggling to assume a posture that was more natural, less rule-violating.

Bosses traditionally received time to monologue. How could he not offer this courtesy?

Die-er didn't need his encouragement and continued un-prompted. "The Skinner Demon comes and goes without a trace, not because I can fly through the skies or disappear into the earth, but rather because every time I finish killing a person, I change into their skin. By wearing these women's skins and imitating their behavior, I can blend into the crowd with none the wiser and search for my next target."

"That's not right," said Shen Qingqiu.

Die-er's expression darkened. "What's not right?"

"Suppose every time you killed a person, you changed skins—for instance, when you killed Die-er and wore her skin, you became 'Die-er.' But Die-er's skinned corpse would still be there. Wouldn't someone find it strange that there are two Die-ers?"

Although, if he thought about it for a moment, he understood.

It wasn't like this world had DNA identification. After skinning someone, all you had left was a messy lump of bloody flesh. Pretty difficult to tell exactly who it had been.

"Looks like you figured that out too," said Die-er. "Not bad. I use the current woman's corpse to substitute for the last woman's. For example, when I killed Die-er, I was wearing Xiang-er's skin, so everyone at that time thought Xiang-er was still alive. After I donned Die-er's skin, I disguised Die-er's corpse to look like Xiang-er's before it was found."

This villain's professional integrity was really impressive. Not only had she exposed her inner thoughts and feelings, she'd also explained her methods and line of criminal reasoning in detail. Offering examples, providing personal experiences—Die-er was more diligently thorough than a college-entrance-exam cram-school teacher!

Luo Binghe had been silently listening the entire time, his eyes glittering with a trace of anger. His juvenile sense of justice had been stirred by this perverse demon's cruel actions.

Meanwhile, Ning Yingying's head was spinning from all the "Xiangs" and "Dies." She couldn't understand it at all, but she didn't dare interrupt.

"After a certain amount of time, you always change skins. Is this all whim, or do you have to?" asked Shen Qingqiu.

Die-er sneered. "You think I'd tell you?"

You've already told me plenty, all right, Sis? (Or is it Bro?) What's one more?

Die-er walked toward where Ning Yingying and Luo Binghe were bound together. Luo Binghe remained calm, but Ning Yingying screamed, "Demon! Don't come near! Shizun, save me!"

Die-er chuckled. "Your master has been bound with my immortal-binding cable. Spiritual energy can no longer flow anywhere in his body. He can't hope to protect himself—how could he save you?"

Ah, that explained it. Shen Qingqiu had been secretly attempting to gather his spiritual power, but it seemed to be obstructed. It didn't feel nearly as plentiful as it usually did.

Die-er had reengaged monologue mode. "Damn, if it weren't for my damaged martial aspect, I wouldn't need to constantly change skins and absorb human qi. You're a brat, but your skin is lustrous and tender, and you're a disciple from a prestigious sect. I expect I'll be able to use you for a good long while. After I suck your skin dry, it'll be your master's turn. That way I'll make sure the Xiu Ya Sword didn't live his life in vain."

Luo Binghe stared, silent.

Shen Qingqiu stared, also silent.

What was that she'd said? *You think I'd tell you,* right?

Not only have you told me, you also seem to have made the astonishing decision to reveal your plan! The professional standards of this world's villains are beyond salvation!

"So, uh…" Shen Qingqiu said in his mind as he shamelessly called out to the System, "if I make a mistake during a quest, and I end up dead, will I get a chance to reload and try again?"

[Only the protagonist is granted the privilege of plot armor,] said the System.

Great. Good thing this villain had the illustrious quality of "must answer every question." If Shen Qingqiu wanted to stall for time, he needed only toss another question at Die-er.

"Haven't you only targeted young, beautiful girls?" he asked.

"I never said I *only* pick young, beautiful women. As long as they're good-looking and their skin is fine and smooth, I'll take anyone. It's just that most of the time, a man's skin isn't as good as a woman's, and the skin of the elderly is never as good as that of the youthful."

As expected, Die-er chattered on and on. Then suddenly her eyes flashed green with envy and her expression grew yearning as she began to run her hands, painted with scarlet nail dye, over Shen Qingqiu's upper body.

"However, cultivators really are different. Even though you're a man, your skin is so glossy and smooth. It's...been so long since I had my male skin..."

As he was felt up by those searching hands, Shen Qingqiu broke out in goosebumps, though he strove to give off the air of the spotless and untouchable. Part of him was disgusted, but another part was sympathetic.

Honestly, this demon was quite pitiful. It sounded like Die-er had originally been a man, but they had to keep using the skins of women due to their condition. After such a long time, of course that would make you a little twisted...

In any case, right in this moment, the demon was wearing the infinitely lovely face of a concubine. Being felt up all over by those lovely hands, Shen Qingqiu inevitably became embarrassed, and he involuntarily shrank back a little.

This vision—that moment—struck Luo Binghe to his core.

Until now, he'd only ever seen Shen Qingqiu's aloof and remote attitude, his derisive expression. But here and now, a faint, uncontrollable red flush formed on that face, and the way those eyes darted away... Also, Shen Qingqiu's upper body was completely bare but for the thin yet unbreakable immortal-binding cable and the red marks it left, and for Shen Qingqiu's long, disheveled, jet-black hair—neither of which concealed anything.

Luo Binghe's chest was burning with a convoluted emotion that was impossible to describe.

If you had let Shen Qingqiu think up an analogy for this emotion, he would have said that it was like watching a beautiful romance movie—only to discover at the end that the protagonist was that English teacher who'd always picked on you to answer questions, and who, if you *failed* to answer, would give your palm three hundred lashes.

In short, it both shattered Luo Binghe's worldview and did him great injury.

Shen Qingqiu suddenly grinned.

"Why are you smiling?" Die-er asked warily.

"I'm amused at you and your poor judgment," said Shen Qingqiu, slow and deliberate. "Pearls before swine, as they say. There are three options here, yet out of them, you keep overlooking the most suitable vessel."

At these words, Luo Binghe's face went pale. He could never have imagined he'd be randomly thrown to the wolves!

However, Shen Qingqiu wasn't speaking thoughtlessly.

Remember who Luo Binghe was: in truth, he was descended from a line of ancient heavenly demons.

Legend had it that these denizens of the heavens had fallen to depravity and become demons, so they were called "heavenly demons" for short. As the future princes of demonkind, their bloodline was first-class. If an ordinary demon got their hands on such a body, forget repairing a damaged martial aspect—would there be anything they couldn't do?

Die-er looked Luo Binghe up and down. The latter strove to appear calm, but inside he was panicking and didn't know what to do. Even though he thought until his wits gave out, he couldn't figure out why he had suddenly become the star of this standoff.

"If you want to trick me, you need a better lie," said Die-er. "This brat's appearance and aptitude may be exemplary, and his skin fresh and tender, but how can he compare to you? You've reached the stage of Mid Core Formation!"

"With your level of insight, it's no wonder your martial training was unsuccessful," said Shen Qingqiu, smiling. "Think about it for a moment. What kind of person am I, Shen Qingqiu? If this child possessed excellent aptitude and a fine appearance but nothing else, why would I accept him as my disciple? If I only wanted a disciple with excellent aptitude, could I not have my pick of the talents who fight to enter Cang Qiong Mountain Sect every year? Though naturally, my thought process cannot be explained to outsiders."

Die-er wavered.

Excellent! This villain's IQ was truly ridiculously low. They were so easy to trick that even though Shen Qingqiu had conjured a hasty explanation riddled with logical holes, they actually seemed to half-believe it!

Shen Qingqiu struck while the iron was hot. "If you're suspicious, there's an easy test. Let me share a method by which you can verify my words. Go over there and strike him on the crown of his head. Then you'll know whether I'm lying."

Luo Binghe's face turned a ghastly white. Though he was mature for his age, he was still a child. Even most grown men couldn't stoically face their deaths, let alone a boy who was only fourteen years old.

Shen Qingqiu tried very hard not to look at him, and he desperately apologized in his heart over and over again.

Bing-ge—you're a man of virtue, please magnanimously forgive my smack-talking and backstabbing just this once, okay, I'll never do it again, I'll definitely make it up to you in the future—

"Shi...Shizun, you...you can't be serious." Ning Yingying was scared witless.

Shen Qingqiu was on tenterhooks; it didn't even occur to him to comfort her. He only smiled at Die-er. "You don't know if I'm telling the truth now, but you'll know as soon as you try. Why hesitate? It's only a single strike against an insignificant boy. Even if I were lying to you, you aren't risking anything, are you? Or are you worried that I'm telling the truth, so you dare not hit him?"

In the eyes of anyone who didn't know the truth, these were the words of a man eagerly pushing Luo Binghe to his death.

Luo Binghe stared in disbelief. He wondered bleakly if Shen Qingqiu's hatred for him had truly become so great.

But if that were the case, why had his master been just a little nicer to him on their trip to the city?

Luo Binghe couldn't help but start struggling with all his might. The ropes restraining his body became tighter and tighter, biting painfully into Ning Yingying, but she didn't dare to even breathe loudly and just quietly sobbed.

Shen Qingqiu's words and tone were powerfully persuasive. Die-er thought for a moment and decided at last that, true enough, they had already killed so many people. How could they be afraid to kill one more?

They snorted. "I want to see exactly what sort of foolish game you're playing."

As they said this, they strode toward Luo Binghe and brought their palm down.

It would be over in an instant! Shen Qingqiu's pupils contracted.

Right as Die-er's strike came down, by curious coincidence, a ceiling beam broke.

If Shen Qingqiu had still been reading *Proud Immortal Demon Way*, upon seeing this described, he definitely would have thrown down his cell phone and started screaming curses.

The System had already declared it so: the one unbreakable, iron-clad rule was that the protagonist *could not* die. Meaning that, as soon as the protagonist's life was threatened, a death flag would be triggered!

Shen Qingqiu purposefully goaded Die-er into attacking Luo Binghe in order to take advantage of this rule. He just used someone else to do his dirty work. Admittedly this was...rather unscrupulous, but Luo Binghe probably hadn't been in real danger. And if Shen Qingqiu hadn't done this, he would have had to pay the price himself. In the long-term, even if he threw Luo Binghe under the bus this one time, there would be more chances to farm his favor in the future.

However.

To "Great Master" Airplane Shooting Towards the Sky:

What do you think of your readers' IQs?! How could a ceiling beam suddenly snap in a perfectly fine, splendid, and beautiful new mansion?!

Even if it was to let the protagonist escape with his life, this twist was still downright contrived. What's the difference between this and a third-rate melodrama where the male and female leads are just about to marry when they're suddenly hit by a car in a tragic twist ending? Downvote!

The practically brand-new ceiling beam fell straight down and just happened to coincidentally smash into Die-er, smacking them flat onto the ground and rendering them unable to get up. The beam *also* coincidentally smashed into the pillar Luo Binghe and Ning Yingying were bound to, causing it to slant. Ning Yingying had already fainted from shock, but after some struggle, Luo Binghe's ropes had, further coincidentally, loosened.

After this string of coincidences, Shen Qingqiu, who was still on the ground and bound by the immortal-binding cable, watched as Luo Binghe stared, unmoving, at the fallen Die-er in a puzzled silence.

Was this...it?

Just as Shen Qingqiu thought that, Die-er overturned the ceiling beam and sprang up.

"Shen Qingqiu!" they snarled, enraged. "The schemers of Cang Qiong Mountain are truly shameless and despicable! What sort of dirty trick did you just use to ambush me from behind like that?"

Shen Qingqiu was in fact completely innocent. This had nothing to do with him, really. If anything, the chief culprit was Luo Binghe.

"So you really were lying to me, trying to draw my attention away so you could sneak attack me," Die-er snapped, unforgiving. "Otherwise, why would a perfectly good ceiling beam come crashing down and just happen to smash into me?"

They also had the wits to notice the parts of this scene that were illogical. So their IQ *wasn't* beyond saving! Shen Qingqiu was a little relieved.

Die-er sneered. "You thought this would be enough to stop me? Keep dreaming. The immortal-binding cable can only be cut by an immortal's sword. You can forget about breaking it via any other means."

I just *praised you, and you goof up again. Don't reveal how to free the enemy, dear!*

Also, did Die-er think that no one could see where they'd put Xiu Ya? They even specifically drew back their cloak to show its place on their hip and patted it.

Shen Qingqiu couldn't contain his exasperation, and he took a chance to communicate a little with the System. "I need to ask. Are all villains in this mold?"

[To guarantee your ability to clear the beginner-level quest, activating easy mode set the villain's IQ to below average.]

So not all bosses would be this easy to fumble through. Shen Qingqiu thought it was a bit of a pity, but he still smashed the like button—thumbs up, thumbs up. "This easy mode of yours is still a bit too user-friendly."

Dier-er gritted their teeth. "I won't listen to you no matter what you say this time! Accept your death, Shen Qingqiu!"

"One last thing!" Shen Qingqiu shouted.

Sure enough, governed by easy mode, Die-er stopped. "What last words do you still have?"

Shen Qingqiu thought for a while. "How does it feel to sleep with a sixty-year-old coot?"

Die-er was struck silent. But they were subsequently so enraged that their expression twisted, their entire body trembling.

Luo Binghe took the chance to suddenly rush the demon from behind. He snatched Xiu Ya from Die-er's hip and drew the sword, filling the entire room with pure-white light. A curved flash of silver and the immortal-binding cable on Shen Qingqiu's body was neatly severed.

Once more betrayed by the IQ loss of easy mode, the mini-boss

Die-er had completely ignored the existence of a living, breathing Luo Binghe standing right behind them.

Die-er cried out in fear. "This is impossible—"

Enough! I'm not the listening type! I don't want to hear a rote analysis of the boss's true motives right before their death!

The corner of Shen Qingqiu's mouth twitched, and he gathered all his spiritual power into his right hand, lashing out with a palm strike and smacking Die-er in the chest. The demon flew back like a kite with a snapped string.

This was the first time Shen Qingqiu had killed someone. But he didn't hold back, not even a little. First, because this was a book; second, because this was a demon who'd killed countless people; and third, because if he didn't, he'd be the one who got killed.

Shen Qingqiu gazed down at the horrible state of "Die-er": four limbs twisted and broken, bleeding from the seven facial apertures. He turned away, bombarding his own brain with a barrage of his three reasons until they blocked out the screen of his mind.

Striving to remain calm, he slowly stood and straightened, settled his heart and breathing, fixed his posture, and turned to Luo Binghe.

"This is your first time seeing someone 'eliminate demons and uphold justice," he said. "Were you scared?"

Luo Binghe's still-childish face was slightly pale.

"If you wish to 'uphold,' you must 'eliminate,'" said Shen Qingqiu, composed.

Luo Binghe gritted his teeth. His voice quavered. "Shizun, if this disciple may be so bold as to ask, just now..."

When the second half of the sentence didn't arrive, Shen Qingqiu spoke. "You want to ask, if that ceiling beam hadn't suddenly come crashing down, what was this master's plan?"

Shen Qingqiu had no choice but to suffer in silence. He yearned to tell Luo Binghe: Don't worry, even if the ceiling beam hadn't collapsed, perhaps the wall would have. Even if the wall hadn't, perhaps the pillar would have. Long story short, you definitely wouldn't have died, the boss definitely would have, and that's all there is to it.

But he couldn't speak these words, so he could only adopt an unpredictable air and evade the question by changing the subject. "If you're asking this, are you blaming this master?"

Luo Binghe shook his head. "No," he said, his expression sincere. "If this disciple could give up his life for Shizun, it would be an honor."

Shen Qingqiu was shaken. This kid really was too much of a white lotus!

"Then this master will promise you in kind," he said after thinking for a moment and settling on properly ambiguous words. "Even if an accident befalls this master, no misfortune will come to you."

This was an absolute truth. Even if Shen Qingqiu died one hundred times—ah, one hundred times—Luo Binghe, the protagonist with impervious plot armor, would go on living in perfect health.

"On this matter, I speak nothing but the truth." His voice resounded as he said this, his expression confident and collected, without the slightest hint of falsehood.

When Luo Binghe heard these words, it was as if his life force had been ignited. The sunflower that had begun to wilt revived, full of renewed vigor.

Holding Xiu Ya in both hands, Luo Binghe lifted the blade until it was even with his brows and presented it to Shen Qingqiu. "Shizun, your sword!"

Shen Qingqiu grasped Xiu Ya, taking it from him. Internally, he wiped away his sweat. For now, this child was way too easy to dupe.

He'd been thrown under the bus and frightened out of his wits, but a couple of words were all it took to restore him to full health in the blink of an eye.

But in the future, he wouldn't be so easy to fool. The path to adulthood truly was tangled with thorns and suffering...

Then a series of System notifications came at him like a succession of cannon blasts, sending Shen Qingqiu to cloud nine.

[Ning Yingying's favor increased. Protagonist satisfaction points +50.]

[Obtained high-level item: Immortal-Binding Cable. Villain's strength +30.]

[Completed beginner-level quest, B-Points +200. OOC feature unfrozen. From this point on, you have full command over the Shen Qingqiu account's controls. Congratulations! Please continue to work hard!]

Shen Qingqiu had fallen a little in love with the sensation of these dramatic ups and downs, the intense joys and sorrows—it was basically gambling.

And now the OOC feature was unfrozen. From this point on, he could finally carry out the great and glorious task of clinging to the male lead's thighs!

Upon returning to Cang Qiong Mountain, the first thing Shen Qingqiu did was ascend Qiong Ding Peak, which was safeguarded by the sect leader, and report his work to Yue Qingyuan.

Previously, Shen Qingqiu had thought Zhangmen-shixiong's existence was basically that of a quest-giving NPC. But as soon as he entered the mountain gates, this impression disappeared without a trace.

Shen Qingqiu had yet to enter the main hall when Yue Qingyuan descended upon him, leading a retinue of Qiong Ding Peak's disciples to welcome him. They had just come face-to-face and smiled at each other, and hadn't yet even said anything, when Yue Qingyuan's right hand grasped Shen Qingqiu's wrist.

Shen Qingqiu was instantly surprised, however Yue Qingyuan made no further movements and instead examined him attentively through his pulse, even inserting a mild spiritual flow of his own to investigate Shen Qingqiu's. He realized then that Yue Qingyuan was only inspecting his spiritual circulation, and he relaxed.

After a moment, Yue Qingyuan let go. He smiled and walked with Shen Qingqiu into the main hall. "How was the training?"

His tone was like that of an eldest brother, which made Shen Qingqiu remember his former self's two brothers. He felt a slight sorrow, but greater still was the comforting sense of warmth, to the point that even his dejected report came out cheery. "Unsatisfactory."

His disciples hadn't so much as glimpsed the Skinner Demon's shadow. Speaking from the angle of disciple-training, the trip really had been a bust.

"No need to rush," said Yue Qingyuan.

Shen Qingqiu nodded before suddenly changing the topic. "Zhangmen-shixiong, I wish to go to the back of Qiong Ding Peak and enter secluded cultivation within the Ling Xi Caves."

Qiong Ding Peak was the head of the Twelve Peaks, and naturally it collected the essence of the heavens and earth. As for the Ling Xi Caves, they were Qiong Ding Peak's best location for cultivating, giving twice the results in half the time. Therefore, the sect's most senior members and outstanding disciples could request permission from the sect leader to enter the caves for secluded cultivation. Only with the sect leader's approval could they act upon this desire.

If Shen Qingqiu wanted to enter seclusion in the Ling Xi Caves, he was sure Yue Qingyuan wouldn't refuse. But the smile on Yue Qingyuan's lips froze a little, his expression changing slightly.

Shen Qingqiu sensed something strange, but this strangeness flashed by quickly.

"For the Immortal Alliance Conference?" Yue Qingyuan asked gently.

"That's correct."

It wasn't only because of the Immortal Alliance Conference, though. The incident with the Skinner Demon had made Shen Qingqiu realize the importance of diligent cultivation. In this world, you only had the right to think about the future if you had the strength to meet it. After all, bosses wouldn't always be on easy mode and saddled with below-average intelligence.

Before entering seclusion, Shen Qingqiu called over Luo Binghe and handed him an actual cultivation manual.

"Why is Shizun giving this disciple a completely different manual?" Luo Binghe asked as he received it.

"Your constitution is a little different, so you can't cultivate properly by following ordinary methods," Shen Qingqiu bullshitted solemnly.

He didn't want to personally reveal the truth—that Shen Qingqiu had inspired Ming Fan to give Luo Binghe a fake cultivation manual—even though eventually the truth would be exposed.

As he stared after Shen Qingqiu's retreating back, Luo Binghe held that manual in both hands, his heart profoundly shaken.

Shizun had specially given this manual only to him!

Shen Qingqiu glanced back a couple of times and saw Luo Binghe still standing there, dumbstruck. He rubbed at the spot between his brows and kept walking.

He didn't know what Luo Binghe was thinking, but the boy was almost certainly thinking *too much*.

The Ling Xi Caves were labyrinthine. After traveling down a thousand twists and turns, Shen Qingqiu emerged in what seemed like a different world, strange and beautiful. Here, there was neither wind nor moon, yet it was cool and quiet. Together, white stones like clouds and green stones like jade created wonders large and small as well as natural stone beds. At the center lay a pool of clear water that reflected this other world like a mirror.

The only thing that marred the beauty was that some cultivator who'd previously gone into seclusion here hadn't properly cherished this public facility. The cave walls were covered in countless gashes and gouges made by both blade and sword glares. The stone walls were further plastered with swathes of dried blood, and the stains had already blackened.

This was only one cavern of many, and though it looked a tad like a murder scene, Shen Qingqiu was very satisfied and had no plans to find another location. He sat on the stone bed and began to cultivate, carefully following the methods he'd memorized from manuals.

Then, as if the heavens didn't *want* him to try to honestly farm B-Points, not long after he began meditating, he heard a strange sound.

Panting.

The panting of a person in pain.

At the same time, he sensed a burst of nigh-rampant spiritual energy.

All right. He knew what had happened.

The Ling Xi Caves were gigantic; of course Shen Qingqiu couldn't be the only person who'd asked permission to enter seclusion. Someone else was cultivating here as well...and they had entered a qi deviation, which was currently at a critical juncture.

I! Only! Wanted! To! Cultivate! In! Seclusion! And! Farm! Martial! Skill! Points! That's! All! Can you not do this?! Can! You! Not!

Shen Qingqiu's eyes snapped open as he decided to investigate. He followed that sound and the waves of spiritual energy as he navigated the various twists and turns. As he went, the disturbances became larger and larger.

At last, he arrived in another cavern. As soon as he entered, he saw a figure clothed in white facing away from him, their longsword stabbed into a rock, all the way to the hilt.

Sword glares flew in every direction, without order or pattern. The smears of blood on the person in white said "victim," but their movements said "crazed murderer."

This person's qi deviation was pretty horrifying!

Shen Qingqiu mulled it over. With his half-assed knowledge, if he tried to smooth this person's spiritual circulation, it was hard to say whether he would be more likely to help or accidentally stab another spiritual knife into the fellow's back.

It was then that he caught sight of that sword. With its master's spiritual energy out of control, the sword trembled unceasingly, pulling itself free a sliver at a time, all while emitting an ear-piercing shriek. Silver light ran down the hilt's engraved incantations and phoenix ornamentation in an unending stream.

Shen Qingqiu needed only a single glance to recognize which sword it was—*whose* sword it was.

Fuck! Of all people, he had to meet *that guy*! Before, he'd wanted to help, but now all he wanted was to flee for his life.

It was too late. The person in white swung his head around, having already detected his presence.

In any other state, Shen Qingqiu might have declared, "What a beautiful man!" But a man could be as beautiful as he wanted, and if he glared at you with crimson eyes and bulging veins, you'd scramble to kneel, okay?!

Shen Qingqiu fled with a flick of his sleeves, but the man slapped the stone wall and sent rubble flying. The longsword finally broke free of the rock, and it shot through the air to stop before Shen Qingqiu's eyes, blocking his path. He barely managed to brake in time. Had he been running even a little faster, he would have been beheaded. In the next instant, the white-clad man rushed him, his eyes devoid of reason.

Shen Qingqiu knew it was too late to run, and he could only steel himself to meet this fight head-on. He drew spiritual energy into his right hand. Putting everything into this one blow, he struck the man's chest.

If this person really was the man the rumors painted him to be, with enough martial prowess to take on the protagonist's OP abilities, this hit would be damn near useless. Not only damn near useless, Shen Qingqiu might be the one sent flying ten meters back while coughing up fresh blood or something.

However, it wasn't useless—and the one sent flying a meter back while coughing up blood wasn't Shen Qingqiu but the other guy.

Shen Qingqiu raised his right hand while staring at the person he'd knocked flat. To think he was already this badass even without making the effort to fake it!

In truth, while those who entered qi deviations were terrifying when berserk, they were also terribly fragile. With luck, a single strike could be the last straw that broke their back.

Expression conflicted, Shen Qingqiu watched the man half-kneel in pain, straining to rise and rip into his foe, only to collapse back onto one knee. At last, Shen Qingqiu sighed and moved closer, placing a hand on the man's back.

"Let me say this first." Shen Qingqiu didn't concern himself with whether the man could understand him; he was saying it for himself. "If I don't help you now, it'll be too late. I'm not familiar with how this works, though, so if you...you know. Anyhow, I'll have tried my best, so don't blame me."

After who knew how long, Shen Qingqiu felt the man's spiritual circulation gradually even out and return to normal. His worry slowly eased, and he withdrew his palm. All that remained was to pray that his slapdash, desperate attempt to help hadn't impaired the man's cultivation.

The man he'd miraculously managed to save remained with his head lowered, still not yet fully conscious.

To be honest, Shen Qingqiu had already guessed this person's identity, but the System's notification provided absolute confirmation.

〚Congratulations! System notification: The scenario "Liu Qingge's Death" has been changed. The villain Shen Qingqiu's grave-digging and hatefulness ratings have decreased, B-Points +200.〛

Yup. Called it.

This was his shidi from the same sect. He was also a sucker who had been done in by the original Shen Qingqiu.

The Master of Bai Zhan Peak of Cang Qiong Mountain's Twelve Peaks, Liu Qingge. He was a character who personified badassery.

The twelve peaks of Cang Qiong Mountain each had their own long histories and distinctive characteristics. For example, the head, Qiong Ding Peak, coordinated the big picture and oversaw the entire group; Shen Qingqiu's Qing Jing Peak was the favorite of scholars and young artists; Wan Jian Peak, with their perfect environment, had produced legions of master swordsmen since time immemorial; Ku Xing Peak's name, "ascetic practice," spoke for itself (even if you whipped Shen Qingqiu, he still wouldn't want to go); Xian Shu Peak, meanwhile, was a droolworthy heaven.

That was because this last peak only accepted female disciples, and historically, their disciples were highly attractive. It was therefore filled to the brim with beautiful girls. There'd been no shortage of lewd fanworks written by perverted readers, blossoming en masse like flowers. Of these, *A Tyrannical Xian Shu Fell in Love with Me* and *My Days Sleeping around on Xian Shu Peak* had been particularly outstanding, filled with grade-school level writing and erotic scenes with no bottom line. The circulation and impact of these fanfics had been enormous, to the point that their popularity compared to that of the original work.

But out of all the peaks, the one youths loved the most, revered the most, and were the wildest about joining was definitely Liu Qingge's Bai Zhan Peak.

It was the most warlike of Cang Qiong Mountain's branches, as well as the branch with the greatest martial ability. Every single generation's Bai Zhan Peak Lord was a world-class swordmaster, a victor of countless battles, an undefeated legend. How hot-blooded—how dashing!

Male readers always fervently admired strong characters. Even though Liu Qingge never officially debuted on page, he hadn't lacked for fans, and Shen Yuan had been especially fascinated with him. In his headcanon, Liu Qingge had been a sharp and manly man, powerful and magnificent. A war god, right?!

Shen Qingqiu looked down at that face, as beautiful as a fine woman's, and his dreams shattered and died. The fantasies he'd always held, destroyed.

How could the invincible Bai Zhan Peak Lord look like his spiritual antithesis? This was clearly the face of a charming young master who arranged flowers and plucked farewell willow branches!

With this appearance, you've totally betrayed the headcanons of your martial prowess fanatics!

Then again, it made sense. Liu Qingge was the older brother of the number one true female lead, the peerless beauty Liu Mingyan. As the protagonist's wife, she absolutely had to be first-class from top to bottom. It was just science for her to have such powerful genes.

Undefeatable in battle, an arrogant disposition, and an attractive face. With Bing-ge around, a second character in the same mold was unnecessary. No wonder "Great Master" Airplane had offed him so early.

Not even the protagonist, yet you dare to share those qualities? Of course you'd be either exceptional cannon fodder or dead in seconds!

It hadn't occurred to Shen Qingqiu in the moment, but as he thought about it now, how might saving this person impact Luo Binghe's satisfaction points?

There were few details on Liu Qingge, but he played a very important role in highlighting the depths of Shen Qingqiu's general scumminess.

Even though the Liu-Shen pair were sect siblings, they didn't get along. This was why Shen Qingqiu had tried to flee at first.

Already unable to see eye to eye on a normal day, throwing Liu Qingge into a qi deviation was just asking him to either chase down and hack Shen Qingqiu to death or, like in the original work, to have Shen Qingqiu sabotage and kill him instead.

Though no one knew why their hatred ran so deep, it was a sure fact that the original Shen Qingqiu had been Liu Qingge's murderer. The exposure of this incident was (one of) the inciting incident(s) that marked the start of Shen Qingqiu's downfall. The specific line they used to condemn Shen Qingqiu went something like, "Taking advantage of an opening during another's cultivation, he intervened, driving the man to his death." So this very moment was likely when he'd made his move.

The original Shen Qingqiu killed the female lead's only family, so of course Luo Binghe took revenge for his wife. Shen Qingqiu's hatefulness quotient was truly extraordinary!

While Shen Qingqiu was crouching there, worrying over his future, Liu Qingge had finished coughing up blood and finally regained consciousness.

As soon as he opened his eyes, he saw Shen Qingqiu sitting before him with a bored expression, looking down his stuck-up nose at him. He definitely didn't look like someone with good intentions.

Alarmed, Liu Qingge violently jerked upright, ready to defend himself. The motion jarred his badly injured internal organs, throwing his qi circulation into chaos. Another mouthful of blood sprayed out of him.

"Shidi, regulate your qi; don't be so agitated," Shen Qingqiu said coolly. "You're the Bai Zhan Peak Lord, how could you let yourself look so wretched? Here! Wipe yourself off." He passed Liu Qingge a handkerchief.

Liu Qingge coughed up more blood. "Shen... What the hell are you planning now...?"

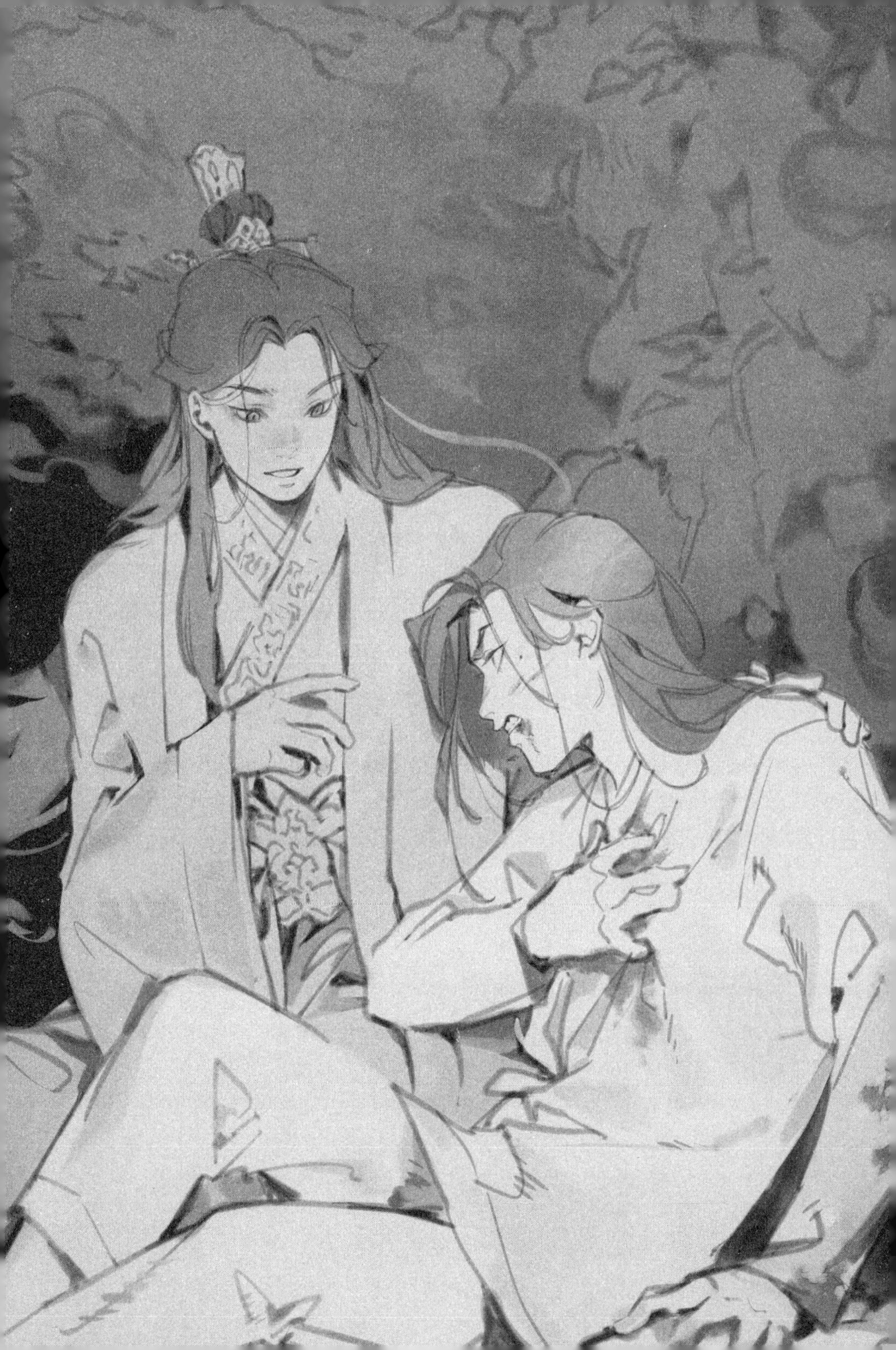

Seeing how much he was suffering, Shen Qingqiu lightly clapped him on the back.

Liu Qingge instantly assumed that Shen Qingqiu intended him harm, but he was helpless to avoid the touch. Only after the palm connected did he feel a clear, steady stream of spiritual energy enter and flow through his body, smoothing his circulation.

Liu Qingge was more aghast than he would have been if Shen Qingqiu had stabbed him in the back. After all, he was used to the backstabbing.

Shen Qingqiu continued to pat his back. "Liu-shidi, to tell you the truth, lately Shixiong has been in seclusion, and he's come to realize many things," he said earnestly. "Seeing you at death's door, a beauty fading—ahem, dying so young, it brought back so many memories. Shixiong is deeply ashamed and filled with regret."

Liu Qingge began to hack up blood even more profusely.

"From this point on, how about we leave our disagreements behind us and move forward hand in hand as a pair of model sect siblings, full of the affection due to fellow sect members?" Shen Qingqiu suggested, tactfully expressing his goodwill. "How do you feel about this, Shidi?"

Laying his objective out straight was a little shameful, but since he hadn't killed Liu Qingge, and had thereby changed the scene and avoided its evil karma, he figured why not go all the way and simply build a good relationship? Maybe Master Liu could even back him up in the future?

Liu Qingge's complexion was abnormally poor. He looked Shen Qingqiu in the eyes for a while. Then, as if he'd finally reached the limits of his tolerance, he said, "You. Go away."

Shen Qingqiu nodded in understanding. After all, they'd hated each other for so long. You couldn't farm favor points so soon after a heel turn. He couldn't rush this thing, only take it slow.

He went as asked, waving behind him without looking back as he walked away. "If Shidi runs into more trouble during training, there's no need to be shy; you can call Shixiong for help. Since we're so close, we should take care of each other."

Liu Qingge looked like he would cough up more blood if Shen Qingqiu said anything further. His glare was terrifying.

Shen Qingqiu wisely shut his mouth and did as he had been told. Liu Qingge was left alone, and he painfully hacked up another mouthful of blood.

They'd always been at odds. Ever since he was young, Liu Qingge had been unable to stand Shen Qingqiu. Both parties had deeply despised each other.

It wasn't the type of vitriol you'd see when a belligerent but happy couple fought and argued, but the type where one wrong word could escalate into violence, even to the point of trying to kill each other. The fact that Shen Qingqiu hadn't kicked him while he was down was inconceivable in itself—but to go so far as to help, even save him?!

But the reality was right before him. Liu Qingge's face couldn't help twisting.

He was unable to remember what had happened after the moment he lost control. But now his spiritual circulation was smooth. He couldn't have straightened it himself during his frenzy. He must have had outside assistance.

Could Shen Qingqiu really have helped him?

Just thinking about this possibility filled Liu Qingge with revulsion. He would rather have died.

Even though the person he'd worked so hard to save was disgusted with him, Shen Qingqiu was incomparably satisfied.

Liu Qingge should have died by his hand, but Shen Qingqiu had saved the man through a series of freak coincidences.

If he could befriend Liu Qingge, even if his plan to raise Luo Binghe into a top-ten best disciple didn't succeed, as the master of Bai Zhan Peak, Liu Qingge could at least stand beside him as a fellow sect sibling and help shield him a little!

Although this was a little utilitarian, as his own sorry life was on the line, it was no time for moral dilemmas.

There was no sense of time within the caves. Shen Qingqiu felt like he hadn't done anything at all when the day to end his seclusion arrived.

Shen Qingqiu sat cross-legged on a stone platform, eyes shut. He kept them closed until the last wisp of spiritual energy had finished circulating through all his limbs and bones.

Having intensively cultivated for several months, he could freely control his spiritual energy and had risen one level above his original cultivation base. This told him that he had obtained one hundred percent command over this body, and even the last shreds of discoordination had been annihilated. Both his eyes shone brightly, and his immortal figure now felt distinctly different from how it had been.

Shen Qingqiu jumped down from the stone platform, his body all the more graceful—as if his four limbs had been instilled with a breeze and filled with vigor.

Of course, it was possible this was only his subjective feeling. After all, the days in seclusion had passed so quickly, as if he'd jumped ahead in the video progress bar. If this were a novel, and not one padded out like that of "Great Master" Airplane's, the plot would have finished in one chapter.

Before leaving, he thought he ought to greet his neighbor, and so he knocked on the stone wall.

"Shidi, how is your situation over there?" he asked. "Shixiong will be leaving first."

His voice echoed in the empty cavern. While not loud, it could be clearly heard by a cultivator like Liu Qingge.

As expected, he received no response. Shen Qingqiu didn't mind. It was enough to express his kind wishes(?). With a sweep of his hem, he exited the caves like the wind whispered beneath his feet, ready to welcome the approaching storm.

If he had correctly calculated the time and date, it was about time for an upcoming story event of critical importance. It could have been considered the first small climax of the early narrative.

The demons would arrive, armed and eager to provoke a fight, thereby triggering mass panic. This small climax also included a brief glimpse of two of the book's important female leads, whereupon they'd start paying attention to Luo Binghe.

The Ling Xi Caves were isolated from the outside world, and the interior of the caves was tranquil—but as soon as Shen Qingqiu exited them, he found the entirety of Qiong Ding Peak consumed by the fire and smoke of war. Panicked disciples ran every which way, and the alarm bells rang in united clamor.

Shen Qingqiu instantly understood: They'd already appeared.

Perfect timing. He'd arrived at just the right moment.

As soon as they saw him, several disciples from some peak or another threw themselves at him.

"Shen-shibo! Shen-shibo, you've finally left seclusion! It's a disaster—monsters from the Demon Realm sneaked onto Qiong Ding Peak and injured many of our sect siblings!"

Shen Qingqiu patted a disciple with each hand. "Settle down. Where is Zhangmen-shixiong?"

"Zhangmen-shibo left the mountain on important business," Disciple A said tearfully. "Otherwise, how else could those monstrous demons have used this chance to invade?!"

"Those monstrous demons are truly despicable!" Disciple B said furiously. "Not only did they take advantage of our vulnerability to invade, they also severed the Rainbow Bridges connecting the Twelve Peaks and set up some strange barrier. Now Qiong Ding Peak is completely unable to receive support from the other peaks!"

Shen Qingqiu knew all of this. He was just asking while passing through. As of now, he had gone through cultivation training—and on top of that had experience punching Luo Binghe and kicking Liu Qingge (*eep!*). With a bearing of heroic resolve that reached the heavens, he said, "No need to panic. Our Cang Qiong Mountain is a majestic, unparalleled sect that has produced countless heroes. We would never fear the dregs of the Demon Realm!"

The disciples instantly felt like they'd found a pillar of support, and they followed behind Shen Qingqiu like a train. Along the way, the disciples who'd been flailing around like headless chickens also rushed to follow—and the ones who didn't know what was happening followed as well. In the end, the procession kept growing longer and longer, until they arrived before Qiong Ding Peak's main hall.

Every single member of Cang Qiong Mountain Sect on Qiong Ding Peak had come to encircle and exterminate the demons who had overtaken it deep within. Due to plot requirements, the disciples of Qing Jing Peak were all "coincidentally" at Qiong Ding Peak to greet Shen Qingqiu as he left seclusion, and they had been gathered there a while now. Shen Qingqiu first sought out Luo Binghe's figure, and indeed he saw him standing within the group, expression solemn.

It had been some time since he'd last seen the boy. He'd grown taller by a fair amount, his youthful figure like a graceful, elongating stalk of bamboo. Along with that handsome little face, he drew a great deal of attention. Having confirmed that the protagonist was at the scene, Shen Qingqiu's heart settled, and he turned his focus to the enemy.

Before the elegant, magnificent Qiong Ding Hall stood more than a hundred unknown individuals, roiling with demonic qi. The leader of this invasion was in fact a young girl who appeared to be no more than fifteen or sixteen.

Shen Qingqiu's heart thumped with excitement. *She's appeared! She's finally appeared!*

Demons loved exotic and unusual dress, but even among them, this girl's fashion sense was exceptionally unorthodox. Her jet-black head of hair had been combed into many small braids; her complexion was fair, her eye makeup bold, her lips abnormally scarlet. Although she was young, it was self-evident that she would grow into a woman of overwhelmingly glamorous bearing.

As it was a hot day, she had dressed lightly, having essentially only wrapped herself in several bolts of gauzy red cloth. Her wrists and ankles were decorated with silver bangles, the tiny bells on every limb jingling with her slightest movements. Her bare, snow-white feet directly touched the ground. Shen Qingqiu couldn't help side-eyeing them a couple of times.

His thoughts weren't indecent, but rather...

You've traveled thousands of miles from the Demon Realm, crossing land and sea, and after arriving you even climbed this tall mountain barefoot? Young miss, do...do your feet really not hurt?

Wait. That wasn't the point!

The point was that this was (one of) the most popular female lead(s) in the novel of *Proud Immortal Demon Way*—Demon Saintess Sha Hualing.

Sha Hualing was a pure-blooded demon, vicious and merciless, crafty and proud, yet she was madly in love with Luo Binghe. After getting involved with Luo Binghe, not only did she kill for him, she even dared to commit an offense as monstrously treasonous as betraying the demon race.

Though these days, a good number of people often denounced this trope of a brainless, lovesick girl, there was nothing you could do. An even larger number of male readers loved it. A pity that a girl this spicy could only be enjoyed by the male lead.

Shen Qingqiu couldn't help glancing at Luo Binghe. At the same time, Luo Binghe inadvertently swept his gaze about as well. Their two gazes met, and they both startled. Luo Binghe seemed about to speak, but he said nothing. Shen Qingqiu nodded at him.

The Rainbow Bridges had been severed. Of the various peak lords, the ones sleeping still slept, the ones in seclusion remained in seclusion, the ones strolling kept strolling, and the ones away on official business did not return. The arrival of Shen Qingqiu, a member of the older generation, was as such powerfully reassuring. The disciples regained confidence.

Ming Fan was the first to yell. "Demoness! My master is here—let's see if you'll dare to be so arrogant now!"

More and more people joined the gathered crowd. Several hundred disciples in uniformly colored robes and furious expressions surrounded the invaders, trapping them in the space before the hall.

Several demons tried to use the chance to break through—perfect training targets for Shen Qingqiu. He casually grabbed them, lifted them up, and threw them back to land at Sha Hualing's feet.

Sha Hualing had always been clever and resourceful. Her earlier arrogance had derived from the fact that, having long enjoyed being the number one sect, Cang Qiong Mountain's defenses were lax and loose. She had also seen Yue Qingyuan depart on official business, leaving Qiong Ding Peak without one of its senior members to guard it.

Sensing that things had taken a turn, she changed her tune. "My people didn't climb this mountain for the sake of battle. It's just that we've long heard that Cang Qiong Mountain produces many talented individuals, so we were curious. We wanted to ascend the mountain for a look, as well as to spar and learn from you."

"How kind of you." Shen Qingqiu flapped his fan. "But if you've come to spar, why do so when the sect leader is away? Why sever the Rainbow Bridges? And why injure so many of our sect's disciples? I've never seen this method of sparring."

Sha Hualing bit her lip, utilizing that weapon exclusive to young girls. She twirled a stray lock of hair dangling beside her cheek around her finger. "This must be the renowned Xiu Ya Sword, Senior Shen Qingqiu," she said, drawing out each word. "As expected, hearsay can't compare to seeing the real person. Ling-er is young and unable to manage her subordinates. If we have offended you or caused misunderstandings, we beg the immortal master to be magnanimous and forgiving."

No matter how softly she spoke, Shen Qingqiu wouldn't be moved the slightest bit. The truth of the situation was clearer to him than to anyone else.

To lay it out plain, this trouble had begun when Sha Hualing was granted the title of a "Demon Saintess"—which had just happened. Being proud and arrogant, she had an exaggerated opinion of her own abilities. She had intended to slaughter the entirety of Cang Qiong Mountain's first peak in one go, then seize the nameplate hanging over Qiong Ding Hall as a war trophy and bring it back as proof of her achievement. At the same time, her exploit would be a demonstration of force directed at the Human Realm.

"Then what is the young miss's conclusion now?" asked Shen Qingqiu.

Sha Hualing pursed her lips in a smile. "Though right now my people are at a disadvantage, that's only because your sect has such great numbers. Ling-er is unable to ascertain who between us would be the victor."

"Oh? Then what would you need to do so?" Shen Qingqiu asked, putting on the air of an elder as smoothly as a fish took to water.

Parting her red lips, Sha Hualing elegantly suggested a method that seemed fair and just: "Why don't we each choose three representatives and hold three matches?"

This suggestion was solid. For many years, the Human and Demon Realms had maintained an uneasy balance and had yet to drop the pretense of peace. Eliminating Sha Hualing and her mob wouldn't be impossible, but it would likely light a fuse. The demons definitely wouldn't let her death go unanswered, and it wouldn't be worth it if they stirred up an even greater conflict. On the other hand, simply letting them go would also generate trouble. They couldn't allow outsiders to come and go as they pleased from Qiong Ding Peak. By setting conditions and holding some matches, each teaching the other party a lesson or two, both parties could back down and save face. It would be the best way to handle this.

Since this was the first small climax in the original work, Shen Qingqiu still remembered it fairly clearly.

The first match was Shen Qingqiu versus the demon Elder "Single Arm" Dubi. To highlight Shen Qingqiu's scummy nature, he of course used despicable and underhanded means to achieve victory. By comparison, Luo Binghe's honorable and upright actions in the third match illustrated a strong contrast for the readers.

Now, however, Shen Qingqiu wasn't about to so pointlessly tarnish his image.

Elder Single Arm's entire body was a dark purple color, and he was taciturn and reticent. At Sha Hualing's command, he walked toward a stretch of open ground.

The sect's disciples cheered and shouted for their Shen-shibo. Shen Qingqiu knew the extent of this Elder Single Arm's strength. "You only have one arm," he said, smiling. "Even if I defeat you like this, it'd be due to an unfair advantage."

"Oh?" Sha Hualing said from behind her hand. "Actually, Ling-er has a solution. How about...you also cut off one of your arms? That way there won't be an unfair advantage anymore!"

Angry protests rose all around them. Unconcerned, Shen Qingqiu smiled slightly and slowly spread his fan. "How about this—I won't use a single hand."

These words threw the crowd into an uproar. Among them, Luo Binghe also stood shocked.

Wouldn't use a single hand?

Sha Hualing snorted, thinking Shen Qingqiu was being full of himself, but she was also secretly filled with endless glee. If her side could win a match so easily, why *wouldn't* they go for it? "Since Senior Shen is so ready, let us start!" she said hurriedly.

A number of bystanders realized then that this girl was actually quite brazen. Though her manner was pure and innocent, her words were vicious and sinister, and she rushed to take advantage of others. As a reader enjoying the drama, Shen Qingqiu had come away with one impression, but experiencing the situation for himself, he came away with another. He'd never really been charmed by Sha Hualing's way of dealing with things, but between her youth and her daintiness, he had at least been able to force himself to regard her behavior as cute loli willfulness—until now.

Under all those gazes, Shen Qingqiu stayed true to his words and didn't draw his sword. Instead, he played with the fan in his hand, smiling at Elder Single Arm.

Elder Single Arm only had the one arm, but that didn't even slightly hinder his ability to swing his beheading saber. But his savage swing didn't actually hit its target. He whipped around to find Shen Qingqiu was already standing behind him, still smiling. In truth, Shen Qingqiu's face was getting sore.

However, Xiu Ya had already left its sheath. Shen Qingqiu hadn't directly touched his sword at all. His left hand had subtly formed a sword seal, commanding Xiu Ya to fly and turn over, brandishing itself.

Elder Single Arm's eyes were struck with pain from the flashes of the sword's snow-white gleam. He rushed to lift his saber and attack again.

Saber and sword clashed in a succession of incessant ringing clangs while sparks sprayed and danced.

The crowd was unable to tear their eyes away. In reality, this was just a competition, but anyone would have called it both captivating and *captivating*.

The first captivating encompassed the impressiveness of the fight, where the use of real weapons made it a matter of life and death. But what made it *captivating* were the magnificent visual effects—especially Shen Qingqiu, who moved with such skill and ease in his pure and scholarly way, surrounded by the glint and flash of blades. On top of this, he continued to gracefully and leisurely fan himself with his paper fan. It was as if any instant, he would compose a poem within seven steps,[3] like a figure of legend. Such utterly breathtaking style! No, achieving this level of badass was far too perfect!

As Luo Binghe watched, his heart practically galloped and his soul trembled. He'd known Shen Qingqiu was incredible, but he'd never anticipated that he was *this* incredible.

So strong!

Surrounded by the cheers of the sect's disciples, Shen Qingqiu attained a complete victory in the first match.

At this moment, Shen Qingqiu realized why the original flavor had clung to being a poser like it was his lifeline—it was unbelievably satisfying.

The disciples' gazes formed a sea of sparkling stars. What an inspiring experience! Shen Qingqiu was certain now—a scum villain could also gain reputation points!

At the same time, the System also gave him good news:

---

3   According to legend, the emperor demanded the poet Cao Zhi compose a poem within seven steps to prove he was innocent of treason. Describes extraordinary literary talent.

[Demonic invasion of the immortals' mountain, first match of the competition, Shen Qingqiu's victory, martial skill rating +50. B-Points +50.]

Shen Qingqiu's pleased smile didn't last long. The System's next notification came like a slap to the face.

[System alert: If Luo Binghe does not participate in the competition, one thousand points will be deducted from the protagonist's satisfaction points.]

"What?!" Completely unprepared, Shen Qingqiu turned pale with shock.

He'd been laboring to earn satisfaction points, huffing and puffing like an old ox dragging a broken cart, and only managed to earn somewhere in the three hundreds—and in an instant he risked losing one thousand?!

System, are you trying to get people killed?!

This competition was an important part of the plot. At the same time, it also served as a small, early-stage climax that debuted two female leads and pitted their splendor against each other—and the consequences of it later enabled the protagonist to get an underling and also allowed him to learn secret techniques. All important things! If Luo Binghe didn't make it on stage this time, he would miss the limelight and be unable to grab everyone's attention. Hence, negative one thousand satisfaction points.

But if Shen Qingqiu named him a sect representative and sent him out to fight, what would he be doing?

The original flavor pushed Luo Binghe onto the battlefield because he was shameless! He didn't care about the sect's reputation! He hated Luo Binghe to the bone, enough to want to vicariously torture him via the hands of demons!

The current Shen Qingqiu didn't share any of those three motives!

And at the end of everything, why was someone else responsible for the oh-so-mighty protagonist's satisfaction points?! Shen Qingqiu was still angrily rebuking the System for its unscientific approach when the time came for the start of the second match.

Sha Hualing had been afraid that Shen Qingqiu would fight all three matches himself and swiftly said, "If the same representative competes in all three matches, we would lose the chance to truly learn from each other. I will be my people's representative for the second match."

No doubt Sha Hualing had entered first because she believed in her own strength, but she also likely thought that Shen Qingqiu wouldn't use his senior position to bully a girl who was his junior. Shen Qingqiu didn't want to concern himself with her thoughts at all and demonstrated as much. Even if he'd originally had the ambition to fight all three matches to earn martial ability points and reputation, the System's notification had extinguished those hopes.

However, the second match did have an impressive, attention-worthy highlight.

"You've all heard her," said Shen Qingqiu. "Who is willing to bear this heavy duty?"

Even though he was asking all the disciples of the sect, his gaze fell on a certain pocket of the crowd.

Within that pocket stood a collection of graceful female disciples. Without a doubt, they belonged to Xian Shu Peak. In this group of pretty girls, each fairer, more beautiful, and more refined than the last, one stood out, a veil draped over her face.

Immediately after Shen Qingqiu asked this question, she slowly stepped forward from the crowd.

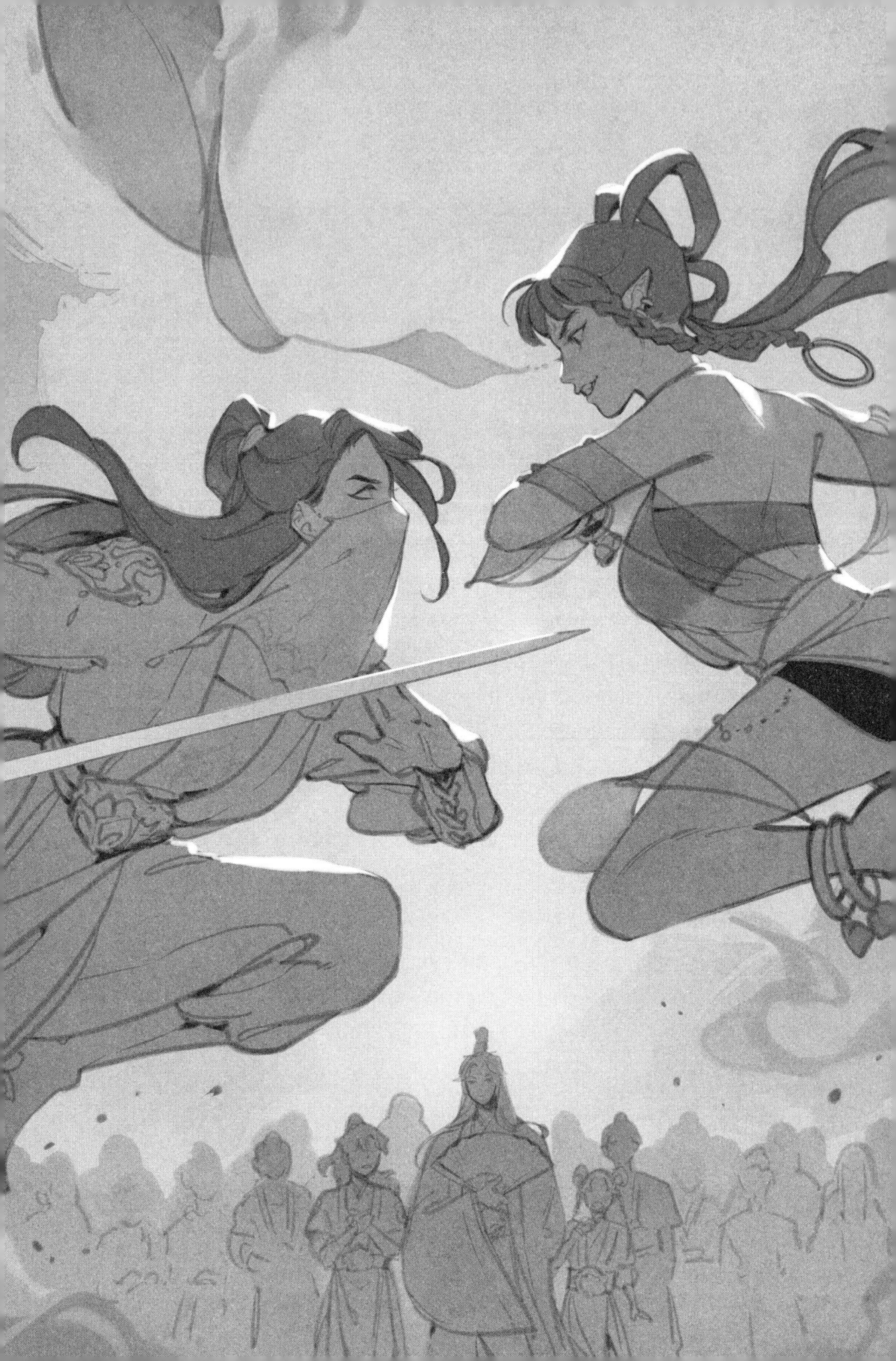

Despite himself, a burst of excitement fluttered in Shen Qingqiu.

It's here! It's almost here! The two biggest female leads in this book, their first 1 vs. 1!

Liu Mingyan was a great beauty—a heaven-and-earth-shattering great beauty at the sight of whom both gods and ghosts would weep. Even though she belonged to Xian Shu Peak, which had produced generations of beautiful women since ancient times, she was still a crane among chickens, rising above and beyond them all.

Her older brother was Bai Zhan Peak's master, but because she was younger, she'd entered the sect later and become a disciple of Xian Shu Peak's next generation.

Because her face was excessively beautiful, capable of stealing souls, she had to hide it behind a veil all year round, rendering her like unto a flower on a high cliff, unattainable and out of reach.

In brief, for the purpose of describing this character's appearance, Master Airplane Shooting Towards the Sky had probably used every single flattering vocabulary word and idiom he'd learned from elementary through to high school. He must have had it hard.

Shen Qingqiu was very fond of this female lead, and it wasn't only because Liu Mingyan's beauty points were the highest. It was also because she had great poise. She always understood the big picture and grasped the general situation, and her conduct was fair and honest. Even in Luo Binghe's gigantic harem, a wife with both intelligence and moral character was rare.

There was one more appeal factor. Liu Mingyan was the only female character for whom Airplane Shooting Towards the Sky didn't write detailed sex scenes. Many readers had been highly dissatisfied with this arrangement, to the point that they spammed the comments with their ranting, but this had given Liu Mingyan something no other female lead had: an image as clear as ice and pure as jade!

Can't be helped, the unobtainable ones are always the best.

¬(̄▽ ̄")ᕗ

This was what made the second match worth watching. An evil demoness naturally demanded a righteous saintess as a rival. Every man dreamed of being caught between an angel and a devil. To watch them jealously vie with each other over him one moment, then risk life and limb for his sake in the next—that was the highest, most sacred, perverted fantasy of every male organism. He could get drunk off the wild, untamed charm of the wicked seductress, and at the same time his heart would ache for the aus- tere taste of the pure saintess who kept pulling him closer only to push him away!

One had to admit, "Great Master" Airplane was genuinely good at nailing what people found satisfying. Shen Qingqiu couldn't help giving Luo Binghe another glance.

Luo Binghe found it very hard to not care about that gaze. Why exactly did Shen Qingqiu keep looking at him? Was it possible that Shizun...really had an interest in him?

What a pity that, under "Great Master" Airplane Shooting Towards the Sky's pen, battles between female characters usually lacked any standout moments, other than ripping [beep—] for the male gaze.

Ah, no, actually, if Shen Qingqiu thought about it, as written by the "Great Master," *none* of the battles had any memorable moments. It was always the same tired phrases, like "light like a lightning flash," "colorful as a rainbow," "sword glares of every color," "horrifying as a monster," etc.

Several incense times later, Liu Mingyan lost. After all, at this time she hadn't yet gone to Wan Jian Peak to claim her personal sword. Even though she did her utmost, her weapon was only a slender, ordinary blade, while Sha Hualing was already a demon saintess with saintly weapons in ready supply at her beck and call. Naturally, there was a gap between their abilities.

Liu Mingyan approached Shen Qingqiu. "This disciple has lost. For failing the mission, I request Shen-shibo's punishment."

"When no one else would come forward, you assumed this responsibility," said Shen Qingqiu. "This fight would never have been easy. Whether you attained victory or suffered defeat, both were acceptable outcomes. You need not be concerned. You need only take back the victory in the future."

Having taken the second round, Sha Hualing's face was glowing, and she laughed delicately. "This last match will decide the overall victor! I wonder who Senior Shen will send out? This time, you must choose carefully."

Shen Qingqiu stood with his hands clasped behind his back. "The young miss need not worry," he said with a profound air. "This one has long since decided on a representative and can guarantee that, no matter if he wins or loses, he will become your life's bane."

Sha Hualing took these words as merely his attempt at intimidation. She clapped her hands. "Which brave warrior will take the third match?"

From the crowd of demons, a giant elder slowly walked out.

He was "giant" because he really was unfairly tall! Definitely more than three meters, wouldn't you say?!

Built like a bear, he had a head of disheveled hair and armor that covered him from head to toe with spikes. He dragged a giant iron hammer behind him. Shen Qingqiu was positive that the ground quaked lightly with every step he took.

"First, to give you all a warning, the spikes on Elder "Sky Hammer" Tianchui's armor are coated with a highly toxic poison," Sha Hualing said gleefully. "This poison is ineffective against demons, but if it enters a human body, there is no cure."

The first thought Shen Qingqiu had was: *Shit, "Great Master" Airplane Shooting Towards the Sky, don't just name things whatever without thinking! Calling the one with only one arm Elder "Single Arm" Dubi, then calling the one whose weapon was a giant hammer, Elder "Sky Hammer" Tianchui—are you afraid of naming things properly?!*

Meanwhile, Sha Hualing's words had had triggered a wave of rage in the onlookers.

"Piece of shit demoness! If you want to compete, then compete! How can you say it's fair to use poison?!"

"I didn't conceal the information, did I?" Sha Hualing retorted. "If you think it's unfair—or are afraid of losing your life—then forfeit the match and admit defeat. Then you won't need to compete anymore. We demons won't mock you—it's human nature to value your lives. But my people value glory over everything else!"

Between the demons' roaring laughter and the disciples' cries of condemnation, Shen Qingqiu rubbed the crease between his brows and silently sighed.

From the reader's perspective, where you could live in the fantasy of being the protagonist, of course you'd love a woman like Sha Hualing and find her satisfying. But once you were a person facing off with her in reality... He couldn't believe anyone could bring themselves to like her!

It wasn't that she was different from how she had been described in the story—in fact, the problem was that she was exactly as advertised!

Cruel and vicious, combined with an infatuation that made her throw her brain away—if you weren't the protagonist, you'd better run the hell away. The moment you threatened her or Luo Binghe's interests even the tiniest bit, she'd want your life. She wouldn't even think of alternatives like chopping off your hands or feet, or gouging out your eyes. Even if you were her father, you had to be careful. In the original work, to help Luo Binghe gain standing in the Demon Realm, she backstabbed the guy...

Shen Qingqiu remained unflappable in the face of Sha Hualing's provocations. He maintained his silence for a stretch, using the time to stare intently at the crowd of demons. Only at the end did he turn, fixing his gaze in a certain person's direction.

"Luo Binghe, come here."

Qing Jing Peak's disciples fell into an uproar.

The disciples from the other branches were calmer, as they weren't familiar with Qing Jing Peak's internal politics. They even thought that Shen Qingqiu had certainly selected a disciple he was proud of, an unparalleled talent. That was the only way they could hope to best this demon elder who appeared to be in his hundreds. It *was* strange that they'd never heard of this person, and he did seem rather young. Was it possible that Qing Jing Peak's disciples weren't yet aware of Luo Binghe's true abilities?

Ming Fan's face had gone white. "Shizun..." he stammered. "To send this little mon—to send Luo-shidi, isn't it...unbefitting?"

"Oh?" said Shen Qingqiu. "Then will you go?"

Ming Fan repeatedly shook his head. Even though he didn't want to offer himself, and he would be happy to see Luo Binghe beaten to a pulp, this matter concerned their sect's honor! To let themselves be invaded and a peak's nameplate taken, *and* to set themselves up to lose this competition? Cang Qiong Mountain would lose face—and Qing Jing Peak would lose a *massive* amount of face!

Ning Yingying was even more anxious, to the point that she teared up. She defiantly grabbed Luo Binghe's arm while stomping and yelling. "No, no, no!"

Luo Binghe had no real battle experience. And if he had to face a demon elder covered from head to toe with spikes and poison, carrying a hammer that weighed at least several hundred kilograms? He'd definitely be beaten to death!

You lot think I want him *to enter? I was also forced into this! I have no choice!* Even so, Shen Qingqiu stated, "I said he'll be our representative, so he will. Are you unsatisfied with this master's decision? Yingying, let go of him."

Ning Yingying saw the stony look on her master's face and knew there was nothing she could do.

Luo Binghe patted her soothingly. "Don't worry, Shijie." He spoke in a steady voice even though his face was stark white. "I may be untalented, but if Shizun has chosen me, I will spare no effort. Even if I must stake my life, I won't lose face for the sect."

Ning Yingying rubbed away her tears and let go of Luo Binghe's arm. As if she couldn't stand to stay there and watch her crush take a beating, she stomped her feet several times and ran off, whimpering.

Shen Qingqiu was overjoyed. Good, run! If she ran, then the trouble she was supposed to make after this drama wouldn't crop up!

The crowd saw that although the youth who approached was upright and honorable in body and spirit, with good potential and foundation, he was clearly a young disciple with shallow cultivation. In contrast, the demon representative Elder Sky Hammer loomed with his bear-like build. Compared to Luo Binghe's still developing figure, he radiated an oppressive aura, his entire body emitting dark, roiling demonic qi. Everyone felt hesitation. Some hypothesized that perhaps Luo Binghe was hiding his strength. But when the fight actually started, they were rendered speechless.

Hiding his strength?! No—this kid really wouldn't be able to beat that guy! This wasn't a match, it was a one-sided beatdown!

From the moment Luo Binghe stepped forward, he essentially had no chance to strike. The demon elder's strength was incomparable, his swings filled with the vigor of a tiger. Even though Luo Binghe did his best to dodge and searched for an opening to attack, from time to time the hammer still managed to smash into him.

Not only were Cang Qiong Mountain's disciples dumbstruck, the demons were also at a loss for words. This was too horrible...

"Isn't this outcome predetermined...?" someone murmured. "What's the point of continuing the match?"

Elder Large Hammer—ah, no, Elder *Sky* Hammer laughed skyward, the sound like a great bell. "Well said! The child should hurry up and admit defeat, then this elder can still spare his life."

"He will win," Shen Qingqiu said lightly.

Bullshit. Luo Binghe was the overpowered protagonist—of course he was going to win. It was only that the path to victory would be difficult.

Shen Qingqiu's voice was neither loud nor soft, but it had just enough volume to carry to the center of the match area. Luo Binghe had directly taken multiple heavy blows, and he was holding back several mouthfuls of blood. When those confident words entered his ears, he somehow managed to swallow it down.

He would...win? Shizun had called on him to enter...because he really thought Luo Binghe would win?

The horde of demons laughed and jeered. They shouted at Luo Binghe to hurry up and admit defeat.

Yet Luo Binghe did not heed their wishes. Even as he took several more blows in a row, he became more and more poised, turning a deaf ear to the jeers and shouts from the crowd. His steps became lighter and more graceful. Soon, nine times out of ten, Elder Sky Hammer's giant weapon couldn't so much as brush him.

The only places on Elder Sky Hammer's body that weren't covered with spikes were his face and fists. This wasn't actually good news. It doubtless meant that the elder had extensively trained these two places so that they wouldn't be vulnerable even without the protection of the poisonous spikes.

At the same time, this was also very likely the only breach in his defenses.

Luo Binghe slowed his breaths and attentively studied his opponent.

On the surface, it had seemed that Shizun had chosen Luo Binghe only to make things difficult for him. However, if Luo Binghe lost this round, not only would he lose face, but the entire sect would as well—and furthermore, as the one who'd chosen to put him forward, Shen Qingqiu would be especially at fault.

That meant that Shizun would only have chosen Luo Binghe for this match if he really did firmly believe he would win!

Thus did Student Luo Binghe's colorful imagination successfully activate the Massive Fog of Misunderstandings System.

No one had ever believed in him like this. If only because he'd been entrusted with something so vitally important, he absolutely had to win and make everyone see!

Once again, that huge hammer came whistling toward him. Luo Binghe's pupils shrank, and gathering energy within his palms, he condensed his qi into an attack.

The audience had been enthralled by this youth who kept persevering without hesitation. Though Luo Binghe had no opportunities to counterattack, he never gave up looking for a chance to do so, and he furthermore refused to admit defeat. At this instant, when the chance to counterattack finally came, Luo Binghe seized it with incomparable precision.

The deadlock had lasted for nearly an hour, but the third match finally came to an end. Other than Shen Qingqiu, no one had anticipated this conclusion.

Elder Sky Hammer, who was covered from head to toe in poisonous spikes and boasted a hundred years' worth of skill, had been defeated by a youth of fifteen years.

Sure enough, Liu Mingyan and Sha Hualing were drawn to Luo Binghe. Two pairs of beautiful eyes fixed neatly upon him, gazing at Luo Binghe's form and unwilling to divert their attention.

[Captured Liu Mingyan and Sha Hualing's interests. Became famous in a fight during the battle with the demons who invaded Cang Qiong Mountain Sect. Protagonist satisfaction points +500.]

Shen Qingqiu was furious.

How dare you! The deduction would have been one thousand, but the profit was only five hundred?! Black-hearted System! Double-standards-holding dog!

However, it was fine, because now everyone was thinking the

same thing: Though young, Luo Binghe was truly worthy of respect! Shen Qingqiu truly had inscrutable depths!

Sha Hualing held herself back for a long while, then finally squeezed out her concession. "Cang Qiong Mountain is certainly full of talent and has produced generations of young heroes. Ling-er... is indeed impressed."

"Well said, well said," said Shen Qingqiu. "Since we have our result, could the young miss withdraw with her people? Please excuse us for being such a mess right now. We're unable to continue entertaining our guests from faraway."

The meaning hidden within his words—well, it wasn't hidden. This was his direct command telling them to get out.

Sha Hualing was filled with anger, but there was nowhere for it to go. Her fingers clenched in the gauzy red cloth on her body for a moment, then she suddenly exploded.

She reached out and gave Elder Sky Hammer a fast and violent slap. "To face Senior Shen's young disciple and yet lose so badly?" her sweet voice said angrily. "You've lost every last bit of face for the demon race!"

Elder Sky Hammer was also pitiable. Hierarchy within the Demon Realm was strict, and Sha Hualing was a saintess of noble birth. He took the slap and could only grovel. He dared not fight back, only saying again and again, "Your subordinate is incompetent and begs the saintess for punishment!"

Shen Qingqiu couldn't stand watching anymore. "Miss Sha, if you wish to discipline your subordinates, please do so somewhere else. Qiong Ding Peak is not a place for the nobility to throw their weight around."

With that slap, Sha Hualing had vented her anger, finally releasing some of her resentment; she turned back, full of smiles. "It is as you say, Senior Shen. It was just, when Ling-er saw the incredible young talent you foster, then looked at the trash under her, her heart was filled with disappointment, so she lost control for a moment. I beg you not to laugh."

She then turned, facing Elder Sky Hammer with the expression of a wicked stepmother, one as cold as a refrigerator. "For Elder Single Arm to lose to Senior Shen in their match was a matter of course. Yet you also lost your match. There is no need for me to say anything; figure out what to do yourself."

As to what she meant by this, Elder Sky Hammer clearly understood.

His heart chilled on the spot. When they arrived, he'd thought that other than Shen Qingqiu, the people of Qiong Ding Peak were a bunch of half-grown children, disciples with shallow cultivation. Hence he'd wanted to take advantage of easy pickings to earn favor before the new saintess. He'd never thought that he'd fail terribly instead, to the point that he would lose his life. He looked up and saw Luo Binghe surrounded by the crowd, all asking concernedly after his well-being. Malice surged within him.

He didn't dare touch Shen Qingqiu, but this child who'd brought him so much misfortune—he absolutely had to make him take his fair share of the blame, to drag him to death as well!

Shen Qingqiu had been paying close attention to the demon's every movement and expression. He didn't miss the flash of nefarious intent in Elder Sky Hammer's eyes. But demons were truly a bold race, taking action immediately and without even the slightest bit of buffering time. Only a second after coming up with the idea, Elder Sky Hammer careened forward, swinging his weapon.

Elder Sky Hammer's body was large and tall, and he quickly closed the distance, like a mountain of metal hurtling toward Luo Binghe. Luo Binghe's injuries weren't light, and so his movements were sluggish. He would certainly be hit. Yet Shen Qingqiu let out a cold humph, and in a flash, his figure suddenly appeared in Elder Sky Hammer's path. With the tip of his fan, he tapped the bend of Elder Sky Hammer's knee.

Elder Sky Hammer collapsed on the spot.

He really collapsed! His entire body crashed to the ground, unconscious. As for that giant hammer, Shen Qingqiu casually scooped it up and held it in his hand, weighing it. As expected, it was a tad hefty. However, given the elegant quality of his image, holding a giant hammer wasn't very aesthetic, so Shen Qingqiu immediately hurled it into the horde of demons. With a muffled thud, the head of the hammer slammed into the ground. The display was significantly shocking, and his intimidating air became even more terrifying.

Shen Qingqiu's smile didn't reach his eyes. "You wanted to kill him? The disciples under my tutelage are not yours to bully."

When he spoke these words with awe-inspiring righteousness, not only were the demons at a loss for words, Shen Qingqiu himself felt that his inner face reddened slightly.

Immortal Master, weren't you the one who sent your disciple out to be abused by others?!

Luo Binghe stared at the teal-clothed back before him, having forgotten to even say thanks. He only knew that his master had saved him yet again.

Shizun was always like this. He would seem to be harsh on Luo Binghe, yet when it came down to the critical moment, he always stood before his student.

Shen Qingqiu threw a glance behind him. "Are you all right?"

Gonna shamelessly try to farm some more favor points...

"This disciple is fine!" Luo Binghe said in a rush. "Many thanks to Shizun for the assistance."

Aiyaaa, this child is so foolishly sweet. Shen Qingqiu's inner face grew even redder, and he quickly turned back to Sha Hualing. "Miss Sha, you need to properly discipline your subordinates. If you can't stand losing, why set yourself up for the potential of it with these three matches?"

Sha Hualing also hadn't predicted Elder Sky Hammer's attack and was slightly embarrassed. She was just about to say a couple of perfunctory words appropriate for an apology, when at that instant, something happened that no one could have predicted.

Elder Sky Hammer, who'd been lying motionless on the ground, suddenly leapt up and hurled himself at Luo Binghe a second time.

Shen Qingqiu had already taken his hammer—did he intend to use his body to crush Luo Binghe?

But as Shen Qingqiu took in Elder Sky Hammer's open arms, and his pose that seemed like he was about to embrace Luo Binghe, his thoughts suddenly made several lightning-like turns, and his entire body broke out in a cold sweat.

Fuuuuuuuuuuuuck me! He's still wearing the poison-spiked armor!

In that instant, Shen Qingqiu completely forgot about Luo Binghe's plot armor. At the moment of truth, subconsciously, he once again moved to protect his student.

Xiu Ya left its sheath, blade flash bright as snow, and pierced Elder Sky Hammer's hulking body. But the demon had an entire body's worth of brute force and all-out effort within him, and he didn't back down even when skewered. Instead, he seemed overjoyed, relentlessly careening forward, forcing Xiu Ya to run clean through him and out his back, his face stretched in a sinister grin.

And he threw himself at Shen Qingqiu.

Shen Qingqiu swiftly made his decision. He promptly withdrew his attack, but it was already too late.

From his right arm came stabs of pain, and his heart chilled down to its depths.

Sky Hammer collapsed to the ground, spat out a mouthful of blood, and laughed madly. "Shen Qingqiu, I've taken you down with me, ha ha ha ha. Worth it! It was worth it!"

"Shizun!" Luo Binghe grabbed Shen Qingqiu's right hand. "You've been pierced?!"

Shen Qingqiu wrenched his hand free. "Nothing's wrong. I wasn't pierced. Don't listen to the ravings of a blowhard." As he spoke, he glanced down, and his heart was once again blotted out by a frantic screen of fuck-fuck-fuck-fuck-fuck.

From the back of his hand to his forearm were rows and rows of tiny pinholes. They were already turning red.

Luckily, he didn't have trypophobia. However, once Luo Binghe saw his arm, his face went completely white.

No one could hear the raging waves in Shen Qingqiu's heart: *Motherfucker, how many times has the male lead screwed you over?! You were already told that he won't die! Remember?! He won't die! Why did you go out of your way to rush to rescue him?! Fuuuuuuck!*

Elder Sky Hammer had finally dragged someone down with him, and it was a heavyweight. "This elder has never spoken only to scare," he said gleefully, no longer even a bit depressed. "If I say this poison has no cure, then it has no cure. Peak Lord Shen, sit back and await your death!"

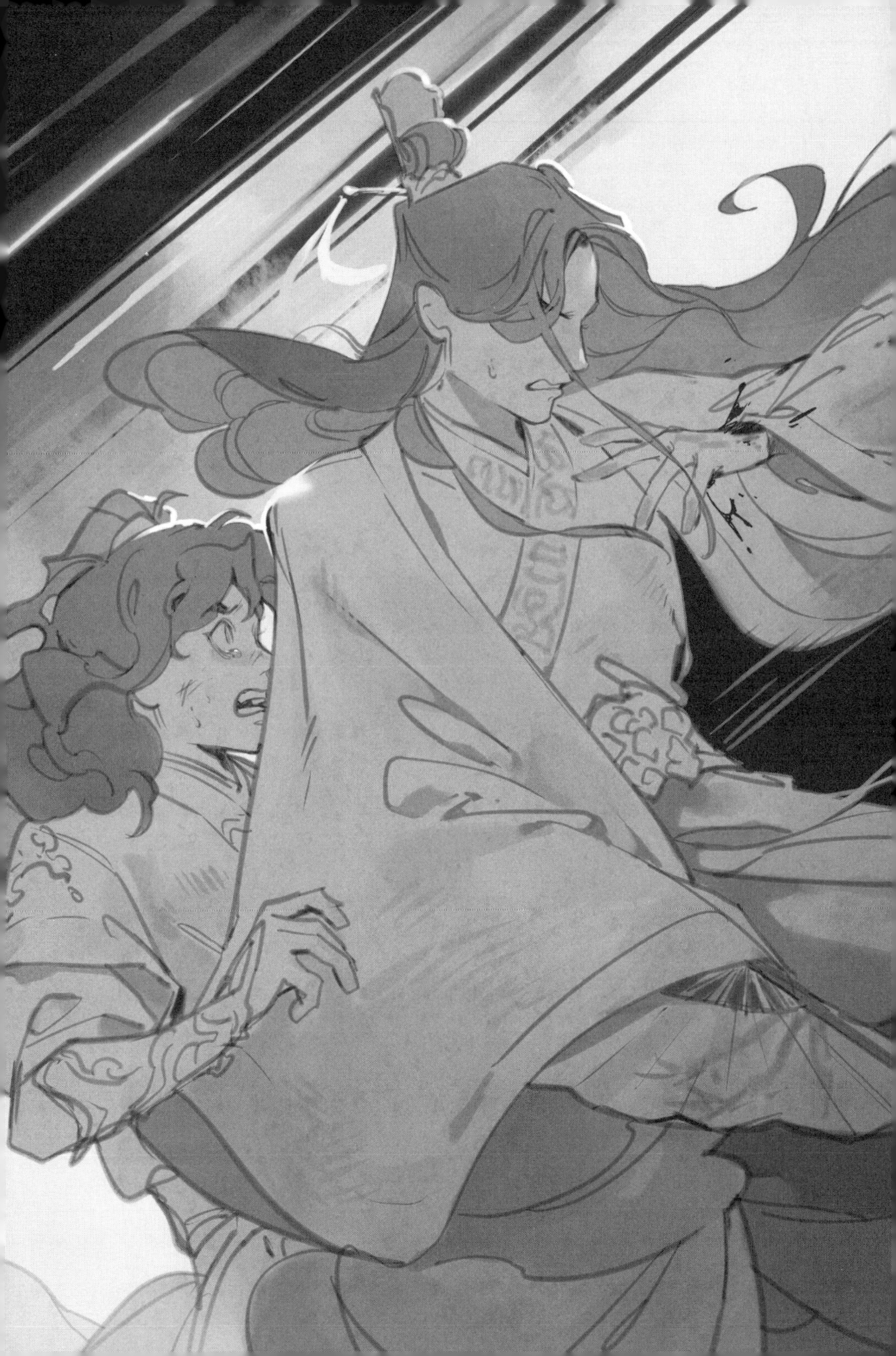

A blade flashed. Luo Binghe pulled out Xiu Ya and held it to the demon's throat, his movements so matchlessly agile that Shen Qingqiu nearly missed them.

It seemed suddenly as if Luo Binghe were another person. "Your people must have a cure," he said coldly. "If you don't hand over the antidote, I'll definitely kill you first!"

"Young master, Elder Sky Hammer truly isn't lying," Sha Hualing interrupted. "This poison is called 'Without a Cure.' When it comes to humans, it indeed has no cure. The elder has lost his match and done something truly disgraceful—he knows only death awaits him. Why would he fear your threat?"

Without a Cure!

Never had less effort been put into naming a poison!

Even though Shen Qingqiu had read the original work and had long known about this rare poison, he couldn't help lampshading and ranting at the pragmatism of "Great Master" Airplane Shooting Towards the Sky's naming sense!

Sha Hualing's eyes flashed. The sudden twist in circumstances had clearly inspired her to resume scheming something malicious. Shen Qingqiu nursed no illusions about her character.

He circulated his spiritual energy to suppress the continuous waves of pain and twitching in his right arm while his lips curved in a smile, purposely putting on a mask of effortlessness. "Your words aren't wrong, but has Miss Sha forgotten that I've already cultivated for many years? Having achieved Mid Core Formation stage, can I still be considered a common person?"

Sha Hualing's expression tightened. However, it quickly settled again, and she laughed delicately. "Whether you're common or not, I don't know. But I do know a method by which we can determine whether Senior Shen has been successfully poisoned. When a person is affected with Without a Cure, starting from their wound, their spiritual flow becomes disconnected. This schism slowly spreads to their entire body. In the end, not only does their spiritual qi coagulate and stagnate, so does their blood. I ask Senior Shen to unleash a spiritual blast with his right hand. Then we will understand."

A spiritual blast, as the name implied, involved amassing a large amount of spiritual energy into a single point, then letting it violently explode, using the waves of the spiritual energy's powerful oscillations as an attack. The effect was similar to pulling a trigger and firing a bullet or hurling a detonator. It seemed that in reality, the impact depended on the cultivation of the user.

Shen Qingqiu had attempted it privately himself and had been able to achieve an effect equivalent to throwing a grenade. But now his right arm was akin to an intricate robot's whose parts had short-circuited.

He nevertheless exerted himself, but his spiritual flow had been completely cut off. Goddammit, he couldn't have been crippled just like that, right?!

Upon hearing the description of Without a Cure, Luo Binghe's lips trembled. In this moment, all the wrongs Shen Qingqiu had committed against him in the past were wiped clean from his heart. The only thing he knew with absolute clarity was that the demons had harmed his teacher to the point that he might be crippled—he might even lose his life.

And all because of him.

Shen Qingqiu saw Luo Binghe's expression fluctuate, and he nonchalantly patted his student's head. "No need to worry."

Then Shen Qingqiu lifted his eyes, smiling slyly. "There's no harm in trying. Only I can't do this without some recompense. Miss Sha, today you ran amok on Qiong Ding Peak, and this one has put up with it thus far. Now I've changed my mind: I can't let you come and go as you please. If I do, won't Cang Qiong Mountain Sect be a laughingstock? How about we exchange a single palm strike under a contract of life and death? No matter who is injured and how, we bear all the blame ourselves. Whatever the result, we must accept it completely. Well?"

He couldn't show weakness now.

All of Qiong Ding Peak was depending on him, the only available member of the older generation, to support them. Sha Hualing would be too merciless to pass up the opportunity if he fell. Best-case scenario, the demons would destroy Qiong Ding Hall, then carry its nameplate and mountain gates back to the Demon Realm, and thereafter their sect's reputation would plummet. Worst-case scenario, it would be a massacre.

He had no doubts that this woman was entirely capable of doing something like that. Better by far to take a desperate risk and make this one last gamble. He could totally take her out too!

Shen Qingqiu hadn't noticed that, unconsciously, he no longer considered the disciples around him—whether they were anxious, resolute, furious, or indecisive—to be mob characters the novel had described in a scant number of words.

Sha Hualing bit at her lip, incredibly torn.

If Shen Qingqiu hadn't really been poisoned, this exchange of blows would directly pit their spiritual strengths against each other, and she would definitely be killed. But if he was only bluffing, and she missed this chance to wipe out Qiong Ding Peak, wouldn't she regret it for the rest of her life?

Shen Qingqiu calmly regarded her. His expression was neither that of anticipation nor avoidance as he awaited her decision.

Luo Binghe tugged on his sleeve. "Shizun, this disciple is willing to take Shizun's place and receive this strike."

Shen Qingqiu yanked his sleeve back, expression unchanging. "In what universe is it acceptable for a master to cower behind his own disciple?"

"Shizun was injured for this disciple's sake..."

Shen Qingqiu glared at him. "Since you know it was for your sake, then put some effort into protecting your life."

Luo Binghe's heart suffered a heavy blow. He was unable to speak, but the rims of his eyes reddened.

At last, Sha Hualing gritted her teeth. "Then, Senior Shen, please forgive Ling-er's rudeness!"

"Come, come, show no mercy and let fate decide who lives or dies!" Shen Qingqiu replied.

Sha Hualing's heart thundered in her chest, and she didn't dare respond. Her fire-red figure rose with a leap and she charged forth, her snow-white, jade-like palm billowing with potent, black demonic qi.

Shen Qingqiu kicked Luo Binghe aside, having made his preparations. With this one strike, he'd ensure there were no winners.

However, he was not sent flying by Sha Hualing's palm strike, nor did he cough up fresh blood as his body self-destructed and killed him.

Roiling with killing intent, the master of Bai Zhan Peak, whose sword had already left its sheath, without even lifting a single finger and using only the spiritual energy bursting forth from his body, blasted away Sha Hualing even as she was attacking with her full strength.

After a short silence, Qiong Ding Peak boiled over.

"Liu-shishu!"

"Liu-shishu left seclusion!"

"The Bai Zhan Peak War God has left seclusion! You demons, let's see if you can still be arrogant now!"

The cheers were greater than the total amount of badass poser points Shen Qingqiu had painstakingly farmed up until now.

A rain of tears showered down on Shen Qingqiu's heart: *You damn show-off! Would it kill you to arrive sooner?! How about you leave some Badass Points for me?!*

Next, this world proved itself to be truly that of a fanservice-packed stallion novel. After Sha Hualing was blasted away, she let out a single delicate scream, and the gauzy red cloth draped over her body—that had barely covered anything in the first place—also tore to shreds, eliciting a series of alarmed cries from the onlookers. She cushioned her landing with a beautifully executed roll, propelling herself to standing in a single movement. Demons were indeed bold and unrestrained; even though her entire body was censored out, Sha Hualing wasn't ashamed in the slightest. She spitefully tore off the cloak of a subordinate beside her, carelessly throwing it over herself.

"I underestimated you today," she said. "But we will definitely meet again in the future! Let's go!"

Liu Qingge sneered. "Coming and going as you please. How shameless! Dream on!"

His posture shifted, and his sword Cheng Luan soared into the sky, summoning sword glares by the hundreds and thousands, which arranged themselves into a glowing array before stabbing downward, descending like rain and hail on the demon horde.

Sha Hualing led her troops and fled while summoning a bolt of red gauze over her head, which she threw upward. Unfortunately, it simply couldn't block the fierce rain of sword glares. The red gauze was quickly pierced full of holes. On top of that, Cang Qiong Mountain Sect's disciples were hemming the demons in, so most of the horde suffered great injuries or were captured. Only the small heart of the group that had kept near Sha Hualing managed to escape down the mountain, thoroughly battered and humiliated.

After returning his sword to its sheath, Liu Qingge turned, stone-faced, to examine the condition of the wound on Shen Qingqiu's arm. The Qing Jing Peak disciples also came to surround them. More than ten faces, all filled with the same anxious expression.

Shen Qingqiu sighed. "It was definitely the right decision to send Yingying to copy Xue Yi and pound on the wall of Ling Xi Caves, wailing until you came out."[4]

"Who's Xue Yi?" asked Liu Qingge.

"World's greatest beauty," said Shen Qingqiu. "How am I?"

Liu Qingge humphed. "You won't die for now."

Though he said this, he didn't stop sending spiritual energy into Shen Qingqiu's body through his left hand, and his expression became increasingly grave.

Shen Qingqiu looked at his hand, and Liu Qingge emphatically clarified, "I'm repaying my debt from the Ling Xi Caves!"

So damn tsundere!

His plan to recruit Liu Qingge as a teammate had promise! But the meridians of Shen Qingqiu's entire body subsequently underwent a series of convulsions, and he was unable to smile.

---

4   Nickname for actress Wang Lin, after the character she played in the Chinese soap opera *Romance in the Rain*. One of her most famous scenes involves her banging on the door to confront the girl who stole her fiancé.

"Liu-shishu, does the poison 'Without a Cure' truly have no cure?" Luo Binghe asked.

Liu Qingge glanced at him, but before he could answer, Shen Qingqiu's knees wobbled, and he almost fell into a kneel.

Luckily, Luo Binghe had been supporting him the entire time. But Shen Qingqiu really couldn't stand anymore. He waved his hand. "Let me lie down...let me lie down for a while."

Luo Binghe had never seen Shen Qingqiu so weak. He knelt beside Shen Qingqiu with bloodshot eyes, choking on sobs. "Shizun..."

With great difficulty, Shen Qingqiu lifted an arm and patted Bing-ge's head like he'd always wanted to. The mouthful of fresh blood he'd been holding back finally spilled falteringly forth.

Even if it was going to be like this, he persisted and tenaciously offered a crucial line to farm more favor. "I knew that...you'd definitely win."

Upon hearing this, a tremor traveled through Luo Binghe's entire body.

Thinking about it afterward, Shen Qingqiu concluded that if he'd been looking at this from an omniscient reader's point of view, he'd have had an outburst, smashing the book down and cursing: *The fuck is with this character, huh? Hurting him one moment and saving him the next! He's messed up in the head! Multiple personalities! Nutjob!*

At this time, the System sent a notification.

[Shen Qingqiu's character complexity rating +20, character depth rating +20, character suspense rating +10, total B-Points +50.]

Shen Qingqiu was horrified. *This* was how character depth was calculated?

Also, please don't randomly create strange point types, thank you!

His vision going dark, Shen Qingqiu lifted his head, and he thought he saw Luo Binghe's tears falling from his eyes like pearls.

He had to be mistaken.

That was his last thought before he lost consciousness.

3

Favor Points

AFTER SLEEPING for an unknown length of time, Shen Qingqiu finally awoke, more dead than alive.

Opening his eyes to the sight of the familiar white, gauzy curtains above his head, he knew that he was on Qing Jing Peak, in his quiet and peaceful residence.

He took a deep breath, wanting to stretch, when he suddenly realized that the door had opened, and someone entered.

Ming Fan held a tray in both hands. Seeing Shen Qingqiu awake, he dropped the tray on the table and started to bawl. "Shizun, you're finally awake!"

Another person was still standing outside. Luo Binghe lingered by the entrance like he wanted to come in, yet he hesitated.

Ming Fan sobbed for a while, soaking a large patch of the bed-sheet, before turning over his shoulder.

"Why are you still standing here? Don't you know that seeing you annoys Shizun?" he rebuked Luo Binghe. Then he said to Shen Qingqiu, "I don't know what's wrong with that kid. He insisted on planting himself there like some kind of stick. He won't leave, no matter how much he's shooed away!"

Shen Qingqiu waved his hand. "No matter. Let him."

"I—I will go and get Liu-shishu, Zhangmen-shibo, and Mu-shishu!" Ming Fan said. "They said to alert them as soon as you woke up!"

After saying this, he scrambled to his feet and rushed outside.

It seemed to Shen Qingqiu that he'd slept for a very long time. Yue Qingyuan had already returned.

As for "Mu-shishu," that had to be Qian Cao Peak's Mu Qingfang. Qian Cao Peak specialized in medication and was proficient in the healing arts, so his presence made absolute sense.

Luo Binghe let Ming Fan pass, but even after Ming Fan had gone a distance, he wouldn't leave his spot. He only stared fixedly into the room, his fist clenched tightly the entire time.

Shen Qingqiu slowly sat up. "Do you have something to say? Then come in."

Luo Binghe complied and entered the room. With a sudden thump, he fell to his knees before the bed.

Shen Qingqiu stared at him in alarm.

Wait a moment, System? What's going on? All I did was sleep for a bit—how did things end up like this? How long have I been asleep for? Is it like ten years in the future or something?

From his kneel, Luo Binghe raised his head, gaze fervent and full of guilt. "Shizun, please forgive this disciple's foolishness and ignorance up until now."

Foolishness and ignorance? You could describe a lot of people with those words, but certainly not Luo Binghe, right?

"Originally, this disciple was under the impression that Shizun didn't care about him at all. Only after the third match did I understand what painstaking efforts Shizun had put in."

No, no, no, your original master really didn't care about you, Shen Qingqiu thought desperately. *He earnestly wished you dead, really! Although, exactly what painstaking efforts of mine have you noticed? Say it out loud; I'm very curious to know!*

But Luo Binghe did not continue speaking on this topic. He only said, entirely earnest, "From this day forth, this disciple will devote himself to carrying out his duty and serving Shizun will all his heart, obeying only Shizun's esteemed commands!"

Shen Qingqiu studied him with a complicated expression.

All that past mistreatment and abuse, completely forgotten because he'd saved Luo Binghe once? Weren't these favor points a little too easy to farm?

To no surprise, at that time, he was unable to understand the course of Luo Binghe's thoughts, with their hundreds and thousands of twists and turns.

Shen Qingqiu was silent for a moment. "As long as you understand. First, why don't you get up?"

He still didn't understand this in the slightest. *Bing-ge, what exactly did you realize?*

He watched Luo Binghe slowly stand, yet the boy remained unwilling to leave. Instead, he seemed bashful, as if there was still something he wanted to say.

"Is there something else?" Shen Qingqiu asked.

"Shizun has slept for many days and only just woke up," said Luo Binghe. "I was wondering, do you perhaps have an appetite?"

In truth, strictly speaking, Shen Qingqiu had long held himself in a state of inedia. Even if he didn't eat, he would be fine. But he was unable to resist his nature, which craved good food. As soon as he heard there were things to eat, his eyes shone with desire.

"Quite a bit. Very much so."

Luo Binghe dashed off to the kitchen. For the past few days, every couple of hours, he'd remade a serving of congee, and now it could finally be put to use. After bringing the congee to the table, still steaming hot, Luo Binghe helped Shen Qingqiu sit up on the bed, so solicitous it made the hair on the back of one's nape stand up. He came just short of spoon-feeding Shen Qingqiu, and a streak of goosebumps ran down Shen Qingqiu's forearms. He ate a few mouthfuls using the ladle himself, and all the while Luo Binghe remained standing by his bedside, silently watching him.

Shen Qingqiu thought for a moment when he was hit by a sudden realization. "It's quite good," he said, reservedly offering a few words of praise.

It wasn't just "quite good." Even Qing Jing Peak's name, "clear and tranquil," told you that this branch tended toward the fresh and light, and the style of their cooks followed this same principle. After eating their food for so long, Shen Qingqiu's tastebuds had become as dull as dishwater. Even though the bowl in his hand was full of mere congee—

Perhaps it was an issue of ingredients and technique, but compared to the watery, meager congee he'd had recently, it was on an entirely different level. Snow-white congee rice, finely chopped scallions, delicious minced pork, and shredded ginger in just the right amount, all at the perfect temperature!

It had been too long. Shen Qingqiu's body wanted nothing but to weep.

At this praise, Luo Binghe's eyes shone. "If Shizun likes it, may I give it to him every day, with variations?"

Shen Qingqiu choked on the spot.

Luo Binghe rushed to pat his back. Shen Qingqiu waved him off, expressing that he was fine.

He was only a little shocked.

Luo Binghe's excellent cooking skills were his foremost lady-killing technique. Shen Qingqiu had never thought that he would have the rare honor to eat as only a few key harem members in the original work got to: "Cuisine a la Luo Binghe."

Even more shocking was that line, ah, that line. This one: *"I'll give it to you every day, with variations."*

Wasn't that what Luo Binghe had used to coax several spoiled young ladies into willingly and ecstatically entering his harem?

Eating whatever you want is fine but saying whatever you want is not!

As Shen Qingqiu's expression had grown strange, Luo Binghe was slightly uneasy. "Shizun dislikes it?" he asked.

You made me free food! Whoever disliked that would be an idiot. Shen Qingqiu said amiably, "This master likes it very much. From today onward, I'll leave this to you."

Finally, he didn't need to resign himself to eating that insubstantial, watery fare. As the oh-so-mighty Qing Jing Peak Lord, why *didn't* he have the privilege of a private kitchen?!

Having received approval, Luo Binghe once again blossomed like a spring flower. Shen Qingqiu watched him bloom, and without knowing why, his hand suddenly itched, wanting to pat that head again. Was it possible that Bing-ge's head had a special magnetic field? That would explain why he couldn't control himself.

After sending a happily beaming Luo Binghe away (returning his goodwill by using him as hard labor), Shen Qingqiu called on the System.

"Is the scenario at the Endless Abyss unavoidable?" he asked.

[If Luo Binghe fails to complete the "Endless Abyss" scenario, ten thousand satisfaction points will be deducted,] said the System.

Upon hearing that number, Shen Qingqiu once again, out of habit, spat up a fountain of blood. Afterward, he wiped his mouth.

Whatever, he'd spat out so much blood that he was used to it at this point.

This was eminently logical. If Luo Binghe wasn't shoved into the Endless Abyss, then he wouldn't be able to activate his golden finger. If the protagonist couldn't become overpowered, then where was the satisfaction?

Therefore, the Endless Abyss scenario was unavoidable. And as this novel's number one loser, number one scum villain, the execution of this glorious task, naturally, absolutely, inescapably, fell to Shen Qingqiu.

Yet unwilling to resign himself to this fate, Shen Qingqiu asked again and ended up sighing, still unable to give up completely. Luo Binghe, who was currently like a little sun, was destined to fall and become that brooding, cold-blooded, demon youth. Even a transmigrator like Shen Qingqiu, who by all rights ought to have access to cheat powers, was unable to change this inevitability.

He had been designated to be the man who threw the protagonist into the Endless Abyss, thereby catalyzing his overpowered, legendary journey!

This job's opportunities for growth were really terrible.

If Shen Qingqiu failed to do this, he would lose ten thousand satisfaction points—he couldn't become more thoroughly dead than that. But if he did do this, once Luo Binghe activated his golden finger, he definitely wouldn't let him off.

The work was difficult, the pay was meager, the benefits—were nonexistent. What the hell was up with this?!

Luo Binghe hadn't left for long when several of Shen Qingqiu's sect siblings came to visit.

Shen Qingqiu lay on the bed, reading a novel hidden inside a copy of the *Daode Jing*.[5] When Yue Qingyuan entered, he shut the books without missing a beat so that the novel was tucked inside, with the *Daode Jing*'s cover proudly exposed. He tried to get off the bed, but Yue Qingyuan hurriedly stopped him.

"Don't move so carelessly," he cautioned. "You shouldn't leave the bed yet. Just keep lying down." Yue Qingyuan turned behind him to Mu Qingfang. "Mu-shidi, come take another look."

While Shen Qingqiu was unconscious, Mu Qingfang had already diagnosed him and provided treatment. This visit was likely for further prognosis.

Shen Qingqiu held out his wrist. "I'm troubling Mu-shidi," he said politely.

Mu Qingfang startled briefly, but he nodded, sitting by the bed and putting his fingers on Shen Qingqiu's pulse. With his medical expertise as the Peak Lord of Qian Cao Peak, no matter how complicated the case, he only needed an instant to make a diagnosis and provide a prescription. But he conscientiously remained there for a long while before finally removing his fingers, his expression solemn.

"How is he?" Yue Qingyuan asked.

As the patient in question, Shen Qingqiu showed no restraint. "So can this poison be cured or not?"

Liu Qingge shook out his sleeves, sitting down next to the table with a humph. "It's called Without a Cure. What do you think?"

Shen Qingqiu sighed. "Then Mu-shidi might as well tell me. How many years do I have left? How many months? Or how many days?"

---

5   More commonly known as the Daode Jing, a famous classical text on the philosophy and religion of Daoism by Laozi.

Mu Qingfang shook his head. "Even though it's Without a Cure, its effects can be suppressed."

His voice was even, neither quiet nor loud, but Shen Qingqiu felt like he'd hit the jackpot.

Even though this poison was called "Without a Cure," in truth there *was* a remedy.

In the original work, at the Immortal Alliance Conference, with its twist after twist, a lovable, graceful, and subdued little shimei from another sect was hit by this rare poison. However, importantly, she was the protagonist's woman.

Was there ever a stallion novel where the male lead let his own woman be poisoned to death? If there was, then he would be a subpar wish-fulfillment protagonist! And that would be a shitty failure of a stallion novel!

The cure was incredibly simple. Let us review the developments in the original work.

Due to the irresistible power of plot, in order to save the male lead—whom she'd known for less than two hours—that graceful little shimei let herself be hit by a demon's underhanded trick, and the poison contaminated her body. Luo Binghe felt an absolute obligation to save her, and therefore he took on the burden of looking for a cure for the graceful little shimei.

It just so happened that, deep within the mountains where the Immortal Alliance Conference was being held, there grew a mythical thousand-year-old flower.

Sorry, Shen Qingqiu had already forgotten exactly what the name was—whatever-flower or whatever-leaf—because the number of mythical flowers in *Proud Immortal Demon Way* numbered at least in the hundreds, and every single one was at least a thousand years old, and when you added on all the mythical grasses and mythical trees, who the hell could remember all those names?!

(Airplane Shooting Towards the Sky, do you think mythical flowers are like Chinese cabbages on sale? Leave mythical flowers at least a little of the dignity that comes with being rare and precious!)

Luo Binghe was sure this legendary flower would cure the poison within the graceful shimei's body. He put a tremendous amount of effort into picking it for her—just doing that took three days (thirty chapters). For those three days, they journeyed to pick the flower while fighting monsters, and through exchanging flirtatious glances, they developed a deep sense of camaraderie.

By the time Luo Binghe finally managed to pick the flower, the graceful shimei's condition had worsened, her entire body fragile and devoid of strength. The two of them were overjoyed, and they hurried to let the graceful shimei eat the flower raw.

However, it was ineffective. The poison wasn't cured! Their hearts sank.

The girl thought, "Since I'm about to die, I must leave behind some memories to ensure that my life won't have been in vain. I don't have many days left, after all, so I won't suppress my feelings anymore."

Then, using her weak and fragile body, she pushed Luo Binghe down.

Luo Binghe put up a brief show of resistance before telling himself "She did it all for my sake. I don't have the heart to reject her final wish." He yielded, still half-reluctant, and went along with it...

Then, in the end, how was the poison cured?

After the down and dirty scene, the girl's poison was naturally cured!

Was it ridiculous? Cliché? Implausible?

...But it was satisfying, right? Ridiculously satisfying, so ridiculously satisfying, ha ha ha ha...

Look, Luo Binghe was of both human and demon blood, right? And the demon half of his bloodline came from their number one Saintly Ruler—from the heavenly demons of old! A wee little demonic poison wasn't even strong enough to get stuck between Luo Binghe's teeth, and he instantly absorbed and digested it during their *you know*.

Incidentally, he even absorbed the nutrients of the mythical flower the girl had just eaten, and so his martial ability once again made great progress—shit!

The so-called protagonist's privilege was that even if he stepped in dog shit, there would probably be a hidden scroll or elixir within it.

As Shen Qingqiu thought back on this segment of *Proud Immortal Demon Way*, his facial expression kept changing erratically. He failed to notice even when the others addressed him. Yue Qingyuan had to repeatedly call his name many times before he finally returned to himself.

"What?"

Mu Qingfang passed him a piece of paper. "Every month, take these four medications, then circulate your spiritual energy with someone who has high quantities of it. This will assist you in maintaining regular spiritual circulation. If you do these things, you shouldn't have any problems." He paused for a moment. "The only thing is, I'm afraid that from today onward, Shen-shixiong, occasionally your spiritual qi will at times suddenly stagnate, or you may suffer other abnormalities in your circulation."

The other three people in the room all paid close attention to his expression.

One must remember that to cultivators, the stagnation of spiritual circulation was a profoundly terrifying problem—especially if it cropped up during a duel between expert practitioners, where a single slip-up could mean your life.

Little did they know, Shen Qingqiu was immensely satisfied with this result.

For somebody in a scum villain role to be poisoned with something like Without a Cure and still be able to live? It was giving him too much confidence.

Like, he knew that going at it with the protagonist could have cured the poison, but like he could do that! Could he? Ha ha ha ha...

Yue Qingyuan sighed. "Had I known any of this would come to pass, I would not have left the mountain."

Shen Qingqiu thought his tone was too solemn. "The Immortal Alliance Conference has always been a massive event that the various sect leaders must work together to organize," he hurried to say. "How could you not have gone, Shixiong? This happened due to the demons' underhanded deceits and my own carelessness; you must not hold yourself responsible."

If he didn't say this clearly here, given Yue Qingyuan's personality, he might never leave the mountain ever again—he'd stay and defend Cang Qiong Mountain Sect to his last. That was all entirely possible.

To his surprise, Mu Qingfang also guiltily declared, "No, the fault is all mine. If I hadn't failed to realize there was a demonic invasion, and if my skill weren't too poor to fully cure Shen-shixiong, it wouldn't have come to this either."

"No, no, no, it has nothing to do with you two," Shen Qingqiu insisted. "Ah, come to think of it, I was a bit indelicate and smashed a giant hole into the ground before Qiong Ding Hall with that hammer..."

The three of them devolved into jumbled apologizing and blame-taking, the scene both chaotic and comical. It left Shen Qingqiu both touched and embarrassed, his entire body breaking out into goosebumps and his scalp going numb.

Liu Qingge stared out the window, face expressionless. He waited until they had exhausted themselves, then finally took a sip of tea and said, "This matter must remain secret to all but the twelve peak lords."

If outsiders became aware that the peak lord of Cang Qiong Mountain Sect's second peak had such a deadly weakness, things would be unfun, to say the least. All three of the others naturally understood this.

"Do you think that the burden of peak lord will be too heavy, Qingqiu?" asked Yue Qingyuan.

The original Shen Qingqiu would most likely have suspected that Yue Qingyuan was trying to undermine his authority or something of that sort. However, the current Shen Qingqiu knew that Yue Qingyuan was genuinely worried about him overworking himself and damaging his health, and he rushed to respond.

"Zhangmen-shixiong, really, don't worry about me anymore. I haven't been crippled to that extent." He smiled. "For now, my hands, feet, and mouth still work, and I still have my cultivation. I am entirely satisfied."

They then discussed a variety of details of the demon invasion before Yue Qingyuan and Mu Qingfang took their leave. Shen

Qingqiu watched them go, thinking it all terribly funny, yet he also felt an unutterable warmth and peace.

Even though his fellow disciples' personalities were all different, with some easy to get along with, some difficult, they all breathed as one. Though split into twelve peaks, whenever something went wrong, they were a dependable family (excepting the original Shen Qingqiu).

Liu Qingge put down his tea, which had long gone ice-cold. "If it weren't for your body's lack of ghostly qi, I would definitely suspect you'd been possessed."

And the one who remained just happened to be one of the difficult ones.

On a certain level, your guess is very correct.

Liu Qingge continued. "You saved me in the Ling Xi Caves. That in itself was inconceivable. During the demon attack, you also rescued some nameless disciple and almost lost your life. You were poisoned to the point of damaging your spiritual energy levels, and you should be furious, yet you've peacefully accepted it. Someone else doing so wouldn't be strange, but *you* doing so upturns everything."

Shen Qingqiu absolutely didn't want to discuss the issues of his own OOC personality with Liu Qingge. He called Ming Fan to refresh the tea, then leaned back and smiled. "Nameless? That's only for now."

"That disciple of yours, his base is indeed excellent," Liu Qingge said. "However, a fair number with his level of aptitude are invited into the large sects every year, and in the end, the number who can become truly outstanding is less than one in ten thousand."

Shen Qingqiu suddenly sensed danger.

What if Liu Qingge became a stumbling block on Luo Binghe's journey to becoming overpowered and, during a confrontation between the two of them, was KO'd in a snap? For everyone's sake, he needed to warn Liu Qingge.

"Believe me," he said patiently, earnestly. "This disciple of mine will definitely be a success. I hope when Liu-shidi has the chance, you can give him a little support and guidance as often as possible."

Ming Fan was half-dead from depression. He had only come to refresh the tea, yet he had been forced to hear Shen Qingqiu, his ally in torturing a shared enemy, heap praise after praise upon Luo Binghe. The level of frustration he felt was akin to that of "the confidante who for years always cursed a little bastard with you suddenly went and coupled up with the same little bastard you'd tormented together." Repulsed, he immediately decided to go be repulsive to others.

A stormy Ming Fan found Luo Binghe in the kitchen, pondering over what food to make Shen Qingqiu the next morning. Ming Fan showered him with verbal abuse before issuing a series of commands.

"Go chop some wood! Chop eighty bundles! Fill the entire woodshed! Fetch water! The water jars in our rooms are all empty! Are you blind? Can't you see?!"

"But Shixiong, if the woodshed is full, where will I sleep?" Luo Binghe asked, perplexed.

Ming Fan stomped his foot, spittle flying everywhere. "Isn't it flat in here?! Isn't that floor enough?!"

"I just filled the water jars in your rooms today..."

"That water isn't fresh anymore—redo it! Refill them all!"

In the past, some grievance and bitterness might have sprouted in Luo Binghe's heart, but today his attitude was completely different. In his eyes, these were all training opportunities.

He already had such a good teacher, one who thought of everything for him, who was even willing to sacrifice his life for him (right...?). What training could he not overcome? What suffering could he not withstand?

Luo Binghe didn't say another word. He turned on his heel to get ready to work.

Ming Fan could derive not even a little satisfaction from his reaction, and instead he felt even more frustrated.

He stormed away while cursing. "I really can't understand what about that brat caught Shizun's eye, for Shizun to suddenly see him in a new light. 'A success'? 'Outstanding'? Even if that brat bewitched Shizun with some potion, Liu-shishu still won't guide or support him! Unthinkable! Bah!"

Though Ming Fan cursed unceasingly as he went, his voice wasn't loud.

But how could Luo Binghe, with his blindingly fast progress and naturally sharp five senses, not hear? Ming Fan's mutterings were largely harsh words and phrases, but in the midst he'd touched on the keywords, and in an instant Luo Binghe took those bits and pieces to guess most of the whole picture.

So Shizun had actually spoken about him like that in front of Liu-shishu...

The feeling of having someone speak about you so highly somewhere you couldn't see—that feeling was truly indescribably wonderful.

Warmth suddenly surged in Luo Binghe's heart; the more it surged, the stronger it became, gradually flowing through his entire body.

Luo Binghe felt like a steady strength had taken root somewhere in the depths of his heart and was starting to bud. Even his hand, carrying the heavy wooden bucket, seemed to become stronger.

At this time, not only did Luo Binghe not feel like other people were making things difficult for him, his expression became joyful and satisfied.

If Shen Qingqiu were there, he would definitely have suspected that, within the depths of his heart, Luo Binghe was actually an extreme masochist.

However, Shen Qingqiu was astoundingly oblivious to the fact that, thanks to the divine wingman abilities of his useless teammate Ming Fan, Luo Binghe's favor had again risen to a new high. For the time being, Shen Qingqiu was lying down in elation.

That day, the always lofty Qing Jing Peak's doorstep almost broke from all the feet rushing across it. The various peak lords all brought their disciples to visit, along with gifts of condolence.

After all, during Sha Hualing's armed provocation, the Rainbow Bridges had been severed, and Qiong Ding Peak had been sealed by a barrier. They had been unable to intervene, and so the burden of the fight had fallen on Shen Qingqiu, who had been the sole representative of the older generation.

Anyhow, Cang Qiong Mountain hadn't lost too much face. But no matter whether their past relationship had been good or bad, the peak lords absolutely had to come and express proper sentiments. Shen Qingqiu calmly received their greetings and used the chance to learn the faces of several peak lords he hadn't yet met, while also taking the opportunity to make some small talk and strengthen his relationships.

That night, he was on cloud nine as he thought: *Finally, I can have a peaceful night's sleep.*

However, four hours later...

Peaceful night's sleep my ass!

Shen Qingqiu stood in the middle of a stretch of chaotic nothingness and stared out at the endless horizon.

He'd definitely just been drunk on satisfied smiles, comfortably sinking into sleep on his bed—so could someone explain why he'd been dragged into this space?!

Shen Qingqiu really wished he had a gong, one he could ring to summon the System so that he wouldn't need to always yell at the top of his lungs within his mind, "System?! Are you online?!"

[The System provides you with 24-hour service.]

"Where is this? What's the situation?"

[This is a world within a dream realm.]

"Of course I know this is a dream realm," said Shen Qingqiu. "Tell me, how could such abstract scenery exist in reality? I'm asking *why* I'm here."

Come on, he thought, *please don't let it be what I'm thinking.*

But this world really wouldn't give him a break. Just as he thought, *don't, don't,* in the next second, he saw a figure that was unbearably familiar.

Luo Binghe stood before him, bewildered, in the middle of a never-ending wasteland.

He also seemed entirely lost as to why he'd appeared here. After a moment of bewilderment, Shen Qingqiu's form came into his view. Luo Binghe startled, then dashed over happily, like a chick who'd seen its mother hen.

(What kind of shitty analogy was that?!)

"Shizun!" Luo Binghe had already been trapped in this world for a long time. He was instantly excited by the sight of Shen Qingqiu and called to him repeatedly, again and again.

As soon as Shen Qingqiu laid eyes on him, he recognized this place and what scenario he'd been thrust into.

Instantly, all of Shen Qingqiu's hopes turned to dust, and even as a shower of tears rained down on his heart, he patted Luo Binghe's shoulder. "I heard you, no need to call me so many times."

"Yes. Shizun," Luo Binghe said hurriedly. "Why are you here too? Do you know where we are?"

Being lazy, Shen Qingqiu directly echoed the System's lines. "This is a world within a dream realm."

"Then why am *I* here?" Luo Binghe asked again.

"Anyone else being here is the strange thing, while your presence is quite natural," said Shen Qingqiu. "This is *your* dream realm."

"Mine?" Luo Binghe startled and backed up a step, looking at the endless, desolate land and sky. "My dream realm, actually...looks like this?"

The dream realm, one's view of the world, reflected one's heart. Luo Binghe was so young, yet his mindscape wasn't filled with the red of flowers and the green of willows, but this bleak scenery. One couldn't help feeling sorrow.

Shen Qingqiu pretended to ponder for a while. "This is not an ordinary dream realm. I'm afraid that while you were unaware, someone tampered with it. The waves of spiritual energy within this dream are strong and unstable. Though this master was inadvertently pulled in by you."

"This disciple is useless and involved Shizun once again." Luo Binghe's face was ashamed, but he considered this carefully. "Exactly who would tamper with my dream realm?"

Shen Qingqiu was ready with an answer, fully enjoying the experience of divulging spoilers. "No need to think too hard. The borders of this dream realm churn with demonic qi, and any entity who would use such crude techniques undoubtedly must be a demon."

Luo Binghe was unsurprised, and these words only deepened his hatred toward that race. "The ways of demons are truly poisonous."

Shen Qingqiu wondered what sort of expression Luo Binghe would make in the future, thinking back on these words, once he learned of his own demonic heritage...

"Not necessarily poisonous," said Shen Qingqiu with a smile. "Perhaps their intentions are the exact opposite."

Someone not in the know couldn't hope to comprehend words spoken from his omniscient perspective.

Luo Binghe didn't understand. What did his master mean? But Shen Qingqiu's smile seemed profound, and the tail of his sentence was inflected lightly upward in a somewhat teasing tone. It was the sort of hint that made people's imaginations run wild. Luo Binghe stopped there, not daring to think about it further.

In truth, Shen Qingqiu didn't intend to tease; he thought himself very straightforward. The one who'd tampered with Luo Binghe's dream realm was Sha Hualing. Though she did have some harmful intentions, her underlying motive was obvious. Naturally, she was driven by a young girl's secret yearning for love.

Otherwise, she would have directed her aggressions toward others, not specifically Luo Binghe. Demons were compelled to viciously bully the person they liked. Only if the object of their affections failed to die would the demon accept them. If their target died, that meant they were useless and not worth nursing any lingering affections for.

"This dream realm is rather complicated." said Shen Qingqiu. "An ordinary nightmare technique couldn't trap me. I can dispel those with a mere thought. But this dream realm was truly meticulously constructed. I'm afraid that until the core of the illusion is destroyed, no one will be able to leave."

"Even Shizun would be trapped in this dream realm forever?" Luo Binghe asked, anxious.

Shen Qingqiu glanced at him. "You will be too."

Luo Binghe's mind jolted, his face going from red to white. "...It's all this disciple's fault."

"The situation is what it is, so there's no use decrying it," said Shen Qingqiu. "We should devise a solution as soon as possible, dispel the barrier, and take our leave."

Luo Binghe silently nodded and followed behind Shen Qingqiu as they headed toward the dream realm's border.

Shen Qingqiu's face was smooth and unchanging, but his mind was a stormy sea. He was having an intense back-and-forth with the System.

[System alert: You are now entering an important subplot scenario, "The 'Dream Demon' Meng Mo's Barrier." During this subplot, please make sure to assist Luo Binghe in defeating Meng Mo's illusion. Otherwise, one thousand satisfaction points will be deducted.]

There it was again. Always deducting satisfaction points, and every time it was a heart-attack-inducing number. After assiduously working for so long, Shen Qingqiu had only managed to scrounge a couple of satisfaction points here and there while the System could remove one thousand points in a single deduction—was this really fair?!

As a person—no, as a System, you shouldn't be so inflexible!

That wasn't the main point, though. The main point was—was that this was the wrong script!

Let us summarize this scenario's original setup: Luo Binghe was pushed into Meng Mo's sphere of influence, but before danger struck, he instinctually sought protection and pulled the person he trusted most into the barrier with him.

Shen Qingqiu urgently called to the System. "Master, Good Master, Esteemed Master! There's a been a bug, right? In this section, Luo Binghe should be cozying up with a maiden, and the maiden is responsible for unraveling his complexes and using love to help him defeat his inner demons. How come I've been thrust into this role?! Where is the promised deep and emotional heart-to-heart where she's accepted into his harem? Where is the promised little shimei who refuses to leave him either in life or in death?!"

〔Our self-inspection failed to find a bug. The System is running normally.〕

No bug. That meant that in this scenario, Shen Qingqiu either had to carry out that role or die.

This was the butterfly effect! Originally, the one who was pulled into Luo Binghe's nightmare was Ning Yingying. As Luo Binghe's closest, most trusted confidante on Qing Jing Peak in the early story, this gate-crashing, intimacy-building task was clearly her job.

What was happening now? How had the hat of "closest, most trusted confidant" nonsensically landed on Shen Qingqiu's head?

I would like to express that I am overwhelmed by this honor, but I don't at all want to accept this special distinction!

"Shizun, what's wrong?" Luo Binghe asked in concern, seeing his unreadable expression.

Shen Qingqiu promptly pulled himself together. "Nothing's wrong," he said calmly. "This master was thinking that demons who manipulate dream realms often target the weaknesses of the human heart. You must be vigilant and on your guard."

Luo Binghe nodded, his expression firm. "This disciple definitely won't allow Shifu to be dragged in again."

This was miserable. Not only had Shen Qingqiu been thrust into a dangerous situation, on top of that, he had to assume the task of playing out the maiden's role.

Shen Qingqiu absolutely didn't want to charge through a mountain of knives or a sea of fire with the male lead to confront the terrifying Master Meng Mo while *also* blocking knives for him and even providing free psychological therapy...

That said, complaining was useless. In the past, when he'd been faced with this kind of situation, his habit had been to cuss out Airplane Shooting Towards the Sky, but honestly, "Great Master" Airplane was also innocent. He was a proper, upright stallion novel author, and he definitely wouldn't have wanted something like this to happen in his work—a healthy maiden being replaced by a scum villain? How disheartening. Ordinary readers would throw the book to the floor.

The two of them kept walking, the clouds above and scenery around them like a kaleidoscope, sometimes lengthening and twisting, and at other times shattering into thousands of fragments, always erratic. The picture formed by the world they walked through was exceedingly eerie, like the people had been illustrated by da Vinci while the backgrounds had been illustrated by Picasso. The style clash was extraordinarily intense.

Suddenly, from within the dense layers of cloud emerged the buildings of a city.

They stopped in their steps. Luo Binghe looked at Shen Qingqiu, waiting for his signal.

"Counter soldiers with arms and floods with earthen dams," Shen

Qingqiu muttered to himself. "We deal with whatever situations arise as appropriate. Forward."

As they walked to the city gates, Luo Binghe raised his head, his expression becoming slightly puzzled.

Shen Qingqiu knew very well what he was thinking: that this city looked very familiar.

Of course it was familiar—this was the city Luo Binghe had wandered while homeless during his childhood.

The city gates naturally had no guards defending them and slowly opened by themselves. Shen Qingqiu led him inside.

This dream realm was frightening in its realism. When abstract, it was so abstract that it became blobs of colors. When photorealistic, it was so photorealistic as to be indistinguishable from reality. The city's streets, markets, residences, vendor stalls—every single one was intricate enough to make your hair stand on end. Lit brightly with lamps, with people coming and going, from a distance it looked bustling and lively, but once Shen Qingqiu drew close, even though he had long prepared himself, his heart still almost escaped his ribcage.

These "people" moving about were, to a one, faceless.

Every visage was a blurry mass, features unclear, and none of them made a sound. They didn't seem like living people at all, yet they still milled around, wandering back and forth. The entire city was deathly silent, its busyness entirely uncanny.

Luo Binghe had never seen a scene like this. "Shizun," he said, aghast, "what are these things?"

Shen Qingqiu was panicking a little from terror, but he still took on the duty of being an expository encyclopedia. "This is an illusory city created via a nightmare. In the dream realm, one can create inanimate objects such as buildings and trees, but not living people. At most, they can be fashioned to this extent, speechless monsters that lack noses and faces. Even so, to be able to construct something on the scope of a city, and to make it nearly like unto reality—I'm afraid it can only be one person."

Luo Binghe was incredibly cooperative, and he humbly sought instruction. "One person?"

"Meng Mo."

Meng Mo the "Dream Demon," was the boss of this instance of a dream realm.

Meng Mo's true identity was that of a famously brilliant and accomplished elder among demons. Several hundred years ago, a bout of divine punishment had destroyed his physical body, but his powerful spirit had endured, undamaged. From then on, he had become a parasite within others' dream realms, subsisting by absorbing their spiritual energy and vitality.

At the same time, he was also one of the protagonist's teachers on his road to becoming a demon. Thus, we can give him a more direct and intimate nickname: the Portable Grandfather.

Meng Mo was the one who, after Luo Binghe broke through the barrier, formulaically took a liking to the protagonist, formulaically taught him everything about his lost arts, and formulaically from that point forth occasionally helped the male lead think up plans for taking care of small fry.

Luo Binghe still wanted to ask a few more questions, but then his eyes involuntarily swept through the crowd and froze for a split second.

Despite knowing the answer, Shen Qingqiu asked, "What's wrong?"

"Faces!" Luo Binghe blurted out. "Shizun! Just now I think I saw people with faces!"

Shen Qingqiu readily heeded his words and kept it concise. "We follow."

They closely tailed the few figures who were incongruous with the people and style of the surroundings, turning and twisting through the city, until they finally stopped before an alley.

In total, there were five people with faces. They appeared to be five youths, each one equipped with noses and features. The four taller figures surrounded one on the ground, and they cursed and yelled incessantly. Words like "little mongrel" and "bastard" poured from their mouths. They completely failed to notice the two people behind them.

"It looks like they can't see us," said Luo Binghe. He looked at Shen Qingqiu as if to ask, *Didn't you say Meng Mo was incapable of creating people with complete features?*

Time for more angst! Shen Qingqiu heaved a sigh in his heart. "Meng Mo indeed cannot create people using nightmares, but he didn't create these individuals. Luo Binghe, look more closely at their faces."

Luo Binghe slowly turned his gaze toward them. Although his expression didn't change much, in a flash, a drop of cold sweat dripped down his forehead.

"These are not illusions created by Meng Mo," said Shen Qingqiu. "They are projections of real people from your memories. Meng Mo only awakened these reflections from the memories sleeping within your mind."

But Luo Binghe could no longer hear him. He placed his hands on his temples, and it seemed as if his head was twitching.

Shen Qingqiu knew that Luo Binghe's inner demons had already struck.

Those four rowdy youths surrounded the child in the alley, who appeared to be only around four or five years old, as they punched and kicked him. That shabbily dressed child had covered his head with both arms and curled up on the ground, soundlessly taking the beating. It really made one worry that they would beat the young one to death.

"Heh, this little mongrel sure is blind, daring to enter our territory and snatch our food!"

"Must be tired of living!"

"Step on him, step on him! He's so pitiful, right? Hungry with nothing to eat, right? Beat him to death, and he won't have to worry about that!"

Luo Binghe's head hurt like it was splitting open.

That small, frail figure on the ground was his young self from the past. Through the disheveled hair and bloodstained face, two bright eyes like stars—like sharp swords lancing forward—met his gaze.

Luo Binghe was completely unable to look away.

"Pull yourself together," Shen Qingqiu said lowly. "It's only an illusion."

However, the terrifying thing about Meng Mo was that he specialized in summoning the human heart's deepest terror, rage, and misery in order to destroy a person's psychological defenses.

To a Luo Binghe who had already activated his god-mode cheats, the power of ten thousand Meng Mos together would amount to little more than parlor tricks. But the Luo Binghe now, whose demonic blood had yet to awaken, was trapped in the dream realm and his dark memories. All he could see was his own powerlessness.

Suddenly, the alley scene distorted, transforming into another one.

Not good, Shen Qingqiu thought. *A second killing blow without time to prepare!*

They were in a broken-down little hut. The hut only had one bed, a crooked little table with a dimly lit oil lamp on top, and a small wooden bench.

On the bed lay a haggard old woman. With great effort, she tried to prop herself up, but from beginning to end, she was unable to do so. A small figure rushed in from outside. A tender-faced Luo Binghe, only a little over ten years old, supported the woman. Around his neck hung that jade pendant.

"Mother, why are you getting up again?" he asked anxiously. "Didn't we say it's fine to rest?"

The woman coughed. "Lying down doesn't help with anything... Might as well get up and wash the clothes."

"I already finished washing," said little Luo Binghe. "Mother, lie down and wait for me to finish simmering your medicine. You can work after you take it and get better."

The woman's face was ashen, her sickness long beyond cure, and she had little time left to live. She smiled while patting Luo Binghe's head. "Binghe is so sweet."

Little Luo Binghe lifted his face, forcing himself to smile. "What does Mother want to eat?"

"These days I have less and less appetite." The woman paused, then hesitantly added, "The last time our house's young master threw out his white congee, I did wish for a bit of a taste. I wonder if the kitchens have any left."

Little Luo Binghe vigorously nodded. "I will go ask for Mother!"

"Just asking is enough," the woman warned him again and again. "If there's none left, then just make something light and soupy.

As long as it fills the stomach, it's fine. Absolutely do not request any from the chef."

Luo Binghe promised profusely, then ran out like the wind, his feet clapping against the ground. After lying down for a while, the woman felt beneath her pillow for a needle and thread and started doing needlework.

The lamplight in the hut became dimmer and dimmer.

While Luo Binghe's mind was unclear, he reached out, trying to grasp something. Shen Qingqiu grabbed his hand.

"Luo Binghe!" he said forcefully. "Look carefully. This isn't your mother, and you are no longer that helpless child who could only endure humiliation!"

One of the things that made this nightmare so lethal was that the more agitated the trapped victim became, the more damage it would do to their mind. Luo Binghe's present extreme instability was terribly harmful to his spirit.

Another dangerous thing that you needed to remember was that you absolutely could not attack the "people" who appeared in your dream realm.

Every single "person" was formed from the mind and consciousness of the dream realm's host. As soon as you attacked them, you would also be attacking your own brain. Many people, not knowing this, or unable to control their emotions, attacked the "people" in the dream realm who'd hurt them in the past and thereby sent themselves into a coma. If Luo Binghe fell into that state, Shen Qingqiu would of course also be trapped in his dream with him.

The scenery around them shifted erratically. This nightmare was a collection of Luo Binghe's misfortunes and traumas from his short decade-plus years of life.

The scene suddenly transformed into little Luo Binghe pleading with the house chef to grant his adopted mother a bowl of congee before being ridiculed by the manor's young master—then it became the time right after he'd joined Qing Jing Peak, when he'd been subjected to exclusion and spite by his numerous shixiong, his frail form straining as he swung a rusty axe or carried pails of water up the long stairs as his steps slowed more and more—then the moment when his treasured jade pendant was snatched away, never to be found...

The disordered scenes piled up as they came one after another without pause. The present Luo Binghe could neither see nor hear anything beyond this maelstrom of images and memories. Within his head, there was only an ongoing explosion of hatred, despair, suffering, helplessness, and fury from those times, churning endlessly within his chest and mind.

The only way to dispel this nightmare would be to undo the tangles in one's heart, thereby causing the nightmare to collapse on itself. But Luo Binghe's fists were tightly clenched. Cracking sounds came from his fingers, his breathing grew increasingly unsteady, his eyes turned an unnatural red, and a faintly discernible current of spiritual power coursed around him, as if his desire to attack were growing near irresistible.

Standing near him was supremely dangerous, thought Shen Qingqiu.

"Don't attack them," Shen Qingqiu said harshly. "Even if you hit them, you'll be the one who's injured!"

Luo Binghe could no longer hear his words. He lifted his right arm, and a powerful spiritual blast flew forth from his palm, hurtling straight forward to destroy the people laughing freely within the illusion.

Shen Qingqiu cried out within his heart. No matter how painful, his body still understood its duties. He rushed over, throwing himself before the illusions, blocking the spiritual blast head on. It struck his lower abdomen.

In that instant, Shen Qingqiu felt like he'd been stomped on by an elephant, his vision going dark. If this weren't the dream realm, he'd have vomited an endless fountain of blood.

As expected of the protagonist!

Shen Qingqiu's face was drenched with tears. Luo Binghe was obviously only a young disciple, so how could he release such a powerful spiritual blast?

It seemed that ever since he'd unlocked the OOC function, not only had he not accomplished any grand achievements, the only thing he'd done aside from blocking blows was block more blows—and also block some blows. He was doing just grand as a self-sacrificial meatshield, wasn't he?!

With this attack of Luo Binghe's, the illusion around them was broken, and the people and objects all shattered like glass into thousands of shards. The illusory landscape transformed into a remote, forested wilderness. The sky was a dark blue, and the lone, cold moon hung high and golden above their heads.

Luo Binghe's mind instantly cleared. He first stared blankly, speechlessly at the half-kneeling Shen Qingqiu, who was unable to stand. Then he lowered his head to look at his own palm, where a shred of remaining spiritual power was still flowing through his fingertips. Vaguely remembering what he'd just done, his face turned stark white.

Luo Binghe threw himself to Shen Qingqiu's side to support him, both worried and regretful. "Shizun! Why, why didn't you hit back?!"

With Shen Qingqiu's level of spiritual power, he would have been wholly capable of returning Luo Binghe's spiritual blast, forcing their powers to collide and directly pitting them against each other until the stronger one won. Not only could he have dissolved Luo Binghe's attack, he could have deflected it back at him.

"Foolish child," Shen Qingqiu said simply, expressing his innermost feelings. Then he continued weakly, "...The point was to ensure you wouldn't be injured. If I deflected it back and injured you, what would be the purpose of that?"

That frail voice made Luo Binghe want to strike his own heart and kill himself. "But now the one injured is Shizun!"

It hadn't been long since they fought those three matches against the Demon Realm, and Shizun had already, again, been injured for his sake. And this time by his own hand!

Shen Qingqiu saw the self-blame and misery on that child's face about to overflow, and unable to stand it, he said consolingly, "Can your cultivation compare to mine? Even if this master took several more blows, it wouldn't matter."

Luo Binghe would have preferred Shen Qingqiu be as he had in the past and vent his anger by viciously beating and cursing him. Even if he were utterly ignored, scorned, and ridiculed, it would have been easier on his heart. On the contrary, Shen Qingqiu's tone and words were unerringly gentle, and so Luo Binghe was struck dumb and speechless, completely at a loss for what to do.

After a long moment, he said in a low voice, "It's all my fault."

The early Luo Binghe indeed walked the path of a brainless moe white lotus. Shen Qingqiu figured he'd once again fallen into the self-flagellating pattern of an anxious people-pleaser.

"It has nothing to do with you," Shen Qingqiu explained patiently.

"The ways of demons are extremely unpredictable and impossible to guard against. However, if you don't want to run into similar trouble in the future, you must become stronger."

These words were spoken purely out of his personal feelings. This was a world of immortals and monsters, where the strong ate the weak. Becoming stronger was the only way to guarantee that you wouldn't become cannon fodder to be pushed around by the world.

Luo Binghe's thoughts shifted, and without speaking, he suddenly raised his head, fixing his steady gaze on Shen Qingqiu.

Shen Qingqiu's heart thumped.

Luo Binghe's eyes, dark like obsidian, flashed with a light more dazzling than the reflection of the moon and stars.

That...that look in his eyes! That kind of protagonist's look, full of "resolute conviction" and "blazing fighting spirit"!

Could it be...I've already become the protagonist's guiding star on his life path going forward?!

Luo Binghe fell into a proper kneeling position by Shen Qingqiu's side. "I understand," he said in a strong, clear voice.

Wait, what did you understand this time? Can you not say only half your words every time? Tell me the rest!

Shen Qingqiu didn't notice that, as Luo Binghe spoke this sentence, he didn't use "this disciple" to address himself.

Luo Binghe tightly clenched his fist. "This kind of thing..." he said, enunciating each word. "I definitely won't let it happen a second time."

Letting Shizun protect his weak self, letting Shizun be injured because of him...this kind of thing absolutely could not happen again!

Shen Qingqiu let out an "oh."

What's going on...? He suddenly had this "the protagonist is protecting me; I feel so safe" kind of feeling. What exactly was going on?!

"Safe" your ass—this person will carve you into a human stick in the future! Wake up!

Shen Qingqiu was filled with a plethora of complex emotions.

Fuck. Originally, this conviction to "become stronger to protect my important person," should have been inspired by the protagonist seeing the female lead's frail, lovely, and delicately panting form after she sustained an injury while helping him.

Was the System...laying all the emotional labor associated with the female lead's role...on Shen Qingqiu?

To hand out the wrong script at this point! Also, if you're giving me extra parts, could you at least offer me complimentary meals?!

Taking on a main character's long and tedious lines while being paid an extra's thin and meager wages. This was labor exploitation!

Out of selfishness, Shen Qingqiu managed to lift a hand and pat Luo Binghe on the head. Luo Binghe's originally stubborn gaze froze, as if a handful of clear spring water had doused his flickering anger.

Shen Qingqiu thought for a moment. "Actually, you need not worry too much. If you cannot become strong, I will stay by your side and protect you."

Instead of letting Luo Binghe become that pitch-black basket case of a young man who made destroying the world his personal mission, it'd be better if he could stay this delicate little white lotus forever. Shen Qingqiu absolutely wouldn't have minded keeping this iteration of Luo Binghe by his side and taking care of him for a lifetime.

These were his simple thoughts, but to the person hearing his words, they didn't sound so simple. Luo Binghe was wholly dumbfounded.

No one had ever made such a straightforward and impassioned promise to him.

Even though the world was large, few people in it could say: *You need not become strong. I am here, and of course I won't let you be bullied.*

And they weren't empty words. If Shizun said he could do it, he could. He had already proven time and again with his actions that he would rather sustain grievous injury than let Luo Binghe suffer even a tiny bit of harm.

Still, the sense of indulgence within these words...was too much to bear. As that first surge of warmth slowly subsided, a burning heat crawled up Luo Binghe's face.

Shen Qingqiu coughed for a while, miserably discovering that coughing up blood within the dream realm was impossible, then pinched Luo Binghe's arm. "All right. First, help me up."

Luo Binghe realized that where his wrist had been pinched neither hurt nor itched. Instead, it tingled. Immediately, he also realized his thoughts were overstepping and scolded himself a little. Thinking such nonsense at a time like this, how disrespectful to Shizun. He hurriedly organized his thoughts and did as he was told.

Suddenly, a voice sounded out of nowhere. That hoarse, aged voice made an inquisitive noise and said, "You're quite something, to actually break through this elder's barrier, boy."

That voice echoed all around them. It was impossible to determine which direction it had come from.

This level's boss had finally appeared!

Luo Binghe was supporting Shen Qingqiu and didn't rise to his feet, his gaze wary. Meng Mo had appeared while Shen Qingqiu was injured, and things were not looking good. Luo Binghe resolved to himself that if Meng Mo tried to attack, even with his paltry strength, he would still give his all to impede him and earn Shen Qingqiu every possible chance of survival.

The instant he made his decision, that voice spoke again. "Come over here and let this elder see what kind of young hero is capable of such a thing."

Luo Binghe looked at Shen Qingqiu. The latter's entire mind was filled with the thought of, *I finished my friendship performance; I can finally leave work now,* and he was extremely cheerful. He even felt like teasing his student.

"The senior is asking for the young hero," he said. "Why don't you reply?"

Luo Binghe's face reddened. He turned and spoke in a clear voice. "You flatter me. The barrier was broken by my master's strength alone."

The voice humphed as if in disdain.

Shen Qingqiu knew why he'd humphed. Though he had blocked an attack for Luo Binghe, this was Luo Binghe's dream realm, and so Luo Binghe had needed to wrest back control of his consciousness before the nightmare could be broken. But Shen Qingqiu couldn't be bothered to explain.

The voice spoke. "This elder wants you to come over, boy, but I don't want this ordinary cultivator from Cang Qiong Mountain to hear our conversation. I'll have him sleep first."

As expected, the circumstances were exactly the same as when Ning Yingying had played this role in the original story. Everyone aside from Luo Binghe would be waved offstage by Meng Mo.

A headache instantly came over Shen Qingqiu, and he collapsed heavily.

Alarmed, Luo Binghe gathered him in his arms. "Shizun?" he called. "Shizun!"

"No need to worry," said Meng Mo. "This elder only sent him into a dream within a dream. He's just in a deeper sleep. Get over here, you!"

This time, it was possible to discern that the voice was coming from a pitch-black cave off to the west.

Luo Binghe couldn't wake Shen Qingqiu. He carefully laid his master on the ground, then turned and spoke in the direction of the voice. "My master acknowledged you as a senior, so I must treat you with the same courtesy. I hope you also won't cause Shizun trouble."

Meng Mo chuckled. "I saw your memories, boy. This master of yours does not treat you well. Why not just let me get rid of him? I would be doing you a favor."

The memories Meng Mo had looked at were mostly those of the interactions between the original Shen Qingqiu and Luo Binghe. Those memories were indeed the greatest in number, but...

Luo Binghe shook his head. "Shizun isn't like you say, Senior. In addition, no matter what, Shizun is my honored master. He can treat me however he likes, but as his disciple, I cannot disrespect him."

Meng Mo humphed. "How backward! The Human Realm's righteous path is full of this type of hypocritical morality. So what if he's honored or not, your master or whatever. If someone mistreats or harms me, they should be killed! He knew your cultivation was not sufficient to face Sky Hammer, yet he still sent you out for that match. Were his intentions not clear?"

"At that time, even I didn't believe I could win," said Luo Binghe.

"But Shizun believed in me. Not only did he give me an opportunity, he even encouraged me during the match. And in the end, I truly did win."

The next sentence he said silently and only to himself: *For my sake, Shizun blocked two attacks meant for me. His goodwill is genuine.*

Meng Mo had only randomly skimmed some memory fragments. He didn't understand Shen Qingqiu's behavior, nor did he want to try unraveling the issue, though he was quite pleased with Luo Binghe's attitude. "You, boy, are a person who values loyalty and bonds."

"Not even a thousandth of how Shizun does toward me," said Luo Binghe.

If Meng Mo had a mouth, its corner would have been twitching. He opted to change the topic.

After murmuring for a moment, he said, "This elder senses that within your body, something is being suppressed. Even though I cannot tell exactly what it is, it must be something surpassingly remarkable."

Luo Binghe was a little shocked. "What sort of thing is it that even you can't tell?"

Meng Mo chuckled. "My race produces master cultivators in droves. It is not impossible that a demon more illustrious than this elder sealed something within your body."

In any case, Meng Mo surely wasn't so eager to throw away his several-hundred-year-old reputation that he'd waste time tricking an impoverished teenager who had nothing. Nevertheless, Luo Binghe stared in disbelief. "Does Senior mean that the thing in my body...is related to demons?"

"What? Are you displeased?" Meng Mo asked sneeringly. "Eager to sever any connections with the demon race?"

Luo Binghe's state of shock didn't last for too long. His thoughts whirled rapidly before he declared, "The Demon Realm does many evils of all kinds and has injured my master multiple times. Naturally, I cannot associate with them."

Meng Mo became depressed. "Can you go three sentences without mentioning that master of yours, boy? Let this elder guess, the next thing you want to ask is 'May I ask this senior if there is a method to remove this something from my body'?"

Luo Binghe smiled wryly. "Even if I ask, would this senior tell me?"

Meng Mo laughed boisterously. "It's not that I don't want to tell you, but that is truly beyond me. I can't even see it clearly—how can I tell you how to remove it? If not for the fact that I couldn't make sense of you, boy, I would have already killed you both. Why else would I care to drag this out for so long? You think I've that much time on my hands?"

Luo Binghe didn't speak. He was thinking, *You don't even have a body anymore, you're just a shade being a parasite on others' dream realms.* If Meng Mo didn't have time, who did?

Meng Mo, unaware that Luo Binghe was internally ridiculing him, continued. "Removing it would be impossible for me, but suppressing it is not out of the question."

"Senior...is willing to tell me how?" Luo Binghe asked tentatively.

"Not only can this elder teach you how to suppress it, he can teach you much more," said Meng Mo leadingly.

This implication was extremely blatant, and Luo Binghe understood. His heart sank. "You want me to cultivate the demonic path?"

As his tone turned cold, Meng Mo's temper flared. "What's wrong with cultivating the demonic path? If you cultivate the demonic path, that thing in your body will bring great benefits to your cultivation. You could leap a thousand kilometers in a day! You could stand above the thousands. These are not empty words. With time, your power could overturn and sweep away the entirety of the three realms, and the heavens and earth within—and it would all be simple!"

At that last part, Luo Binghe's heart jolted.

A thousand kilometers in a day, stand above the thousands. The entirety of the three realms, swept away before him. That was to say... He'd become strong, the strongest!

He quickly rejected this thought.

Shen Qingqiu hated the way of demons more than anything. If he couldn't resist this Meng Mo's temptations to become a demonic cultivator, how could he face his master? Whether Shen Qingqiu would be thunderously angry or drown in depression, either way, Luo Binghe definitely didn't want to find out.

"No." So, he resolutely refused.

Meng Mo sneered. "If you refuse to learn from me, you won't be able to suppress the demonic energy in your body. It's hidden deeply now, and you're fine because it can't be seen, but this elder senses that the seal in your body is weakening. One day in the future, when that power breaks through, how will that good shifu of yours treat you? He who abhors evil and makes 'eliminating demons and upholding justice' his mission?"

Even as Meng Mo articulated Luo Binghe's greatest worry, Luo Binghe clenched his teeth. "This junior is but an ordinary cultivator, for whom achieving even Foundation Establishment is full of perils and hardships. Why do you insist I cultivate the demonic path?"

This question was way too high-level. Other than the author, who could explain why all the great geniuses and masters were always crying and pleading for the protagonist to be their apprentice/disciple/son-in-law?

No, in fact, even most authors probably didn't know the answer to this eternal riddle.

"You should appreciate others' kindnesses, boy! This elder can see that you are extraordinary. Would you rather all my knowledge vanish like smoke along with my physical body? How many people would beg for it to no avail?!"

Luo Binghe showed no feeling on his face. At his refusal to reply, Meng Mo felt a rush of ominous premonition.

Sure enough, the next time Luo Binghe opened his mouth, he did so with a pure and harmless smile.

"Surely Senior isn't so eager to teach me because he's unwilling to let his knowledge vanish without a successor, right?" he asked, slow and composed.

Meng Mo cried to himself: *Not good!*

"If one lives by feeding off of others' dream realms, and one often changes hosts, one's spirit will weaken and suffer damage during the transfers," said Luo Binghe. "But if one were to live long-term within a set host's body, one could instead preserve and nurture the spirit to stabilize it." He paused. "Senior Meng Mo, could it be that you're already approaching your limit, and that's why you have to pick me to be the host you'll raise?"

Having been seen through, Meng Mo neither denied it nor became angry. Instead, he grandly admitted, "That's right! Who'd have thought, boy, that you were actually so well-learned and knowledgeable that you'd even know something like that."

Luo Binghe's expression was unperturbed.

Unable to intuit what this boy was thinking, Meng Mo continued. "However, don't assume that this elder absolutely must have you as a host. Wonderfully gifted demons number in the millions. Any one of them would beg on their knees for this special honor! You're the one who should carefully consider whether you can afford to miss this opportunity."

In truth, over these long years, Meng Mo's spirit had steadily degenerated. He had originally resided within a demonic device and happily lived there. With a hundred and eighty years of meditation, he would have been brimming with energy again—but it had just so happened that Sha Hualing, unaware of this, had at the end of a series of absolute coincidences used the device as a weapon and unloaded it on Luo Binghe. Consequently, Meng Mo had not the strength to search for another host.

But on the road to his doom, he'd unexpectedly discovered that, buried within the body and consciousness of the boy he newly resided in, lay concealed a faintly discernible yet incredible power. He'd been ecstatic. How could he have let this go?

He'd already decided that no matter how adamantly Luo Binghe refused, he'd wheedle and pester, make threats and promises. Even if it meant exhausting every single method he had, he would persuade the boy to learn his demonic techniques in order to make Luo Binghe's body and consciousness an even more suitable residence for him.

"This elder will give you time, so think through it carefully," said Meng Mo. "Otherwise, I'll trap your and your master's consciousnesses within the dream realm forever. This elder is capable of that much!"

Luo Binghe's head snapped up. For an instant, as cold light flashed in the youth's eyes, Meng Mo froze, intimidated.

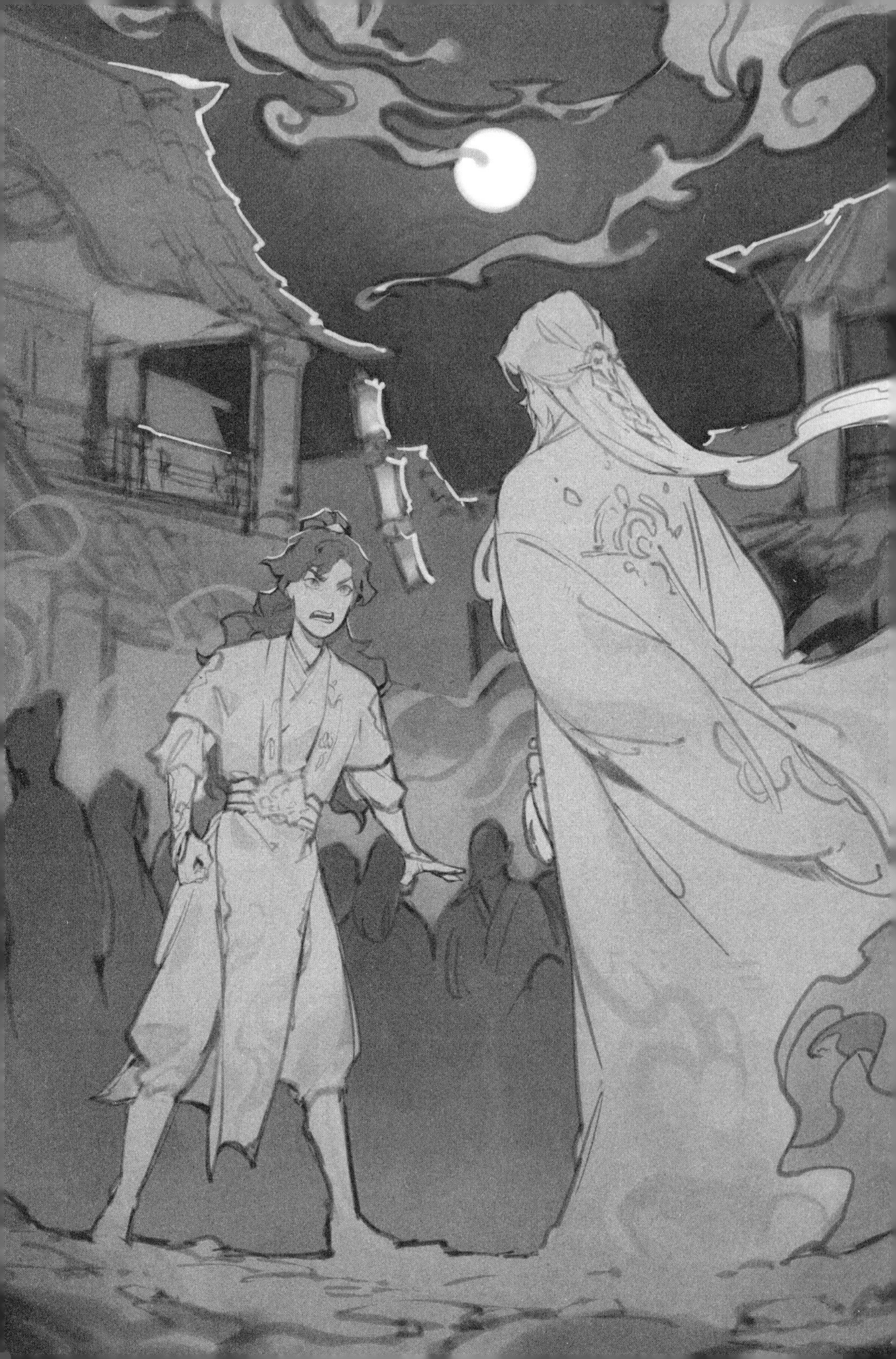

"Right now, you are discussing terms with me, and you are free to say anything." Luo Binghe's gentle and humble demeanor from moments before was entirely gone, his voice bitterly cold. "But if you harm Shizun, any agreement is void!"

Meng Mo was frozen for a long time before he finally returned to himself, stunned that he'd actually been terrorized by the presence of an ordinary, insignificant cultivator of the Human Realm. He had intimidated souls throughout the three realms for hundreds of years. Even in the miserable battle where his corporeal body had been destroyed, he had not lost to anyone in terms of *presence*.

How could he have known that in future generations this presence would be called (the protagonist's exclusive) Aura of Badassery!

The cave exploded with a sudden bellowing laughter. "Boy, you really have quite the temper!"

As that ancient voice said those words, Luo Binghe felt his limbs become heavy, the scenery around him spinning before he was plunged into darkness.

In a flash and with a start, Luo Binghe awoke inside the woodshed, his back utterly drenched with sweat.

At the same time, Shen Qingqiu also sprang up in bed, like a corpse coming alive after death. Head dizzy and vision spinning, he gasped for breath for a while, and only then did he finally relax.

Horrible, horrible, horrible. Horrible enough to die!

How come?! How come when, in the original work, Meng Mo dragged Ning Yingying into a dream within a dream, her dream was a comforting childhood memory wherein her parents let her pick flowers and ride horses? How come on his turn, he had first been surrounded by fist-sized man-eating wasps, then been dashing madly through the narrow passages of a tomb while closely pursued by a giant ball of fire?!

The most terrifying thing was that, in the final part of the dream within a dream, Meng Mo had woven in Shen Qingqiu's greatest fear.

Within a damp, dark dungeon, he had been suspended in midair by a ring around his waist, unable to feel his limbs. When he opened his mouth, no sound came out, and he could only helplessly hiss. His entire body burned with pain.

Only after an unknown length of time had passed did the sound of a stone door opening drift from outside the dungeon. Footsteps neither fast nor slow steadily approached, then the shadow of a person was cast on the floor before him.

On an ink-black hem, exquisite motifs were embroidered in silver thread. From that person emanated an ice-cold pressure, more stifling than the dungeon's airless darkness.

Shen Qingqiu couldn't clearly see that person's face, but he knew very well who they were.

Meng Mo truly deserved to be a legend among demons—that dream realm had been far, far too realistic. Even now, the damp odor of decay seemed to linger in Shen Qingqiu's nose, nauseating him.

Shen Qingqiu managed to keep sitting for a while, then he rolled off the bed and began to retch.

Ding-dong. Now of all fucking times, a System notification sprang up: [Congratulations on completing the scenario "Meng Mo's Barrier"! The System awards you +500 satisfaction points! Please continue to work hard!]

Shen Qingqiu made a "stop" gesture and still had enough in him to try settling debts.

"Let's have a proper discussion," he said. "When you threatened to deduct satisfaction points, it wasn't five hundred, right? Why not set it at five hundred for both? Are large punishments and small rewards really fair? And I went through the extra scenario of the dream within a dream, so why haven't you awarded any extra B-Points to me? System? System! System, don't play dead, let's sign a new contract!"

At this moment, someone slammed open the Bamboo House's front door and rushed inside like a gust of wind.

"Shizun!"

Shen Qingqiu knew who it was just from the sound. He miserably rolled his eyes. He really didn't want to see that face right now!

Luo Binghe had already thrown himself to Shen Qingqiu's side, overflowing with anxiety. "Shizun, how are you? Do you feel the least bit unwell?"

Truthfully, not too terrible... If you could stay a bit farther away I'd feel even better... Shen Qingqiu averted his face and, with unyielding strength and poise, stood by himself. "Everything is well with this master."

Luo Binghe had wanted to help him up, yet his hand had been reflexively shoved away. He couldn't help but freeze.

Shen Qingqiu didn't notice these small shifts in Luo Binghe's emotions. He tidied his clothes, verifying to himself that even though he wore only an inner robe, his image remained spotless. "Did that Meng Mo trouble you further afterward?"

Trouble my ass. Meng Mo would have been falling over himself to lick Luo Binghe's boots. Shen Qingqiu was asking despite knowing.

Luo Binghe hesitated a bit before he replied. "That demon elder's spiritual strength seems to have been lacking. This disciple was expelled from the dream realm after a short while. Shizun, did you encounter anything inside the dream within a dream?"

"Even if I did encounter something, could this master not handle it?" Shen Qingqiu boasted shamelessly.

Of course he couldn't handle it!

Even now the shadow of being a human stick remained. With Luo Binghe so close to him, his entire body was tingling, and he couldn't help averting his gaze to suppress his fear.

Unsure of the reason for this, Luo Binghe only saw that Shen Qingqiu's expression was odd, his gaze no longer calmly looking straight at him like he usually did these days. It made his heart both fretful and anxious.

Luckily, Shen Qingqiu adjusted his attitude with superlative quickness, remembering that he was a teacher and what he should do at this time. In the next instant, he reached out and took Luo Binghe's wrist. "Being attacked by a demon is no joke," he said firmly. "This master will examine you for a moment. We cannot be negligent."

"Yes," said Luo Binghe obediently, his wrist firmly held.

His heart had just known a moment of ease, but now it was once more suspended. On the off-chance Shen Qingqiu uncovered Meng Mo and exposed the peculiarity within his body afterward...

But though Shen Qingqiu diligently examined Luo Binghe for a time, he didn't detect anything off. Of course he didn't—Meng Mo had several hundred years' worth of skill and experience, and his celebrated reputation wasn't exaggerated in the slightest. However, Shen Qingqiu still had to go through the motions.

His examination fruitless, he nevertheless repeatedly urged Luo Binghe to visit Qian Cao Peak and Qiong Ding Peak the next day to let other people examine him and, finally, to absolutely say something if an issue arose.

Yet Luo Binghe had no intention of leaving. With the appearance of someone full of worries, he started and stopped speaking several times before asking, "Shizun, demons…are they all wicked beyond redemption? Must every last one of them be exterminated?"

Shen Qingqiu didn't reply to this question right away. He stood in place, indeed finding it difficult to answer.

Seeing Luo Binghe petrified, forcibly keeping calm while also somewhat anticipating his teacher's answer, Shen Qingqiu spoke slowly. "Humans can be good or bad, so naturally demons too can be good or evil. We often see demons victimizing people, but that doesn't mean there aren't cases where humans harm innocent demons. Don't put too much weight on race."

This was the first time Luo Binghe had heard a teacher express this kind of opinion. He listened in a daze, heart thumping wildly. "Shizun means, even if someone is closely connected to demons, that doesn't mean the heavens find them intolerable—is that right?"

"How can you claim they're intolerable to the heavens in the first place?" Shen Qingqiu countered. "If they're intolerable, why would the heavens let them exist? Who has the authority to say whether they ought to be tolerated or not?"

During this chain of questions, Luo Binghe's eyes gradually lit up. There was within him a faint sense of burning passion.

"Luo Binghe, you may choose to ignore the words this master tells you from here on out," Shen Qingqiu said at last, "but you must always remember what I've told you here today. In this world, there is nothing intolerable to the heavens. This is true for all races, as it's true for humans."

At this time, though Luo Binghe's heart leaned toward the righteous path, he wasn't a pedant. In any case, since whatever was within him couldn't be removed, why not put it to good use?

He absolutely had to become stronger! So strong that he would never be powerless—strong enough that he could protect Shizun from any hand that dared reach for him.

Seeing Luo Binghe's eyes so dazzlingly bright, Shen Qingqiu couldn't imagine what he was thinking, but his own thoughts were a jumbled mess.

His advice this time wasn't coming purely from a place of having developed an addiction to being the sage guiding the protagonist's life journey.

The idea of the heavens' magnanimity was a universal concept, older than time itself, and it had been recycled like reheated old rice for decades by the historical, wuxia, and xianxia genres without the slightest hint of progress. But in this world of ocean-deep hatred between humans and demons—who were unable to coexist and who had engaged in countless great wars in the past up to the present—the concept was extremely unconventional. Anyone who espoused it risked unilateral condemnation.

As someone of mixed lineage, it had been extremely difficult for the original Luo Binghe to avoid being impacted by human hatred of demons and vice versa. Since the greater half of his life had been harsh and full of misfortunes, he'd even begun to despair and think that perhaps the world and heavens both found his existence intolerable—that he should have never been born.

Shen Qingqiu hoped that, from this point forth, these words could plant a seed within Luo Binghe's heart and broaden his perspective. That in the future, when facing the truth of his heritage, he could remain optimistic and not take attacks on his lineage to heart. Perhaps then his behavior wouldn't trend so extreme, and he wouldn't become bent on taking revenge on the world.

Perhaps, even if someday in the future, Luo Binghe had to face a Shen Qingqiu who would throw him down into the Endless Abyss, he would be able to understand that this betrayal wasn't *his* fault.

If that was possible...then even if the scenario arrived and the System forced Shen Qingqiu to say lines like, "Humans and demons cannot coexist, their hatred is ocean-deep and cannot be overcome, you fucker, hurry up and die," thereby slapping himself so hard that he sent himself flying, well, that would be that!

Now that the atmosphere had grown heavy, Shen Qingqiu felt he'd gone overboard with his cool act. With his terror of embarrassment about to erupt, he coughed once.

"That said, demons are naturally gifted with spiritual strength, far more so than humans," he said. "If their strength could be used for good and was dedicated to the righteous path—to the common people—then how could that not be a good thing?"

Demons had exceptional talent for cultivation and absolutely crushed the Human Realm in that arena. As the races were different, so too were their energy systems. Humans relied on spiritual qi where demons relied on demonic qi—though Shen Qingqiu reckoned that the two were basically the same, with only the color and names being distinct.

Maybe the Demon Realm had good feng shui or something, but the vast majority of demons were born fully charged with demonic qi. At age three, they could rip apart a human with their bare hands, and at age eight, they could split mountains and crack stone—ahem, this was a bit of an exaggeration.

However, the truth was that many humans had only mediocre aptitude. Even after cultivating for several decades, they could often only achieve the skill level of a small demon infant. Even more humans were like dried-up ponds, their spiritual strength practically a perfect egg, i.e., zero. These humans were often said to be "lacking spiritual roots" or "absent the lot for immortality." It couldn't get worse than that.

If it weren't for the humans' comparative love of propagating, and for demons being generally sparse in number, the Human Realm would have long ago been colonized by demons. Honestly, they were just coasting on the fact that demon family planning was so strict.

After suffering the torments of this world-changing journey, Shen Qingqiu hadn't slept the entire night. Two dark bags had already appeared under his eyes. He waved his hand. "It's very late. If there's nothing else, then go and rest."

Luo Binghe obediently asked to be excused. But he hadn't walked far when he heard Shen Qingqiu call from behind, "Come back."

Luo Binghe immediately turned back. "Does Shizun have any other instructions?"

"The dorms are that way," said Shen Qingqiu. "Why are you walking in the other direction?"

The disciples' dormitories and the woodshed were both a left turn out the door, yet Luo Binghe had turned to the right.

"This disciple wants to go to the kitchen first, to prepare tomorrow's breakfast for Shizun," said Luo Binghe.

Shen Qingqiu was in a bind. He really wanted to eat Luo Binghe's breakfast, but having a child cook for him instead of sleeping when it was already so late at night—didn't that sound like Cinderella and her stepmother...? Either way, it seemed inhumane.

In the end, Shen Qingqiu's conscience won over his stomach. He coughed. "Nonsense. It's the middle of the night, what is there to cook? Go back and sleep."

Luo Binghe knew his master was worried about him not resting enough and agreed with a smile—but he still planned to sneak off to the kitchen to work later.

Shen Qingqiu wanted to ask him if he was still sleeping in the woodshed, but after mulling it over for a moment, he concluded that youths still had their dignity. Asking him outright would be embarrassing. Moreover, even if he had Luo Binghe sleep in the disciples' dorm, the other students would take Ming Fan's lead and bully him—steal his blankets and hide his shoes or whatnot, the poor thing.

"Tomorrow, pack your things and come here," said Shen Qingqiu before Luo Binghe left.

At first, Luo Binghe didn't understand what he meant. "Shizun?"

"There's a side room in the Bamboo House. Starting tomorrow, you can move in there."

If Luo Binghe lived a little closer, then in the future, it would be easier to have him make breakfast and clean up around the house.

Shen Qingqiu's adaptability was, as always, as incredible as a record-breaking dick. Just a moment ago, he had been unable to even look Luo Binghe in the face, but now he dared to scheme how to make the great protagonist wait on him hand and foot—serve his tea, carry his water, wash his clothes, fold his blankets, etc. Being in the middle of fantasizing, he hadn't noticed said protagonist's reaction.

Suddenly, Luo Binghe pounced on him like a tiger, capturing him in a tight embrace.

Caught off guard, Shen Qingqiu jumped in surprise. Then his face reddened. For the first time in his life, someone had wrapped him in a full-bodied embrace, and it wasn't a warm and gentle jade-skinned maiden, but a youth brimming with tyrannical energy, ahhh—

"Shizun! Shizun!" Overflowing with happiness, Luo Binghe hugged him around the neck and refused to let go, crying in his ear over and over.

Shen Qingqiu didn't know where to put his hands. After floundering for a bit, he placed them on Luo Binghe's head and stroked his hair. "All right. You've cried out to me, hugged me, and made all this racket, and you aren't even embarrassed. You're already so big—it's not like you're a ten-year-old child. How do you think this looks?"

Luo Binghe hadn't thought about it that deeply. When it was put that way, he grew suddenly ashamed. If he hadn't been overcome by a torrent of joy, he would never have dared to treat his normally aloof and removed Shizun like this. Though reluctant, he hurried to peel himself from Shen Qingqiu's body, his whole face red.

"Yes—I—this disciple has overstepped."

When it came to asking for hugs, children under the age of ten were moe, but the fifteen-year-old Luo Binghe…was still moe!

With a fresh and tender face like this handsome little sprout's, anything you did would be moe!

Luo Binghe floundered for a while, at first a little flustered, but then he noticed that Shen Qingqiu's complexion didn't look particularly good.

Even though Shen Qingqiu had the immortal body of a cultivator, he was haunted by old injuries and a lingering poison. Then because of Luo Binghe, he had been dragged into Meng Mo's dream realm. He hadn't rested properly and was at his limit, so of course he looked a bit haggard. Luo Binghe didn't dare interfere with Shen Qingqiu's rest any longer and grudgingly said his goodbyes.

Nevertheless, he didn't return to the woodshed, though this time he made sure to take a detour before going to the kitchen. He promised himself that for the next long while, he would carefully watch over his master's diet and recuperation.

As soon as Luo Binghe stepped out of the room, a System notification arrived.

[Protagonist satisfaction points +50.]

Shen Qingqiu was mystified. Why add another fifty? System lag? Or had the System discovered its conscience and concluded it had given him too little before?

Whatever. He was exhausted. So what if points were added? To the point, there was no way his admittedly great self had earned that fifty with a single hug, ha ha ha ha ha ha...

The next day, Shen Qingqiu hadn't yet slept as long as he wanted before the fragrant scent of fish and rice wafted into his room and tempted him awake. Outside of the Bamboo House, Luo Binghe had spent long hours preparing a meal with utmost care. The scent drew in a great number of Qing Jing Peak disciples, who were used to eating bland food. They hid off to the side, snooping.

Enraged, Ming Fan and the others chewed their sleeve hems while watching the scene unfold—especially when Shen Qingqiu sat at the table and affectionately sang praises to Luo Binghe for his efforts and handiwork. As the two blissfully smiled at each other, their audience's grief and resentment reached its peak.

Utterly shameless! To use these licentious schemes and unorthodox methods to curry Shizun's favor!

That evening, when Luo Binghe moved his things into the side room of Shen Qingqiu's house, every last one of the Qing Jing Peak disciples who had bullied Luo Binghe were wiped out. It was as if they had been struck by lightning from a clear sky, leaving their corpses scattered across the field.

Though the words were "moved his things," in truth it was only Luo Binghe moving himself. From the beginning, he'd never really had anything in the woodshed.

His pillow? He had rested his head upon a bundle of straw he found there. Blankets? His outer robes had covered him.

And, of course, Shen Qingqiu had prepared the real deal for him already.

Shen Qingqiu had always thought that Luo Binghe's life was unbearably miserable—just a textbook case of child abuse. Cang Qiong Mountain Sect was one of the major sects in the cultivation world. How could people's hearts have grown so dark in such a place? How could their resources be so lacking?

That night, Luo Binghe lay on a normal bed for the first time in his life. Before, he had laid in a wooden basin floating down an icy river, then on the damp, cold ground, then between noisy streets, and then even in mountain caves while roughing it out in the wild—it had become normal. Conversely, now that he was sleeping on a soft and tidy bamboo bed, his entire body felt light, floaty, like none of this was real.

It was especially unreal when he thought of Shen Qingqiu sleeping in the main room, just a wall away.

That night, perhaps because Luo Binghe had too much on his mind, Meng Mo didn't appear in his dream realm.

So, Luo Binghe remained composed and waited. Sure enough, a few days later, Meng Mo appeared once more.

This time, Meng Mo didn't set up some mysterious barrier, having not intended to hide in the first place. Instead, he appeared directly in Luo Binghe's dream, though he did so in the form of a cloud of black mist.

This cloud of black mist expanded and contracted before Luo Binghe's eyes, endlessly transforming, and that aged voice echoed from within it. "What have you decided in these three days, boy?"

"Does Senior Meng Mo not know my decision?" Luo Binghe replied.

Meng Mo chuckled. "You have chosen a path you definitely won't regret. Remember this day, boy—today is the beginning of your meteoric rise!"

What youth didn't dream of meteoric success? Meng Mo's words rang with grand heroic spirit.

But Luo Binghe was unmoved. He only cupped his fist and bowed. "This junior has one more request."

"What is it? Out with it! Hurry up and finish so you can finally become my apprentice." Meng Mo urged him on, not realizing that he was being far too optimistic.

"That is precisely what this junior wanted to speak about," said Luo Binghe. "My master treats me with utmost kindness. I really can't apprentice under anyone else without his permission—"

"Fine, fine, fine!" Meng Mo interrupted before he could finish, at the end of his patience. "This elder won't demand the titles of master and apprentice, is that enough?!"

Had any extraordinary master ever come away with a worse deal? He was falling over himself to teach someone his people's techniques, yet he wouldn't even get to hear his student call him "Shifu."

How was his plight any different from that of an absolutely devoted yet bitterly suffering concubine who couldn't gain official status?!

Luo Binghe smiled. "Then many thanks to Senior."

He wasn't remotely willing to call anyone other than Shen Qingqiu "Shizun."

As he eyed Luo Binghe, Meng Mo was sure that if he still had a physical body, his nose would have gone crooked with rage.

This Luo Binghe was all cute and obedient in front of his master, just like a little white lotus. So then why was he so hard to deal with for other people?! Two completely different faces—he was practically a different person!

This elder is going to die of rage!

4
Conference

TIME FLEW LIKE AN ARROW, the sun and moon alternating back and forth like a weaver's shuttle.

Shen Qingqiu really didn't want to use such a worn-out saying, but he just couldn't find a better phrase.

Every day on Qing Jing Peak, he played the guqin, read books, wrote calligraphy, painted paintings, practiced his cultivation, occasionally nitpicked Luo Binghe's food, occasionally bickered or sparred with Liu Qingge, and from time to time reported on his work to Yue Qingyuan. The days flew by, perfectly in synch with his life goal of "idling away to a ripe old age."

Until the Immortal Alliance Conference finally arrived.

In the end, this day really did dawn. Shen Qingqiu had been too carefree; he'd forgotten about the first major climax of the novel.

The first step of Luo Binghe's climb to the top, on his journey to marrying every ideal woman, as well as his first step toward his blackened heart, after which his soul would never again be washed clean—and he had actually managed to forget it!

So when Shen Qingqiu received the gilded invitation, he stared at it in shock for a long time.

The Immortal Alliance Conference was *Proud Immortal Demon Way*'s first major climax. At the same time, it was also an important turning point in the novel.

The conference was held once every four years, and it was an excellent opportunity for cultivators to pick out new talent, or for said new talent to establish their reputation. Before every conference, the major sect leaders conducted discussions, and the exact structure of the proceedings differed, but there was always a list of the top rankers.

Whether you came from a prestigious sect or from the poorest parts of the jianghu, as long as your performance at the conference was outstanding, your name would be inscribed in gold upon a tablet, and you would become renowned across the land.

Before this event, *Proud Immortal Demon Way*'s performance online had been steadfastly lukewarm. But once the Immortal Alliance Conference Arc debuted, the reviews, comments, subscriptions, and tips all soared into the heavens.

It wasn't only because from that point forward, "Great Master" Airplane Shooting Towards the Sky abandoned the last of his already minimal moral principles and poured woman upon woman into the story, adding interminable sections of titillating descriptions and blush-inducing, barely legal passages one after another—there was another important "it" factor. It was, in fact, the main element that had first compelled Shen Qingqiu to follow the novel until the end.

The demonic beasts!

The reason "Great Master" Airplane Shooting Towards the Sky—an author who hadn't even properly researched cultivation settings and was often confused as to whether characters were at the Foundation Establishment or Nascent Soul stages—rarely received straight-man scolds on this element was because the cultivation setting wasn't the selling point of his novel.

Instead of being categorized as a "cultivation" novel, *Proud Immortal Demon Way* should have been called a "monster fighting" novel. The "fighting" component way outweighed the "cultivation" component. As a cultivation novel, it was out-and-out filled with landmines, but as a monster handbook, it was pretty entertaining.

To the point, very soon, Sheng Qingqiu would directly face those savage monsters who came in all shapes and sizes, as described in the book.

More importantly, very soon, it would be time for him to personally, mercilessly strike Luo Binghe, his demonic heritage revealed, into the Endless Abyss.

The gears of fate (a.k.a., the plot) had already started to turn...

Shen Qingqiu was silent for a long time. He finally tossed the invitation into Ming Fan's arms for him to file away.

Luo Binghe was receiving Meng Mo's guidance within the dream realm every day, and he was progressing at lightning speed. He had long since assumed responsibility for many things. Shen Qingqiu often happily assigned some of Cang Qiong Mountain's trivial internal tasks to him. Once he became older, he had also been tossed missions to eliminate demons or help people down the mountain—in part so that he wouldn't spend every day tagging after Shen Qingqiu.

Though Shen Qingqiu was comfortable being waited upon, he wasn't sure if Luo Binghe's development had gone awry or something. Wasn't he sticking to his master a little too closely...?

Shen Qingqiu would often wonder: *Was it because I doted on him too much? Should I besmirch myself a little, as appropriate, to prove to the System that I'm firmly a villain?*

If things kept going as they were, he was afraid that when the time came, he would be unable to harden his heart and throw Luo Binghe into the Endless Abyss.

However, though Shen Qingqiu told himself this, every time he finished thinking about it, the next time he saw Luo Binghe—and that pure and innocent face, that hard-working figure—he would always, immediately, praise him out of habit.

"You finished copying the scrolls/rescued the people/found the things/are done cooking? Hm, well done."

After that praise, he'd forget his original intentions.

Ming Fan filed the invitation away and saw that Shen Qingqiu's complexion wasn't especially good. It occurred to him that since that stinking brat Luo Binghe had gone down the mountain, Shizun had only picked at the kitchen's fare. In the last few days, he hadn't eaten properly at all.

"Shizun, shall this disciple prepare some congee?" Ming Fan asked.

Shen Qingqiu really had no appetite and waved him away. "No need. You can go."

Ming Fan didn't dare say more, and he obediently took his leave, but his heart flooded with tears. In the last couple of years, that brat Luo Binghe had become Shizun's absolute favorite.

I can't serve Shizun even a single mouthful of congee!

Notably, Ming Fan didn't consider that perhaps the issue was with his own cooking skills.

After some time, more footsteps approached.

"Didn't I say there was no need?" Shen Qingqiu asked.

"This disciple rushed a considerable distance, all the way from the outer provinces, and Shizun won't give me even a single glance before refusing me?"

The voice was gentle and clear, and it even carried a hint of teasing dismay. Upon hearing it, Shen Qingqiu almost fell to the ground along with his chair. He jerked his head around.

A seventeen-year-old youth, slim and tall and graceful, dressed in white robes, lips turned upward in the hint of a smile, gazed at him with a pair of shining eyes.

The longsword on Luo Binghe's back was Zheng Yang, drawn from Wan Jian Peak. Its name, "righteous sun," complemented the current Luo Binghe's temperament well. The sword's blade glistened with a sacred light, and it was a good, high-quality weapon. When Luo Binghe had pulled it free from the rock wall, it had elicited a wave of surprised exclamations and praise from various sect members.

But compared to Luo Binghe's true personal sword, it was a toothpick.

Shen Qingqiu composed himself. "Why have you returned so quickly this time?"

Luo Binghe sat in the seat next to his and steadily poured a cup of tea, then pushed it toward Shen Qingqiu's hand. "The disaster wasn't difficult to handle. I also missed Shizun terribly, so I rushed back without stopping to rest."

These words sounded rather slick and insincere, but since Luo Binghe was the male lead, he had the ability to make the slickest of smooth-talking matchlessly warm and genuine.

On Shen Qingqiu, this attack was...super effective!

Shen Qingqiu picked up that cup of tea and took a sip. It was a fragrant snowy mountain blend plundered from Qiong Ding Peak, but he couldn't taste it at all.

"The Immortal Alliance Conference is about to begin," he said.

Luo Binghe had long known about this. "Would you like this

disciple to draft a list of Qing Jing Peak's participating disciples and give it to Shizun to check?"

These past couple of years, Shen Qingqiu had handed all manner of miscellaneous tasks big and small to Luo Binghe to deal with. After all, for now Luo Binghe was so sweet, obedient, and useful, his work thorough and meticulous. Shen Qingqiu could think of absolutely no reason why he should do these things himself.

Before finalizing anything, Luo Binghe always conscientiously asked Shen Qingqiu to look over his work to check for any problems. Shen Qingqiu always wanted to say: Actually, you don't need me to check it, seriously—you're much better at handling these things than I am!

Instead, Shen Qingqiu said, "When you finish the draft, report directly to Zhangmen-shixiong."

Luo Binghe nodded. He had more to say, but he sensed something slightly off. Shen Qingqiu seemed to be paying extra attention to him today. He couldn't help but smile.

"Why does Shizun keep looking at me?" he asked. "Could it be that this disciple was gone for so long that Shizun also missed him?"

"I'm not allowed to look at someone I raised?" asked Shen Qingqiu.

Luo Binghe chortled. "Of course Shizun is allowed. Am I pleasing to look at?"

Shen Qingqiu shook his head while smiling, and he considered his next words. "Binghe."

"Yes?" Luo Binghe's expression instantly turned serious. He had realized that Shen Qingqiu had something important to say.

Shen Qingqiu stared into his eyes. "Do you want to become stronger? Stronger until you are without rival, until no one beneath the heavens would dare challenge you?"

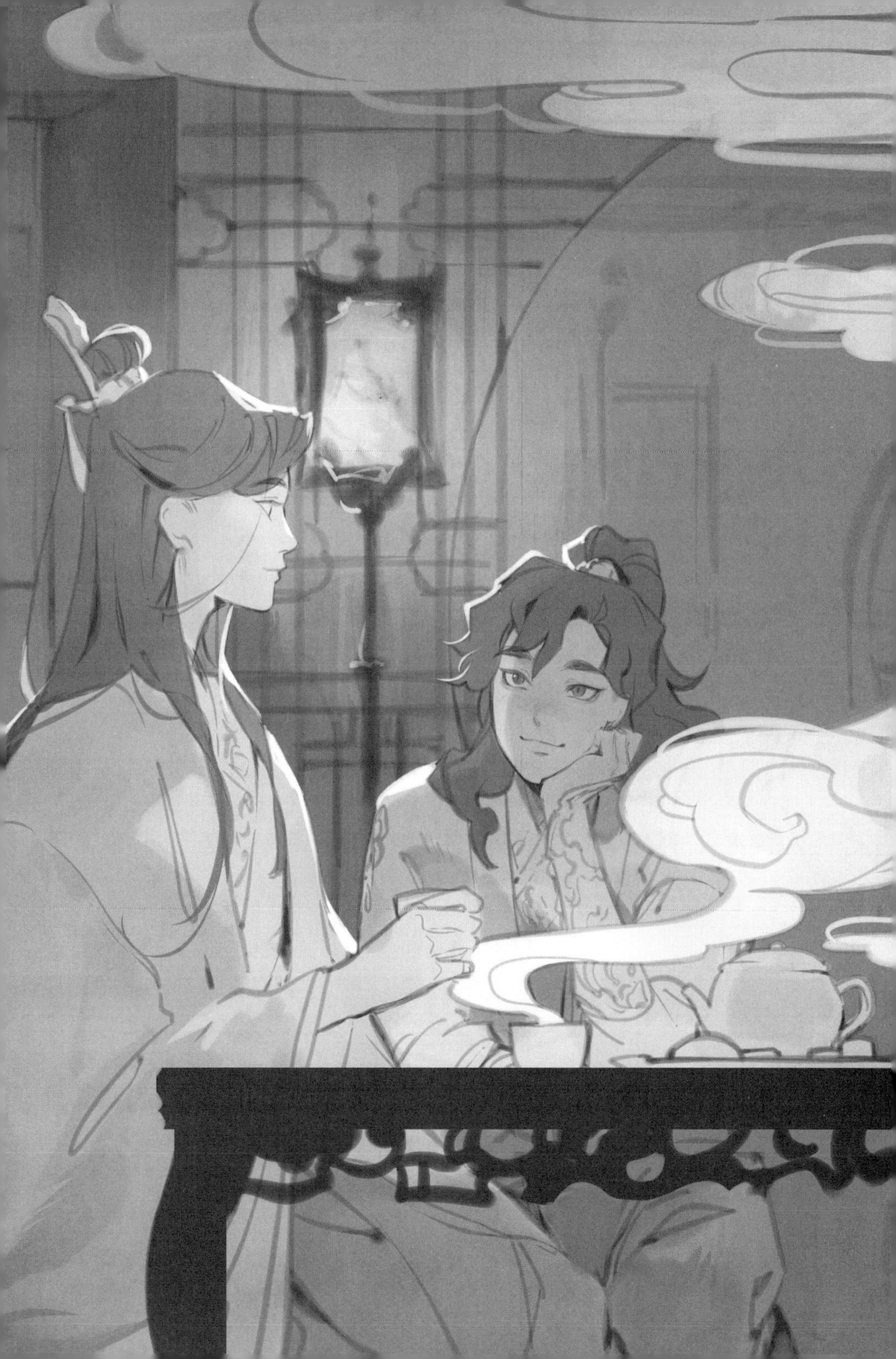

Luo Binghe had possessed an answer to this question for a long time now. Sitting squarely, without the slightest hesitation, he looked straight back. "Yes!"

This resolute answer made Shen Qingqiu release a breath of relief within his heart. "Even if in order to achieve that, you had to suffer through pain, torment, and countless tribulations, to the point that your body and heart were about to collapse—you would still want to become the strongest?"

"Binghe does not fear suffering and tribulations," Luo Binghe said slowly. "I only wish to be strong enough to protect the people and things important to me!"

This answer finally settled Shen Qingqiu's thoughts a little.

That's right. Luo Binghe, for the sake of protecting the myriad harem of jade- and flower-like beauties you'll embrace in the future, you must become strong!

Shen Qingqiu's heart was still unwilling, but when he remembered that this suffering was something the protagonist had to experience in order to break free of his chrysalis and become a butterfly, he had no choice but to adjust his mindset.

Although he was already adept at brainwashing himself thus, it wasn't like he felt the slightest bit of happiness at the thought, just because he'd forced himself to think it so many times.

Three days later, each of Cang Qiong Mountain's Twelve Peaks had prepared their participant rosters and headed to the conference.

This time, the Immortal Alliance Conference was set to convene at Jue Di Gorge, a rolling mountain range with complex terrain that extended for many kilometers.

People of established reputation were conscious of their rank and didn't participate in the conference, i.e., they didn't compete with their juniors for the limelight. There was no need, and it would have been beneath them. Therefore, the twelve peak lords and members of their generation didn't sign up. The cap on the number of spots was nevertheless high—naturally, the more the better—and in the end, around one hundred well-equipped individuals set out in grand style for Jue Di Gorge.

So many people flying on their swords would have been too high-profile and disturbed civilians, so they did travel by carriage.

A cultivation novel where they sat in carriages and rode horses all day! Shen Qingqiu still couldn't understand why Airplane Shooting Towards the Sky had stuck to this setup, but no matter how much it merited roasting, after three years, one simply ran out of words. At this point, he was numb to it.

The majority chose to ride horses, their bearing heroic and valiant. However, firstly, Shen Qingqiu wasn't good at riding and didn't want to fall and break his neck. Secondly, he disdained all exposure to the wind, sun, and rain. It wasn't comfortable, nor elegant, and so he wormed his way into a carriage under a crowd of watchful eyes.

Someone else had long since entered the carriage before him.

"A big, strong man like you trying to steal my spot!" she said with contempt as he lifted the curtain with his fan and slid inside.

This woman with beautiful eyebrows, a full chest, and thick, gorgeous hair was Xian Shu Peak's master, Qi Qingqi.

In the original work, Qi Qingqi and Shen Qingqiu had no real relationship and very few interactions. However, over the past few years, Shen Qingqiu had occasionally worked with her. He found her straightforward and fierce, and he got along with her decently well.

"I am frail and indisposed," Shen Qingqiu said with perfect composure as he used his fan to shoo her into giving him room.

Qi Qingqi moved to do so, but she refused to spare him her words. "Pampered and spoiled! Being so delicate and coddled is totally unbefitting of a cultivator at Core Formation stage! Will you also be needing someone to serve you snacks later?"

Shen Qingqiu looked like he'd just had an epiphany. "Right. Many thanks to Shimei for the reminder."

While speaking, he rapped on the carriage wall with his fan's guard.

A short while later, the carriage curtain lifted. Luo Binghe smiled. "Shizun. Snacks, water? Or is your waist sore?"

A lively and energetic white horse; a handsome and extraordinary youth. With the sun beaming down from above, both seemed to shine before their eyes.

"Your Qi-shishu would like some snacks," said Shen Qingqiu.

Luo Binghe immediately withdrew an exquisitely wrapped snack from his robe and offered it to them. It looked like he'd long been prepared for this. "If Shizun has any more orders, please call for me."

Only then did he let down the curtain.

Liu Qingge spurred his horse on past them with a powerful and resounding humph.

"Of course," said Shen Qingqiu. He lowered his head and opened the wrapping. "Dragon's beard candy. Not bad." He turned to pass the snack to Qi Qingqi. "Want some?"

Qi Qingqi found it difficult to describe her current emotional state.

More or less, it was indignation. Luo Binghe was a good disciple, so considerate and with such immense spiritual energy, and *Shen Qingqiu*, of all people, was the one who had raised him.

In truth, "indignation" didn't cover it. She just didn't know there was a phrase that nailed the feeling, and it was "my damned dog eyes!"[6]

Qi Qingqi refused to look at Shen Qingqiu as he ate the dragon beard's candy, but she made one final attempt.

"Even Mingyan is riding a horse!" As long as she could make Shen Qingqiu feel a scrap of shame, she would claim victory!

It just so happened that Shen Qingqiu had nothing better to do, so he looked outside. Indeed, Liu Mingyan sat straight on her horse, her face covered with a veil, her personal sword Shui Se on her back. A faint breeze blew by, fluttering the veil and giving her an air of ethereal lightness.

This picture was far too pleasing to the eye. Shen Qingqiu couldn't help but gaze at her for a while, sighing. "Beautiful beyond comprehension."

"*Pah!*" Qi Qingqi snapped at his face. "Don't look at my beloved disciple with such covetous eyes!"

Luo Binghe heard this back-and-forth, and his face paled.

But Shen Qingqiu didn't notice his expression at all and continued eating while gazing at Liu Mingyan. He was in the mode of someone in a theater before a movie, eating popcorn and drinking soda while waiting for the ads to end and the film to begin.

That was Liu Mingyan! The male and female leads were in the same venue—how could there *not* be sparks flying and amorous feelings budding between them?!

---

6   Originally "this is blinding my dog-eyes." "Dog" is commonly used as a curse, similar to "damn" in English.

As Luo Binghe saw his master staring fixedly at Liu Mingyan, the hand with which he held his reins couldn't help but tighten, the knuckles turning white.

"Beautiful beyond comprehension?" he muttered. She wasn't even showing her entire face. No matter how beautiful she was, could she be better-looking than him?

Luo Binghe honestly wasn't a narcissist, he'd just always been very self-aware of how he looked to others. He didn't gleefully revel in his appearance, but he also wouldn't downplay it for the sake of false humility.

After a long time, during which Shen Qingqiu showed no sign of diverting his gaze, Luo Binghe could no longer stand it. He lightly urged his mount with his whip, and the white horse quickly moved forward until its bridle was even with Liu Mingyan's.

Luo Binghe inclined his head and smiled in greeting. "Liu-shimei."

Liu Mingyan startled, then nodded shallowly, returning the greeting. "Luo-shixiong."

Oh, oh, oh—oh, oh, oh! It's started, it's started!

A once in a lifetime chance had actually come—with his own eyes, Shen Qingqiu could watch a peerlessly handsome man and a beautiful woman from a book ride together bridle to bridle. He was secretly overjoyed, and he couldn't resist leaning out further to watch.

Luo Binghe saw in his peripheral vision that Shen Qingqiu's gaze hadn't moved, and in fact he was staring at them even more intently. His face grew shadowed, his heart stuffy and teeth itchy. So he laughed and chatted with Liu Mingyan while sneakily urging their horses faster and faster, until they were far enough away that Shen Qingqiu could no longer see them without leaning his whole torso out of the carriage.

Shen Qingqiu could only resume his proper seat, disappointed.

How could he forget? When male and female leads were cooing sweetly at each other, a third wheel could never hang around like a glaring fluorescent light, nor could there be a meddlesome audience.

Although, if that child had grown up so far that he wanted to hide his romances from his elders...was it possible that his rebellious stage had finally arrived?

Jue Di Gorge.

It spanned seven mountain peaks and overflowed with verdant greenery. Scattered every which where within it were bright springs and dark rivers, waterfalls and wondrous stones, deep valleys and soaring peaks. As the name "Hopeless Land" implied, some of its terrain represented "the brink of despair"—yet in the next moment, as if confirming that every cloud had a silver lining, you would spot paths winding through the peaks, indelible and unerasable. In Shen Qingqiu's eyes, such a reminder was vital for both adventurers and homebodies.

The new talent participating in the conference followed the agreed-upon arrangements and stood in well-ordered rows surrounding a gigantic, natural stone platform before the gorge.

Disciples from the four great cultivation sects made up the main share of participants. Cang Qiong Mountain was in the lead, followed closely by Zhao Hua Monastery, Tian Yi Temple, and Huan Hua Palace.

Of the four sects, Cang Qiong Mountain was the most comprehensive. The twelve peaks each had their own strengths in a variety of fields. Meanwhile, the monastery and temple sects were naturally those who fostered Buddhist monks and Daoist priests, respectively.

Huan Hua Palace was more complicated. Their sect followed the teachings of a number of different schools, had an aptitude for the Daoist art of concealment, and interacted the most with the secular world. The level of their techniques was unclear, but on one point there was no doubt: they were absolutely the wealthiest of the sects. They contributed the most funds to every conference.

Other than these four, numerous small and mid-sized sects were also participating. Therefore, the final number of those who had signed up and gathered at Jue Di Gorge was well over one thousand.

What had been a cold and silent gorge entrance suddenly burst to life with more than one thousand people. Animals that had never seen people before were all frightened away. It was unusually lively in all meanings of the word.

A high dais had been constructed at the entrance to the gorge, and from there, all the non-participating cultivators would observe the battles. Various colored flags representing each of the sects fluttered and swayed upon it. Seats for the sect leaders were at the highest level. Cang Qiong Mountain's delegation, led by Yue Qingyuan, took their place on the dais.

Shen Qingqiu sat in the back next to an elderly man of great poise and a head of white hair. This man had greeted their group earlier and nodded to him again now.

"Immortal Master Shen," he said.

Huan Hua Palace's Old Palace Master was also the master of Luo Binghe's birth mother. Shen Qingqiu returned the greeting in the mode of someone meeting the emperor's relative.

Not long after, a member of Huan Hua Palace walked onto the stone platform. After all, they'd contributed the most money, so no one could argue with their choice of host. Below the platform, the over one thousand competitors gradually quieted, focusing their attention on listening to the host describe the proceedings.

The host's martial foundations were deep, his breaths plentiful and long-lasting. Every last person at the mouth of the gorge, including those on the soaring dais, could clearly hear his voice in full.

"The conference will last for seven days. Once everyone enters the gorge, we will erect a giant barrier and cover the entirety of Jue Di Gorge. For those seven days, the participants who enter Jue Di Gorge will be isolated from the outside world and will remain ignorant to what happens there. The observers will follow the situation within via the spirit eagles let loose above the valley.

"Over a hundred varieties of demonic creature have been loosed within the valley. The total number nears five thousand. Every time you take down a creature, you will receive a prayer bead from its body. The creatures are of different difficulty levels, and the spiritual qi within the prayer beads will likewise vastly differ. Is everyone wearing a gold cord around their wrists?"

The people beneath the platform raised their wrists together, revealing a sea of gold cords. It was quite a magnificent sight.

The host continued. "When you obtain a bead, thread it onto the cord. Your scores will automatically be displayed on the ranking charts outside."

The ranking charts were displayed opposite the dais. Although there were eight charts in total, the crowd's attention would be squared on the names of the top one hundred scorers on the first, gold-inscribed tablet at the top—and at times, they would be watching only the top ten. This embodied the principle of "No first place among scholars, no second place among martial artists."[7]

Finally, the Huan Hua Palace host delivered a severe warning. "Sect disciples are forbidden from fighting over and stealing each other's beads! The moment anyone is found to be fighting or using underhanded methods to steal beads, their right to participate will be revoked, and they will be banned from the conference for three sessions!"

Three sessions meant twelve years.

This group of new talent was like a mix of carp and dragons. Many were young and inexperienced, but quite a few were slippery old bastards, scoundrels who'd scurried about for years and years. If duels weren't forbidden, the organizers had reason to fear that the entire conference would devolve into incomparable chaos, and lives might well be lost. Therefore, this rule was exceptionally necessary.

Shen Qingqiu was bored to the point that his bones itched. Though he seemed to be staring intently at the scene beneath him, his mind had long since wandered off.

Suddenly, from the side, several female members of a certain sect leader's entourage whispered amongst themselves.

"Which sect is that disciple from? He's incredibly handsome."

"Those white robes really suit him. Maybe even better than they do Gongyi-shixiong."

"But Gongyi-shixiong isn't just extraordinarily handsome, he also possesses incredible spiritual strength. How can you compare them?"

"Tut-tut, you just can't stand when anyone criticizes Gongyi-shixiong, can you? Sure enough, you defended him right away—admit it!"

---

7   文无第一，武无第二. *Scholars must uphold modesty and so can't claim first place, while martial artists are all about competition and so only first place matters to them.*

"A-admit what? Stupid girl, what did you just say? I dare you to say it again!"

A burst of mortified, frustrated anger was followed by giggling play-fighting.

As soon as he'd heard them, Shen Qingqiu knew who they were eyeing. The figure in the crowd dressed all in white: the refined, outstanding Luo Binghe.

In truth, they weren't the only ones secretly watching and discussing him. Even a number of the girls in the crowd of participants below the stone platform were glancing stealthily at Luo Binghe, their jade-like cheeks dusted with blushing red.

The girls kept their voices very low, but given the quality of cultivators present, their five senses all incredibly sharp, of course they were overheard. These girls were too young to be careful, and they let others hear their private conversations. Fortunately, their seniors were all very considerate and let their sect leader, who was already holding a hand to his forehead and feigning sleep, keep his dignity. Everyone pretended that they hadn't unintentionally eavesdropped, their gazes straight and unflinching.

In an effort to break the awkward pall, someone coughed twice. "Why don't we do as we have before and make our predictions about which of these new talents will stand out the most?" he said with a smile.

Shen Qingqiu's spirits rose.

The words "make our predictions" weren't actually referring to divining fortunes, but instead to *gambling*.

To be clear, it was about betting on the talent you had your eye on. Cultivators needed entertainment too, after all.

Also, the stakes used in these bets weren't tacky, monetary items like gold and silver, but artifacts, spirit stones, or even the names of disciples who would be sent to study under other sects. They also wouldn't bet anything of vital importance—but it was still one of the Immortal Alliance Conference's traditional entertainment activities.

Anyone as dignified as a first-class sect leader, like Yue Qingyuan, had to be conscious of their status and wouldn't indulge in things like this, but naturally many others were willing to join the fun. A short moment later, the dais was roaring with enthusiasm, dozens of bets being laid. Quite a few bet on their own disciples—for example, Qi Qingqi bet on Liu Mingyan's victory.

Shen Qingqiu didn't even need to think, and straightaway he bet five thousand spirit stones on Luo Binghe.

Such a daring move caused quite a ripple. Even Yue Qingyuan paused in his polite exchange of greetings with the abbot from Zhao Hua Monastery, his gaze shifting toward Shen Qingqiu.

Shen Qingqiu saw the way Yue Qingyuan seemed about to speak but didn't. "Zhangmen-shixiong, this is just a bit of fun," he said. "To encourage Binghe a little."

"Just for fun." Liu Qingge sneered. "If you shattered the entirety of Qing Jing Peak, would you even find a thousand spirit stones in the rubble?"

Shen Qingqiu clammed up. Indeed, he wouldn't!

When placing a bet here, you only needed to write it down. The accounts were settled afterward, and you didn't need proof of funds. Because everyone here had name and reputation, there was no fear that debts would be blown off. Shen Qingqiu knew that betting on Luo Binghe was a sure win, and so he had raised the stakes. After all, no one else knew exactly how many assets he possessed.

Yue Qingyuan was probably afraid of the sect being embarrassing before outsiders, and he rushed to smooth things over. "All right. Lower your voices. Of course there would."

"Zhangmen-shixiong, you'll be his guarantor?" Qi Qingqi butted in, getting right to the point.

"I will," said Yue Qingyuan.

"If you lose, who pays?" Liu Qingge asked.

"Me," said Yue Qingyuan.

"If I win, who keeps the payout?" asked Shen Qingqiu.

"You," said Yue Qingyuan.

An agreement was reached, and everyone other than Liu Qingge rejoiced. Shen Qingqiu happily went to make his bet.

The gathered cultivators quietly wondered why they'd never heard of Luo Binghe. You couldn't really blame them. The current Luo Binghe's modus operandi was low-key and modest, and he was unwilling to claim credit. Every time he did a good deed or completed a task, he quietly took his leave. This prevented his reputation from growing, so his skills and talents had never shone. Those unaware of the situation assumed Shen Qingqiu was doing exactly as he'd claimed and just making a show of good faith to encourage his disciple.

Below the dais, after the participants took their oath together, they formally entered the venue. There were many of them, so twelve different entrances had been erected, through which the participants would enter in assorted groups of mixed sects. The participants, shaking with nerves, stepped into Jue Di Gorge and began their expeditions.

On the dais, the members of the older generations, who'd long since achieved success and made their reputations, had finished their round of betting. They sat with unruffled composure, some of them even exchanging pointers, chatting, or chewing on melon seeds.

Within the venue flew more than a hundred spirit eagles controlled by experts. The silver rings around their talons were inlaid with special crystals. As they soared, a panoramic view of the people and scenery below was projected onto the dais's numerous crystal mirrors, the effect similar to that of surveillance equipment.

Someone smiled from ear to ear. "As expected, Gongyi Xiao is in first place right after entering!"

On the gold-inscribed tablet, the first ten names all shone with bright light. At this time, "Gongyi Xiao" had already reached the first-place position. Right after his name was the number twelve. That is to say, a mere hour in, he'd already eliminated twelve demonic creatures and obtained twelve prayer beads.

Even Liu Mingyan, close behind in second, had only obtained six prayer beads. A large gap had already appeared.

A youth dressed in white was reflected on a crystal mirror, his figure elegant and unrestrained like drifting clouds and flowing water, yet his actions were quick as lightning. In an instant, he shredded a shrilly screaming vengeful ghost into scattered smoke.

An unceasing stream of excessive praise rose in response, and Shen Qingqiu smiled without speaking.

This Gongyi Xiao, although he looked favored and blessed, over-flowing with incredible presence—actually, enh, he was at best only half a dollar better than his fellow cannon fodder.

He was the typical character trope who was handsome, of good lineage and surpassing talent, loved by girls, full of mettle, and accomplished in his youth—but unfortunately, there was also the protagonist, so he was doomed to serve as the lead's cannon fodder foil. Though most bets for top ranker had been placed on Gongyi Xiao, sorry to say, he wouldn't be first for long before Luo Binghe kicked him off the spot.

Luo Binghe's name was currently in the middle of the pack. The number after it was a mere "one." Yet Shen Qingqiu wasn't worried at all. He knew that once tonight arrived, and once the curtains lifted on that breathtaking, climactic event, Luo Binghe's name would soar unstoppably up the charts!

The first day of the Immortal Alliance Conference approached midnight. A round, golden moon hung high in the sky, and the dais gleamed bright beneath the lamplight.

Among the many crystal mirrors, Shen Qingqiu finally found one displaying Luo Binghe. Currently, he was slowly moving through the forest, spotlessly clean and without a trace of exhaustion. His eyes were like stars, and it seemed as if they could see right through the crystal mirror.

However, he wasn't alone.

Most of the participants moved by themselves. If people teamed up to fight the monsters, how would they divvy up the beads? At most, they might cooperate with those they were familiar with, forming teams of two or three shixiong and shidi.

There were also some incredible female cultivators, but on the whole, these girls' strength and mental fortitude was lacking, and they often required help. Their teams were mainly composed of shimei and shijie who got along well, and they spent their time playing around instead of actually working. Basically, they looked quite hopeless.

Yet following after Luo Binghe were seven or eight other individuals, and all of them were either delicate girls or young disciples.

This group drew a great deal of attention. Some of the audience even stopped watching Gongyi Xiao's heroic exploits, switching over to size up this bloated team and finding it too strange to look away.

In the group, the one walking closest to Luo Binghe was a Huan Hua disciple in light yellow robes, holding a night pearl to light the way.

The girl was graceful and elegant, but she walked with a slight limp, like she had sprained her ankle. It was probably an injury she had sustained while fighting monsters.

"Luo-shixiong, I truly apologize," she said. "You saved us, and now we're troubling you. If you weren't protecting us, you would be so far ahead already... We are a burden."

"We are all cultivators. It's our obligation to look after each other," Luo Binghe said, eminently proper.

Shen Qingqiu had come to know Luo Binghe's early-stage white lotus mindset like the back of his hand, and he didn't find this strange.

His student was fighting monsters while also looking after this crowd of weaker fighters—women and young disciples. Hence, he hadn't shot up in the rankings. Otherwise, with his ability, he would have already effortlessly defeated Gongyi Xiao. Even Ming Fan ranked higher than Luo Binghe right now... But it didn't matter—Luo Binghe would have a second wind!

My disciple is the most awesome in the world! If he weren't so good, so kind, and so easy to take advantage of, none of you could even dream of defeating him!

Shen Qingqiu never thought to reflect on what this agitated attitude of his meant.

Yue Qingyuan smiled. "Qingqiu, that little disciple of yours has great moral character."

Shen Qingqiu smiled behind his open fan, quietly accepting the compliment.

Qi Qingqi humphed. "Exactly. It's impossible to tell that *he* was the one who taught the boy."

Other observers said a few additional words of praise. However, they weren't necessarily sincere. What use was good moral character? The Immortal Alliance Conference valued power. In their eyes, Luo Binghe's actions seemed rather childish.

But when Huan Hua Palace's Old Palace Master, sitting by Shen Qingqiu's side, saw Luo Binghe's face through the crystal mirror, he let out a barely audible "eh?" and almost stood up.

Shen Qingqiu didn't glance over, but he understood well enough. Luo Binghe was beautiful, and he looked quite like his birth mother. The Old Palace Master had seen this face and, thinking the junior disciple's similar appearance only coincidental, had become nostalgic about his own favorite. He could scarcely have imagined that Luo Binghe was the child of precisely that beloved lost pupil.

On the other side, in Jue Di Gorge, Luo Binghe was calmly considering what to do with this crowd of vulnerable disciples.

From a moral standpoint, he couldn't just abandon them; they were from Huan Hua Palace and had barely started training. But he also didn't want to miss the chance to shine in the Immortal Alliance Conference and win honor for Shizun.

As Luo Binghe was mulling over how to extricate himself from this situation, Shen Qingqiu thought he was rolling around with maidens and making sparks fly.

There was the first maiden to sleep with Luo Binghe! Qin Wanyue, the graceful and subdued little shimei!

The biggest impression this maiden had left on Shen Qingqiu was her role in helping Luo Binghe lose his virginity. Later, her role was to be a victim in the constant harem intrigue. Only someone as...special as Airplane Shooting Towards the Sky could manage to occasionally write a stallion novel's harem more in the flavor of *The Legend of Zhen Huan*.[8]

I'd rather read ten thousand words describing how ghost-head spiders mate than read about Sha Hualing tearing into Qin Wanyue! Thank you!

Watching this parade of people trailing close behind Luo Binghe, treating him like their personal savior, Shen Qingqiu grew unhappy.

Some of these disciples honestly hadn't acclimated and so couldn't yet demonstrate their skills. They would be fine after a little more time to adjust. But some were truly ignorant and incompetent, yet they refused to back out of the competition. They wanted to ride Luo Binghe's coattails so they could fumble together some beads and rise in the ranking.

If this were the black-hearted Luo Binghe, he'd have slaughtered them all in seconds without even blinking.

People sure do take advantage of kindness, huh!

They pressed forward for a while, and every low-level monster that leapt from the darkness to attack them was eliminated with pretty much only flicks of Luo Binghe's fingers. His sword never left its sheath. Yet he still couldn't pick up the pace.

Why?

A female disciple from Huan Hua Palace leaned on Qin Wanyue and began to hiccup and cry. "Jiejie, my feet hurt so much."

---

8 甄嬛传, English name *Empresses in the Palace, is a 2011 television series centered on harem scheming and infighting.*

In front, Luo Binghe stopped, but he didn't turn around. He lowered his head and rubbed his temples.

Nervous, Qin Wanyue lowered her head and spoke quietly to the girl. "Wanrong, endure it for a bit longer, all right? We have to walk a little faster."

"But my feet really hurt—I can't walk anymore!" Wanrong-meimei whined. "We've been walking all day, and there's nowhere to take a bath. I'm so uncomfortable."

A number of untrained disciples in the group agreed, one after another. If Shen Qingqiu had been the one in charge, he would have long since revoked their right to participate and kicked them out of Jue Di Gorge.

If your feet are so delicate, don't sign up for the Immortal Alliance Conference. And if you do, then whatever, but why drag others down? Look at Liu Mingyan! The difference between you is vast. No wonder she's the number one female protagonist!

But there was nothing he could do about Qin Wanrong. After all, the beautiful sisters Qin Wanyue and Qin Wanrong were members of Luo Binghe's harem. Therefore, according to universal convention, no matter how dedicatedly they dug their own graves, they wouldn't die.

Shen Qingqiu's heart filled with a strange annoyance.

Luo Binghe, you... In the future, when you're gathering your harem, can you put more thought into quality? Don't welcome just any decent-looking girl into your arms. The inconsistency in your harem's standards makes this master's heart hurt for you!

Qin Wanyue sent another look at Luo Binghe's back. "Little Sister," she said quietly, "we've already made a lot of trouble for Luo-shixiong..."

She still wanted to rely on Luo Binghe and try to make a name for herself in the Immortal Alliance Conference and earn some reputation. If her sister foolishly annoyed Luo Binghe, it would go badly for her.

"Luo-shixiong is such a good person—he won't mind," Qin Wanrong said innocently. "Isn't that right, Luo-shixiong?"

Luo Binghe finally turned, a faint smile still on his face—peerlessly handsome, utterly faultless—and did not speak. But for some reason, Qin Wanyue inwardly shivered in fear.

However, Qin Wanrong had cotton for brains and took his smile as acquiescence. Singing a carefree tune, she swept over to a nearby creek like a gust of wind.

It's coming! Shen Qingqiu's gaze tensed.

Luo Binghe started. Given what she'd just said, he thought she was going to bathe. Fortunately, this little girl wasn't that eccentric, and she only shook off her shoes and socks to dip her feet into the creek.

Those were the river's upper reaches. What if someone downstream wanted to drink…?

Shen Qingqiu mentally lit a candle for any such unlucky disciples.

A number of the other disciples soon followed Qin Wanrong's example, and just like that, the little crowd started to laugh and play.

Luo Binghe was completely helpless as he watched. It would have been awkward to approach them, so he could only call from far away, "Wading in the water at night isn't safe. It's best if we finish and leave right away."

Shen Qingqiu felt this was a bit odd. In the original novel, surely Luo Binghe hadn't stood so far away? He didn't think he had remembered wrong. At this time, Luo Binghe, out of worry (or out of

"Great Master" Airplane Shooting Towards the Sky's selfish desire to write fanservice) went to the creek with the others. Then he enjoyed the alluring show of all the women slowly rolling down their stockings... Textbook foot fetish material!

Luo Binghe pleaded with the disciples, but a few had even crossed to the other side of the creek, chatting and laughing.

"It's all right! Luo-shixiong, you come too!"

Even the sect leaders watching through the crystal mirrors were speechless.

Shen Qingqiu had no expression on his face.

Luo Binghe, you still won't go? If you don't, you'll miss the plot!

Qin Wanyue knew her little sister was being rather inappropriate, and she cautiously apologized to Luo Binghe.

"Luo-shixiong, I'm so sorry," she said. "This is the first time Shimei and the others are participating in the Immortal Alliance Conference..." Truly lovable and pitiful. She bit her lip like she was making an excruciating decision. "If Luo-shixiong feels burdened, leave us and go. It's all right..."

These words, together with that expression on the verge of tears, were wildly insincere. But after hearing her plea, any man with a bare minimum of virtue would find himself unable to do as she suggested.

Before Luo Binghe could reply, an ear-piercing scream came from the creek. His face suddenly changed, and he shoved past Qin Wanyue, whose beautiful face had lost all color, as he dashed toward the creek's bank.

The audience watching from the crystal mirrors stood in terror.

"What's going on?" Luo Binghe asked in a forceful voice, his sword before him.

Five or six disciples had been washing their feet and playing in the creek. Now two of them had disappeared, and one of the missing was Qin Wanrong.

You see! Told you that you should have gone earlier! Wonderful, a perfectly good wife is now gone, just like that! Shen Qingqiu thought, frustrated and disappointed. *Now you can't complete the Qin Sisters bouquet for that grand threesome scene in the future. Now what?!*

Moreover, despite everything, he'd never thought that a member of the protagonist's harem could actually get herself killed.

"I don't know what happened!" a disciple screamed. "The water suddenly turned black, and Shijie and the other were swept under by something!"

Luo Binghe rapidly dragged the stupefied disciples still in the creek up onto the bank. But just as he reached out to grab the last person, they fell over like they had lost their footing. Everyone stared as the water closed over the disciple's head and they disappeared with their eyes wide open.

At the same time, a black smog billowed through the creek. Shen Qingqiu peered through the crystal mirror. The smog was actually countless black strands, smooth and silky like a woman's dark hair. From between the strands seeped scarlet blood, diluted by creek water. They were thicker and more disgusting than Sadako's[9] hair.

Someone on the dais cried out in shock. "Nu Yuan Chan!"

In Jue Di Gorge, Luo Binghe had quickly identified the monster in the creek as well. He sent sword glares into the water as he cried, "Get far away from the water! It's the Demon Realm's Nu Yuan Chan!"

---

9   A ghostly character who appeared in the Japanese horror movie Ringu; famous for her long, bedraggled black hair, which obscured her face.

For a while, the billows and billows of the hair-like demonic creature's body swirled within the water. Suddenly, like they were burping after a full meal, the black strands spat out a few objects with a stream of bubbles: three bodies that had been sucked clean of flesh and blood, leaving only drenched corpses of skin and bone.

The pores on the dead bodies were abnormally large. That was because many strands of hair were still attached to their skin, thrust into their pores, hungrily sucking out the bodies' remaining flesh, blood, and spiritual essence.

Leaving no pore uninvaded, diving into any opening it could find—this was one of the Nu Yuan Chan's most terrifying characteristics.

This scene scared the disciples by the creek witless. Wails and screams filled the forest as they threw themselves behind Luo Binghe to hide. At the sight of the horrible state of her sister's body, Qin Wanyue nearly fainted.

Luckily, she was smart enough to not faint for real. Otherwise, in all this chaos, who would bother to help her escape?!

Nu Yuan Chan was an amphibious creature. After sucking three people dry underwater, it was itching to climb the bank and search for new targets. Luo Binghe's expression was icily severe. He snapped his fingers, igniting a burst of flames at his fingertips. Then, boosting the flames with spiritual energy, he flicked them toward the lurking demonic beast. As soon as they touched the beast's hair-like strands, the flames flared into an inferno, forcing the black mass of hair to retreat into the water with all speed, leaving it afraid to come onto the bank.

Luo Binghe executed this set of actions in a single smooth sequence, radiating formidable might, utterly relentless. Shen Qingqiu internally held up a sign: Ten points to Luo Binghe!

Luo Binghe picked up the night pearl that Qin Wanyue had dropped in her panic and raised it high. Like a shining beacon, it calmed everyone's hearts.

"Don't stray, stay together!" he shouted.

Then he took out a piece of the standard equipment all the participants had been given, a rescue firework, and fired it into the sky.

The rescue fireworks were given to disciples to call for help if they encountered a monster that they were unable to handle. The Immortal Alliance Conference hadn't released any excessively dangerous monsters, and if a participant fired a rescue firework three times, they automatically forfeited their right to participate. Therefore, in all past conferences, no one had really used the fireworks unless they were really backed into a corner. However, at that moment, glittering bursts of fireworks rose one after another in the sky over Jue Di Gorge. This should have been a beautiful scene, but at that moment, not only did these fireworks not seem gorgeous, they made the onlookers' insides twist in fear.

Every blossoming firework represented a disciple who had encountered an exceedingly dreadful monster—whose life was in danger.

"The crystal mirrors! Look at the crystal mirrors!"

Bloodcurdling shrieks and wails of distress came in an unending stream from the mirrors. Some disciples were already corpses on the ground, some were still struggling, soaked with blood, gazes full of terror.

"Why? Why here... There shouldn't be!"

"Someone, help! Shifu, save me! Shige, save..."

A hoarse cry burst from one mirror, followed by the mournful shriek of a spirit eagle. The picture went out, becoming a flat, black screen.

Everyone stared, uncomprehending.

"What's going on?"

That hoarse cry had definitely been the cry of a Demon Realm bone eagle, a type of aerial demonic beast that was as fierce as it was bloodthirsty. It had no doubt torn apart the spirit eagle, shattering its crystal into dust.

Beasts that swam in the water, beasts that walked on land, beasts that flew through the air... These fierce demonic entities had absolutely not been part of the conference's plan.

Though Shen Qingqiu had mentally prepared for this long ago, as he watched the all-encompassing scene of chaos play out before him, his scalp went numb, and his fingers chilled. He realized that he would be unable to do as he'd expected. He couldn't just pretend he was watching the climax of an ultra-realistic show.

Outside Jue Di Gorge, pandemonium had broken out on the dais. Tian Yi Temple's cultivators said sternly, "What's happening? The demonic beasts chosen for the Immortal Alliance Conference were determined via strict rules and meticulous selection. How could something like the Nu Yuan Chan, which resides only in the Demon Realm, find its way in?!"

Many Huan Hua Palace disciples had already died. The Old Palace Master shot to his feet. "Open the barrier!"

The giant barrier over Jue Di Gorge was supported by nearly a hundred monks from Zhao Hua Monastery. The Zhao Hua Monastery abbot immediately began to cast a long-distance voice transferral spell to tell the monks to release the barrier

"You cannot!" Yue Qingyuan said.

The Old Palace Master started. "Sect Leader Yue, what is the meaning of this?"

Over a hundred of Cang Qiong Mountain's disciples were in Jue Di Gorge, yet Yue Qingyuan refused to open the barrier to let the trapped escape. Obviously he had an exceptional reason.

Shen Qingqiu had long since figured it out. He responded in Yue Qingyuan's place. "Once you release the barrier, the disciples will be able to escape, but so will the demonic beasts trapped within—and they will scatter. There are villages only a few kilometers from here. The situation would become even more grave. Sect members and disciples at least have the ability to contend with the beasts, but the common people with no spiritual energy at all..."

No elder or sect leader on the platform had the words to retort, and they fell into a dead silence. At this time, no matter how great one's cultivation, Core Formation or Nascent Soul stage or anything between, there was no way to reverse the course of events.

"If we cannot open the barrier to let them out, then...then what should we do?" asked a cultivator, at a loss.

"If they can't leave, then we must enter," said Liu Qingge.

The members of Cang Qiong Mountain exchanged a look in tacit agreement.

"Fellow cultivators," Yue Qingyuan said gravely. "Someone must be behind today's incident. They hope to use these demonic beasts to wipe out the new talent of the cultivation world, eliminating its future pillars in one fell swoop. For now, we can only maintain the barrier. But are any of our fellow cultivators willing to enter the gorge with Cang Qiong Mountain Sect to clear out the demonic beasts and rescue the participating disciples?"

To carve a path of blood into the gorge, clearing out all the demonic beasts, would require not only martial power but a great deal of courage.

The Old Palace Master was the first to respond. "It would dishonor Huan Hua Palace to refuse."

Huan Hua Palace had sent the most participants to this year's conference and had invested the most as well. They were the party least able to take the loss.

Once someone took the lead, others followed, volunteering one after another. Even if a scant few cowards were in the crowd, by now they had been reminded that their own precious, talented disciples were also trapped.

Shen Qingqiu stepped forward, ready to stand with the group volunteering to provide assistance, when Liu Qingge also stepped forward slightly and used his sword sheath to block Shen Qingqiu's way.

Expression unchanging, Shen Qingqiu pushed the sheath aside with two fingers. "What is the meaning of this?"

"Your poison," Liu Qingge said succinctly.

"That's right," Yue Qingyuan agreed. "Your ailment from Without a Cure has yet to be resolved. Entrust the safety of Qing Jing Peak's disciples to us."

If Shen Qingqiu's condition suddenly acted up after he entered Jue Di Gorge, and his spiritual energy stalled while he was surrounded by swarms of demonic beasts, then neither heaven nor earth would be able to help him.

Shen Qingqiu shook his head. "How can a master hide and relax on a dais while his disciples are in danger? If I can't even protect my own disciples, I don't deserve to be the Peak Lord of Qing Jing Peak."

Also, he was a vital character who needed to trigger a crucial plot point. If he wasn't on the scene, they couldn't keep filming, you know?

Ding-dong, System notification: [Making the villain more three-dimensional by crafting an honorable image, B-Points +30.]

Shen Qingqiu internally rolled his eyes. *Are you handing me a piece of candy before you stab me?*

Yue Qingyuan had failed to dissuade him, as had everyone else. "Then you must be careful," he said reluctantly. "If you can't manage it, you must use a voice transferral spell to call us for help."

Shen Qingqiu wasn't so pessimistic about his ability to handle demonic beasts. His confidence in his own cultivation and spiritual power aside, his interest in the demonic beasts of *Proud Immortal Demon Way* had far surpassed his interest in all those flavors of women. He might not have remembered where any given female protagonist liked to go stargazing with Luo Binghe after being slighted, and he sometimes was unable to match names to characters, but he definitely remembered every demonic beast's attributes and weaknesses with exacting clarity!

His knowledge of the plot aside, if you had to call something Shen Qingqiu's golden finger...it could only be this!

In Jue Di Gorge, Luo Binghe had just calmed a crowd of terror-stricken junior disciples. In this sort of situation, they couldn't afford to fall into disarray. If they encountered a new demonic beast or any of them strayed off, the situation would only grow more disastrous.

The night wind whipped by, carrying wails and howls from all around. It was impossible to tell if they came from human or demonic throats. The faint-hearted were already curled up and sobbing, and Qin Wanyue's face was deathly pale. But at the sight of Luo Binghe leaning against a tree, Zheng Yang clasped hilt-up within his crossed arms, calm yet alert, protecting them against any attacks that came from the darkness...she couldn't stop the trace of tender fondness welling up within her.

If Shen Qingqiu were there, he would have grown incredibly excited, his gossip's soul on fire: *Girl, you've fallen in love with him!*

Suddenly, rustling noises came from the nearby shrubbery. Luo Binghe's gaze sharpened, and he gathered spiritual energy in his palm, ready to strike.

The rustling in the brush grew louder and louder, closer and closer. Everyone's hearts climbed into their throats. Perhaps they were terrified beyond belief, because not a single one let out a scream.

Suddenly, there was a plop, like someone had collapsed to the ground. A round object rolled out of the bushes.

It was a human head.

Both of the head's eyes were tightly closed, its face covered in blood, its hair disheveled like a chicken's nest. Normally, this sight would have been frightening. But at present, a harmless corpse head was much better than a man-eating demonic beast, so quite a few disciples even sighed in relief.

"This... Does anyone know which sect this shixiong belonged to?" Qin Wanyue asked, her voice trembling.

Disciples from the various sects stepped closer to check, one after another, but all of them sighed in relief.

"Not one of ours."

"Never seen him before."

Luo Binghe gazed into the dark depths of the shrubbery, thinking. If the head was here, the body was also nearby. It would be better to go check its sect uniform. He strengthened the spiritual flow in his palm and walked into the dark.

As expected, a stiff corpse lay beyond the shrubbery, wearing aqua-blue cultivator robes. One of Tian Yi Temple's newly accepted disciples. Luo Binghe saw only the hem of his robes before sighing. Newly accepted disciples like this one only came to the Immortal Alliance Conference to gain experience. They had never imagined that they'd be drawn into such an unpredictable catastrophe and lose their lives.

He looked farther up and suddenly froze in shock.

There was still a perfectly good head on top of the corpse's neck.

Then where had that other head come from?

Zheng Yang had already left its sheath before Luo Binghe doubled back. As its white light overflowed, he yelled, "Get away from the head!"

Before he finished speaking, the head lying quietly askew on the ground suddenly opened its eyelids.

It met the disciples' gazes with wide, glowering eyes—then eight spindly spider legs, segmented and barbed, stretched forth from somewhere at the bottom of its neck, and it leapt up in a single bound.

The closest person couldn't dodge in time, and the monster jumped onto the disciple's head. With a crazed howl, the disciple drew his sword and wildly swung it around, forcing everyone nearby to hurriedly duck away. Luo Binghe dared not attack carelessly in case he stabbed the disciple's head instead of the monster. The result would be too horrible to imagine.

The sensation of something so terrifying crawling back and forth on your head would be enough to frighten anyone to death. In complete despair, the disciple changed the direction of his sword and swung it toward his own head. Before he could strike, those eight spindly spider legs had found their target and ferociously speared into his temples.

He went instantly stiff, and like his tongue had twisted into knots, he was unable to yell a single word. The spider legs sticking into that human head bored deeper and deeper, and the disciple's whole body began to twitch unceasingly. After only a moment, the eight legs drew back out, leaving nothing but twin rows of gory holes in his temples. Everything within his skull had been sucked clean, leaving it completely empty.

The scene was utterly horrible. Even Luo Binghe remained frozen for a while, unable to react.

Having eaten its fill of brains, that human-headed spider monster crawled up and down the corpse, letting out a mournful scream like an infant's wail.

Just then, an arrow of light made of pure spiritual energy flew through the night and pierced its still howling mouth, skewering a hole clean through it.

Amidst the sudden silence and everyone's dazed stares, Shen Qingqiu rubbed his sore ears, slowly shook out his sleeves, and with a snap of his fan, murmured, "Shut up."

This arrival of his was truly quite low-key.

"Shizun!"

At the sight of Shen Qingqiu, Luo Binghe was far happier than shocked.

After all, since the mayhem began, he'd anticipated that Shen Qingqiu would absolutely be so worried that he would personally enter the gorge to rescue them.

Shen Qingqiu swiftly righted himself. He swept his gaze over the many disciples coming to surround him and asked, "Is anyone injured?"

"Other than those shimei at the riverside...and the shidi who died just now, we've thus far suffered no other casualties," said Luo Binghe.

"You've been through a lot," said Shen Qingqiu.

Luo Binghe smiled, his eyes shining brightly. "This disciple was only doing his duty."

Shen Qingqiu glanced at Qin Wanyue, whose eyes were still red. *You can still smile? Smile?! Don't you know that one of your wives is dead?!*

Now that a powerful senior had appeared to rescue them, every one of the disciples acted like they'd seen their mother, stopping just short of clinging to Shen Qingqiu's thighs and wailing.

"There's no need to panic, nor reason to fear," said Shen Qingqiu. "The sect leaders know the situation within the barrier, and a large number of seniors have already entered the gorge to help. Protect yourselves well. We'll be able to break out soon."

His words were like a narcotic. The youths who'd been frightened out of their wits absorbed them and became at ease.

"Shizun, what exactly was that thing?" asked Luo Binghe.

When it came to *Proud Immortal Demon Way*'s demonic beasts, he'd really asked the right person. Shen Qingqiu spoke with great familiarity, like he was listing his family treasures. "It's no surprise you've never seen one; that was a ghost-head spider. Mean-tempered and terrifying to behold, it can mimic the sound of crying infants and uses that to lure prey. Once the prey approaches, it uses the suction pads below its head to firmly grip the top of its prey's skull. Its eight legs are incredibly sharp and can pierce right through bone, allowing it to drain the brains of living creatures."

As Luo Binghe listened to this excruciatingly detailed explanation, he was filled with both admiration and awe. "To think such an evil creature exists in this world. This disciple is truly too ignorant."

Ever since Luo Binghe apprenticed under Meng Mo, Shen Qingqiu had been able to provide him with less and less guidance on martial and sword techniques. This rare chance to show off as a master before his disciple secretly left Shen Qingqiu feeling an immense sense of satisfaction. It was like he'd finally found his long-lost teacher's halo.

"Ghost-head spiders are a demonic rarity," he went on. "Being unsuited to the Human Realm's environment, it's been many years since any sightings of them, so naturally they don't appear in most reference guides. Next time you see one, remember to directly strike its temples. The one we just saw was a male, and that's fortunate. The females are even more terrifying—"

They hadn't yet said much to each other when more rustling came from the leaves overhead.

One by one, heads suspended upside down from threads of white silk descended from the trees.

Shen Qingqiu's expression completely changed.

Ghost-head spider cries attracted large numbers of them to encircle and attack their prey.

He swept his fan, releasing a powerful gust of wind and snapping dozens of silk threads. The ghost-head spiders smashed into the ground and thudded like overripe fruit.

"Go!" yelled Shen Qingqiu.

Luo Binghe sprang to action. While the ghost-head spiders were dazed and reeling, the entire group broke out into a run. Master and disciple, one in the lead carving a path, the other bringing up the rear, together sandwiched the bloated procession. The two ends slaughtered foes until it rained blood, the air thick with the stench of carnage. Ghost-head spiders were agile and possessed incredible jumping ability.

But as they flew and leapt through the air, the barrage of spiritual blasts fired by master and disciple punctured them like sieves.

Once Luo Binghe knew how to deal with these beasts, it was like he had been blessed by divinity. He could practically pierce two or more in a single blow with his eyes closed. The scene overhead was a mess of blood and gore, anguished wails and monstrous howls.

Even with all they accomplished, in the end, there were still too many, and they proved impossible to defend against. Just as Shen Qingqiu started to worry about when that goddamned hack of a poison would next act up, he felt his spiritual power stagnate, and his next strike came up empty.

Truly, speak of the devil!

Shen Qingqiu swiftly redirected the flow of his energy into a physical attack. With a flip of his hand, his fan sliced the ghost-head spider lunging toward him horizontally in two.

Luo Binghe had been paying keen attention to Shen Qingqiu's condition. He noticed something was off and asked, "Shizun?"

"It's nothing," Shen Qingqiu rushed to say. "Focus on yourself."

Fortunately, under Shen Qingqiu's leadership, they'd already reached a particular area. As if the ghost-head spiders had encountered an invisible barrier, they didn't dare advance and instead wailed and howled while falling back, until they at last withdrew into the shrubbery and trees—and vanished.

Shen Qingqiu let out a sigh of relief.

Delicately panting, her expression uncertain, Qin Wanyue asked, "Senior Shen, why were those demonic beasts unwilling to approach this place?"

"Have you forgotten what kind of mystical flower grows in Jue Di Gorge?" asked Shen Qingqiu.

In truth, the one who'd forgotten was him.

Forgive me for not remembering the flower's name!

Luo Binghe very considerately remembered for him, speaking the name right away. "Thousand-Leaves Fresh-Snow Lotus!"

Shen Qingqiu finally realized why he had been unable to remember the name.

The number of mystical flowers named "Something Snow Whatever" or "This and That Lotus" was such that they were more numerous than old memes. Like hell anyone could remember!

"Correct..." said Shen Qingqiu. "This is indeed the Thousand-Leaves Fresh-Snow Lotus. This flower has grown within the depths of Jue Di Gorge for thousands of years. Its spiritual qi is extraordinary, and furthermore, it is the natural bane of creatures from the Demon Realm. It emits an innate barrier that repels demonic beasts. Therefore, as long as we're within its protected zone, we won't suffer too many attacks."

"The natural bane of demonic creatures?" Luo Binghe suddenly asked. He'd been listening with rapt attention the entire time. Now intense sparks seemed to ignite within his gaze, which flickered faintly with a peculiar quality.

Shen Qingqiu thought it strange. "Yes?"

"Then Shizun, could this spray of Thousand-Leaves Fresh-Snow Lotus cure demonic poison?" Luo Binghe asked.

Shen Qingqiu was horrified. That look... Luo Binghe couldn't be...hoping to pick the mystical flower and cure him, right?

Stop. Do not pass go. The girl you're supposed to pick the flower for, Qin Wanyue, is right next to us, watching—and you want to deflower it in her presence, and for a big, strong man to boot?

Leave your wife some dignity, all right?!

"We should handle the crisis before us first," Shen Qingqiu said quickly.

But Luo Binghe wouldn't let it go. "This disciple asks for Shizun's instruction."

"It cannot do what you imply," said Shen Qingqiu.

"Has Shizun tried it before?" Luo Binghe pushed. "If we don't try, how can we know? This disciple knows that Shizun doesn't want him to take chances, but if we don't take this one, this disciple will never be at peace!"

This really isn't the time! Why must you be so filial at this critical juncture?! I can't tell you that the only way to completely cure the poison is to take a trip to pound town with you, okay?!

Shen Qingqiu couldn't say any of this in such terms. His expression became cold. "Has this master indulged you such that you think you can willfully fool around even at a time like this?"

To tell the truth, over these past few years, due to Shen Qingqiu's strange desire to preemptively atone—along with certain other sentiments—he'd never spoken to his disciple with even the slightest bit of harshness. So, once he did, Luo Binghe first startled. Then, as expected, he obediently shut his mouth. But his gaze remained obstinate, and he refused to sheath Zheng Yang, obviously unwilling to back down.

Just as the two reached a deadlock, the dense overgrowth of grass and leaves rustled, and a person stepped out. Behind him came a group of battered and exhausted disciples who had no doubt endured a bloody struggle.

On guard, Shen Qingqiu looked his way. As soon as he came face-to-face with the newcomer, he felt like a giant hammer from the sky had smashed into his temples.

In truth, this person's appearance could have been considered proper and handsome, it was just that in his every word and action there was an inescapable air of sleaziness. At the sight of Shen Qingqiu, he smiled and returned his sword, flowing with light, back to its sheath.

"So it was Shen-shixiong," he said. "Meeting up with you puts my heart at ease."

At ease. At ease my ass. With you here I can't be "at ease," okay?!

The person in front of him was the main culprit behind this catastrophe!

Shang Qinghua, a character that Shen Qingqiu had mentally roasted before with "He goes to Qinghua University, well I even took Beijing University's exam,"[10] was the Peak Lord of An Ding Peak. At the same time, he had another important identity: he was a spy, a pawn planted many years ago by the demons, and he had orchestrated the disaster at the Immortal Alliance Conference.

Long ago, Shang Qinghua had been only one of An Ding Peak's many insignificant and nameless disciples. Then he'd been captured by the demons, who had forced him to become a mole.

Ah, no, he hadn't really been *forced*—he happily took on the important task of being a mole without even a hint of discomfort.

Secretly backed by the demons, Shang Qinghua's road became smooth sailing. He swiftly rose through the ranks until he actually attained the position of Peak Lord of An Ding Peak.

However, he still wasn't satisfied. And why not? Because it was An Ding Peak!

---

10   The word "shang" can mean "to go to" in the sense of "going to a university," so the name Shang Qinghua read aloud sounds like "goes to Qinghua University." Qinghua (or Tsinghua) University and Beijing University are two top schools sometimes referred to as "the MIT and Harvard of China."

As soon as you heard the name, "stable and settled," you knew it wasn't a place for the ambitious. This peak's tradition and specialty was completely in line with its name—logistics.

So of course, the entire peak from top to bottom, including the peak lord, were like bricks, to be moved wherever they were needed. Send some cheap laborers here today, assist with supplies there tomorrow. Mountain gates broken? Get An Ding Peak to fix it. Missing a carriage driver? Get An Ding Peak to send someone. This month's expenses over budget and you need money? Get An Ding Peak to file a report.

Even if this kind of peak lord's professional competence trounced that of Lanxiang and New Oriental,[11] could they be called impressive? Were they imposing? Were they cool, awesome, insane, badass, or hyped?

Did they have the dignity of a peak lord?

Even a talented, low-level disciple from another peak would have more to brag about.

So, Shang Qinghua became a demon flunky without hesitation. He took it upon himself to help the demons conquer the Human Realm and committed all kinds of evil.

Shen Qingqiu's stomach hurt as soon as he saw the guy. "Shang-shidi," he said. "As you approached, did you see a large demonic beast nearby?"

Shang Qinghua froze. "A large demonic beast? That... There wasn't one."

Shen Qingqiu's heart thumped. There wasn't?

The large demonic beast in question was one of the plotline's key

---

11   Refers to Shandong Lanxiang Vocational School and New Oriental Education and Technology Group Inc. They're well known because of their ads, so this is a derogatory reference.

devices. In the original work, Luo Binghe's demonic heritage was exposed because someone released a Black Moon Rhinoceros-Python at the Immortal Alliance Conference.

To protect the innocent, Luo Binghe engaged it in a life-or-death struggle. The Black Moon Rhinoceros-Python's destructive power and body were both enormous. Of course he couldn't defeat it. What to do if he couldn't win?

Activate SEED[12] mode.

In so doing, Luo Binghe exposed himself to Shen Qingqiu. Only then did Shen Qingqiu have the excuse to strike him down: eliminating one's companion for the sake of justice. And when he struck his student down, he enabled Luo Binghe to level up.

Thus far, Shen Qingqiu hadn't sensed the demonic qi of the Black Moon Rhinoceros-Python, much less heard its signature moonward howl—described in enigmatic fashion as "like that of both a python and a rhinoceros." Now Shang Qinghua said he hadn't even seen it. Shen Qingqiu couldn't help being on his guard. Without this key plot device, surely the System couldn't ask him to suddenly strike Luo Binghe without any justification?

He couldn't help but glance at the silent, unspeaking Luo Binghe. The child was still struggling with the matter of whether he should pick the flower to cure his master's poison. There was a stubborn glint in his eyes, as if he still felt a little discontent.

Discontent my ass! Come on, I'm doing this for your own good. If you're going to pick flowers, don't give them to the wrong person, thank you!

"On my way here, we lost quite a few disciples from various sects," said Shang Qinghua, tone full of grief and lamentation. "They were

---

12 Reference to an ability in the series Mobile Suit Gundam SEED that allows someone to enter an enhanced state.

all future pillars of the cultivation world. The person who released these demonic creatures is truly poisonous and shameless, underhanded and vulgar, cruel to the point of insanity!"

Shen Qingqiu was speechless. *Weren't you the one who released those creatures? Are you really okay with using these lines to attack yourself? Although if you don't mind, that's fine…*

He hadn't finished his mental roast when, without warning, the earth began to shake.

People staggered and fell all over the place, terrified and confused, their questioning voices merging into one.

Shen Qingqiu's pupils contracted.

There was no mistaking the sensation of a magnitude 7.5 earthquake. The Endless Abyss had finally been opened.

The so-called Endless Abyss was on the boundary between the Human and Demon Realms. A liminal space, it was full of peril and the unknown. Twisting, tearing vortices through space, raging flames, and burning magma were everywhere to be found.

The disciples on the scene had fought the entire way there, and their bodies and hearts had long been completely exhausted. After that violent quake, most of them tumbled to the ground. Only Shen Qingqiu, Luo Binghe, and Shang Qinghua managed to stay standing.

Since the Endless Abyss had been opened, that meant something demonic would definitely appear from the other side. The three held their breaths in anticipation, silently waiting and on full alert.

The figure of a man slowly emerged from the shadows.

As soon as Shen Qingqiu saw that ice-cold face and aloof expression, he knew who it was. He shot a glance at Shang Qinghua, whose whole face had gone white. Shen Qingqiu wanted to laugh, but he was unable to.

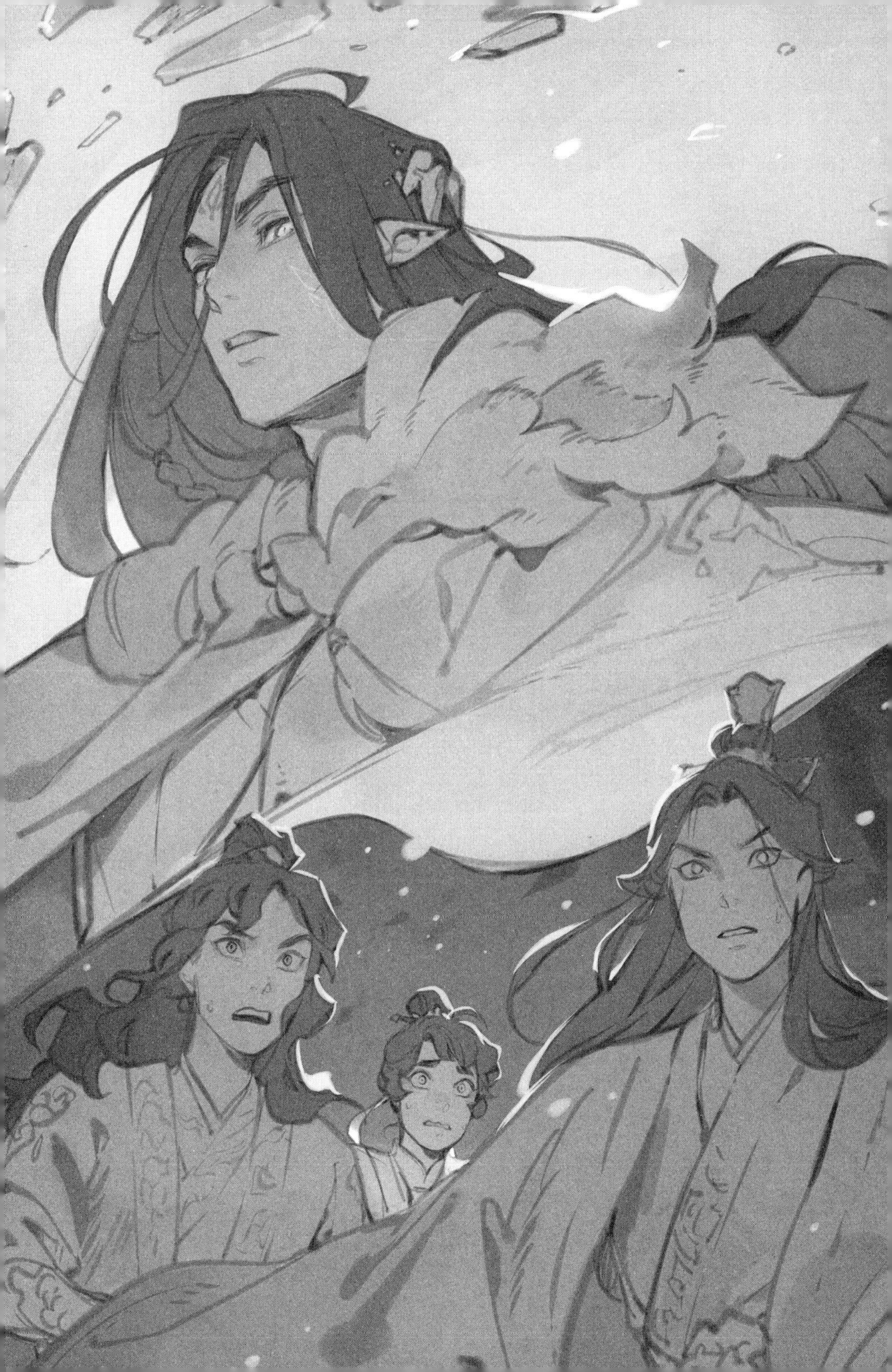

Why would Luo Binghe's future subordinate, his magnificent right hand—and best buddy for committing evil deeds, murder, and mayhem—show up right here and now?!

Mobei-Jun was a pure-blooded demon, a supremely orthodox demonic second-gen. In the future, he would inherit his family's territory on the demonic border in the north, and after that, he would spend all his time appearing and disappearing at will, idling his life away, completely indifferent to everyone else. However, this maverick was destined to get beaten up by a Luo Binghe who had suddenly activated his overpowered abilities. Thereafter, he would mysteriously capitulate to the protagonist, to the point of letting himself be ordered about. From then on, Luo Binghe would have an exceptionally badass-looking errand boy and loyal sidekick.

But to be clear, according to the original timeline, there are still five hundred chapters before it's your turn to debut, Great Master!

"Who is this distinguished one?" Shang Qinghua yelled as he rushed forward. "Why have you come to this place?"

Isn't that your real boss? Wasn't he the one who ordered you to release those dangerous creatures into Jue Di Gorge? No, no, please go right ahead and keep pretending.

Mobei-Jun tilted his head. Half of his handsome silhouette sank into the darkness, a chilling sight. With a half-hearted flick of his finger, he flung Shang Qinghua into the air with sudden force. Shang Qinghua crashed into an old tree and fainted, blood spurting unceasingly from his mouth—spurting until Shen Qingqiu couldn't help but sigh with respect.

Such effort, such dedication. Bro, you sure do a lot for your career!

After paying his respects, he sighed again. He'd known it would go this way. In the end, he would still need to step in.

Holding his sword before him, Shen Qingqiu spoke, neither humble nor haughty. "A demon?"

This line was pointless bullshit. Anyone who couldn't see those murky billows of demonic qi would have had to be blind.

A white figure flashed past him. Without saying a word, Luo Binghe had moved to stand in front of his teacher.

They'd just argued, and they now faced a powerful enemy, yet he still played the role of a human shield without hesitation. It would have been a lie to say Shen Qingqiu was entirely unmoved.

But the more moved he was, the more he felt that what he was about to do was just too cruel. Shen Qingqiu wished that his student had done nothing at all.

"Binghe, stand down," he said.

Luo Binghe did not reply, and he did not leave. He calmly met eyes with Mobei-Jun, entirely unaffected by his imposing aura.

Mobei-Jun let out an "eh?" of curiosity, like he'd found something that aroused his interest a little.

"What disciple has to shield his master?" snapped Shen Qingqiu.

"You are a disciple of Cang Qiong Mountain?" asked Mobei-Jun.

"Disciple of Cang Qiong Mountain's Qing Jing Peak, Luo Binghe, thanks this distinguished one for his guidance," Luo Binghe replied coldly, his tone sarcastic.

Mobei-Jun sneered. "The immortal acts unlike an immortal, and the demon acts unlike a demon. Interesting."

At this, Shen Qingqiu finally caught on to something. Could it be…that Mobei-Jun's appearance was a substitute for the Black Moon Rhinoceros-Python's role in advancing the main storyline?

"Immortal" probably referred to Shang Qinghua, who was lying off to the side and playing dead while occasionally remembering to cough up blood. Though clearly a cultivator, he tirelessly labored for the Demon Realm—indeed completely unlike an immortal. That was a fair accusation. As for the "demon," who on the scene could this refer to other than Luo Binghe?

Shen Qingqiu's thoughts turned and whirled. He wasn't sure if Mobei-Jun could really see Luo Binghe's hidden bloodline with a single glance.

Luo Binghe saw his master's furrowed brow and feared he was angry at his own disobedience. "Shizun, he won't let any of us go. It'd be better to use all our strength and fight this battle together."

That's true, but it'd also be fucking useless. But Shen Qingqiu said, "If you stay here, you'll lose your life in vain."

"Dying for Shizun or dying together with Shizun, either one is something this disciple would gladly do," said Luo Binghe.

Mobei-Jun scoffed. "You'd do battle with me?" The following "such foolish arrogance" was left politely unspoken.

Good thing you didn't say it out loud, thought Shen Qingqiu. *In three years, Luo Binghe will be able to single-handedly beat you until you can't get up—and won't you still become his diligent henchman? You'd really be slapping your own face.*

"Fine," said Mobei-Jun. "Then let me see."

Before he had finished speaking, the killing intent in the air around them spiked.

His steps agile and unreadable, Shen Qingqiu flashed in front of Luo Binghe. With his left hand, he tossed forth Xiu Ya to hold off Mobei-Jun for a bit, even if it would be largely ineffective. At the same time, with his right hand, he lifted Luo Binghe like an eagle would a chick and hurled him away. Once he'd sent Luo Binghe outside the range of Mobei-Jun's demonic qi, he turned and met palms with Mobei-Jun.

When their palms connected, blood churned in Shen Qingqiu's chest as if someone had punched him there. The spiritual energy in his body surged like it was boiling over. Though he had already formed a core and his cultivation wasn't low, what was a golden core against the right hand of the future demon lord, Luo Binghe?

But he had to go all out and try.

Throwing himself into a desperate battle to the death without regard for his own life was the only way to survive this. According to Shen Qingqiu's experience from ten-plus years of reading all sorts of wuxia and xianxia novels, temperamental chuunis[13] had a modicum of respect for hardheaded types who fought bloody battles to the end and refused to admit defeat. But they definitely didn't show any mercy to cowards and weaklings!

Having been caught off guard and hurled away by Shen Qingqiu, Luo Binghe doubled back, unsheathing Zheng Yang. Mobei-Jun spared one hand to flick away the white sword glare he threw. Zheng Yang couldn't withstand the massive influx of demonic energy, and in an explosion of white light, it shattered into pieces on the spot.

Mobei-Jun held off both of Shen Qingqiu's hands with just one of his own, his power overwhelmingly superior. Bored, he blasted Shen Qingqiu away.

"Unusually inferior talent," he said. "Foundation and techniques inflexible. Leave."

Shen Qingqiu said nothing.

He wasn't some unmatched genius in the Human Realm, but his talent was still at least one in a thousand. And Cang Qiong Mountain's foundation and techniques weren't *inflexible*, they

---

13 Shortened form of Japanese "chuunibyou," or "middle school second-year disease." Describes people who are "edgy" or have delusions of grandeur. Used as a loanword in the Chinese text.

were orthodox! Mobei-Jun still described them as he would a pile of garbage. If the original Shen Qingqiu had heard this, he would have coughed up three liters of blood and run away crying to make a voodoo doll.

Luo Binghe didn't care that his sword was broken. When he saw Shen Qingqiu injured by this palm strike, blood dripping from between gritted teeth, Luo Binghe's gaze frosted over, his aura changing in an instant. Sensing this shocking change, a cold flash of interest shot through Mobei-Jun's pale blue eyes. He abruptly summoned a pure-black sword of ice out of thin air. That one blade became two, two became four, four became eight, instantly dividing into an array of hundreds of ice swords—which shot at the surrounded Shen Qingqiu from all directions.

No normal defense technique could possibly block these ice swords; they were crystallized from the purest demonic qi. Shen Qingqiu's spiritual qi was nearly exhausted. If his power collided with Mobei-Jun's, it would be like a single spark against a towering wave. The end result went without saying.

Just as the sword array was about to come down like sheets of rain, Shen Qingqiu snarled within his heart.

I've done my best, but he still thinks I'm low-level trash, so what can I do?!

How loathsome! If I have to die, couldn't it at least be in a better-looking way? After being stabbed with hundreds of black swords, I'm going to be a sieve! Who could bear to look?!

However, even long moments after, the pain of being skewered by thousands of swords did not arrive.

Unless Mobei-Jun had suddenly lost his mind and revoked the sword array, there was only one explanation—only one person who could have blocked this attack that seethed with murderous intent.

Shen Qingqiu steadied himself and slowly raised his head.

As expected.

In the air all around him, the forest of swords had shattered.

They'd splintered so completely that it was like they'd disappeared without a trace, leaving only a night sky full of black ice crystals. Reflecting the moonlight, they fell one by one.

This scene could have been described as beautiful.

However, Luo Binghe, standing in the middle of it, was the center of a blizzard that seemed to roar around him and within his gaze. He could only be described as terrifying.

Shen Qingqiu collapsed next to a large tree, swallowing mouthfuls of blood. He circulated energy to heal his wounds while watching this earthshaking showdown between two demon lords.

The seal on Luo Binghe's blood had yet to be removed. Mobei-Jun was only testing him, but still this battle darkened the sky and earth, blotting out all light. Raging waves of demonic energy overflowed from both of them, enough to cloak the entire sky.

Wasn't this area within range of the—the Thousand-Leaves Fresh-Snow Lotus? That was what that thing was called, right? Right, demonic creatures were supposed to be afraid to approach its proximity. But as soon as this inescapable smog of demonic qi touched the flower, the Snow Lotus that brimmed with spiritual qi wilted and rotted down to its roots.

All the demonic creatures hiding in the dark crept out one by one, greedily inhaling what to them was a fragrant scent.

Several ghost-head spiders stealthily crawled onto a few of the Cang Qiong Mountain disciples, hairy legs poised to stab into their temples. Shen Qingqiu was nearly out of spiritual energy and was unable to use spell attacks. He could only directly grab the beasts by their filthy, tangled hair and throw them aside. He aimed before he threw, making sure to toss them toward that traitor, Shang Qinghua.

Meanwhile, Mobei-Jun had pretty much finished testing Luo Binghe, and he prepared to wrap things up, sending out one last blow. With a flick of his finger, he fired a stream of scarlet light at the center of Luo Binghe's forehead.

Once that stream of light touched Luo Binghe's brow, it seeped into his skin, turning into a fiery red mark. Luo Binghe was lost to his bloodlust. He didn't know why, only that his head ached like it was about to explode, and he nearly collapsed to his knees. His entire body roiled with a desire to inflict savage cruelty. Unable to vent it, he threw out his hand, and as if shot out of a cannon, an eruption of demonic qi descended upon Mobei-Jun.

This last strike was extremely powerful.

Yet Mobei-Jun waved it away with one hand, a bit surprised. "Not bad." Ignoring whether Luo Binghe was in a state to understand him, he continued. "The Human Realm isn't where you belong. Why not return to your origins?"

Now Shen Qingqiu was finally one hundred percent sure. Mobei-Jun's sudden appearance was indeed a substitute for the Black Moon Rhinoceros-Python. But compared to the original, Mobei-Jun had done a far more thorough job.

He...he...he...he'd actually directly removed the seal suppressing Luo Binghe's demonic blood!

And after completing his task, he turned right around and left.

This NPC really was so straight to the point, not a moment spared—completely in line with his modus operandi in the original work. He'd show up wherever Luo Binghe needed him without rhyme or reason. His actions were just that forced, a total maverick, needing not a shred of logic!

Speaking of forced, that could only be how Shen Qingqiu would face his next task: the last level.

Having fought a harsh battle, Luo Binghe was half-kneeling in the midst of a ruined landscape, his eyes vacant, but it looked like his placid veneer would at any moment tear. Right now, his mind was like a dormant volcano, one that had suddenly erupted after being silent for many years, the magma in its veins starting to flow. Just thinking about this made Shen Qingqiu feel like he was burning up along with it, until his bones and head began to ache and pound.

The System sent a shrill notification the likes of which he'd never heard before.

[Warning! The critical quest "The Endless Abyss and Endless Hatred, a Sky Filled with Crystal Frost and Tears of Blood" has officially begun! If it is not successfully completed, twenty thousand protagonist satisfaction points will be deducted!]

Was it Shen Qingqiu's imagination, or were the quest names getting more and more absurd every time, to the point that Shen Qingqiu didn't even know where to begin roasting them?

And hey, when I confirmed with you a while back, wasn't it ten thousand? It's been like five minutes, and now it's doubled?

Swaying, Shen Qingqiu walked over to Luo Binghe, who was still in a half-crazed state. He unleashed a couple of palm strikes on his back, channeling some of his own remaining spiritual energy into his student's body.

You think it's going to be that easy? Dream on!

Not only did Luo Binghe fail to regain consciousness, the demonic qi within his body rebounded Shen Qingqiu's efforts, forcing Shen Qingqiu to cough up the mouthful of blood he'd been holding back for so long.

Only at this moment did Luo Binghe finally recover some awareness.

He slowly pulled himself out of his muddled state and managed to piece together a couple of mangled words. That familiar face also gradually came into focus.

Shen Qingqiu saw Luo Binghe's gaze clear a bit and let out a sigh of relief. He wiped at the blood by his mouth and asked in an even tone, "You're awake?" After a pause, "If you're awake, let's have a thorough discussion. Luo Binghe, tell me honestly, exactly how long have you been practicing demonic cultivation?"

As soon as he said this, it was as if Luo Binghe had been plunged from the stifling upper heavens into a bone-chilling pool. It would have been impossible for him to not return to complete consciousness.

He stared at Shen Qingqiu's wintry face, and his heart sank straight down. In the past, Shen Qingqiu had always called him Binghe—he had never been addressed by his full name.

"Shizun," he said quietly, "this disciple can explain."

Though Luo Binghe was still a youth, he'd always remained calm and unperturbed, often acting mature beyond his years. Now actual panic surfaced on his face, like he was frantic to explain but didn't know where to start.

Seeing the oh-so-mighty male lead reduced to this state, Shen Qingqiu couldn't stand to watch anymore. He burst out to cut him off. "Silence!"

His voice had only just left his mouth, and he already felt like he hadn't properly controlled himself—that his tone had been overly harsh. He seemed to have scared Luo Binghe. The boy stared at him blankly with pitch-black eyes, like a child who'd been slapped, muddled and confused, and indeed he obediently went silent.

"When did you start?" Shen Qingqiu stiffly recited the line, unable to harden his heart enough to look his student in the eyes.

"Two years ago."

Shen Qingqiu went silent and didn't speak. To answer his question so quickly, and so honestly to boot—it seemed Luo Binghe really was scared witless.

Unbeknownst to him, Luo Binghe automatically took this silence to mean: "Is that so? You wicked disciple, you managed to hide this from me for so long!"

"Two years," Shen Qingqiu said quietly. "No wonder you were able to progress by leaps and bounds, and to such an extent. You truly live up to your reputation, Luo Binghe. You are gifted with spectacular talent."

In truth, these words he spoke were purely an expression of the regrets within his heart. As the male lead, Luo Binghe was indeed blessed with spectacular talent. If Shen Qingqiu had to describe what he was feeling with absolute honesty, it was admiration, with the tiniest bit of envy.

But to Luo Binghe's ears, his meaning was completely different. He instantly fell to his knees before Shen Qingqiu.

Shen Qingqiu's soul almost left his body. If a man kneeling was worth his weight in gold, the male lead kneeling was worth your life. Letting him kneel at this critical juncture—when Luo Binghe remembered it in the future, wouldn't his hatred be compounded?

"Get up!" Shen Qingqiu waved his sleeve at once.

Hit by the gust from this wave, Luo Binghe couldn't help but stand again and back up a few steps, even more stunned out of his senses.

Had he done something wrong? Something so wrong that it couldn't be absolved—that he didn't even have the right to kneel and plead Shizun for forgiveness?

"But Shizun, you said before that just as people can be good or bad, demons can be good or evil," he mumbled. "That in this world, there is no one...intolerable to the heavens."

I said that? It had been many years. Shen Qingqiu thought intently for a while.

It seemed like he really had said that!

But that had been then, when he'd been considering a far-off future. This was now, in the midst of a crisis with a blade suspended above his throat.

This was a last resort, but would it be too shameless to slap his own face by doubling down?

"You are no simple demon," Shen Qingqiu said. "That mark on your forehead is a mark of sin—the mark of the demons who fell from the heavens. These demons have murdered countless humans, and moreover, their temperaments are impossible to contain. From ancient times, they've been the cause of calamity upon calamity. Under no circumstances can they be spoken of in the same breath as other demons. I cannot wait and hope my earlier words were true while you develop a taste for slaughter and lose all control."

As these words touched his ears, Luo Binghe's hopes shattered, and the rims of his eyes reddened. His voice quivered. "But you said..."

I've said a lot of things, okay? I even once made several hundred posts in bright red font about wanting to castrate Shen Qingqiu—

It wasn't the least bit funny.

Shen Qingqiu, who'd always been so good at mental gymnastics, reached a new high in his number of mental roasts, madly smashing through his old records—yet he still couldn't put himself at ease, and instead he only grew more tired and worn out.

He relentlessly told himself to the point of auto-brainwashing: the suffering and torment Luo Binghe endured now was all necessary in order for him to stand above the masses in the future.

Without enduring the bone-chilling cold / How could fragrant plum blossoms hope to bloom / Without three years' training in realms below / How could a demon king over worlds loom?

Xin Mo in hand, he would possess everything beneath the heavens / With a harem innumerable, he need not be an incel...

But it was useless.

It was completely useless. Nothing could lift his spirits.

Shen Qingqiu raised his head and formed a sword seal to summon Xiu Ya, and he held it within his hand. The hand wielding the sword shook slightly, thin veins surfacing through his skin.

"Shizun, do you really want to kill me?" Luo Binghe couldn't believe it.

"I don't want to kill you." Unable to look at his expression, Shen Qingqiu's gaze went right through him.

Luo Binghe searched his memory, but he'd never seen Shen Qingqiu so cold and emotionless, not toward him. Even back when he'd just entered Cang Qiong Mountain Sect, when Shizun had disliked him, his eyes had never been this empty—like he was looking at nothing.

His gaze held not even a trace of warmth. It was exactly the way he'd looked at heinous demons whom he had executed with that same sword.

"It's only, what that man said wasn't wrong," said Shen Qingqiu. "The Human Realm is no longer a place for you. You ought to return to the place you belong."

He stepped forward, and Luo Binghe stepped back. Shen Qingqiu pressed him backward until they were right on the edge of the Endless Abyss.

If one looked into the ravine, they would see the simmering demonic qi roiling unceasingly within it, and they would hear the anguished wailing of tens of thousands of spirits. Hundreds and thousands of deformed arms reached up from the cracks toward the Human Realm, hungering for fresh blood and flesh. The deeper regions faded into black fog and eerie scarlet light.

"Will you go down yourself, or must I force you?" Shen Qingqiu asked, Xiu Ya pointing toward the abyss.

He selfishly hoped that Luo Binghe would go of his own volition. In this kind of scenario, characters who chose to jump from cliffs were always caught on something—then Shen Qingqiu could go on believing his own lies that this scene would have a happy end.

Better that than this moment being carved into Shen Qingqiu's memory from here on out, forcing him to remember night and day that he had shoved Luo Binghe down with his own two hands.

But Luo Binghe refused to give up hope.

He refused to believe that the teacher who had been so kind to him would actually hurt him. He refused to believe that all those years of companionship every day, morning to night, could lead to this conclusion.

Even as Xiu Ya stabbed into his chest, he clung to a last strand of hope.

Shen Qingqiu hadn't meant to stab him.

He really hadn't. He was only steeling himself, waving his sword around in order to scare Luo Binghe. If Luo Binghe had stepped back once more to avoid his swings, he'd have naturally fallen in. Shen Qingqiu had never predicted that Luo Binghe would simply silently stand there, taking the blade head-on.

It was all over. In the original work, Luo Binghe was only kicked into the abyss—now there was this extra stab to add to his grudge!

Luo Binghe lifted his hand to grip the blade, but he didn't use any of his strength and only lightly held it. If Shen Qingqiu decided to exert force, Xiu Ya would continue to stab into him until it pierced straight through his chest.

Luo Binghe's throat lightly bobbed; he said not a single word. The blade point clearly hadn't pierced his heart, yet Shen Qingqiu felt like he could feel that heart's pained thumps, traveling up the blade and into his hand, spreading through his entire arm, until they arrived directly at his own heart.

Shen Qingqiu suddenly withdrew the sword.

With that action, Luo Binghe's body swayed a little, but he quickly steadied himself. Realizing that Shen Qingqiu hadn't dealt him a killing blow, his eyes, which had dimmed faintly, shone once more, like sparks struggling within burnt ashes. The corner of his mouth also managed to twitch. Perhaps he was trying to smile.

Then Shen Qingqiu unleashed a final strike, which extinguished the last trace of light within Luo Binghe's eyes.

He knew he would never forget Luo Binghe's expression from the moment of his fall.

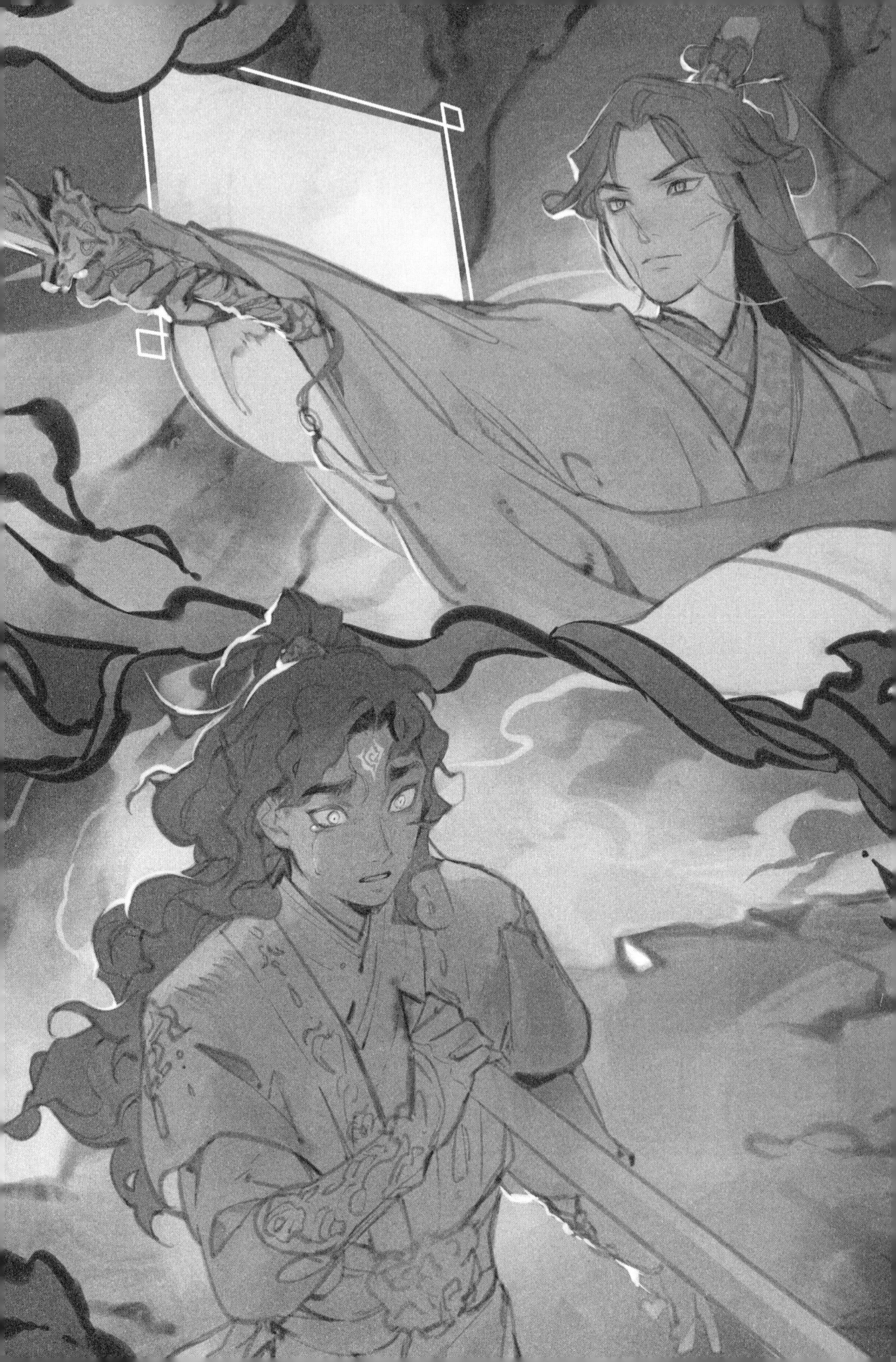

By the time the sect leaders and other cultivators arrived, having finished clearing out the demons within Jue Di Gorge, the spatial rift caused by the Endless Abyss had long since closed.

Other than Shang Qinghua, who was playing dead, Shen Qingqiu had stabilized the injuries of everyone who'd passed out, but he hadn't really paid attention to his own. His robes splattered with blood, his face expressionless and stark white, he looked quite wretched.

Yue Qingyuan stepped forward to check Shen Qingqiu's pulse and condition, then frowned and asked Mu Qingfang, as the expert, to examine him. The cultivators of each sect picked out their disciples from among the bodies scattered across the ground, then whisked them away for further treatment.

Liu Qingge sensed that they were short one person. Then he realized it was the person who was always flitting around Shen Qingqiu, impossible to miss.

"Where's that disciple of yours?" he asked.

Head lowered, Shen Qingqiu didn't answer. He picked up the shattered pieces of a longsword lying on the ground, which had broken into many fragments.

Qing Jing Peak's disciples had hurried to the scene. The sharp-eyed Ming Fan, who had been leading them, looked at that sword and stammered, "Shizun, that sword can't be..."

Ming Fan had yearned for the Zheng Yang sword on Wan Jian Peak, and he had spent many years thinking about it. After Luo Binghe had claimed it, his entire body had burned with envy, and for many nights he'd cursed while tossing and turning. He definitely couldn't mistake it.

Ning Yingying let out a sudden loud wail. "Shizun, d-don't scare me. Is that...is that A-Luo's Zheng Yang? It can't be, right? It can't be!"

A wave of whispers flowed around them.

"Zheng Yang?"

"They're talking about Peak Lord Shen's beloved disciple, Luo Binghe?"

"A sword shares its existence with its master. If the sword is broken, then where is he?"

"Could he have...ahem."

Someone sighed. "If this is really what happened, that's truly a great pity. In the midst of all this, Luo Binghe had become the Immortal Alliance Conference's top ranker."

"Heaven envies talent, heaven envies talent!"

There were those who sighed in pity, those who were stunned, those who were sorrowful, and those who rejoiced in the misfortune of others.

Ning Yingying burst into wailing tears on the spot.

Though Ming Fan hated Luo Binghe and was always cursing at him to go die, he'd never really wanted him dead. Moreover, when he thought about how much Shizun had adored him, and how this shitty brat had died without even leaving a corpse—Shizun had to be terribly sad, and Ming Fan couldn't be happy about that either.

Gloom and anxiety fell over the entirety of Qing Jing Peak's delegation. Xian Shu Peak's group of women, with Qi Qingqi as their head, were also deeply moved.

Liu Qingge wasn't good with words. He patted Shen Qingqiu's shoulder. "Your disciple is gone, but you can still accept more."

Though he knew Liu Qingge was trying to comfort him, Shen Qingqiu still wanted to feebly roll his eyes at him.

People who hadn't kicked their favorite disciple—who was also the male lead—into the Endless Abyss were all just commentating from the sidelines!

Whatever. What's done is done.

"Qing Jing Peak's disciple Luo Binghe," Shen Qingqiu said slowly, "fell to the demons and perished."

That year's Immortal Alliance Conference was a greater disaster than nearly any since its inception.

Over a thousand new talents from every sect had participated in the conference. Of the four great sects, the members of Zhao Hua Monastery, who'd focused on supporting the barrier spell, had luckily been spared, while Huan Hua Palace had suffered the greatest losses, to the tune of nearly a hundred participants. Cang Qiong Mountain had taken the least damage, with only thirty or so injured.

The newcomers with low skill and meager cultivation largely hailed from the other assorted sects and clans. This was the group that had been hit hardest and taken the most casualties.

Getting your name on the gold-inscribed tablet should have been a joyous occasion, but this year, many of the people listed on that tablet had perished in Jue Di Gorge. Most heartbreaking of all was the first-ranked name, high at the top of the list—a member of Cang Qiong Mountain's Qing Jing Peak and Shen Qingqiu's beloved disciple, Luo Binghe, deceased, his sword broken.

This was to say nothing of the casualties among the cultivators who had joined the fray to give aid during the incident. In this battle, each sect had suffered major losses.

A red ranking chart was delivered to Qing Jing Peak. "Luo Binghe" was written high at the top in first place, glittering in gold.

Ming Fan walked in to report. "Shizun, ten thousand spirit stones were delivered, what should be done with them?"

Ten thousand spirit stones? Shen Qingqiu stared at him blankly. "Why would they suddenly send so many spirit stones up the mountain?"

"Shizun, have you forgotten?" Ming Fan asked carefully. "At the Immortal Alliance Conference, you bet five thousand..."

Now Shen Qingqiu remembered. It was the bet he had placed on Luo Binghe. Yue Qingyuan had said that any losses would be his to pay, while Shen Qingqiu could keep any winnings for himself.

Sure enough, Luo Binghe had made a good showing, and in the final hour, he had shot past the first- and second-ranked Gongyi Xiao and Liu Mingyan to perch at the head of the rankings, thereby earning his master double his initial investment.

At the time, Shen Qingqiu had thought that profit was profit and that he might as well receive a consolation prize, but now he was at a bit of a loss.

In the past, he had always given these things to Luo Binghe to handle—where the gift should be saved or whether it should be used to trade for something else, and if so, how to do so. He'd never had to worry about such things himself. Now Ming Fan was asking him what to do.

Shen Qingqiu thought for a while, then said, "Put them away for now."

Ming Fan was silent. He actually wanted to ask for more instruction, like "*Where* should I put it?" But his master's face really didn't look too good, so he was afraid to press for answers. He thought, *It should be fine if I put them where Luo Binghe used to put things,* and immediately withdrew.

For many days, Qing Jing Peak's disciples walked on eggshells, doing their best to avoid the elephant in the room, afraid of touching their master's sore spot. They all thought that after a few days, things would eventually take a turn for the better.

Then, after half a month had passed and Shen Qingqiu seemed to be gradually returning to normal, one day, right before mealtime, they suddenly heard Shen Qingqiu call Luo Binghe's name a few times from the Bamboo House.

With a thud-thud-thud, Ning Yingying burst inside, giving Shen Qingqiu a scare.

"What are you doing?" he asked. "Charging in here so suddenly— it's unsightly for a lady to act so rough and undisciplined."

Ning Yingying's eyes were red, like that of a little bunny's. "Shizun, you—whatever you want to eat, I'll make it for you!"

Shen Qingqiu coughed. "No need. Go out and play."

"Shizun!" Ning Yingying stamped her foot. "Even if A-Luo is gone, you...you still have the rest of your disciples. You're so...out of your mind with grief, we disciples—we disciples are worried to death!"

Shen Qingqiu would never have expected someone to use the words "out of your mind" to describe him.

Actually, now that he'd reached the Core Formation stage, it didn't matter whether he ate or not. He'd just had a sudden craving and wanted to eat some snacks, and he had for a moment forgotten that he'd already thrown Luo Binghe into the Endless Abyss. How did that count as being "out of his mind"?!

Shen Qingqiu opened his mouth, a hundred words of protest ready to spill forth, but seeing Ning Yingying nearly about to cry from anxiety, he hurriedly went to comfort her instead. Only after he swore solemnly that his calls just now had been a mere slip of the tongue did she calm down.

After coaxing her back outside, Shen Qingqiu let out a long sigh. He suddenly felt that this little miss, who in the original novel had always been pampered and childish, only capable of getting in trouble and being a burden, had in fact grown up quite a bit.

After all, she was one of Luo Binghe's harem. *She* was the one who was supposed to be clawing at the ground, wailing to the heavens—but instead she'd come to comfort her master.

Had his instruction actually had some effect?

Either way, things couldn't go on like this any longer.

Clearly Shen Qingqiu was the one who'd raised that little lamb of a protagonist, so why did it seem like the protagonist had been the one looking after him? He was scaring his disciples, putting on the act of a grieving widow whose husband had just died. Hadn't it been only a couple of days since he'd last seen that child?

No! Bah! Shen Qingqiu mentally slapped himself. *Who are you calling a grieving widow?! Whose husband died?! That's not something you should just* say—*you're really getting worse by the day. A negative mindset produces nothing good. You* deserve *a slap!*

But, perhaps because Luo Binghe had left, he really was a bit lonely. Especially when he thought about how five years from now, when they reunited, a relationship that had once been that of a compassionate teacher and filial disciple (or something) would become defined by veiled murderous intent and daggers hidden within smiles.

Shen Qingqiu had brought the broken pieces of Zheng Yang back with him. He messily dug a hole behind Qing Jing Peak's Bamboo House, erected a tablet, and set up a sword mound. When others saw him lost in thought as he faced that empty tablet, they thought he was reminiscing about his beloved disciple, and they could only sigh. What a deep master-and-disciple bond! Fate toys with us all.

Only Shen Qingqiu knew that the one he was mourning was in truth within that sword mound, buried underneath and never to return: that youth as warm as the sun.

What truly broke him and caused him to weep at the heavens was that, after several days of silence, the System sent him a message truly devoid of all humanity.

[Congratulations! You have successfully completed the key quest, "The Legend Begins: Luo Binghe's Fall and Rebirth." Reward: Protagonist satisfaction points +10,000.]

Before Shen Qingqiu even had the chance to be pleased, it continued:

[However, due to extraordinary circumstances, a new point value has been activated: Luo Binghe's heartbreak points. Due to excessively high heartbreak level, protagonist satisfaction points have been reset to zero. Please continue to work hard!]

Reset to zero... Reset to zero... Reset to zero...

Those three large words looped endlessly within Shen Qingqiu's mind.

What the hell are these heartbreak points?! Didn't I tell you not to randomly activate strange point values?! Fuck off! So Luo Binghe really is your darling son—even his heartbreak gets a point value of its own?!

Years of slaving away at the System's every command, and he was back to square one in a single night.

Being a villain was true misery / Grievances enough to fill the ocean.

Being so unhappy, naturally Shen Qingqiu had to go take it out on someone else. So, he had Ming Fan deliver a message inviting Shang Qinghua to the Bamboo House.

Shang Qinghua placed down the porcelain tea bowl and smiled. "Shen-shixiong's Qing Jing Peak is truly elegant and secluded. Even this mere tea bowl is exquisite. Such sophistication truly makes Qinghua feel ashamed."

Qing Jing Peak and An Ding Peak had always minded their respective business. Shen Qingqiu was reserved and aloof and very rarely took the initiative to invite guests, but this time he had actually sent a disciple to An Ding Peak with an invitation. Shang Qinghua was unable to discern what he wanted. But no one slaps a smiling face, so he started out with compliments. At least that couldn't be a misstep.

Shen Qingqiu dismissed the disciples, closed the door, and sighed. "Shidi, with these words of yours, everything I see begins to bring up old memories. Every plank, every dish in this Qing Jing Bamboo House was personally arranged by that disciple of mine."

Shang Qinghua said nothing but sighed along with him. "Ah, Luo-shizhi was a heroic youth, such a pity. Those demons brought such disaster upon us; they are truly hateful. The whole world mourns with us. Shen-shixiong, my condolences."

"If Shang-shidi truly felt it was a pity, this tragedy would not have occurred," Shen Qingqiu said faintly.

At this, Shang Qinghua stiffened. After a moment, he seamlessly smoothed things over with a smile. "What does Shen-shixiong mean by that? Is he rebuking our An Ding Peak for inadequate administration? If so, Shidi should truly apologize."

Shen Qingqiu refilled his teacup. "How was it inadequate? You clearly overexerted yourself. You even found demonic creatures like the ghost-head spiders, Nu Yuan Chan, and bone eagles—none of which ever enter the Human Realm of their own volition. How could Shixiong rebuke you for inadequacy?"

"Peak Lord Shen—to make such outrageous accusations!" Shang Qinghua shot to his feet, his face rapidly changing colors.

Shen Qingqiu put his hand on Shang Qinghua's shoulder. "Why is Shang-shidi getting so excited?" he asked solemnly. "Let's sit down and talk. Let me say something. Do you dare respond?"

"Why wouldn't I? I have a clear conscience. Why would I fear a false accusation?" With a sneer, Shang Qinghua brushed away his hand.

"Airplane Shooting Towards the Sky?" asked Shen Qingqiu.

In that instant, it was like a bolt of lightning from the heavens had struck Shang Qinghua in the head, rendering him unable to speak.

After a long time, he managed to stammer out, "You... How do you know my ID?"

In that moment, it was like Shen Qingqiu had also been burnt to a crisp by the aforementioned bolt of lightning.

He'd only wanted to study Shang Qinghua's reaction to this name to determine if he had also read *Proud Immortal Demon Way*—but given his reaction...he wasn't just a reader, was he?!

After three long seconds, Shen Qingqiu jumped on him.

"It's you?! How could I not know your ID after reading your entire fucking novel?! If you hadn't let something slip when Mobei-Jun appeared, I really never would have known what hole you'd really crawled out of, 'Great Master'!"

5
Bai Lu

THE MOMENT Shang Qinghua had seen Mobei-Jun suddenly appear, he had accidentally let out a "WTF!"

At the time, Shen Qingqiu hadn't heard him particularly clearly, so he hadn't paid it any mind. But afterward, the more he'd thought about it, the more suspicious he'd grown.

As the one who'd masterminded the event (or the logistics of it), Shang Qinghua was subject to the irresistible pressure of the plot—yet he hadn't released the Black Moon Rhinoceros-Python that should have starred in numerous scenes. This was suspicious in itself, but if you considered the possibility that he had failed to do this intentionally in order to hinder the development of the plot—to sever the tragedy of Luo Binghe's fall into the Endless Abyss at its roots—it made sense.

The two stared at each other, speechless, competing for most stunned.

"Digging plot holes and not filling them!" Shen Qingqiu finally burst out. "Foreshadowing gone to waste! Landmines all over the place! The writing style of an elementary schooler! If you're going to write a stallion novel, then write a proper stallion novel—don't fool around writing whump!"

"I'm also a victim here," Shang Qinghua said slowly. "At the end of the day, I'm still the author. Even if I didn't transmigrate into the protagonist, I should at least have transmigrated into the role of a System in itself, right? But all of a sudden, I try to plug in a cord, I get electrocuted, and the System assigns me a character at random—and I end up cannon fodder."

"Still better than me," Shen Qingqiu sneered. "After you're exposed as a spy, Mobei-Jun kills you outright to silence you. At least it's a straightforward death. Don't you remember the state I'll be in after I get carved up by Luo Binghe?

"You only transmigrated here how many years ago?" Shang Qinghua countered. "Right upon rebirth, you already had the rank of a great master, right? I transmigrated into an infant. A childhood where I was destitute and miserable, and years as a disrespected outer disciple—have you really gone through more than I have?"

This competition had no winner, because in the end, it was six of one, half a dozen of the other.

Shang Qinghua sighed. "I've actually met a reader. Must be fate, must be fate. One of the four joys in life is meeting an old friend in a foreign place. What was your Zhongdian ID? Maybe we were old acquaintances."

"Peerless Cucumber," said Shen Qingqiu.

Shang Qinghua thought for a while. "I vaguely remember you. Weren't you especially vicious in one of those threads that was demanding I castrate the villain? It was when you, ahem, when the original Shen Qingqiu wanted to do...to Ning Yingying..."

At first, Shen Qingqiu emphatically said nothing. "I refuse to believe you only remember that one thing. Don't dwell on the past." More importantly, he had a resolution. "Enough blathering. I wanted to have a real discussion with you today—because after the

Immortal Alliance Conference, I suddenly had an idea. Perhaps it can solve our shared problem."

Shang Qinghua froze. "For real?"

"You think joking about something like this is funny?" Shen Qingqiu asked. "I'm talking about a guaranteed fix. As long as we keep it absolutely secret, we'll avoid any trouble. It all depends on you. Do you still remember creating a plant that only appears every thousand years?"

Shang Qinghua was speechless. "Your description is way too broad. Bing-ge's eaten at least eighty, if not a hundred plants like that."

So you know too!

Shen Qingqiu sighed, then spoke four words into Shang Qinghua's ear.

Shang Qinghua listened, shocked. After a moment, he gave Shen Qingqiu a deeply meaningful glance.

"What are you looking at?" asked Shen Qingqiu.

"Nothing," said Shang Qinghua. "It's only, long ago, I began to suspect that Cucumber-bro was a faithful reader, just one who didn't like expressing his feelings in a normal way. To think you were able to recall an obscure, throwaway plot point that I used only once. I'm very moved."

Shen Qingqiu refused to respond to that. "Tomorrow, leave the mountain with me. We'll go search out its place of origin."

"Tomorrow? This... Isn't this a little too sudden?" Shang Qinghua stammered. "Truthfully I—I can't remember its exact location and description. The entire work was nearly twenty million words long, and it was only mentioned in a single paragraph. Let me think for a while. I'll tell you once I remember."

"Then take your time remembering until Luo Binghe murders his way back, with Mobei-Jun under his command," said Shen Qingqiu with utmost sincerity. "At that time, one will kill me, and the other will kill you. I'm sure it won't be too late then either."

"All right... I'll definitely remember by tomorrow!"

Thankfully, on An Ding Peak, trivial matters like assigning rooms and uniforms to newly accepted disciples didn't require the peak lord's involvement. Shang Qinghua went back, and he thought long and hard the entire night, racking his brain, shifting and overturning the contents of his mind. Finally, before daybreak, an epiphany struck, and he circled a location on a map.

Upon seeing the map, Shen Qingqiu slapped the table, then grabbed Shang Qinghua and set off down the mountain. They spent part of the journey eating, part of it playing, traveled partly by sword and partly by carriage. All in all, it should have been quite pleasant. The only part that was just a tiny bit *un*pleasant was that Shang Qinghua moaned and groaned as he sat in the coachman's seat.

"Why am I the one paying for all the food and lodgings?" he asked. "Why, whenever we're taking a carriage, am I also the one driving?"

"Don't you feel any shame?" Shen Qingqiu asked from inside the carriage. "The funds are communal, provided by Zhangmenshixiong. All you're doing is taking them from your waist pouch."

Shang Qinghua's heart grew especially sour when he thought back on the words of instruction Yue Qingyuan had given him before they left.

"Shang-shidi, for the journey's duration, Qingqiu will be in your care. He's frail, so please watch over him."

What was up with that?

As the author "Great Master" Airplane Shooting Towards the Sky, who'd put his all into portraying Shang Qinghua as lowly scum, he finally understood this character's pain.

Logistics really got no respect. Everyone treated him like a nanny! Who wouldn't understand the original Shang Qinghua's desire to climb the ranks by any means? It was all too sympathetic!

"You have hands and feet," said Shang Qinghua. "Why don't you use them your—fuck, fuck!"

Shen Qingqiu felt the carriage suddenly pitch forward, like Shang Qinghua had abruptly reined in the horse. He raised the curtains, on the alert. "What's wrong?"

The carriage was currently passing through a stretch of dense forest. All around them, ancient trees soared into the sky while fallen leaves were scattered everywhere. Most of the sunlight was blocked by layers upon layers of branches. On the ground, it was difficult to find even specks of light.

Shen Qingqiu saw nothing strange, but he didn't lower his guard. "What were you screaming about?"

Shang Qinghua was still panicked. "Just now I saw a woman on the ground, slithering by like a snake! If I hadn't stopped the carriage, I would've run her right over!

This did sound rather eerie.

"That is indeed worth screaming over," said Shen Qingqiu.

The forest was still and quiet. As of right now, nothing seemed off. Shen Qingqiu didn't dare relax, though. Instead of getting back inside the carriage, he joined Shang Qinghua in the driver's seat. Forming a sword seal with one hand, he observed their surroundings in silence while his other hand pulled out a handful of melon seeds from the snacks bag, which he shoved at Shang Qinghua. "Be good, go inside, eat and play."

Shang Qinghua could be ordered about and used for odd jobs, but when it came to fighting monsters, he was pretty much useless. He knew his own capabilities and obediently took the melon seeds and started eating. With every step the horse took, he ate a seed.

As such, after an incense time, they finally...realized a very serious problem.

The two of them wordlessly looked at the ground and at a trail of familiar melon seed hulls.

"Mm, no doubt about it. Cang Qiong Mountain Sect's Qian Cao Peak's Dragon-Bone Cantaloupe seeds are red in color with golden insides," said Shang Qinghua. "This is definitely the trail of seed hulls I left."

"I am aware that peddling melon seeds is one of your peak's side jobs. Enough."

So, here was their problem: how had they returned to their original location?

The two of them stared at each other.

They were going in circles, a classic—and very tired—scenario.

Shang Qinghua suggested an old folk remedy. "How about we try sprinkling a male virgin's pee into the horse's eyes?"

"Horses have dignity too. Why sprinkle urine in its eyes?" Shen Qingqiu asked. "And where am I supposed to find a male virgin's pee out in the middle of nowhere?"

Once these words left his mouth, he realized that Shang Qinghua was gazing intently at him.

"Why are you looking at me?! As for my former self—let's not talk about that for now. You wrote Shen Qingqiu's original character yourself. He's unsullied without, degenerate within, always burning with lust. He had an affair in his youth and sought prostitutes as an adult. You think I'm still a virgin? And don't point at yourself, Shang Qinghua was written the same way."

Shen Qingqiu frowned, thinking carefully, then slapped his thigh. He turned and entered the carriage, but he abruptly heard Shang Qinghua howl again from outside. Shen Qingqiu grabbed the thing he was looking for and scurried back out.

"What is it?!" he yelled.

Shang Qinghua was so terrified that his words no longer had any punctuation marks. "When you went in I felt something hairy brush my neck and when I raised my head I saw it was a mass of hair and underneath it was a huge white face that I couldn't see clearly fuck me!"

Shen Qingqiu lifted his head, and of course he couldn't see anything. He sat down properly, opened the map in his hands, and raised an eyebrow. "Whatever it is, it's quite clever."

"Why so?"

"It knows to pick off the weak and so chose the easier one to scare." He patted Shang Qinghua's shoulder again. "No matter how terrifying the creature, you wrote it yourself. Why are you scared?!"

"I don't remember writing..." Shang Qinghua trailed off. "Cucumber-bro, are you looking at the map? Take a good look; this is a map of the mainland—the *entire* mainland. Bai Lu Forest may be marked, but it's only the size of a dot."

"Look for yourself." Shen Qingqiu pointed at the lower portion of the map.

Cang Qiong Mountain and Zhao Hua Monastery were in the east, Tian Yi Temple was in the center, and in the south was the territory belonging to Huan Hua Palace. The dot representing Bai Lu Forest just happened to fall on a border with the last, which had been outlined in diluted ink.

Shang Qinghua suddenly understood. "Bai Lu Forest was allotted to Huan Hua Palace and its sphere of influence? So right now, we aren't walking in circles, we've just entered their protective array?

To prevent random passersby from intruding and stirring up trouble, all the large sects had their own security spells. Take, for example, Cang Qiong Mountain's Heaven-Ascending Stairs: common folk who didn't know the path would be stuck climbing thirteen thousand steps, unable to reach the peak, until they were nearly dead. They could only wait for the disciples defending the mountains to escort them back down.

Thus, so long as they were trapped in this spell and without guidance, they would only keep running in circles.

Shen Qingqiu called out mentally. "System? You there?" After a while with no response, he called again. "Didn't you promise 24-hour online service? If you don't respond, I'll leave a negative review."

[Hello, the System has entered Hibernation Mode. You are speaking to the AI assistant. If you require service, please help yourself.]

Hibernation. Shen Qingqiu split his sides laughing.

Now that he thought about it, these past few days, the System hadn't granted him any B-Points or various other bizarre, newly activated point varieties.

[The System was disconnected from its central power source, "Luo Binghe,"] the AI assistant explained. [It is currently undergoing maintenance and updating itself in the background. The System will reactivate once it has been reconnected. We wish you a pleasant self-service experience. Thank you.]

The current version was already frustrating enough—wouldn't a new version just straight up kill him in the future? No, wait, the main point was—

Luo Binghe was your central power source?! The fuck!

Shen Qingqiu had more questions, but he soon realized that the assistant only repeated the same thing over and over.

What kind of fucking "AI assistant" is this? Isn't this basically like QQ's[14] *automated response? And you still have the nerve to call it an "AI"!*

Shen Qingqiu nudged Shang Qinghua. "Call your System. Is it still connected?"

Shang Qinghua blinked. After a moment, he said, "It says it's undergoing maintenance."

So not only was Luo Binghe the central power source of Shen Qingqiu's System, once he was disconnected, *all* the Systems went down.

One could have said this matter was serious, but in truth it wasn't *that* serious. It only meant that while Luo Binghe was in the Abyss, Shen Qingqiu couldn't acquire B-Points. If he thought about it, this was good. If he couldn't acquire them, he also couldn't lose them, which meant that all restrictions were off!

Shen Qingqiu was still consoling himself when he suddenly sensed the shrubbery by the side of the road rustling and moving. He snapped his fingers. "Come out!" he yelled.

At his waist, Xiu Ya left its sheath, controlled by the orders from Shen Qingqiu's sword seals, flipping, stabbing, and slashing. The creature hidden in the shrubbery seemed to swim like a fish, more slippery than a loach, evading all his stabs.

Suddenly, a blinding ray of light flashed before Shen Qingqiu's

---

14 A widely-used Chinese instant messaging app, which also offers various entertainment services.

eyes. The creature let out a shrill whine and leapt backward several meters.

The shrubbery had been slashed into shambles and was no longer capable of hiding anything, but that thing had long since escaped. There were no further movements.

He hadn't used any flashy techniques just now, right? Presumably he'd just momentarily reflected a ray of sunlight.

"It's afraid of light?" Shang Qinghua asked, bringing his head close to Shen Qingqiu's. "Damn, it really is a female ghost! But I didn't write about one—I absolutely didn't write about one!"

The two of them were about to discuss this when they heard the subtle sound of footsteps.

This person's footwork was excellent. If Shen Qingqiu and Shang Qinghua had been of any shallower cultivation, they definitely wouldn't have noticed them approaching.

From the depths of the woods emerged a youth dressed in white. That youth held his sword unsheathed, his expression alert. On seeing his visitors, his face grew astonished, and he quickly sheathed his sword to greet them.

"This junior sensed some unusual fluctuations around the barrier and henceforth hurried over, not knowing Immortals Shen and Shang were here. Please excuse us for not coming to receive you."

Shen Qingqiu saw that he was quite handsome but that he looked unfamiliar. "This young hero is?" he asked politely.

The youth almost fell over.

"There's a limit to how little dignity you can leave others," Shang Qinghua whispered in his ear. "That's Gongyi Xiao."

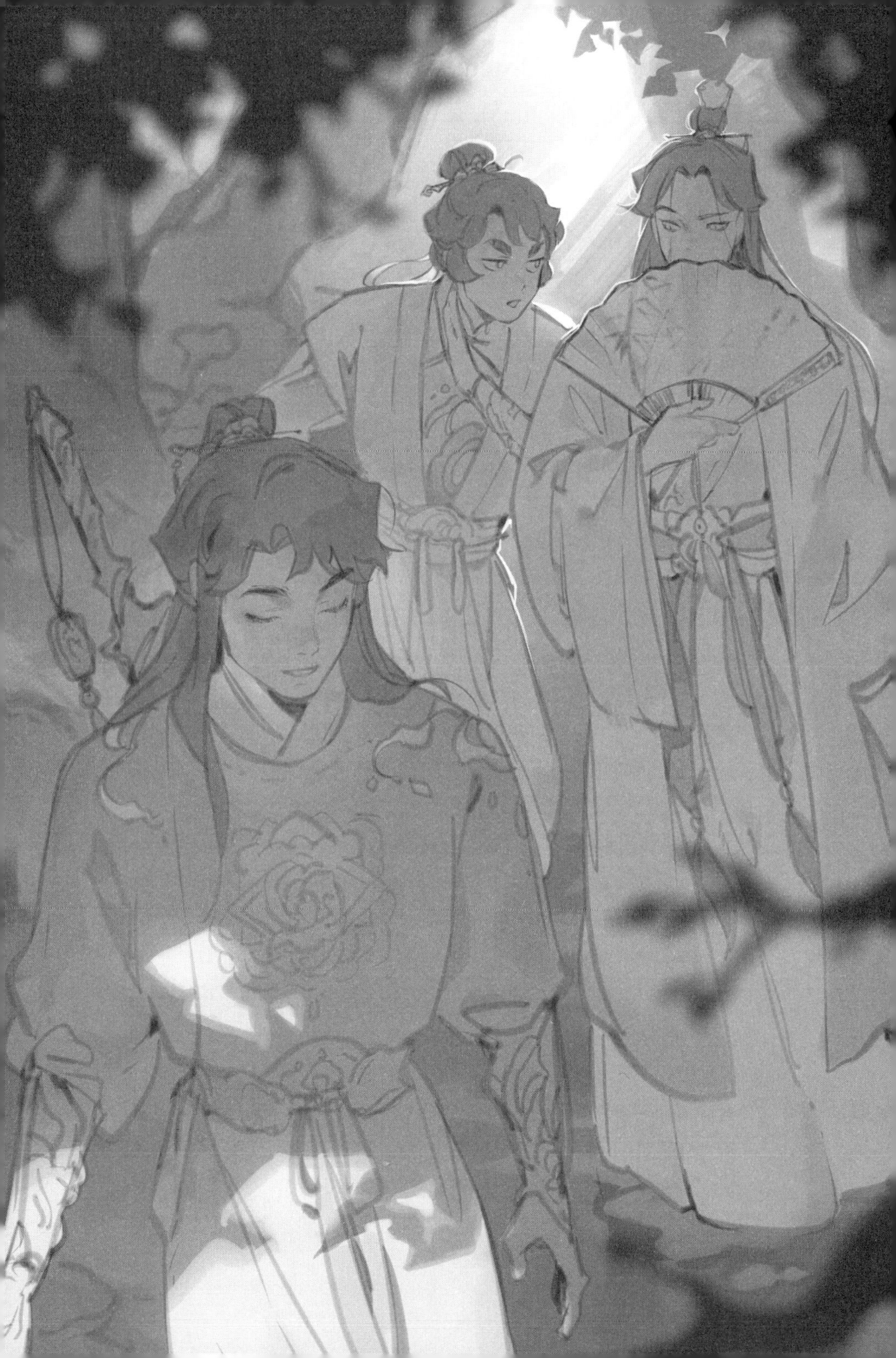

Gongyi Xiao was a little depressed. Though he had been number one before Luo Binghe kicked him off that place on the golden tablet, no matter what, he was still number two.

His achievements were remarkable, and he had been the favorite for first place, so he had greeted each sect's high-ranking members alongside the Old Palace Master. Therefore, Shen Qingqiu's failure to recognize him came as a surprise.

"As expected, one's heroism is evident even in youth," Shen Qingqiu said, offering praise.

"I don't dare presume," Gongyi Xiao demurred. "Still, for two peak lords to enter Huan Hua Palace's territory unannounced—why didn't you inform us beforehand? We've neglected our seniors. Our hearts are burdened."

He was truly treating Bai Lu Forest as his sect's territory. As a favored disciple on the Huan Hua Palace payroll, he had an obligation to ascertain the intentions of two visiting peak lords from Cang Qiong Mountain Sect. Why would they skulk around the border of his sect's sphere of influence?

"We have no intention of visiting Huan Hua Palace and are only dealing with a small matter within Bai Lu Forest," Shen Qingqiu said.

By informing Gongyi Xiao that they had come for business but neglecting to say what the business was, he clearly indicated that he was unwilling to discuss it. In general, Gongyi Xiao would be expected not to ask further questions. After all, a junior interrogating his seniors about their activities would be improper.

Gongyi Xiao wavered for a moment. "This junior doesn't know what matter the two seniors are seeing to, and he is unskilled. But may he be so bold as to request permission to come along to assist?"

"If we refuse him now and let him leave, it won't be just one person coming to look for us later." Shen Qingqiu's face held a smile, his lips barely moving, as he muttered to his teammate. "It's better if we bring him along. Anyhow, he can fight."

Shang Qinghua, who admittedly couldn't fight, muttered in response. "In the event he won't let us walk away with the Sun-Moon Dew Mushroom, what will we do? 'If it grows in my garden, of course it belongs to me. If it grows along my fence, it also belongs to me.' Don't say that I didn't warn you of Huan Hua Palace's logic."

"Are you an idiot?" Shen Qingqiu asked. "When we find it, we take it and leave. He can't forcibly snatch it from us. If he goes back and tattles to his teacher, that's a problem for future us. We'll be long gone by then. Like we'd wait for them to catch us."

"What if our sects become hostile?"

"Your life or diplomatic relations, choose one."

Shang Qinghua didn't hesitate in the slightest. "Let's bring him!"

Shen Qingqiu raised his head and decisively said to Gongyi Xiao, "Let's go!"

And so, the hard work of driving was handed to the junior.

"Senior Shen, there's something junior doesn't understand," Gongyi Xiao said curiously as he was maneuvering the reins.

"Please, speak," said Shen Qingqiu.

"With Senior's level of cultivation, he would need only a moment to break our sect's protective array, and he could do it without anyone knowing any better. Why did you emit such a large spiritual fluctuation?"

"That fluctuation wasn't my attempt to break the spell," said Shen Qingqiu. "It occurred while I fought a mysterious demonic creature."

"A mysterious demonic creature?"

"In truth, it was hard to tell if it was demonic, but it had an evil appearance unlike that of normal creatures from our realm."

Gongyi Xiao frowned. "There are human settlements within a five-kilometer radius from Bai Lu Forest, but we've never heard word of any demonic attacks. Even fierce beasts are uncommon."

"Then what exactly was that?" Shen Qingqiu muttered to himself. "It had loose hair draped all over its head, an oddly flexible skeleton, and a bloated face like that of a starved, drowned corpse."

"No matter what it is, it's for the best if it doesn't appear again," Gongyi Xiao said. "If it does, the two seniors need not trouble themselves and can leave it to this junior."

The respect within those words wasn't a pretense. Though Gongyi Xiao's understanding of his senior who carried the Xiu Ya sword was limited, and they'd only met once or twice from afar during the last Immortal Alliance Conference, Shen Qingqiu's personal disciple had surpassed Gongyi Xiao to secure the top rank. That same disciple had also saved quite a few of Huan Hua Palace's disciples, and therefore Gongyi Xiao felt no lack of reverence for him.

Shen Qingqiu took in that proper bearing, which lacked not the slightest bit of appropriate humility. Moreover, Gongyi Xiao's appearance was of the same type as Luo Binghe's—gentle and emotional, a handsome youth with a smile in his eyes. It was horribly difficult not to be reminded of Luo Binghe, his unblackened, lovable disciple; it was also horribly difficult not to come away with a favorable impression of the boy.

With Gongyi Xiao's guidance, the three quickly broke through Huan Hua Palace's protective array and pinpointed their location.

The original novel had not described the place where the Sun-Moon Dew Mushroom grew in much detail, just briefly mentioned that it was "in a stone cave covered by dense greenery." Merely recalling this sliver of content had cost Shang Qinghua half his soul. In his defense, this mushroom wasn't reserved for Luo Binghe. Rather, it was supposed to be for one of his opponents.

It was precisely because of this that Shen Qingqiu dared to seek it for himself. If it were a thing that affected the main plotline, or if it were some mystical flower or herb meant to provide one of Luo Binghe's power-ups, he wouldn't have had the guts to try and steal it. Trying to snitch resources from the male lead didn't lead to the kind of sweet and forgiving conclusion you got when you lost a handful of rice for trying to swipe a chicken. But since they were both villains, he figured it should be fine if they reappropriated it.

Fortunately, though Bai Lu Forest was large, there was only one stone cave. This saved them quite a bit of trouble.

Shen Qingqiu snapped his fingers, and a bright yellow flame sprang to life at his fingertips. With a flick, the flame swam off into the depths of the damp, pitch-dark cave, a bright tail leisurely swishing behind it to illuminate the path before them.

At first, the stone path was wide enough for three people to walk shoulder to shoulder, but the farther they went, the narrower it became, until they had to turn sideways to get through. It twisted this way and that, like the coiled intestines of some giant beast.

The lighting was poor. Even Shen Qingqiu's ball of flame flickered between bright and dim. He flicked out a few more, and the balls of fire chased each other around. Gongyi Xiao took up the rear. Shang Qinghua had wanted to wait outside the cave, but Shen Qingqiu had dragged him in. Maybe he was scared or something, because he touched Shen Qingqiu's arm from time to time, making goosebumps run down it whenever he did.

Finally, Shen Qingqiu couldn't take it anymore. Because they were with an interloper, he lowered his voice to hiss, "Can you stop pinching me?"

There was no reply, but at least the touches stopped. Shen Qingqiu continued to grope his way forward, but Shang Qinghua suddenly kicked him in the calf.

Shen Qingqiu couldn't help letting a "Fuck!" slip from his mouth.

Shang Qinghua's voice sounded from far behind. "Shen......shi...... xiong! What......did......you......say?"

His voice echoed through the winding corridors like it had been stretched by the distance. It seemed that Shen Qingqiu had been unconsciously walking faster and faster while Shang Qinghua had dawdled, meaning Gongyi Xiao, who was taking up the rear, was also unable to pick up the pace. He'd already left the other two quite a ways behind.

But if Shang Qinghua hadn't been touching his arm, then who had?

Or, in other words, *what* had been touching his arm?

Shen Qingqiu ground to a halt. With a blank expression on his face, he patted his arm, attempting to brush off the goosebumps. A few balls of flame were still suspended in midair, burning faintly.

The enemy's in the dark. I'm in the light.

With a flip of his left hand, Shen Qingqiu silently produced two paper talismans from his sleeve while his right hand slowly drew Xiu Ya. The sword grew increasingly bright, but the only thing in front and behind him was dark stone, which gave off a damp, rank odor.

Then Shen Qingqiu realized that, when something had collided with his calf a second before, it hadn't felt like a kick from a foot. Rather, it had been more like...a headbutt.

Shen Qingqiu jerked his head down, and his gaze met that of a deathly pale and bloated face on the ground.

Shen Qingqiu threw his talismans at the face, and in an instant, the narrow stone pathway lit up with bursts of fire and flashes of lightning. He wanted to draw his sword, but he hadn't realized that the space was too narrow. Before he'd even drawn it halfway out of its sheath, his right arm knocked against the wall of the tunnel, and the hilt of his sword hit the stone with a clang.

The thing on the ground was soft and boneless, slithering back and forth like a giant snake. It was more agile than Shen Qingqiu, and it evaded his attacks so quickly that even at this point-blank range, the talismans failed to hit it. In the short time Shen Qingqiu had lost attempting to draw his sword, it had already reversed course with a swish and slithered away, heading right in the direction of Shang Qinghua and Gongyi Xiao.

"Watch out!" he yelled. "There's something heading your way!"

At this, Shang Qinghua immediately turned around and yelled. "Young hero, quick! Let's switch places!" He worked in logistics—how could he be the front line of an assault?!

Gongyi Xiao tried to do as instructed, but the pathway was already narrow enough to raise the hair on one's nape. There was only enough space for one person to walk with a fist's width of margin besides. He couldn't get around at all.

Shen Qingqiu yelled again. "On the ground! Look at the ground! It's crawling on the ground!"

When Shang Qinghua turned his head back, he saw a snake-man slithering toward them. He made a swift decision and collapsed on the spot.

Gongyi Xiao had never seen such an eerie monster either, and he froze for a moment. But upon seeing Shang Qinghua's sudden collapse, his face twitched.

"My apologies!" he cried as he leapt over Shang Qinghua.

Though it was done in an unsightly way, the logistics guy and the vanguard finally at least managed to switch places.

"Don't draw your sword—" Shen Qingqiu yelled again.

Before he could finish the word "sword," Gongyi Xiao had carelessly tried to draw. Of course, he ended up suffering the same disastrous consequence. His hilt hit the stone wall before the sword was halfway out.

Shen Qingqiu finally arrived, holding his own blade. "Ah, idiot!" he blurted out.

Gongyi Xiao was rather aggrieved. In truth, Shen Qingqiu also knew that the issue was that the boy's reflexes were too fast, leading him to move before he finished listening. Anyone else would have done the same. But in the past, on the few occasions Shen Qingqiu had partnered with Luo Binghe, his disciple had understood exactly what Shen Qingqiu wanted, and he had always responded perfectly without his master needing to offer a single word of clarification. The contrast was as clear as day. Shen Qingqiu couldn't help but miss the benefits and ease working with Luo Binghe had afforded him.

The stone corridor meandered back and forth, and moreover it was dark, which made for an extremely advantageous environment for that thing to move through. Shen Qingqiu drew out another handful of talismans, but the thing had already slithered away and disappeared.

"Senior Shen, that...snake, was that the demonic creature you encountered in Bai Lu Forest?" Gongyi Xiao asked in disbelief.

"It was," said Shen Qingqiu. "I still don't understand how that thing managed to escape our pincer attack."

"By squeezing past me." Expression unchanging, Shang Qinghua got up from the ground and patted the dust from his robes.

Gongyi Xiao pointedly said nothing.

"...Let's go," said Shen Qingqiu. "This time, stay close to me."

His reminder wasn't necessary. This time, even on threat of death, Shang Qinghua refused to stray more than an arm's length away from him.

After a dizzying number of twists and turns, the three finally made their way out of the stone corridor. Deep in the belly of the cave, they suddenly came upon a wide cavern.

Before, Shen Qingqiu hadn't really understood how anything called the "Sun-Moon Dew Mushroom" could be found in the depths of a cave, which presumably had neither sunlight nor moonlight. The name clearly indicated a thing that gathered spiritual energy from nature and from the essence of the sun and moon, so how could it grow in this place? Now he finally got it.

As it turned out, at the cavern's highest point, a giant opening in the ceiling yawned up toward the sky. Sun and moonlight fell through this opening like a spotlight to hit a single point at the heart of an underground lake.

A little mound of soil surrounded by glittering water was naturally a hallowed location with excellent feng shui, and it was where the Sun-Moon Dew Mushroom grew.

"The Dew Lake," Shang Qinghua said with conviction. "I'm certain."

Having received confirmation, Shen Qingqiu let out a sigh of relief. They had found the right place.

The lake before them was filled with no ordinary water but rather with unsullied morning dew. This unsullied water collected from morning dew, brimming with spiritual energy, and nourished the Sun-Moon Dew Mushroom. After the mushrooms matured, their mycelia sunk into the water and soil to nourish the dew water in return. In this way, the spiritual energy cycled back and forth undiminished, never to be exhausted.

Admiring the beautiful scene, Gongyi Xiao finally understood the peak lords' objective. But he still found it a bit odd.

Cang Qiong Mountain was a major sect that produced mystical herbs and elixirs, and surely they gathered a number of rare and treasured flowers every day. Though this mushroom was scarce and precious, it didn't look like something that could grant immortality, nor a breakthrough to ascension—so how did it merit two peak lords personally taking a long journey to collect it?

Meanwhile, Shen Qingqiu's eyes were fixed solely on the small, white, fleshy pods in the center of the lake. With a sweep of his sleeves, he stepped resolutely into the water. After a few dozen steps, the dew water reached his waist, neither warm nor cold, soaking his skin. It felt as if it could soak right through to the heart.

Though these mushrooms were small and looked just like bean sprouts, once they were planted somewhere with excellent feng shui and a bounty of spiritual energy, and nurtured according to plan...

Shen Qingqiu hesitated at the sight of the dozen or so white mushrooms growing on the little dirt mound, small and tender. Come to think of it, these mushrooms were a natural wonder; to harvest every last one seemed a bit immoral. But on second thought, if he didn't pick them all now, another villain would pick them later, which would be even more immoral. And if they messed up and destroyed one, it would be good to have a few extra as backup, just to be absolutely safe. Insurance was critically important.

Having made his decision, he carefully pulled up each mushroom together with a little soil and stored them in his sleeves.

When the last mushroom was in his hands, Shen Qingqiu suddenly heard the sound of a sword being drawn behind him before he could properly stow it.

When he turned around, Gongyi Xiao had his sword in hand, and he was staring straight at Shen Qingqiu.

At first Shen Qingqiu thought Gongyi Xiao was protesting his slapdash approach to harvesting, but Shang Qinghua was in the same stance. It was then that he knew something had gone wrong, and he held his breath.

Suddenly, something long and large leapt out of the surface of the lake. It looked like a giant fish, and it pounced straight toward Shen Qingqiu.

A pale and deadened face flew right at him. It was that thing that had been following them since they reached the forest.

At the same time, Gongyi Xiao finished forming his sword seal, and his sword flew at the thing like a bolt of lightning. But once the thing missed Shen Qingqiu, it sank into the lake and did not resurface, stirring up the long-settled silt at the bottom until the water became turbid and murky.

Gongyi Xiao recalled his sword. "Senior Shen, come back to shore, quick!"

But Shen Qingqiu smiled. "Don't panic. I want to go fishing."

He stood in place without moving, and he slowly extracted a talisman from his robe.

"A single talisman probably isn't—" Gongyi Xiao started.

Before "enough" could leave his mouth, Shen Qingqiu rubbed the talisman like he would rub a bill, and the single talisman abruptly became an entire stack. Holding that stack of talismans, Shen Qingqiu thrust his fist into the water.

A chain of booms followed.

The surface of the lake exploded, sending up over twelve sprays of water into the air, each several meters tall.

This explosion also threw the snake-man hiding on the lake bottom into the air. It was tossed up high before crashing heavily to the ground by Shang Qinghua's feet.

Shen Qingqiu dripped his way back to shore. After being given a meaningful look, Gongyi Xiao used the hilt of his sword to turn the creature over.

Once it had been, all three were horror-struck.

After a long time, Shen Qingqiu turned to look at Shang Qinghua. "What is this?"

Shang Qinghua squeezed out three words. "...I don't know!"

He really didn't.

The creature was vaguely human-like. It had a full head of long hair, but it seemed to be entirely composed of cartilage. Its skin was rough, hard, and covered in patches of scales here and there, like a python half-scraped of its scales.

Though Shen Qingqiu had originally thought it was a female ghost, upon taking a closer look at its face, though it was bloated, he could faintly discern that it was that of a man.

Shang Qinghua gave Shen Qingqiu a questioning look. "Did I...?" he asked.

Meaning: Did I write about this kind of thing?

Shen Qingqiu frowned. "...I don't think so."

If the original novel had given this thing more than ten words of description, there was no way he wouldn't have remembered!

The two looked hopefully at Gongyi Xiao. Gongyi Xiao didn't recognize it either, and he felt a bit awkward. "If the two masters cannot recognize this creature, it is even more unfamiliar to this junior."

"Let me say something," Shang Qinghua said suddenly. "What if this isn't this creature's natural form?"

That made sense. It was so grotesque that it certainly didn't seem like a normal creature but rather a deformed specimen or a crossbreed.

"Punishment from the heavens, a curse, or a cultivator who failed to cultivate a forbidden technique?" Shen Qingqiu muttered.

"All three of those events could indeed result in this kind of monster," said Gongyi Xiao.

The snake-man on the ground seemed to be irritated by the word "monster," and its tail-like back half furiously slapped the ground.

Shang Qinghua hurriedly dodged away. "Young Hero Gongyi, Young Master Gongyi, don't say such irresponsible things—it seems like it can understand us. Use a different word, a different word!"

The creature's gaze remained fixed on Shen Qingqiu's sleeve.

At that moment, Shen Qingqiu noticed that, although this creature looked sinister and terrifying enough to make one retch, the eyes gazing through its curtain of tangled hair were incomparably clear, just like the water of the Dew Lake.

He had a sudden realization.

"No wonder it attacked us. Look." He pointed. "Its eyes. They probably look like that because it drinks the unsullied morning dew every day. Now look at its scales—there's lichen growing between the cracks, green with a bit of red, the exact same kind that grows on the stone walls. It's been visiting this cave for a long time. Perhaps it's been living off the spiritual dew within the Dew Lake."

And if the Sun-Moon Dew Mushroom was picked, the main force driving the circulation of spiritual energy in this lake would be destroyed. The spiritual energy in the Dew Lake would gradually be depleted, and eventually it would become a pool of mere wastewater—it might even dry up completely. That was why this creature had been following them, waiting for a chance to attack.

"But Senior Shen, if that monster has been living off the dew water, wouldn't it be better to eat them directly?" Gongyi Xiao asked. "Why did it never pick the mushrooms for itself?"

"When we were in Bai Lu Forest, it kept obstructing us," said Shen Qingqiu. "At first, it only retreated after it was burned by the sunlight reflecting off my sword blade. Perhaps it can't stand light, especially light from the sun and moon. So it can only move within the shade of forests, inside caves, and beneath the water." He pointed at the shaft of light beaming down from the cave's domed ceiling. "The Sun-Moon Dew Mushrooms are steeped in sunlight and moonlight all day and all night. Of course it couldn't approach them."

As confirmation, he withdrew a tender mushroom and swung it back and forth. As expected, the snake-man's eyes lit up, and it urgently craned its neck toward it, baring a mouthful of dense white teeth.

Gongyi Xiao prodded it with the hilt of his sword and flipped it over again. The snake-man strained, struggling and wriggling on the ground, but it couldn't turn back over. Gongyi Xiao turned his sword point down, seemingly preparing to stab it through.

"Wait," Shen Qingqiu said hurriedly.

As expected, Gongyi Xiao stopped. "Senior?" he asked in confusion.

"You said before that the common people within a several-kilometer radius of Bai Lu Forest had never suffered demonic attacks?" Shen Qingqiu asked tactfully.

"Yes."

"Then that means this creature has never done anything malicious. There's no need to exterminate it. Moreover, all it's ever done has been to drink the dew water in this cave. We were the ones who intruded and disturbed it."

Since his senior had spoken, of course Gongyi Xiao had to obey. Shen Qingqiu spoke true; if this monster really had killed or harmed humans, Huan Hua Palace would have discovered and eradicated it long ago. It was precisely because it had never done any harm that it had not yet been killed. Therefore, Gongyi Xiao sheathed his sword as he observed Shen Qingqiu looking at the creature on the ground with a benevolent gaze. Gongyi Xiao believed that Shen Qingqiu was cut from the same cloth as the masters from Zhao Hua Monastery, who believed in mercy and charity. He could never have guessed that Shen Qingqiu's interest in such strange creatures was equivalent to the average Zhongdian reader's interest in the hundreds of flower-like maidens, each more beautiful than the last.

Even after they had left the depths of the cave, no one noticed that the snake-man strenuously struggling on the ground had stopped writhing and was instead ever so slightly shivering.

Pressed under its deformed body was a tiny, thin Sun-Moon Dew Mushroom sprout. In that pair of incongruously bright eyes, a raging fire began to burn.

After exiting Bai Lu Forest, Gongyi Xiao invited the two peak lords to visit Huan Hua Palace—he could also notify the Old Palace Master.

Shen Qingqiu declined. "After all, we've already enjoyed your assistance. It would be impolite to trouble you further."

You're joking! Go to Huan Hua Palace? For what? A mushroom-viewing party? What if your higher-ups take things too seriously and insist on discussing property rights?

Realizing that Gongyi Xiao still wanted to detain them, Shang Qinghua took the lead. "Young Hero Gongyi, let's dispense with courtesy today—we can visit properly next time. If you come to Cang Qiong Mountain in the future, you can visit Qing Jing Peak. Your Senior Shen will definitely look after you well."

Shen Qingqiu gave him a look. Shang Qinghua immediately shut up.

Shen Qingqiu finally recovered his expression and smiled. "As Shang-shidi says, Qing Jing Peak awaits your arrival."

Gongyi Xiao knew that just like its name, the people of Qing Jing Peak were fond of peace and quiet and didn't like to be disturbed by guests. He wasn't sure if these were just words of courtesy, but he smiled either way.

"I will remember Senior Shen's words," he said. "I may indeed have the chance to disturb you in the future. When the time comes, to whom should I send the message announcing my arrival?"

Without a second thought, Shen Qingqiu said, "Give it to my disciple, Luo Bing—"

After he spoke, everyone fell silent. The atmosphere turned a bit odd.

Though he was stuck for a moment, Shen Qingqiu slowly flapped his fan twice and stiffly continued. "—he's shixiong, Ming Fan."

Gongyi Xiao's heart filled with conflicted feelings.

Rumor had it that after the peak lord of Qing Jing Peak lost his beloved disciple at the Immortal Alliance Conference, he had for a time fallen into inconsolable heartbreak, being out of his mind with grief. The man before him right now didn't seem like one who had accepted that Luo Binghe was really gone. Perhaps Shen Qingqiu hadn't come here primarily to pick the mushroom but rather to take his mind off things so he could briefly forget Luo Binghe's existence. Otherwise, why would two peak lords pursue this task in person? Senior Shang must have come to supervise Senior Shen and make sure he didn't do anything rash. Then, after Shen Qingqiu had forced himself to smile this whole trip, Gongyi Xiao had managed to poke his sore spot and stir up melancholy thoughts... As expected—what a deep master-and-disciple bond!

Until they parted ways, Gongyi Xiao kept looking back at Shen Qingqiu every ten steps, his gaze a tangled mix of awkwardness, sympathy, sorrow, and admiration.

Shen Qingqiu was a bit creeped out by this gaze. It had only been a slip of the tongue. What stories was Gongyi Xiao making up in that head of his?

"It's true," Shang Qinghua sighed when they were again alone. "It's actually true."

Shen Qingqiu gave him a kick that was neither heavy nor light. "What's true?"

"I've been watching you for a while, and I have something to say. Besides, keeping it in is uncomfortable," said Shang Qinghua. "Cucumber-bro, did you really see Luo Binghe as the apple of your eye? Did you adore him as your darling baby and disciple?"

He went on, analyzing the evidence piece by piece. "I heard your Qing Jing Peak disciples say that ever since returning from the

Immortal Alliance Conference, Shen-shixiong has been out of his mind with grief, his thoughts wandering all over the place. Time after time, you call Luo Binghe's name, and you stand in front of that sword mound and sigh in sorrow. I didn't believe it, but just now I finally witnessed it with my own eyes. Cucumber-bro, I really never thought that you were this sort of person."

Fuck, "out of your mind" again?! Is this phrase going to be the eternal stain on my lifetime of hard work?! My disciples all supposedly walk the path of scholarly detachment—when did they turn into such gossips? Spreading this sort of nonsense everywhere! What are you doing with your master's image?!

Shang Qinghua continued to dig his own grave. "Cucumber-bro, can I ask, how did you see Luo Binghe? I remember you were one of his fans, right? You roasted a huge number of the characters I wrote, but even so, you never roasted him. To you, is he a character, or is he a..."

A chill ran down Shen Qingqiu's back.

This bizarre interrogation from "Great Master" Airplane Shooting Towards the Sky was identical in tone to high-school girls gossiping in the dorms after lights-out.

"Tell me! Do you have a crush on ___?" "N-no, what are you talking about!" "Dodging the question~ Don't be shy O(∩_∩)O ha ha~" "I hate you, go to bed!"

Lightning. Lightning from the nine heavens!

Shang Qinghua was in fact innocent. He was honestly asking and was interested in discussing the matter. It was Shen Qingqiu who was overthinking the skeletons in his closet.

"Why aren't we moving?" Shen Qingqiu snapped, interrupting him.

Shang Qinghua stared. "What?"

Shen Qingqiu stared back, then shoved the reins into his hand. "Gongyi Xiao left, so we need a driver."

"Why haven't you driven even once?" Shang Qinghua asked suspiciously.

"You should be considerate toward the poisoned invalid."

Invalid my ass! thought Shang Qinghua. *Who was happily fighting monsters and blowing up spiritual lakes just now?! Have some dignity!*

Shen Qingqiu relaxed within the carriage and shook out his sleeves.

There were still five years before Luo Binghe would leave the Endless Abyss and return to the Human Realm. If nothing went wrong, the mushrooms they had just harvested would definitely be enough to save Shen Qingqiu's life.

However, he had forgotten the fundamental stupidity of *Proud Immortal Demon Way*. If nothing went wrong at such a crucial junction in a novel's storyline, that meant it wasn't exciting enough!

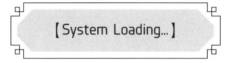

【System Loading...】

THE STORY CONTINUES IN
The Scum Villain's Self-Saving System
VOLUME 2

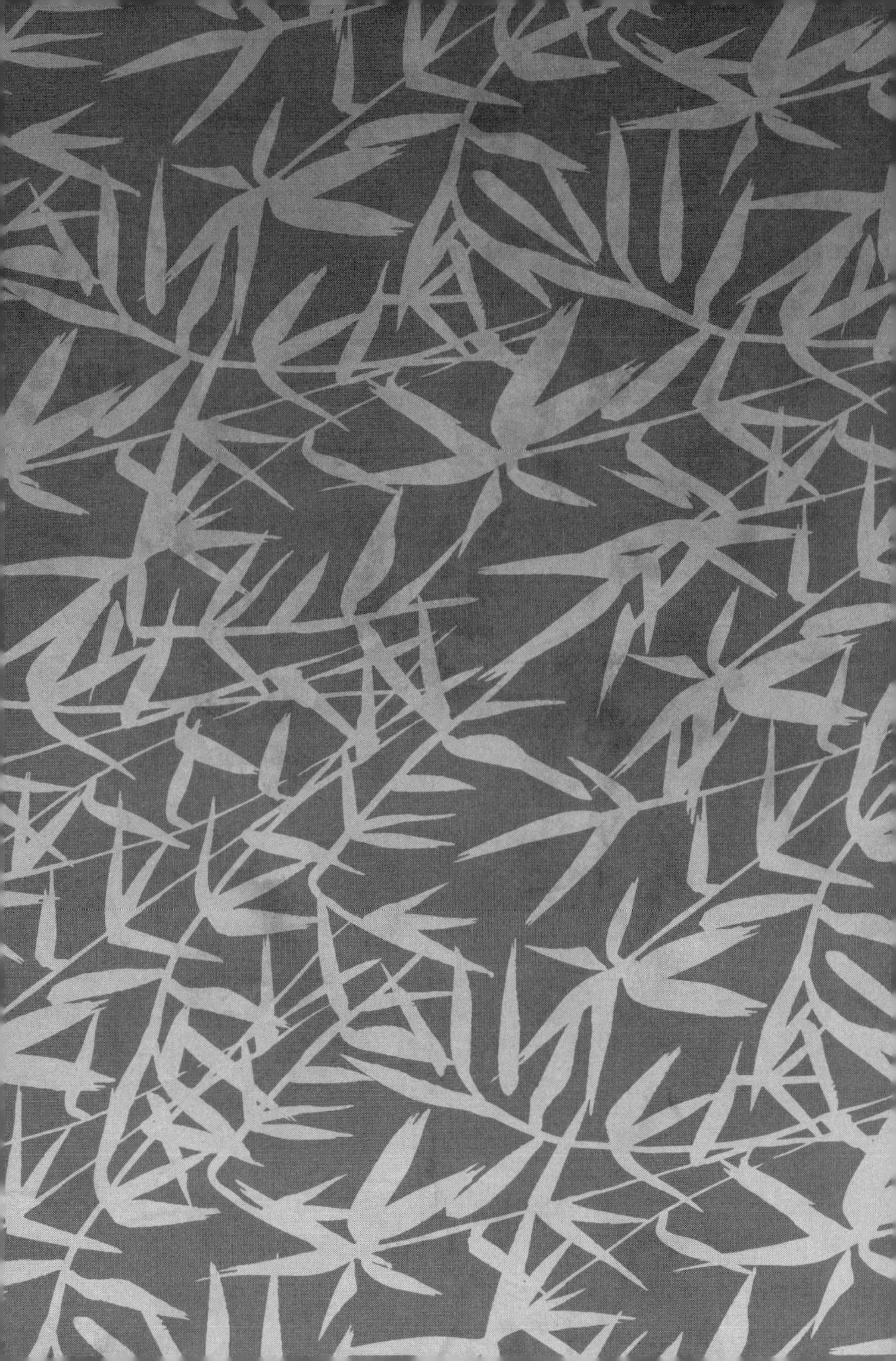

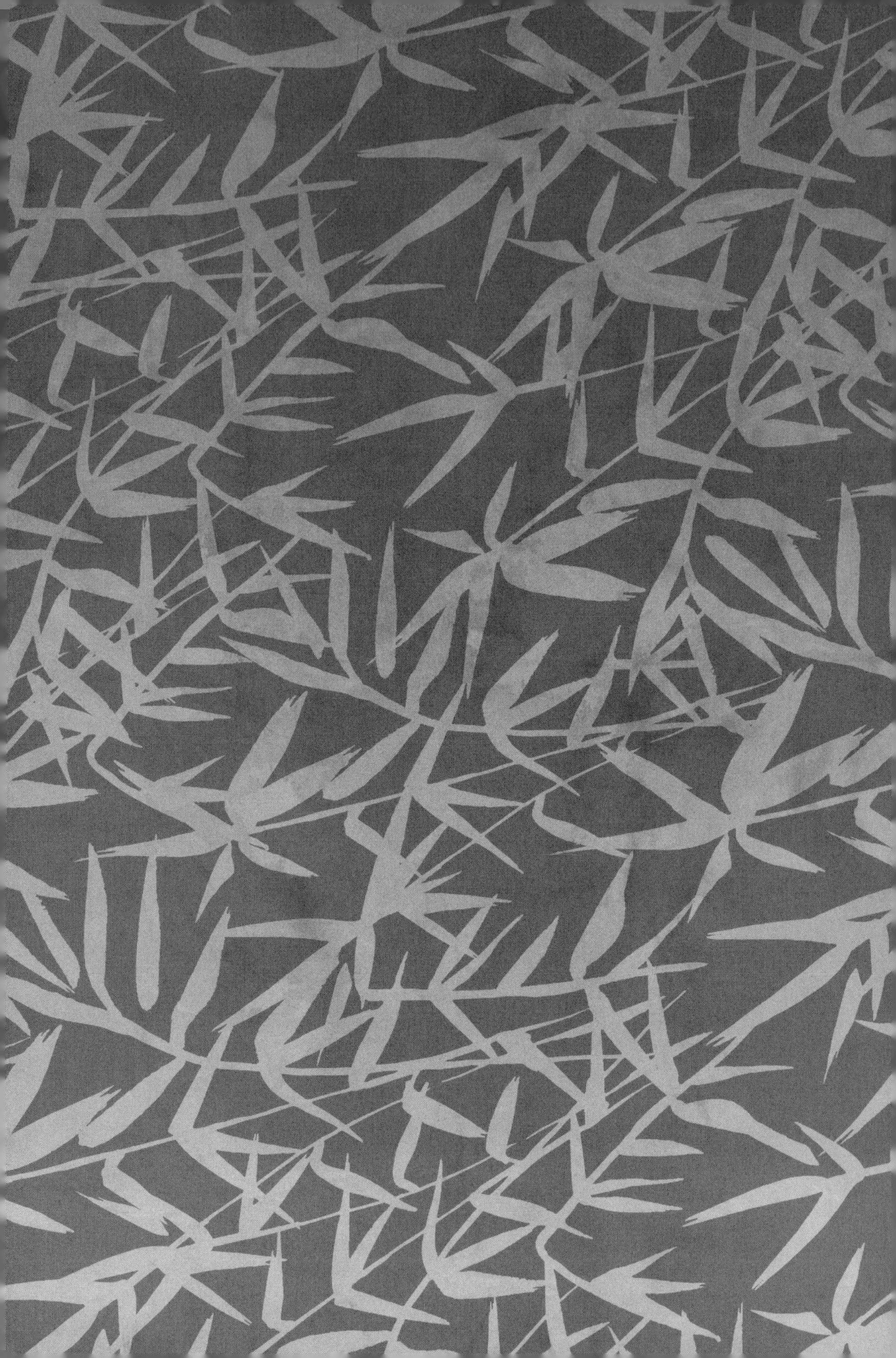

The Scum Villain's Self-Saving System

REN ZHA FANPAI
ZIJIU XITONG

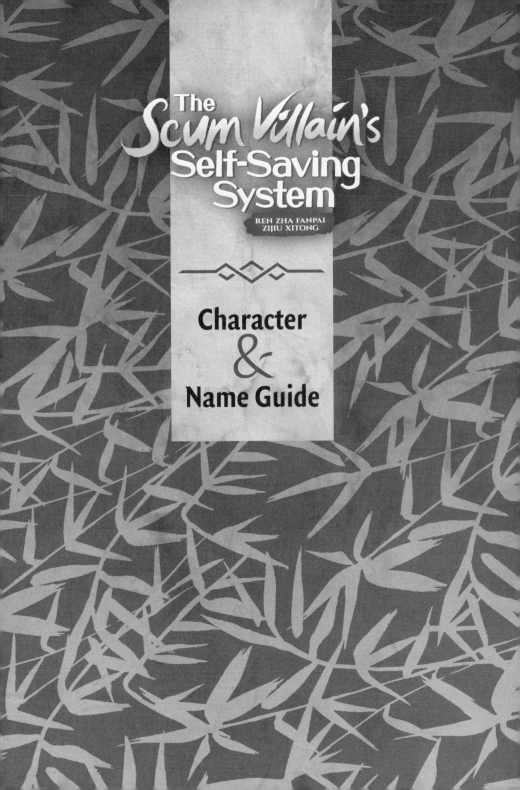

Character
&
Name Guide

Characters

The identity of certain characters may be a spoiler; use this guide with caution on your first read of the novel.

Note on the given name translations: Chinese characters may have many different readings. Each reading here is just one out of several possible readings presented for your reference and should not be considered a definitive translation.

MAIN CHARACTERS

Shen Yuan (Shen Qingqiu)
沈垣   SURNAME SHEN, "WALL"

TITLE: Peerless Cucumber (web handle)

RANK: *Proud Immortal Demon Way*'s Most Supportive Anti

Probably the most dedicated anti-fan of *Proud Immortal Demon Way*, Shen Yuan was baited by its cool monsters and charming protagonist to read millions and millions of words of the hit stallion novel, though he cussed out the author's sellout tendencies the whole way. After his untimely death during a fit of rage over the novel's ending, he was rewarded with the chance to enter the world of the story and fix it his own damn self.

However, instead of transmigrating into the stallion protagonist—or even an innocuous side character—he found himself waking up in the body of the scum villain Shen Qingqiu! Now things are looking a little difficult, but Shen Yuan is confident he can use the upcoming years to suck up to Luo Binghe hard enough to be spared when the boy begins his quest for revenge...right?

As the transmigrated Shen Qingqiu discovers that his glorious quest of thigh-hugging may not be as easy as he imagined, the line between story and reality begins to blur—more and more, he starts to treat those he meets in his new world not as mere characters in a story but as *people*. Will his knowledge as a reader of the original novel be enough to stay afloat as his actions divert the plot further and further from its path?

Luo Binghe
洛冰河 SURNAME LUO FOR THE LUO RIVER, "ICY RIVER"

RANK: White Lotus Disciple (Qing Jing Peak)
SWORD (CURRENT): Zheng Yang (正阳 / "Righteous sun")
SWORD (FUTURE): Xin Mo (心魔 / "Heart demon")

As the protagonist of *Proud Immortal Demon Way*, the original Luo Binghe rose from humble origins to reign as tyrant over the three realms, his innumerable harem at his beck and call. However, at the beginning of *this* story, he is still a young disciple who manages to stay sweet, earnest, and hard-working despite the horrible mistreatment he suffers. Though a childhood of poverty has already planted the seeds from which a dark, twisted personality might soon grow, he still yearns for love and acknowledgment. When the transmigrated Shen Qingqiu offers him kindness, he is willing to forgive and forget his master's prior abuse.

Though Luo Binghe holds some misconceptions about his master's sudden change of heart, he still turns the force of his protagonist's conviction toward a new goal: become stronger—so he can protect Shizun in the future! In the meantime, he's content taking over all the housework, cooking, and general peak management for Shen Qingqiu.

CANG QIONG MOUNTAIN SECT MEMBERS

Shen Qingqiu
沈清秋   SURNAME SHEN, "CLEAR AUTUMN"

TITLE: Xiu Ya Sword (修雅 / "Elegant and refined")

RANK: Peak Lord (Qing Jing Peak)

Shen Qingqiu, the refined and elegant peak lord of the peak of scholars, was also the scum villain who seemingly made it his life's mission to make Luo Binghe's life miserable in the original *Proud Immortal Demon Way*. He beat the young Luo Binghe for the slightest infraction and encouraged his peers to bully him. Furthermore, under his pure and unsullied exterior, he was (supposedly) a lustful degenerate who went so far as to target his own female disciple.

Shen Qingqiu got away with his misdeeds under the implicit permission of Sect Leader Yue Qingyuan, but the sect leader's favoritism couldn't protect him from his body becoming a permanent host for the transmigrated Shen Yuan.

Yue Qingyuan
岳清源   SURNAME YUE, "CLEAR SOURCE"

TITLE: Xuan Su Sword (玄肃 / "Dark and solemn")

RANK: Sect Leader, Peak Lord (Qiong Ding Peak)

As Sect Leader of the foremost major cultivation sect, Yue Qingyuan normally lives up to his responsibilities as a levelheaded leader and respected authority. But when his shidi, Shen Qingqiu, is the one asking for a favor, he can never deny the man anything... though this clear favoritism wasn't enough to keep the scum villain from causing Yue Qingyuan's death in the original *Proud Immortal Demon Way*.

Though the transmigrated Shen Qingqiu is no longer the intended recipient of this favor, Yue Qingyuan becomes something of a guide to him in the early days of his transmigration—even if Shen Qingqiu keeps debasing his sect leader a bit by mentally relegating him to the role of quest-giving NPC.

Ning Yingying
宁婴婴   SURNAME NING, "INFANT"

RANK: Youngest Female Disciple (Qing Jing Peak)

Luo Binghe's shijie and childhood friend. In the original *Proud Immortal Demon Way*, she was the first maiden to be accepted into Luo Binghe's harem after she helped him confront his inner demons. Ning Yingying starts out as a cute and naive young girl who can't always comprehend the consequences of her own actions and frequently gets herself and others into trouble. But as the world evolves away from the constraints of the stallion genre, Ning Yingying also begins to grow up into a fine young woman who cares deeply for the people around her.

Ming Fan
明帆   SURNAME MING, "SAIL"

RANK: Most Senior Disciple (Qing Jing Peak)

One of Luo Binghe's tormentors in *Proud Immortal Demon Way*, Ming Fan was a loyal lackey and coconspirator to the original Shen Qingqiu. But aside from his worrying habits of antagonizing the protagonist, the transmigrated Shen Qingqiu finds him to be a promising young man who doesn't let his spoiled upbringing interfere with his respect for his master. Unfortunately, he'll be eternally left to wonder why the master who favored him so suddenly left to shack up with Luo Binghe instead.

Liu Qingge
柳清歌 SURNAME LIU, "CLEAR SONG"

RANK: Peak Lord (Bai Zhan Peak)

SWORD: Cheng Luan (乘鸾 / "Soaring phoenix")

Despite being a character who never made an official appearance in *Proud Immortal Demon Way*, Liu Qingge had a legion of fanboys for his legendarily unparalleled skill in battle. This time around, Liu Qingge is rescued from a once-lethal qi deviation by the transmigrated Shen Qingqiu and gets to play a role in the story long past his original counterpart's death. Though baffled by Shen Qingqiu's mysterious attitude change and initially wary, he warms up to him in his own standoffish way. He's the older brother of Liu Mingyan.

Mu Qingfang
木清芳 SURNAME MU, "CLEAR FRAGRANCE"

RANK: Peak Lord (Qian Cao Peak)

A master of the healing arts, who feels a sense of responsibility for the well-being of his sectmates. Serious injuries? Supposedly incurable poisons? Come see Mu-shidi.

Qi Qingqi
齐清萋 SURNAME QI, "CLEAR AND LUSH"

RANK: Peak Lord (Xian Shu Peak)

A woman with a straightforward and fierce temperament; a sectmate the transmigrated Shen Qingqiu gets along with well in his new world. Though she won't hesitate to speak her mind, she cares deeply for her sect.

Liu Mingyan
柳溟烟 SURNAME LIU, "DRIZZLING MIST"

RANK: Disciple (Xian Shu Peak)

SWORD: Shui Se (水色 / "Color of water")

The number one true female lead of *Proud Immortal Demon Way* and younger sister of Liu Qingge. Because of her peerless beauty, Liu Mingyan typically wears a veil to hide her face. Even as an unskilled young disciple, she has the courage to stand up and fight for her sect's honor and the poise to accept defeat with dignity. Later, she is well on the way to growing into abilities that befit her position as the younger sister of the war god. What other aspirations could she be nursing beneath that pure and chaste exterior?

Shang Qinghua
尚清华 SURNAME SHANG, "CLEAR AND SPLENDID"

RANK: Peak Lord (An Ding Peak)

Overworked and underpaid, the Peak Lord of An Ding Peak takes on a thankless job as the head of the sect's "housekeeping" department. One might wonder...is there a reason he is willing to toil for this dubious honor?

DEMONS

Many demons go by titles instead of personal names. Titles styled like XX-Jun are for high-ranking demon nobility, and some titles may be hereditary.

CHARACTER & NAME GUIDE

Tianlang-Jun
天琅君　"HEAVEN'S GEMSTONE," TITLE -JUN

RANK: Saintly Ruler (former)

Luo Binghe's birth father, a heavenly demon. Now sealed beneath a great mountain by the righteous sects.

Sha Hualing
纱华铃　"GAUZE," "SPLENDID BELL"

RANK: Demon Saintess

A crafty and vicious pure-blooded demon who is eager to prove herself after being appointed as demon saintess, she first takes notice of Luo Binghe after invading his sect and becomes determined to capture his attention. Of course, the demonic way of flirting may seem rather alien to humans.

Meng Mo
梦魇　"DREAM DEMON"

RANK: Luo Binghe's Teacher in Demonic Techniques

Once a legendary master of dream manipulation, Meng Mo is now Luo Binghe's underappreciated "Portable Grandfather." Oh, the things a teacher will suffer to pass on his techniques.

Mobei-Jun
漠北君　"DESERTED NORTH," TITLE -JUN

RANK: Demonic Second-Gen

Luo Binghe's future eccentric sidekick. A proud ice demon-turned-plot device for Luo Binghe's power-up arc.

OTHER SUPPORTING CHARACTERS

Old Palace Master

RANK: Master of Huan Hua Palace

The master of Luo Binghe's birth mother. When he sees Luo Binghe for the first time, he seems to recognize the shades of someone familiar in the young disciple's face...

Luo Binghe's Birth Mother

RANK: Former Disciple (Huan Hua Palace)

Expelled from her sect on suspicion of having secret ties to demons, Luo Binghe's birth mother set young Luo Binghe adrift on the Luo River before her death.

Gongyi Xiao
公仪萧   SURNAME GONGYI, "MUGWORT"

RANK: Head Disciple (Huan Hua Palace)

"Young hero" Gongyi is a favored disciple of Huan Hua Palace, a dutiful and respectful young man whose glowing prospects are clear to everyone who meets him.

Qin Wanyue
秦婉约   SURNAME QIN, "GRACEFUL AND SUBDUED"

RANK: Disciple (Huan Hua Palace)

The "graceful and subdued little shimei" who shared a tender moment with the original Luo Binghe during the Immortal Alliance Conference.

Qin Wanrong
秦婉容   SURNAME QIN, "GRACEFUL COUNTENANCE"

RANK: Disciple (Huan Hua Palace)

Qin Wanyue's eccentric little sister.

Locations

CANG QIONG MOUNTAIN

Cang Qiong Mountain Sect
苍穹山派 "BLUE HEAVENS" MOUNTAIN SECT

Located in the east, Cang Qiong Mountain Sect is the world's foremost major cultivation sect. The mountain has twelve individual peaks that act as branches with their own specialties and traditions, each run by their own peak lord and united under the leadership of Qiong Ding Peak. Rainbow Bridges physically connect the peaks to allow easy travel.

The peaks are ranked in a hierarchy, and disciples of lower-ranked peaks call same-generation disciples of higher-ranked peaks Shixiong or Shijie regardless of their actual order of entry into the sect, though seniority within a given peak is still determined by order of entry. Disciples are separated into inner ("inside the gate") and outer ("outside the gate") rankings, with inner disciples being higher-ranked members of the sect.

Qiong Ding Peak
穹顶峰 "HEAVEN'S APEX" PEAK

The peak of the sect's leadership; the Peak Lord of Qiong Ding Peak is also the leader of the entire Cang Qiong Mountain Sect.

Qing Jing Peak
清静峰 "CLEAR AND TRANQUIL" PEAK

The peak of scholars, artists, and musicians.

An Ding Peak
安定峰 "STABLE AND SETTLED" PEAK

The peak in charge of sect logistics, including stock transportation and repair of damages.

Bai Zhan Peak
百战峰 "HUNDRED BATTLES" PEAK

The peak of martial artists.

Qian Cao Peak
千草峰 "THOUSAND GRASSES" PEAK

The peak of medicine and healing.

Xian Shu Peak
仙姝峰 "IMMORTAL BEAUTY" PEAK

An all-female peak.

Wan Jian Peak
万剑峰 "TEN THOUSAND SWORDS" PEAK

The peak of sword masters.

Ku Xing Peak
苦行峰 "ASCETIC PRACTICE" PEAK

The peak of ascetic cultivation.

OTHER CULTIVATION SECTS

Huan Hua Palace
幻花宫 "ILLUSORY FLOWER" PALACE

Located in the South, Huan Hua Palace disciples practice a number of different cultivation schools but specialize in illusions, mazes, and concealment. They are the richest of the sects and provide the most funding to each Immortal Alliance Conference.

Tian Yi Temple
天一观 "UNITED WITH HEAVEN" TEMPLE

Located in the central territories, the priests of Tian Yi Temple practice Daoist cultivation.

Zhao Hua Monastery
昭华寺 "BRIGHT AND SPLENDID" MONASTERY

Located in the East, the monks of Zhao Hua Monastery practice Buddhist cultivation.

MISCELLANEOUS LOCATIONS

Bai Lu Forest
白露森林 "WHITE DEW" FOREST

A forest on the edge of Huan Hua Palace's territory where the Sun-Moon Dew Mushroom can be found.

The Endless Abyss
无间深渊

The boundary between the Human and Demon Realms; the hellish location of Luo Binghe's five-year training arc before he reemerges as the overpowered protagonist.

Jue Di Gorge
绝地谷 "HOPELESS LAND" GORGE

A mountainous region with all sorts of treacherous terrain, perfect for adventure.

Name Guide

NAMES, HONORIFICS, & TITLES

Courtesy Names

A courtesy name is given to an individual when they come of age. Traditionally, this was at the age of twenty during one's crowning ceremony, but it can also be presented when an elder or teacher deems the recipient worthy. Generally a male-only tradition, there is historical precedent for women adopting a courtesy name after marriage. Courtesy names were a tradition reserved for the upper class.

It was considered disrespectful for one's peers of the same generation to address someone by their birth name, especially in formal or written communication. Use of one's birth name was reserved for only elders, close friends, and spouses.

This practice is no longer used in modern China but is commonly seen in wuxia and xianxia media, as such, many characters have more than one name. Its implementation in novels is irregular and is often treated malleably for the sake of storytelling.

It was a tradition throughout some parts of Chinese history for all children of a family within a certain generation to have given names with the same first or last character. This "generation name" may be taken from a certain poem, with successive generations using successive characters from the poem. In *Scum Villain*, this tradition is used to give the peak lords their courtesy names, so all peak lords of Shen Qingqiu's generation have courtesy names starting with Qing.

Diminutives, Nicknames, and Name Tags

XIAO-: A diminutive meaning "little." Always a prefix.

> EXAMPLE: Xiao-shimei (the nickname Ming Fan uses for Ning Yingying)

-ER: A word for "son" or "child." Added to a name, it expresses affection. Similar to calling someone "Little" or "Sonny." Always a suffix.

> EXAMPLE: Ling-er (how Sha Hualing refers to herself when she is trying to be cute)

A-: Friendly diminutive. Always a prefix. Usually for monosyllabic names, or one syllable out of a two-syllable name.

> EXAMPLE: A-Luo (the nickname Ning Yingying uses for Luo Binghe)

FAMILY

DI: Younger brother or younger male friend. Can be used alone or as an honorific.

DIDI: Younger brother or a younger male friend. Casual.

XIAO-DI: Does not mean "little brother", and instead refers to one's lackey or subordinate, someone a leader took under their wings.

GE: Familiar way to refer to an older brother or older male friend, used by someone substantially younger or of lower status. Can be used alone or with the person's name.

GEGE: Familiar way to refer to an older brother or an older male friend, used by someone substantially younger or of lower status. Has a cutesier feel than "ge."

JIE: Older sister or older female friend. Can be used alone or as an honorific.

JIEJIE: Older sister or an unrelated older female friend. Casual.

JIUJIU: Uncle (maternal, biological).

MEI: Younger sister or younger female friend. Can be used alone or as an honorific.

MEIMEI: Younger sister or an unrelated younger female friend. Casual.

SHUFU: Uncle (paternal, biological) Formal address for one's father's younger brother.

SHUSHU: An affectionate version of "Shufu."

XIAOSHU: Little uncle.

Cultivation and Martial Arts

-JUN: A suffix meaning "lord."

ZHANGMEN: Leader of a cultivation/martial arts sect.

SHIZUN: Teacher/master. For one's master in one's own sect. Gender neutral. Literal meaning is "honored/venerable master" and is a more respectful address.

SHIFU: Teacher/master. For one's master in one's own sect. Gender neutral. Mostly interchangeable with Shizun.

SHINIANG: The wife of a shifu/shizun.

SHIXIONG: Older martial brother. For senior male members of one's own sect.

SHIJIE: Older martial sister. For senior female members of one's own sect.

SHIDI: Younger martial brother. For junior male members of one's own sect.

SHIMEI: Younger martial sister. For junior female members of one's own sect.

SHISHU: The younger martial sibling of one's master. Can be male or female.

SHIBO: The older martial sibling of one's master. Can be male or female.

SHIZHI: The disciple of one's martial sibling.

Pronunciation Guide

Mandarin Chinese is the official state language of China. It is a tonal language, so correct pronunciation is vital to being understood! Below is a simplified guide on the pronunciation of select character names and terms from MXTX's series to help get you started.

Series Names

SCUM VILLAIN'S SELF-SAVING SYSTEM (REN ZHA FAN PAI ZI JIU XI TONG):
   ren jaa faan pie zzh zioh she tone

GRANDMASTER OF DEMONIC CULTIVATION (MO DAO ZU SHI):
   mwuh dow zoo shrr

HEAVEN OFFICIAL'S BLESSING (TIAN GUAN CI FU):
   tee-yan gwen tsz fuu

Character Names

SHEN QINGQIU: Shhen Ching-cheeoh

LUO BINGHE: Loo-uh Bing-huhh

WEI WUXIAN: Way Woo-shee-ahn

LAN WANGJI: Lahn Wong-gee

XIE LIAN: Shee-yay Lee-yan

HUA CHENG: Hoo-wah Cch-yung

XIAO-: shee-ow

-ER: ahrr

A-: ah

GONGZI: gong-zzh

DAOZHANG: dow-jon

-JUN: june

DIDI: dee-dee

GEGE: guh-guh

JIEJIE: gee-ay-gee-ay

MEIMEI: may-may

-XIONG: shong

Terms

DANMEI: dann-may

WUXIA: woo-sheeah

XIANXIA: sheeyan-sheeah

QI: chee

General Consonants & Vowels

X: similar to English sh (**sh**eep)

Q: similar to English ch (**ch**arm)

C: similar to English ts (pan**ts**)

IU: yoh

UO: wuh

ZHI: jrr

CHI: chrr

SHI: shrr

RI: rrr

ZI: zzz

CI: tsz

SI: ssz

U: When u follows a y, j, q, or x, the sound is actually ü, pronounced like eee with your lips rounded like ooo. This applies for yu, yuan, jun, etc.

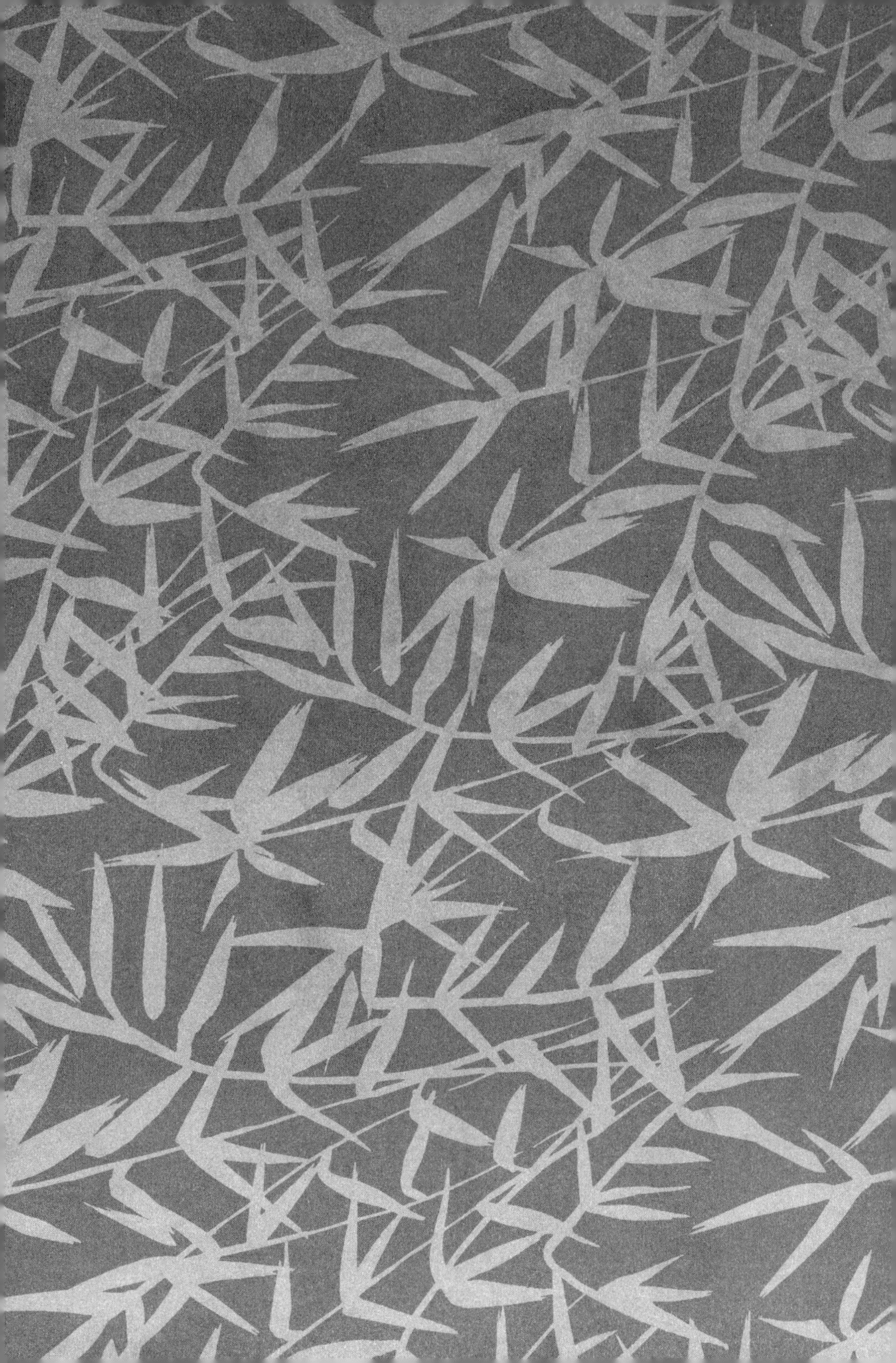

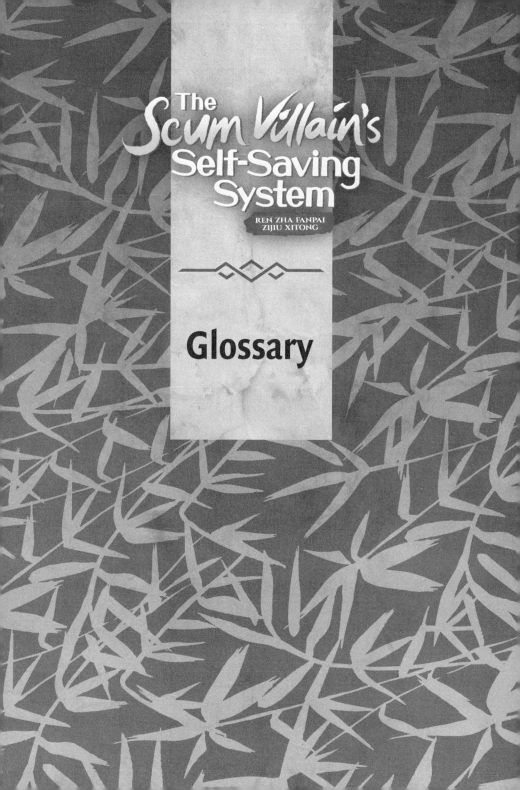

The Scum Villain's Self-Saving System

REN ZHA FANPAI
ZIJIU XITONG

Glossary

Glossary

While not required reading, this glossary is intended to offer further context to the many concepts and terms utilized throughout this novel and provide a starting point for learning more about the rich Chinese culture from which these stories were written.

GENRES

Danmei

Danmei (耽美 / "indulgence in beauty") is a Chinese fiction genre focused on romanticized tales of love and attraction between men. It is analogous to the BL (boys' love) genre in Japanese media. The majority of well-known danmei writers are women writing for women, although all genders produce and enjoy the genre.

Wuxia

Wuxia (武侠 / "martial heroes") is one of the oldest Chinese literary genres and consists of tales of noble heroes fighting evil and injustice. It often follows martial artists, monks, or rogues, who live apart from the ruling government, which is often seen as useless or corrupt. These societal outcasts—both voluntary and not—settle disputes among themselves, adhering to their own moral codes over the governing law.

Characters in wuxia focus primarily on human concerns, such as political strife between factions and advancing their own personal sense of justice. True wuxia is low on magical or supernatural elements. To Western moviegoers, a well-known example is *Crouching Tiger, Hidden Dragon*.

Xianxia

Xianxia (仙侠 / "immortal heroes") is a genre related to wuxia that places more emphasis on the supernatural. Its characters often strive to become stronger, with the end goal of extending their life span or achieving immortality.

Xianxia heavily features Daoist themes, while cultivation and the pursuit of immortality are both genre requirements. If these are not the story's central focus, it is not xianxia. *The Scum Villain's Self-Saving System*, *Grandmaster of Demonic Cultivation*, and *Heaven Official's Blessing* are all considered part of both the danmei and xianxia genres.

Webnovels

Webnovels are novels serialized by chapter online, and the websites that host them are considered spaces for indie and amateur writers. Many novels, dramas, comics, and animated shows produced in China are based on popular webnovels.

Examples of popular webnovel websites in China include Jinjiang Literature City (jjwxc.net), Changpei Literature (gong-zicp.com), and Qidian Chinese Net (qidian.com). While all of Mo Xiang Tong Xiu's existing works and the majority of best-known danmei are initially published via JJWXC, *Scum Villain's* series-within-a-series, *Proud Immortal Demon Way*, was said to be published on a "Zhongdian Literature" website, which is likely intended as a parody of Qidian Chinese Net, known for hosting male-targeted novels.

Webnovels have become somewhat infamous for being extremely long as authors will often keep them going for as long as paying subscribers are there. Readers typically purchase these stories chapter-by-chapter, and a certain number of subscribers is often required to allow for monetization. Other factors affecting an author's earnings include word count which can lead to bloated chapters and run-on plots. While not all webnovels suffer from any of these things, it is something commonly expected due to the system within which they're published.

Like all forms of media, very passionate fanbases often arise for webnovels. While the majority of readers are respectful, there is often a more toxic side of the community, one exacerbated by the parasocial relationship that some readers develop with a given author. Authors often suffer backlash from these fans for things such as a plot or character decisions that the readers don't agree with; events the readers finds too shocking (often referred to as landmines); writing outside the genres or tropes the readers expect the story to cleave to; openly disagreeing with another creator; abruptly pausing or ending a story; posting a chapter late; or even simply posting something on their social media accounts that these fans in some way dislike.

Fan toxicity is a particularly troublesome problem for webnovel authors in part because they are reliant on subscriber support to make a living. Furthermore, this abuse can follow them across platforms, and often the only way to escape it is to stay off public social media altogether, which is a decision often made by the most popular of writers.

In *Scum Villain*, Shen Yuan could be considered one of these toxic fans due to his scathing commentary about the story of *Proud Immortal Demon Way*. However, he did seem to relegate his criticism to covering the story itself and continued to pay for all the content he consumed, making him a lesser evil in the scheme of things.

TERMINOLOGY

ARRAY: Area-of-effect magic circles. Anyone within the array falls under the effect of the array's associated spell(s).

BOWING: As is seen in other Asian cultures, standing bows are a traditional greeting and are also used when giving an apology. A deeper bow shows greater respect.

BUDDHISM: The central belief of Buddhism is that life is a cycle of suffering and rebirth, only to be escaped by reaching enlightenment (nirvana). Buddhists believe in karma, that a person's actions will influence their fortune in this life and future lives. The teachings of the Buddha are known as The Middle Way and emphasize a practice that is neither extreme asceticism nor extreme indulgence.

CHINESE CALENDAR: The Chinese calendar uses the *Tian Gan Di Zhi* (Heavenly Stems, Earthly Branches) system, rather than numbers, to mark the years. There are ten heavenly stems (original meanings lost) and twelve earthly branches (associated with the zodiac), each represented by a written character. Each stem and branch is associated with either yin or yang, and one of the elemental properties: wood, earth, fire, metal, and water. The stems and branches are combined in cyclical patterns to create a calendar where every unit of time is associated with certain attributes.

This is what a character is asking for when inquiring for the date/time of birth (生辰八字 / "eight characters of birth date/time"). Analyzing the stem/branch characters and their elemental associations was considered essential information in divination, fortune-telling, matchmaking, and even business deals.

CHRYSANTHEMUM: A flower that is a symbol of health and vitality. In sex scenes, specifically for two men, it's used as symbolism for their backdoor entrance.

CLINGING TO THIGHS: Similar to "riding someone's coattails" in English. It implies an element of sucking up to someone, though some characters aren't above literally clinging to another's thighs.

Colors:

WHITE: Death, mourning, purity. Used in funerals for both the deceased and mourners.

BLACK: Classy, scholarly. Considered masculine, representing the Heavens and the dao.

RED: Happiness, good luck. Used for weddings.

YELLOW/GOLD: Wealth, prosperity. Often reserved for royalty.

BLUE/GREEN: Health, prosperity, and harmony.

PURPLE: Divinity and immortality.

CONCUBINES: In ancient China, it was common practice for a wealthy man to possess women as concubines in addition to his wife. They were expected to live with and bear him children. Generally speaking, a greater number of concubines correlated to higher social status, hence a wealthy merchant might have two or three concubines, while an emperor might have tens or even a hundred.

CONFUCIANISM: Confucianism is a philosophy based on the teachings of Confucius. Its influence on all aspects of Chinese culture is incalculable. Confucius placed heavy importance on respect for one's elders and family, a concept broadly known as *xiao* (孝 / "filial piety"). The family structure is used in other contexts to urge similar behaviors, such as respect of a student towards a teacher, or people of a country towards their ruler.

CORES/GOLDEN CORES: The formation of a jindan (金丹 / "golden core") is a key step in any cultivator's journey to immortality. The Golden Core forms from and replaces the lower dantian, becoming an internal source of power for the cultivator. Golden Core formation is only accomplished after a great deal of intense training and qi cultivation.

Cultivators can detonate their Golden Core as a last-ditch move to take out a dangerous opponent, but this almost always kills the cultivator. A core's destruction or removal is permanent. It cannot be re-cultivated, as there is no longer a lower dantian to form it from. Its destruction also prevents the individual from ever being able to process or cultivate qi normally again.

COUGHING/SPITTING BLOOD: A way to show a character is ill, injured, or upset. Despite the very physical nature of the response, it does not necessarily mean that a character has been wounded; their body could simply be reacting to a very strong emotion. (See also Seven Apertures/Qiqiao.)

COURTESY NAMES: In addition to their birth name, an individual may receive a courtesy name when they come of age or on another special occasion. *(See Name Guide for more information.)*

CULTIVATORS/CULTIVATION: Cultivators are practitioners of spirituality and martial artis who seek to gain understanding of the will of the universe while attaining personal strength and extending their life span.

Cultivation is a long process marked by "stages." There are traditionally nine stages, but this is often simplified in fiction. Some common stages are noted below, though exact definitions of each stage may depend on the setting.

◇ Qi Condensation/Qi Refining (凝气/练气)
◇ Foundation Establishment (筑基)
◇ Core Formation/Golden Core (结丹/金丹)
◇ Nascent Soul (元婴)
◇ Deity Transformation (化神)
◇ Great Ascension (大乘)
◇ Heavenly Tribulation (渡劫)

CULTIVATION MANUAL: Cultivation manuals and sutras are common plot devices in xianxia/wuxia novels. They provide detailed instructions on a secret or advanced training technique and are sought out by those who wish to advance their cultivation levels.

CURRENCY: The currency system during most dynasties was based on the exchange of silver and gold coinage. Weight was also used to measure denominations of money. An example is "one liang of silver."

CUT-SLEEVE: A term for a gay man. Comes from a tale about an emperor's love for, and relationship with, a male politician. The emperor was called to the morning assembly, but his lover was asleep on his robe. Rather than wake him, the emperor cut off his own sleeve.

DANTIAN: *Dantian* (丹田 / "cinnabar field") refers to three regions in the body where qi is concentrated and refined. The Lower is located three finger widths below and two finger widths behind the navel. This is where a cultivator's golden core would be formed and is where the qi metabolism process begins and progresses upward. The Middle is located at the center of the chest, at level with the heart, while the Upper is located on the forehead, between the eyebrows.

DAOISM: Daoism is the philosophy of the *dao* (道 / "the way") Following the dao involves coming into harmony with the natural order of the universe, which makes someone a "true human," safe from external harm and who can affect the world without intentional action. Cultivation is a concept based on Daoist superstitions.

DEMONS: A race of immensely powerful and innately supernatural beings. They are almost always aligned with evil.

DISCIPLES: Clan and sect members are known as disciples. Disciples live on sect grounds and have a strict hierarchy based on skill and seniority. They are divided into **Core**, **Inner**, and **Outer** rankings, with Core being the highest. Higher-ranked disciples get better lodging and other resources.

When formally joining a sect or clan as a disciple or a student, the sect/clan becomes like the disciple's new family: teachers are parents and peers are siblings. Because of this, a betrayal or abandonment of one's sect/clan is considered a deep transgression of Confucian values of filial piety. This is also the origin of many of the honorifics and titles used for martial arts.

DRAGON: Great chimeric beasts who wield power over the weather. Chinese dragons differ from their Western counterparts as they are often benevolent, bestowing blessings and granting luck. They are associated with the Heavens, the Emperor, and yang energy.

DUAL CULTIVATION: A cultivation method done in pairs. It is seen as a means by which both parties can advance their skills or even cure illness or curses by combining their qi. It is often sexual in nature or an outright euphemism for sex.

FACE: *Mianzi* (面子), generally translated as "face", is an important concept in Chinese society. It is a metaphor for a person's reputation and can be extended to further descriptive metaphors. For example, "having face" refers to having a good reputation, and "losing face" refers to having one's reputation hurt. Meanwhile, "giving face" means deferring to someone else to help improve their reputation, while "not wanting face" implies that a person is acting so poorly or shamelessly that they clearly don't care about their reputation at all. "Thin face" refers to someone easily embarrassed or prone to offense at perceived slights. Conversely, "thick face" refers to someone not easily embarrassed and immune to insults.

FENG SHUI: *Feng shui* (風水 / "wind-water"), is a Daoist practice centered around the philosophy of achieving spiritual accord between people, objects, and universe at large. Practitioners usually focus on positioning and orientation, believing this can optimize the flow of qi in their environment. Having good feng shui means being in harmony with the natural order.

THE FIVE ELEMENTS: Also known as the *wuxing* (五行 / "Five Phases"). Rather than Western concepts of elemental magic, Chinese phases are more commonly used to describe the interactions and relationships between things. The phases can both beget and overcome each other.

◇ Wood (木 / mu)
◇ Fire (火 / huo)
◇ Earth (土 / tu)
◇ Metal (金 / jin)
◇ Water (水 / shui)

FOUNDATION ESTABLISHMENT: An early cultivation stage achieved after collecting a certain amount of qi.

THE FOUR SCHOLARLY ARTS: The four academic and artistic talents required of a scholarly gentleman in ancient China. The Four Scholarly Arts were: Qin (the zither instrument *guqin*), Qi (a strategy game also known as *weiqi* or *go*), Calligraphy, and Painting.

GOLDEN FINGER: A protagonist-exclusive overpowered ability or weapon. This can also refer to them being generally OP ("overpowered") and not a specific ability or physical item.

GUANYIN: A bodhisattva is a Buddhist who achieves enlightenment and, rather than release into nirvana, returns to show others the way.

GUQIN: A seven-stringed zither, played by plucking with the fingers. Sometimes called a qin. It is fairly large and is meant to be laid flat on a surface or on one's lap while playing.

HAND SEALS: Refers to various hand and finger gestures used by cultivators to cast spells, or used while meditating. A cultivator may be able to control their sword remotely with a hand seal.

IMMORTALS AND IMMORTALITY: Immortals have transcended mortality through cultivation. They possess long lives, are immune to illness and aging, and have various magical powers. The exact life span of immortals differs from story to story, and in some they only live for three to four hundred years.

IMMORTAL-BINDING ROPES OR CABLES: Ropes, nets, and other restraints enchanted to withstand the power of an immortal or god. They can only be cut by high-powered spiritual items or weapons and often limit the abilities of those trapped by them.

INCENSE TIME: A common way to tell time in ancient China, referring to how long it takes for a single incense stick to burn. Standardized incense sticks were manufactured and calibrated for specific time measurements: a half hour, an hour, a day, etc. These were available to people of all social classes.

"One incense time" is roughly thirty minutes.

INEDIA: A common ability that allows an immortal to survive without mortal food or sleep by sustaining themselves on purer forms of energy based on Daoist fasting. Depending on the setting, immortals who have achieved inedia may be unable to tolerate mortal food, or they may be able to choose to eat when desired.

JADE: Jade is a culturally and spiritually important mineral in China. Its durability, beauty, and the ease with which it can be utilized for crafting both decorative and functional pieces alike has made it widely beloved since ancient times. The word might cause Westerners to think of green jade (the mineral jadeite), but Chinese texts are often referring to white jade (the mineral nephrite). This is the color referenced when a person's skin is described as "the color of jade."

JIANGHU: A staple of wuxia, the *jianghu* (江湖 / "rivers and lakes") describes an underground society of martial artists, monks, rogues, and artisans and merchants who settle disputes between themselves per their own moral codes.

KOWTOW: The *kowtow* (叩头 / "knock head") is an act of prostration where one kneels and bows low enough that their forehead touches the ground. A show of deep respect and reverence that can also be used to beg, plead, or show sincerity.

LILY: A flower considered a symbol of long-lasting love, making it a popular flower at weddings.

LOLI: Anime fandom slang for a female character with cute and childish (or childlike) traits.

LOTUS: This flower symbolizes purity of the heart and mind, as lotuses rise untainted from the muddy waters they grow in. It also signifies the holy seat of the Buddha.

MERIDIANS: The means by which qi travels through the body, like a magical bloodstream. Medical and combat techniques that focus on redirecting, manipulating, or halting qi circulation focus on targeting the meridians at specific points on the body, known as acupoints. Techniques that can manipulate or block qi prevent a cultivator from using magical techniques until the qi block is lifted.

MOE: Anime fandom slang for an endearing character or character traits that evoke a feeling of protectiveness in the viewer. Similarly, "gap moe" describes when this feeling is aroused because a character has behaved in a way that seemingly contradicts their persona— for example, when an otherwise scary demon wants a hug.

NASCENT SOUL: A cultivation stage in which cultivators can project their souls outside their bodies and have them travel independently. This can allow them to survive the death of their physical body and advance to a higher state.

NIGHT PEARLS: Night pearls are a variety of rare fluorescent stones. Their fluorescence derives from rare trace elements in igneous rock or crystalized fluorite. A valued gem in China often used in fiction as natural, travel-sized sources of light that don't require fire or qi.

NPC: Shortened for "Non-Player Character". An individual in a game who is not controlled by a player and instead a background character intended to fill-out and advance the story.

Numbers

TWO: Two (二 / "er") is considered a good number and is referenced in the common idiom "good things come in pairs." It is common practice to repeat characters in pairs for added effect.

THREE: Three (三 / "san") sounds like sheng (生 / "living") and also like san (散 / "separation").

FOUR: Four (四 / "si") sounds like si (死 / "death"). A very unlucky number.

SEVEN: Seven (七 / "qi") sounds like qi (齊 / "together"), making it a good number for love-related things. However, it also sounds like qi (欺 / "deception").

EIGHT: Eight (八 / "ba") sounds like fa (發 / "prosperity"), causing it to be considered a very lucky number.

NINE: Nine (九 / "jiu") is associated with matters surrounding the Emperor and Heaven, and is as such considered an auspicious number.

MXTX's work has subtle numerical theming around its love interests. In *Grandmaster of Demonic Cultivation*, her second book, Lan Wangji is frequently called Lan-er-gege ("second brother Lan") as a nickname by Wei Wuxian. In her third book, *Heaven Official's Blessing*, Hua Cheng is the third son of his family and gives the name San Lang ("third youth") when Xie Lian asks what to call him.

OTAKU: Anime fandom slang for individuals who are deeply obsessed with a specific niche hobby, e.g., anime. Generically, refers to those fixated on anime.

PEACHES: Peaches are associated with long life and immortality. For this reason, peaches and peach-shaped things are commonly eaten to celebrate birthdays. Peaches are also an ancient symbol of love between men, coming from a story where a duke took a bite from a very sweet peach and gave the rest of it to his lover to enjoy.

PEARLS: Pearls are associated with wisdom and prosperity. They are also connected to dragons; many depictions show them clutching a pearl or chasing after a pearl.

PEONY: Symbolizes wealth and power. Was considered the flower of the emperor.

PHOENIX: *Fenghuang* (凤凰 / "phoenix"), a legendary chimeric bird said to only appear in times of peace and to flee when a ruler is corrupt. They are heavily associated with femininity, the Empress, and happy marriages.

PILLS AND ELIXIRS: Magic medicines that can heal wounds, improve cultivation, extend life, etc. In Chinese culture, these things are usually delivered in pill form. These pills are created in special kilns.

PINE TREE: A symbol of evergreen sentiment or everlasting affection.

QI: *Qi* (气) is the energy in all living things. There is both righteous qi and evil or poisonous qi.

Cultivators strive to cultivate qi by absorbing it from the natural world and refining it within themselves to improve their cultivation base. A cultivation base refers to the amount of qi a cultivator possesses or is able to possess. In xianxia, natural locations such as caves, mountains, or other secluded places with beautiful scenery are often rich in qi, and practicing there can allow a cultivator to make rapid progress in their cultivation.

Cultivators and other qi manipulators can utilize their life force in a variety of ways, including imbuing objects with it to transform them into lethal weapons or sending out blasts of energy to do powerful damage. Cultivators also refine their senses beyond normal human levels. For instance, they may cast out their spiritual sense to gain total awareness of everything in a region around them or to feel for potential danger.

QI CIRCULATION: The metabolic cycle of qi in the body, where it flows from the dantian to the meridians and back. This cycle purifies and refines qi, and good circulation is essential to cultivation. In xianxia, qi can be transferred from one person to another through physical contact and can heal someone who is wounded if the donor is trained in the art.

QI DEVIATION: A qi deviation (走火入魔 / "to catch fire and enter demonhood") occurs when one's cultivation base becomes unstable. Common causes include an unstable emotional state and/or strong negative emotions, practicing cultivation methods incorrectly, reckless use of forbidden or high-level arts, or succumbing to the influence of demons and evil spirits. When qi deviation arises from mental or emotional causes, the person is often said to have succumbed to their inner demons or "heart demons" (心魔).

Symptoms of qi deviation in fiction include panic, paranoia, sensory hallucinations, and death, whether by the qi deviation itself causing irreparable damage to the body or as a result of its symptoms such as leaping to one's death to escape a hallucination. Common treatments of qi deviation in fiction include relaxation (voluntary or forced by an external party), massage, meditation, or qi transfer from another individual.

QILIN: A one-horned chimera said to appear extremely rarely. Commonly associated with the birth or death of a great ruler or sage.

SECOND-GENERATION RICH KID: A child of a wealthy family who grows up with a large inheritance. "Second-generation" in this case refers to them being the younger generation (as opposed to their parents, who are the first generation) rather than immigrant status.

SECT: A cultivation sect is an organization of individuals united by their dedication to the practice of a particular method of cultivation or martial arts. A sect may have a signature style. Sects are led by a single leader, who is supported by senior sect members. They are not necessarily related by blood.

SEVEN APERTURES/QIQIAO: (七窍) The seven facial apertures: the two eyes, nose, mouth, tongue, and two ears. The essential qi of vital organs are said to connect to the seven apertures, and illness in the vital organs may cause symptoms there. People who are ill or seriously injured may be "bleeding from the seven apertures."

SHIDI, SHIXIONG, SHIZUN, ETC.: Chinese titles and terms used to indicate a person's role or rank in relation to the speaker. Because of the robust nature of this naming system, and a lack of nuance in translating many to English, the original titles have been maintained. *(See Name Guide for more information.)*

SPIRIT STONES: Small gems filled with qi that can be exchanged between cultivators as a form of currency. If so desired, the qi can be extracted for an extra energy boost.

STALLION NOVELS: A genre of fiction starring a male protagonist who has a harem full of women who fawn over him. Unlike many wish-fulfillment stories, the protagonist of a stallion novel is not the typical loser archetype and is more of an overpowered power fantasy. This genre is full of fanservice aimed at a heterosexual male audience, often focusing on the acquisition of a large harem over individual romantic plotlines with each wife.

The term itself is a comparison between the protagonist and a single male stud horse in a stable full of broodmares. *Proud Immortal Demon Way* is considered a prime example of a stallion novel.

SWORDS: A cultivator's sword is an important part of their cultivation practice. In many instances, swords are spiritually bound to their owner and may have been bestowed to them by their master, a family member, or obtained through a ritual. Cultivators in fiction are able to use their swords as transportation by standing atop the flat of the blade and riding it as it flies through the air. Skilled cultivators can summon their swords to fly into their hand, command the sword to fight on its own, or release energy attacks from the edge of the blade.

SWORD GLARE: *Jianguang* (剑光 / "sword light"), an energy attack released from a sword's edge.

SWORN BROTHERS/SISTERS/FAMILIES: In China, sworn brotherhood describes a binding social pact made by two or more unrelated individuals of the same gender. It can be entered into for social, political, and/or personal reasons and is not only limited to two participants; it can extend to an entire group. It was most common among men, but it was not unheard of among women or between people of different genders.

The participants treat members of each other's families as their own and assist them in the ways an extended family would: providing mutual support and aid, support in political alliances, etc.

Sworn siblinghood, where individuals will refer to themselves as brother or sister, is not to be confused with familial relations like blood siblings or adoption. It is sometimes used in Chinese media, particularly danmei, to imply romantic relationships that could otherwise be prone to censorship.

THE SYSTEM: A common trope in transmigration novels is the existence of a System that guides the character and provides them with objectives in exchange for benefits, often under the threat of consequences if they fail. The System may award points for completing objectives, which can then be exchanged for various items or boons. In *Scum Villain*, these are called B-points, originally named after the second sound in the phrase *zhuang bi* (装逼 / "to act badass/to play it cool/to show off").

TALISMANS: Strips of paper with incantations written on them, often done so with cinnabar ink or blood. They can serve as seals or be used as one-time spells.

THE THREE REALMS: Traditionally, the universe is divided into Three Realms: the **Heavenly Realm**, the **Mortal Realm**, and the **Ghost Realm**. The Heavenly Realm refers to the Heavens and Celestial Court, where gods reside and rule, the Mortal Realm refers to the human world, and the Ghost Realm refers to the realm of the dead. In *Scum Villain*, only the Mortal Realm is directly relevant, while the Demon Realm is a separate space where all demons and their ilk reside.

TSUNDERE: Anime fandom slang for a character who acts standoffish (tsun) but secretly has a loving side (dere), similar to "hot and cold" in English.

TRANSMIGRATION: (穿越 / "to pass through") is analogous to the isekai genre in Japanese media. A character, usually from the modern world, suddenly finds themself in the past, future, or a fantasy world, most often by reincarnation or teleportation. The character often uses knowledge from their former life to "cheat" in their new one, especially if they've transmigrated into a novel or game they have recently finished and thus have knowledge they can use to their advantage. These individuals are referred to as transmigrators.

VINEGAR: To say someone is drinking vinegar or tasting vinegar means they're having jealous or bitter feelings. Generally used for a love interest growing jealous while watching the main character receive the attention of a rival suitor.

WEDDING TRADITIONS: Red is an important part of traditional Chinese weddings, as the color of prosperity, happiness, and good luck. It remains the standard color for bridal and bridegroom robes and wedding decorations even today.

A bride was always veiled when she was sent off by her family in her wedding dress. Veils were generally opaque, so the bride would need to be led around by her handmaidens (or the groom). The veil is not removed until the bride is in the wedding suite with the groom after the ceremony and is only removed by the groom himself. During the ceremony, the couple each cut off a lock of their own hair, then intertwine and tie the two locks together to symbolize their commitment.

WHUMP: Fandom slang for scenarios that result in a character enduring pain—emotional and/or physical—especially if the creator seems to have designed that scenario explicitly for that purpose.

WILLOW TREE: A symbol of lasting affection, friendship, and goodbyes. Also means "urging someone to stay," and "meeting under the willows." Can connote a rendezvous. Willows are synonymous with spring, which is considered the matchmaking season, and is thus synonymous with promiscuity. Willow imagery is also often used to describe lower-class women like singers and prostitutes.

XUANDUAN: A formal style of men's robes that was worn as court dress in certain eras of history. The top was made of *xuan* (玄 / "dark") cloth with a proper, square cut and no excessive ornamentation, and a red, yellow, or dark skirt was worn underneath.

YIN ENERGY AND YANG ENERGY: Yin and yang is a concept in Chinese philosophy that describes the complementary interdependence of opposite/contrary forces. It can be applied to all forms of change and differences. Yang represents the sun, masculinity, and the living, while yin represents the shadows, femininity, and the dead, including spirits and ghosts. In fiction, imbalances between yin and yang energy can do serious harm to the body or act as the driving force for malevolent spirits seeking to replenish themselves of whichever they lack.

ZHONGDIAN LITERATURE: Likely intended as a parody of Qidian Chinese Net, a webnovel site known for hosting male-targeted novels.

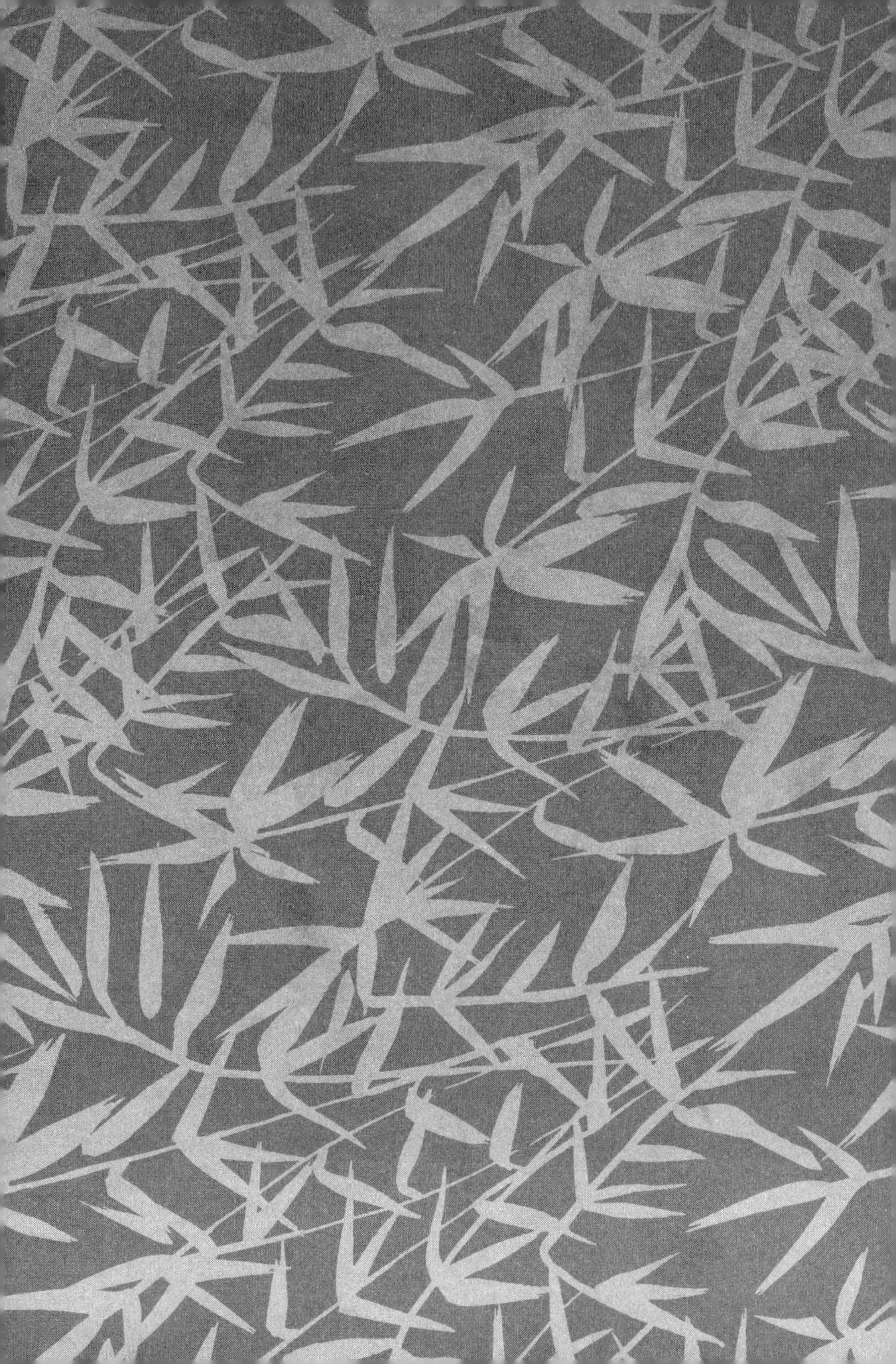

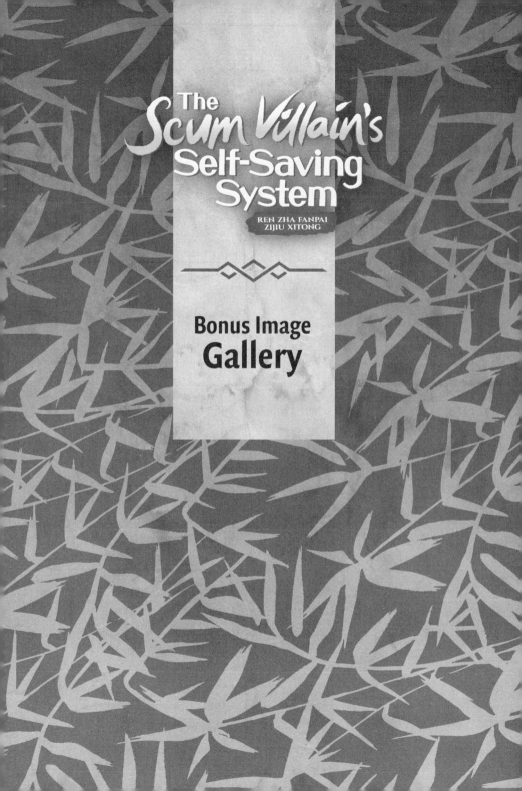

The Scum Villain's Self-Saving System

REN ZHA FANPAI
ZIJIU XITONG

Bonus Image
Gallery

Shen Qingqiu

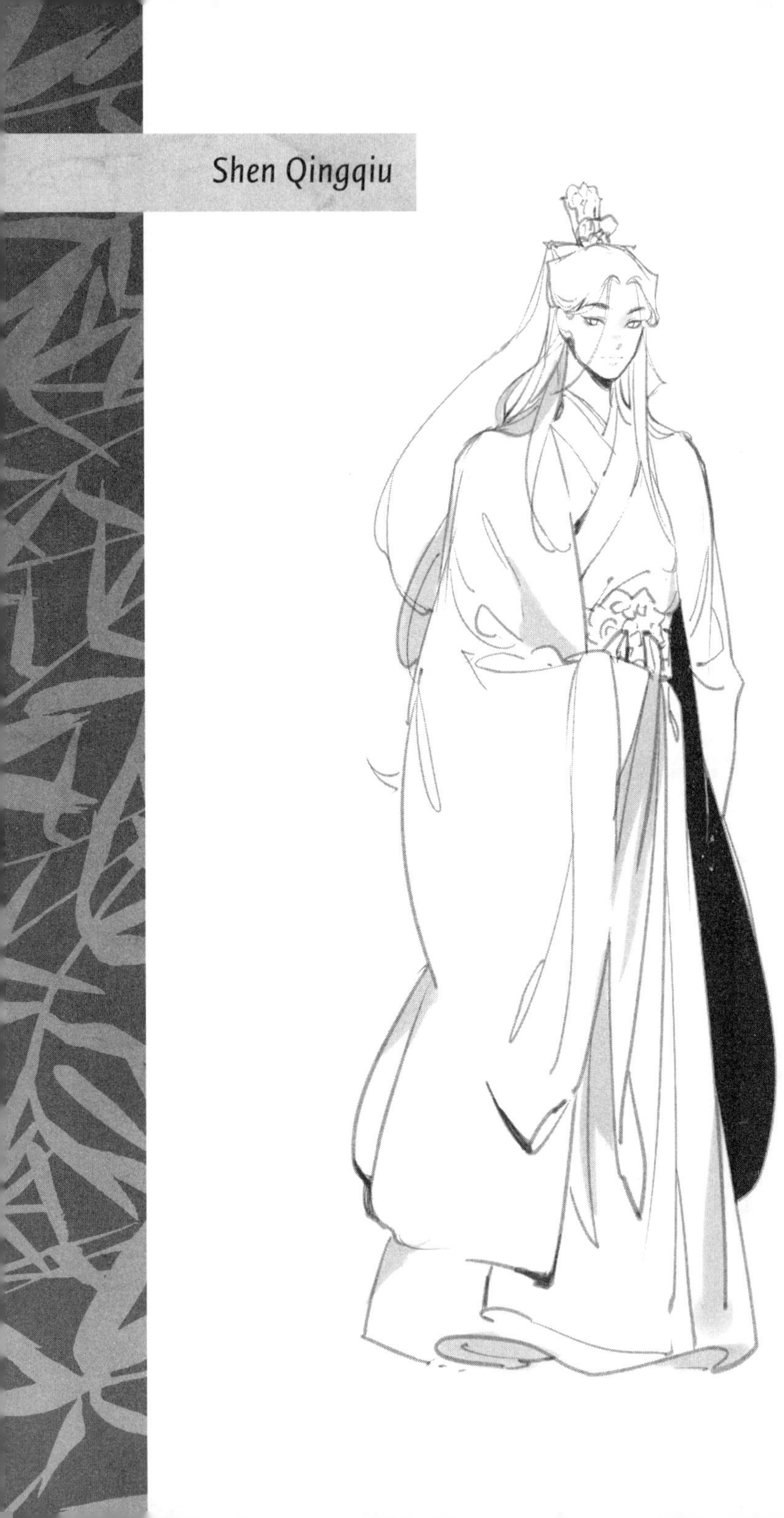

Luo Binghe

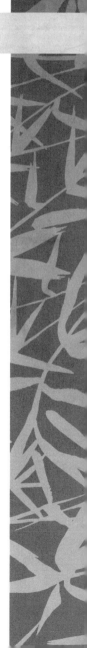

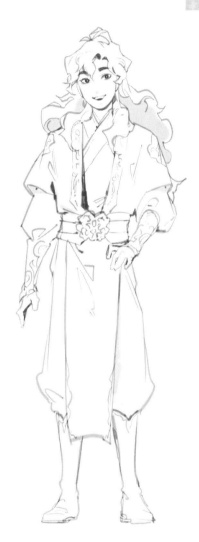

Yue Qingyuan

Liu Qingge

Ming Fan

Ning Yingying

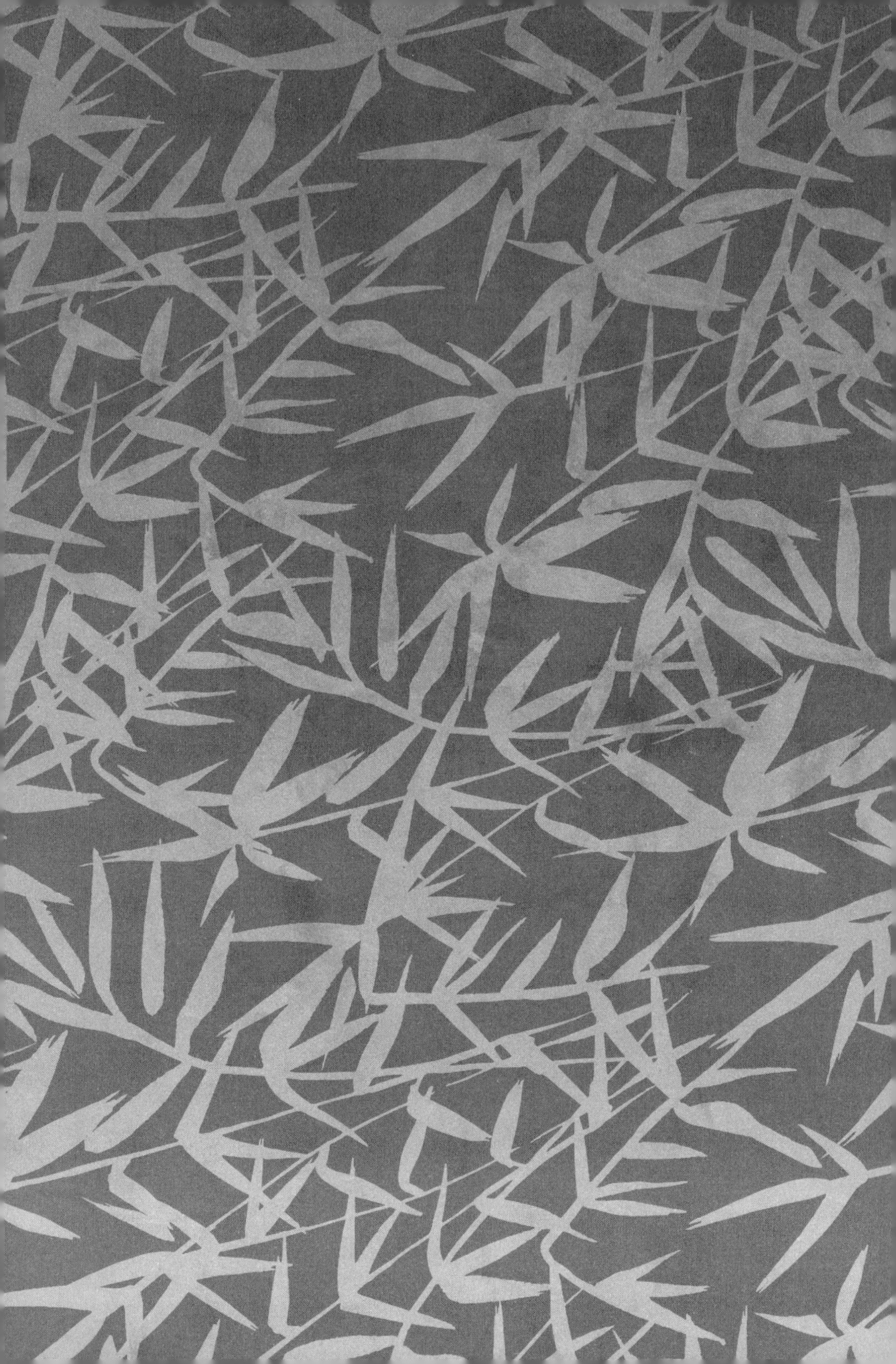

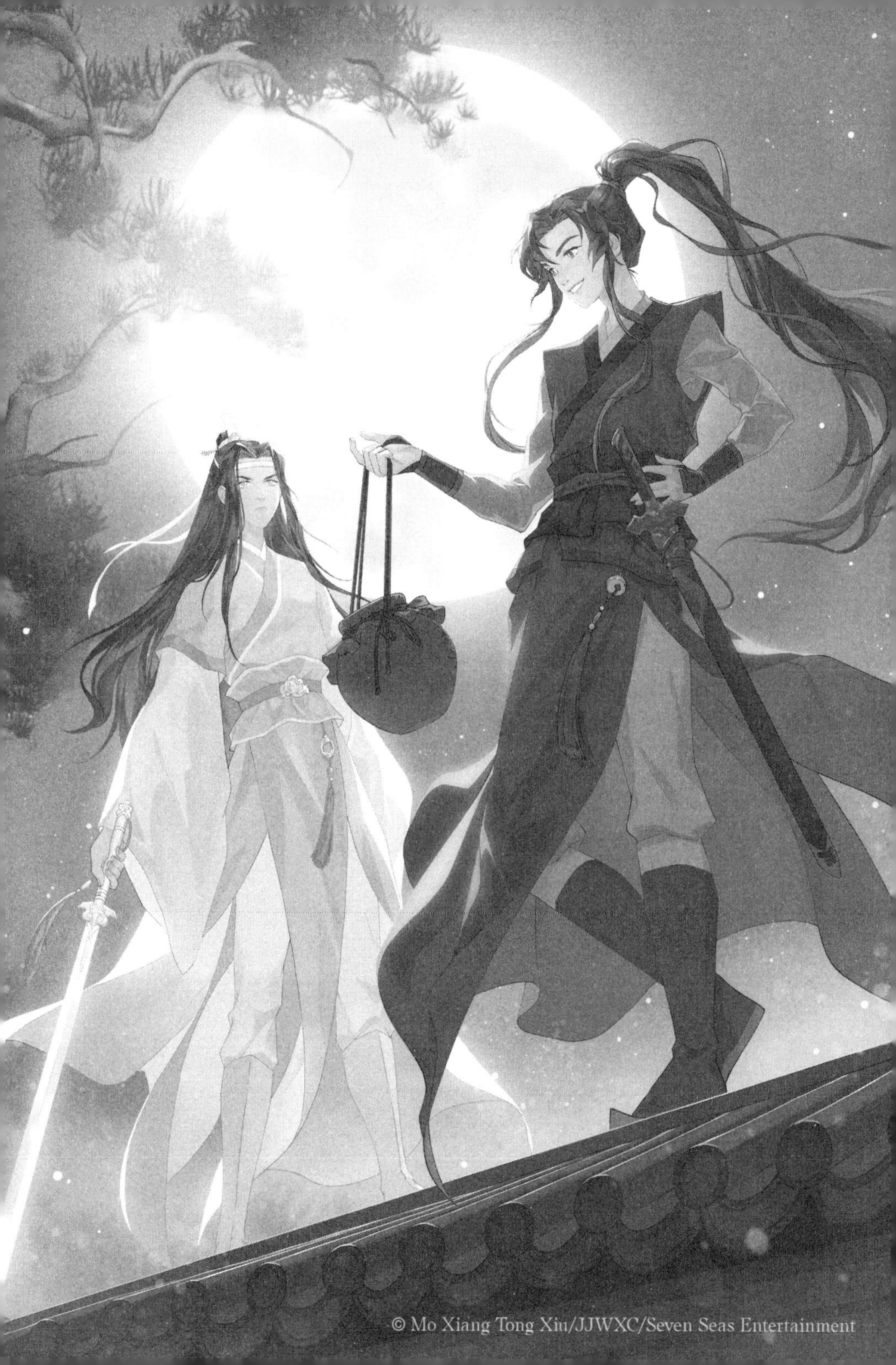

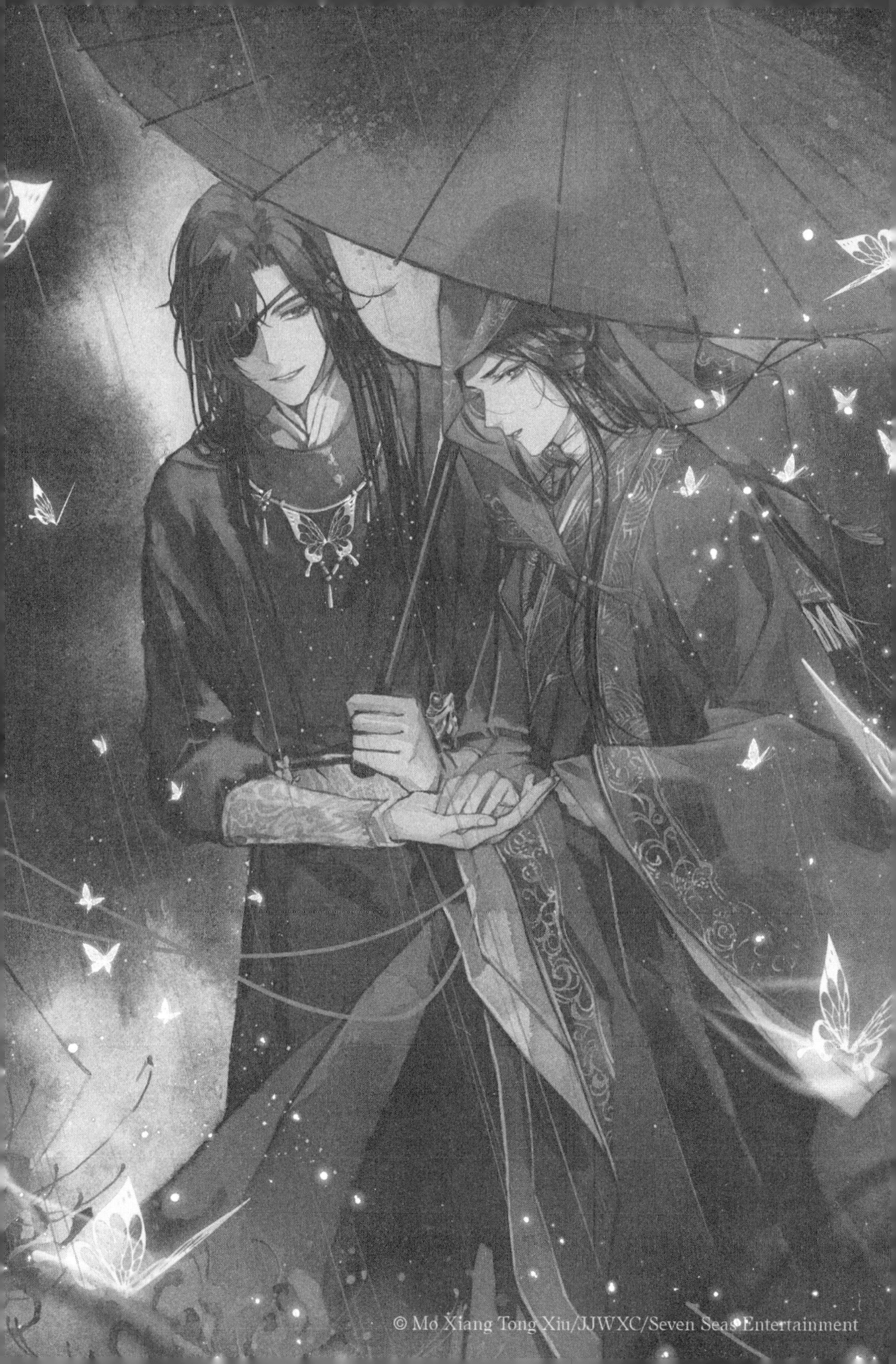